NO TURNING BACK

"A pity we didn't meet before the war," Sterling heard himself say. He didn't know what made him say it. He could feel himself digging a hole deeper and deeper with each word she spoke, each smile she rewarded him with.

"Or at least that you weren't on the wrong side," Reagan answered.

His laugh echoed in the paneled chamber. "It's tempting."

She shook her head. "That's a red uniform you wear. To . . . " Her cheeks flushed. "It would be betraying my country. I couldn't do it."

Sterling came to her. She made no advance toward him, but she did not push him away. She knew it was wrong. She hated all he stood for. But he made her feel wonderful somewhere deep inside.

"May I kiss you?" Sterling asked. One kiss, he told himself. Just one.

"If I say no?"

He lifted a lock of auburn hair from her shoulder and brought it to his lips. "Then I won't."

"Liar. Soldiers take what they want." She lifted her chin, daring him to kiss her, her pulse racing . . .

Temptation's Tender Kiss

COLLEEN FAULKNER

ZEBRA BOOKS
KENSINGTON PUBLISHING CORP.

ZEBRA BOOKS

are published by

Kensington Publishing Corp.
475 Park Avenue South
New York, NY 10016

First printing: June, 1990

Printed in the United States of America

We have a natural right to make use of our pens as of our tongue, at our peril, risk and hazard.
                                              — *Voltaire*

Prologue

New Castle, Delaware
December 24, 1777

Captain Grayson Thayer stepped from the covered carriage into the swirling snow. Just ahead, a lantern glowed in a doorway, illuminating the tavern's entrance. "I won't be long," he called to the huddled driver. "Wait for me here."

"Aye, sir" came a muffled voice.

Grayson hurried across the frozen yard, his polished leather boots crunching in the snow. Flinging open the tavern door, he stepped inside and shook the snow from his cloak.

"Capt'n?" an ancient gravelly voice questioned.

The British officer eyed the sailor standing in the shadows. "Who's asking?"

The old grizzled man chuckled. "Yer party waits for ye above." He gestured with a clay pipe.

Ignoring the other tavern patrons, Grayson crossed the room and started up the wooden staircase.

"First door to yer left," the sailor called after him.

Turning on the landing, Grayson rapped his knuckles on the paneled door and pushed in. A bare-chested man, face lathered with shaving soap, raised

7

a flintlock pistol and aimed it steadily at Grayson.

"God a mercy!" A maid holding a shaving razor gave a squeal and fell to her knees behind a chair.

Grayson closed the door, a hint of a smile crossing his handsome face. "Playing with fire, asking me here, brother." He shook a finger. "Sooner or later, you're going to get burned."

Sterling Thayer lowered the pistol. "It's all right, Sary. You can go. I'll finish myself."

The frightened maid peered over the back of the chair. "By the king's breeches, Master Sterling! You're as alike as two peas in a pod!"

Sterling came to his feet, laying down the pistol. "I said that will be all."

Bobbing her head, Sary dropped the razor in a basin of water and scurried from the room.

For a moment the two brothers regarded each other coolly. Each was a mirror image of the other with their startling blue eyes and golden hair.

Sterling retrieved his razor from the washbowl and concentrated on his reflection in a piece of broken mirror propped on the mantel. He scraped his chin methodically. "You surprise me, Brother. What made you come?"

"What made you ask? They catch you here and you'll be hanging by dawn." Grayson walked to the center of the room, brushing a bit of imaginary lint from his heavy woolen cloak.

"Just thought we might have a drink between brothers before you report to duty. After all, it's been two years." Sterling wiped the remaining soap from his clean-shaven face.

"How did you know I was bound for Philadelphia?"

Sterling laughed, his rich tenor voice echoing in the tiny room. "You're my brother, for Christ's sake!" He hit Grayson on the back. "I make it my business to know."

Grayson's eyes met Sterling's. "I haven't time to dally. I've an engagement."

"So let the young lady wait a few minutes. When do you report?"

"Tomorrow."

"Christmas Day? Droll fellows aren't they . . . your commanding officers." He poured a clear liquid from a pitcher and added water, turning the concoction cloudy. "Just one drink before you go. It wasn't easy finding this." He pushed the handleless pewter cup into Grayson's hand.

Grayson took a swallow, savoring its warmth as it burned a path to his stomach. "A *palm toddie?* God's bowels, how did you manage?"

It hadn't been easy for Sterling to find the arrack, but it had been necessary. "For my brother, nothing but the best."

"You'll not have a draught?"

"Nah. You know what drink does to me. Makes me bloody unpredictable."

Grayson tipped his glass again. "Makes you bloody foolish, you mean." Finishing the arrack, he peered into the cup. Slowly he lifted his head. Suddenly the room was spinning and his brother's voice seemed to be coming from far in the distance. "W-what have you done to me?" The empty pewter vessel slipped from his fingers. Then his eyes met Sterling's. "S-son of a b-bitch . . ."

A few minutes later the uniformed British officer came down the flight of wooden steps. The sailor at

9

the door opened it and stepped back out of his way. " 'Ave a good night, Master Sterling."

The officer stopped. "You must be mistaken, fellow. I'm Captain Grayson Thayer. It's my brother who goes by the name of Sterling."

The sailor grinned. "Right you are, sir. Mistaken I must be." He opened the tavern door. "Have a good evenin' to you then . . . Capt'n."

Chapter One

Philadelphia
December 25, 1777

Cloaked in darkness, Reagan Llewellyn hurried along the cobblestone walk, her basket clutched in her mittened hands. The sound of Christmas bells echoed somewhere in the city, and in the distance she could hear the voices of merry carolers. Raucous male laughter filtered onto Chestnut Street from a three-story brick house, and she hurried to make her way past. Just as she walked beneath the last window, the front door flew open and she spun around.

A lamp hanging in the doorway cast bright light onto the street illuminating the figures of a Hessian soldier and a woman. The woman giggled, snatching the feathered hat off the soldier's head, and he swatted her playfully on the bottom. "Lead the way, mine pretty," he bellowed drunkenly. "Lead the way."

Holding her basket tightly in her hands, Reagan turned the corner, pressing her back to the wall. The soldier and the doxy walked by without noticing the cloaked figure in the shadows.

Heaving a sigh of relief, Reagan crossed Chestnut and made several turns, up Fourth, west on Market, up Sixth, weaving her way through the streets of the city. Snow began to fall lightly, the dusty flakes covering her forest-green cloak in a layer of shimmering white.

Suddenly there were footsteps. "Halt, traitor!" came a voice from behind.

Reagan lowered her head, giving no heed to the warning. She walked faster, and the heavy footsteps behind her quickened.

"I said, you! Halt! Or I shoot!"

Terrified, Reagan broke into a run. One shot was fired, filling the air with the sickening smell of black powder, and then came a second. Catching the toe of her boot on a rain-barrel, Reagan fell headlong into the snow, her basket skittering across the icy cobblestone walk. Chunks of gingerbread flew from the basket. In terror, she rose on her knees and grabbed the basket, trembling in anticipation of the next shot. She knew the soldiers would not miss again.

But a long minute passed and then another and no soldiers appeared. Behind her she could hear their voices. Scrambling to her feet, Reagan ducked behind the rain-barrel, daring a glance down the street. In the dim light she spotted two soldiers leaning over a prone body.

Heart pounding, Reagan jerked back out of sight. They hadn't been after her! She took a deep breath. Slowly she got to her feet, and taking one final glance at the redcoats, she slipped around the corner and into the darkness.

A few minutes later Reagan ran up a short flight of steps and knocked on a door decorated with tree boughs and red ribbon. Pausing, she waited, watching as candlelight passed by the windows.

The door swung open and a comfortingly familiar face appeared.

"Mistress Claggett!" Reagan panted.

The elderly woman glanced left and then right down Mulberry Street. "Come in! Hurry, child, before you're seen. They've doubled the patrols!" Reagan stepped inside the front hall and Mistress Claggett slammed it shut, sliding the bolt home. "What is it? What's happened?"

Reagan laughed shakily. "Nothing but my own foolery. There were soldiers chasing some poor man on the street, only I thought they were after me. I think they killed him."

Mistress Claggett shook her head, making a clicking sound between her teeth. "I told you I'd come for it." She took the basket of gingerbread from Reagan's hand. "Since the British have occupied our dear old city it's not been safe for a young woman to walk the street. Next time you've a batch, you let me know."

Reagan's cinnamon eyes met Mistress Claggett's. "You know Papa'd never allow it. It's not safe."

The elderly woman gave a snort. "Not safe! You think I'm afraid of those bloody redcoats? I could do the job and do it well!"

Reagan pushed back the hood of her cloak. Her rich auburn hair was pulled back in a neat singular braid, but wisps of bright curls had escaped to frame her oval face. "And what if you were caught? We could never forgive ourselves if something happened to you. You've been too important to the patriot cause."

"Who'd stop a poor senile woman on the street? I could slip right beneath their noses, the poor stupid bastards!"

Reagan couldn't help but laugh. "Oh, I do so enjoy

coming to see you once a week! But I'd better be going; Papa will be worried."

"Very well." Mistress Claggett waved a wrinkled hand laden with gold rings. "Just let me return your basket." She removed the linen cloth from the top and began to take squares of gingerbread out and lay them on a silver tray on a table. "So tell me, how is that dear, sweet sister of yours?"

"Elsa? Just fine. She loves the spinet. She has me play it by the hour. It was so good of you to give it to us."

"Nonsense. I told you. I haven't played in years. The thing was rusting in my parlor." Emptying the basket of gingerbread, Mistress Claggett removed another linen cloth and retrieved a handful of paper leaflets.

"Wait until you read the latest piece on Major Burke! It's quite humorous."

Carefully the older woman laid the stack on the table and returned the linen cloths to the basket. "I'll see they go out tomorrow, have no fear of that." She handed Reagan the container.

"I know you will." Lifting her hood, Reagan walked to the door. "I hear they brought in another shipment of officers from London. Hilda and John Gatler have had to put one up."

Mistress Claggett shook her head, reaching out to tug at the strings of Reagan's hood. "Thank the good Lord we've been spared! I just can't understand how they can do that, forcing us to take soldiers in and provide them with food and shelter. They send one of those dandies here and he's liable to die of food poisoning!"

Reagan unlocked the door. "You wouldn't!"

The older woman shrugged, drawing her woven shawl tighter around her shoulders. "What could they do to me? Whose fault would it be if they lodged a soldier with a senile old woman? No telling what can happen once a person's mind goes."

Reagan laughed, stepping out the door into the falling snow. "Merry Christmas to you, Mistress Claggett," she said loudly. "I hope you enjoy your gingerbread. I'll see you next week."

Mistress Claggett patted her gently on the shoulder. "Godspeed, child."

Reagan came in through the back door of her father's house and into the kitchen, shrugging off her cloak. She picked up an apple from a wooden bowl on the worktable and took a bite.

"Where've you been, Sister?" Elsa asked softly, turning from the fireplace. "I was worried."

"Delivering gingerbread. I told you I was going to Mistress Claggett's, don't you remember?"

Elsa smiled prettily. At eighteen years old she was a picture of loveliness. Petite and dark-haired, she bore no resemblance to her elder sister. "Oh. Yes, I think you did."

Reagan dropped her cloak over a chair, munching on her apple. "Did you have a nice day?"

"Mmmhmmm." Elsa beamed. "Westley brought me a kitten." She clasped her hands in childlike excitement. "I'm going to call him Mittens."

"Westley was here?" She glanced at her sister. "Today?"

Elsa nodded. "He said he was sorry he couldn't stay, but he wished you a Merry Christmas. Would

15

you like to see my kitten? Papa said he could sleep here by the fire." She knelt and lifted a mewing kitten from a wooden box on the floor. "He purrs when I pet him."

Reagan stroked the kitten absentmindedly. "Westley shouldn't have been here," she said more to herself than to her sister. "I wonder what's about."

"Papa says I can give Mittens milk, but not too much because it will give him belly pains."

Reagan smiled. "He's sweet, Elsa. Put him back in the box and let him sleep."

The dark-haired girl did as her sister told her. "I'm making sassafras tea for Papa. Would you like some?"

"Sure. Where is he?"

"Papa?"

"Yes, Elsa," Reagan responded patiently. "Where papa?"

"In the parlor. Scribbling. You know he's always scribbling."

Reagan tossed her apple core into the fire. "Bring the tea to the parlor, will you?"

Elsa nodded her head vigorously. "And gingerbread. I'll bring gingerbread."

"You do that," Reagan answered as she left the kitchen.

"Papa?" Reagan walked into the parlor. Her father sat at a writing desk near the fireplace, his head bent in concentration.

"What took you so long? I was worried." Uriah Llewellyn peered over his spectacles.

"It didn't take me any longer than it usually does." She perched herself on the corner of an upholstered chair and stretched her hands out to warm them by the fire. She saw no need to tell her father of the incident on the street. After all, no harm had come to her; it was her own silliness that had caused her fright.

"Well, thank God you're back because I need some help with this piece." He gestured to the paper on the desk in front of him. "I have a good idea, but nothing sounds right."

"Papa, it's Christmas. Haven't we done enough for today? Put it away and I'll work on it tomorrow."

Uriah sighed, returning his quill to the inkwell. "I suppose you're right." He pushed back in his chair, stroking his graying beard. "We could all use a rest."

"Elsa said Westley was here; I thought he'd gone to New York. Is there a problem?"

Uriah patted his waistcoat, searching for his pipe. "Nothing to worry about. He just had some trouble with his pass."

"Trouble?" Reagan leaped up. "What kind of trouble? We pay dearly for those passes out of the city."

"Now settle yourself, Daughter." Uriah waved a hand. "No one's in any danger. He simply passed the leaflets on to another party."

Reagan paced the worn Persia carpet that covered the floor. "The more people we take into this, the more people at risk. I don't understand why we can't do it ourselves."

Uriah patted his waistcoat again. "Where's my pipe? Have you seen my pipe?"

Reagan picked the clay pipe up off the writing table. "Right in front of you."

He snatched it from her hand. "We've been over this time and time again. We can't do it alone any longer. Not since we increased the print run."

"I know." She smoothed the soft wool of her burgundy skirts. "It's just that it frightens me. I can take the risk for myself, but for others . . ." She shook her head.

"There is no one we've recruited who doesn't know the danger he or she invites." Uriah filled his pipe bowl with pungent tobacco and tamped it down with his finger. "But they feel as we do. The people of this land need our kind of support just as sure as Washington needs our supplies in Valley Forge."

"Just the same—" Elsa stepped into the parlor carrying a tray and Reagan cut herself off in midsentence. Her sister had no idea that Reagan and Uriah were actively involved in the patriot cause and they had no intentions of letting her know. "Tea! Wonderful." Reagan rubbed her hands together. "It was so cold outside. I'm still chilled."

Elsa set down the tray and began to pour three cups. "Do you think we could play a game now, Papa? It's my birthday. You promised."

Uriah studied his younger daughter's face, a bittersweet sadness coming over him. It was this time each year that he grew empty inside. Memories of his dear wife Anna washed over him. It was today, Christmas day eighteen years ago, that she had died in childbirth and their newborn babe had come down with a fever. Though his little Elsa had recovered from the illness, her mind had never grown as it should. She was an innocent who would forever need the protection of her father and sister.

"Papa!" Elsa repeated. "Can we play?"

Uriah blinked back the moisture that glistened in his eyes. "For my birthday girl?" He clapped his hands. "Of course!"

18

Reagan's dark eyes met her father's and she smiled in understanding. She knew how difficult Christmastime was for him, even if Elsa didn't. She took a cup of tea from the tray. "So what shall it be, birthday girl?"

A loud pounding came at the door, and Reagan jumped, spilling her tea. "W-who could that be?" She brushed at her skirt.

"I'll go!" Elsa volunteered happily. "Maybe it's Westley come back again. You think he can play my birthday game, too?"

The pounding came again, followed by a man's voice. "Open up in there!"

"No, Elsa." Reagan stood, setting down her teacup. "I'll go. You stay here with Papa." She heard Uriah crumble the piece of paper he'd been writing on and toss it into the fire.

Refusing to meet her father's gaze, Reagan hurried out of the room. As she neared the front door, the pounding became more insistent. "Open up in there, I say!"

"Who is it?" Reagan demanded in a steady voice.

"Jack Mulligan." The man banged on the door. "You're to open up under the orders of Lieutenant Litheson."

Reagan rested her hand on the doorknob. Lieutenant Joshua Litheson had been a childhood companion. The Lithesons and the Llewellyns had been friends for years. Everyone had expected her and Josh to marry, but then the war had broken out and he was now an officer with a loyalist regiment. Reagan had never been in love with Josh, so in a way she was relieved when the families had parted, but she still missed him sometimes.

19

Reagan took a deep breath. She hadn't talked to Josh in months. "And what is it the lieutenant wants, Mr. Mulligan?"

"Open the bloody door or I'll break it down!" the man bellowed.

Then came a calmer voice. "Reagan, it's Josh. Open up."

Unlocking the door, she yanked it open. "What do you want?" she asked coldly. Behind her old friend stood two cloaked, uniformed officers.

"You've been chosen to give aid to the king's men," Josh said in an official-sounding voice. "These gentlemen will be staying with you."

Redcoats! Here! How could she and her father continue their work with the enemy so near? Her brown eyes met Josh's stubbornly. "I think not. We've hardly enough food for ourselves. Your army cleaned our larder out in the *name of the king* two weeks ago. My father isn't well and Elsa . . ." She dropped her hands to her hips. "You certainly can't expect me to have them here with Elsa the way she is."

"Reagan, it's sleeting. Let us come inside. We can discuss the matter."

"I'm telling you, I'll not have their stinking hides in my house. You take them elsewhere. Let your Tory friends house them."

Josh came up the steps, lowering his voice. "You haven't got a choice, Reagie. It was only because of me that my commanding officer didn't make his request sooner. You've got to lodge them or—"

"Or what?"

Joshua looked away, unable to withstand the scrutiny of her gaze. "Or you'll be arrested, both you and your father for obstructing." There was a pause and then their eyes met. "Who'd care for Elsa then?" he asked quietly.

Reagan flung open the door in angry defeat. "I never thought I'd see the day British soldiers stepped foot in this house." She moved back as the officers started up the brick steps. "All right, Lieutenant. I'll let them in, but you tell them to wipe their damned feet!"

Chapter Two

Sterling Thayer walked into the front hall of the Llewellyn home and flung back his elegant cloak. Unlacing the ties, he offered the woolen garment to the young woman.

Reagan lifted a feathery eyebrow shrewdly, her hands resting on her hips.

"My cloak," Sterling enunciated.

" 'Tis your cloak," she replied.

Sterling's eyes met hers, and for a moment he was lost in their russet depths. Never in his life had he witnessed such controlled fire and brimstone in a female's face. Reminding himself that he was now portraying his brother Grayson, he gave the bundle of damp wool a shake. "Take my cloak; it's wet."

Reagan tried not to stare. The British officer standing in her entranceway was the most finely formed man she'd ever seen—no enemy redcoat surely, but some Greek god stepping fullblown from the pages of Homer. His classic face was angular with a sloping nose and a chiseled chin. His eyes were a heavenly blue and his hair the color of spun gold.

She blinked, feeling suddenly awkward and foolish. "T-take it yourself," she snapped, glancing away. "And you, see to your own cloak as well." She motioned to the officer coming in the door just ahead of Josh. "I'll be no man's servant."

The men wiped their polished boots on a reed mat. But when Jack Mulligan stepped through the door, Reagan pressed her hand against his chest. "I have to let them in, but not you," she said stubbornly.

"Reagan," Josh reasoned. "He works for me. It's bitter cold out. Just let him stand in the hall."

She shook her head. "I hear a Tory by the name of Jack Mulligan turned Larry Peabody in just last week."

"The bloke was buyin' King's Army rations on the blackmarket," Mulligan argued.

"Outside," Reagan repeated. "I'll have no such filth in my house. Larry was just trying to feed his family and now he's spending Christmas in the Walnut Street jail."

A twitch of a smile crossed Sterling's face, disappearing as fast as it had come. *Remember the role you play,* he reminded himself. *You're here to infiltrate the British Army and learn what you can of their intentions come spring. General Washington needs to know where and when General Howe would strike. You can't afford to allow anyone to know who you really are. There are too many lives at stake.*

Sterling turned to Josh. "Lieutenant, your man can stand in or out, it makes no difference to me, but shut the bloody door before I catch a chill!"

Reagan glanced at the blond officer. "Mind your knitting! The house is mine to leave the door open all night if I so choose."

"Lieutenant," Sterling said. "I think perhaps you should have a discussion with our hostess. She obviously is not aware of my position . . . nor hers."

Josh groaned, snatching his hat off his head. "Jack, outside." He closed the door, turning to Reagan. "Reagie, the captain is right. You shouldn't speak to him in such a manner. He's an influential man."

"This is my house."

"And if you wish it to remain so—" Sterling spoke with his brother's arrogance—"you will show some respect. This house can easily be confiscated and then it will be you, mistress, and your family, who will be looking for lodging elsewhere."

Reagan lifted her dark lashes to meet the officer's gaze and Sterling nearly took a step back. Her brown eyes were brimming with hatred, and for some reason he found it distressing. *Take care,* he warned himself. *This is neither the time nor the place for infatuations. A chit like her could get you killed.*

Stepping between the two, Josh cleared his throat. "Captain Thayer, I've not properly introduced you. This is Mistress Reagan Llewellyn. Reagie, Captain Grayson Thayer of the Grenadier Company, 64th Regiment."

Sterling removed his cocked hat mockingly. "At your service, ma'am."

Reagan turned away, speaking to the other officer. "And you, sir?"

The dark-haired man swept off his hat and took her hand, brushing his lips against it. "Lieutenant Roth Gardener." He straightened, smiling. "And I do hope that we can all make the best of this situation."

She snatched her hand from his, wiping it on her

skirt. His lips were wet and he reeked of whiskey. "Very well, gentlemen. You can hang your wraps in the room behind the kitchen."

"Reagie . . ." Josh rested his hand on her shoulder. "Please . . . Call Nettie."

She stepped aside. "Nettie's gone out for the evening to visit an ill friend."

Exhaling slowly, Josh took the officers' cloaks himself. "Why don't you show these gentlemen into the parlor then, and I'll take these into the kitchen."

Reagan turned to Sterling and Roth and lifted a hand, gesturing in the direction of the parlor. Her smile was painstakingly artificial. "Come right this way. I'm certain my father can hardly wait to meet you."

Hours later Reagan paced the floor in Uriah's bedchamber, her hands tucked behind her. "Father, I don't know what to do. They can't stay here."

"Don't you see, child? We've no choice! We both knew it would happen sooner or later." Uriah spoke in a hushed voice.

She shook her head, refusing to give in so easily. "There's got to be a way . . ."

"Give it up!" Uriah exhaled, watching the smoke from his pipe rise in the air. "We're finished. There'll be no more publications coming from you or me. The Cause will have to find a new penman to plead their case with the citizens. Our printing days have come to an end."

Reagan spun around. "An end? What do you mean they've come to end? We've just begun!"

"You certainly don't think we can continue, not

with these soldiers in our house."

"We'll just have to be more careful, that's all, Papa." Reagan crossed her arms over her chest, pacing faster.

"And you don't think those men will become suspicious with our deliverers coming day and night to pick up the material?"

"We could work strictly from your printing shop."

"Impossible. The risk is already too great. You know what we've had to put up with to keep our doors open. We should have just carried our press out of the city before the soldiers marched on us, like the others did. Major Burke still thinks we intend to start up that Tory paper; when he realizes I've made no pledge of allegiance he may well close me down. He's suspicious of everyone these days. That piece you wrote on him last month was the last straw. He's now actively searching for whoever is printing so-called treasonous materials."

"That's been the scuttlebutt for weeks," Reagan argued. "We've seen no soldiers actively seeking anything but the nearest ale house."

"They closed John Goodmen down just last week for refusing to print that Tory paper. They thought that because he was Quaker, he'd do their bidding. Threw his press, piece by piece into the street and dumped his ink into the sewer."

"Then we'll print here."

Uriah caught his daughter's hand as she walked by. "Reagan. This is your life you speak of. Yours, mine . . . Elsa's."

She dropped down on one knee before her father, taking both of his hands in hers. "I know. But it's

26

also the life of our new nation," she said passionately. "We may not be able to take up arms for our patriots, but this is something we can do." Her eyes glistened with tears. "Something we must do."

Uriah stroked his daughter's cheek with his ink-stained fingertips. "Aye, Reagie, you're as stubborn as your mother was. She could never take no for an answer, either."

"Papa, you might as well help me because I'll continue with or without you. I don't care if I have to write each and every leaflet by hand. The words of men like Mr. Thomas Paine must be heard."

Uriah sighed, suddenly feeling old. "And tell me, Daughter, how could we manage this?" He held up a finger. "Now I'm not saying I'm in agreement, but if I were . . . ?"

Reagan bounced up. "The secret room below the carriage house."

Uriah yanked his pipe out of his mouth. "The secret room, is it? And how might you know about the secret room?"

"Nettie told me. I'm certain it's big enough."

"You've been down there?"

"A few times. It was dark and dusty, but with a broom and a mop . . ."

"And just what did Nettie tell you about the secret room?" Uriah asked, caught between being amused and angry.

"That Grandpapa had it dug so that he could hide from Grandmama without actually having to go anywhere." She hesitated. "Nettie also said he had assignations with other women there, but I don't know that that's true."

Uriah stuffed his pipe back in his mouth. "Nettie

27

has a loose tongue."

"It would work, wouldn't it?" Reagan stood in front of the fireplace warming her backside.

"I'm not sure that it's safe. The whole thing could cave in. The ceiling joists would have to be checked; I haven't been down there in years."

"Westley could help. He knows a bit about building."

Uriah leaned back in his worn chair, tucking his hands behind his head. "And if I did agree to this crazed idea, and if the building was safe, where on God's green earth would we get another press? I can't very well pack mine up at the shop and carry it over here."

Reagan added another log to the fire. "We could build one."

"Build one!" her father scoffed.

"You said yourself that the soldiers tossed John Goodmen's press into the street. Most of the pieces are still in the alley. He's packed up and gone to New Castle. You know he wouldn't mind." She spoke faster as her excitement grew. "And the pieces that are broken or missing, we can get Westley to replace. You know he can scrounge up anything in this city."

Uriah shook his head. "It will never work, Daughter. You just might as well put the whole idea out of your head."

"I could run the press."

Uriah's yes widened. "You?"

"You . . . you could show me how to do the printing and I could work during the day when the officers are gone. Surely they must have some duties elsewhere."

"I don't know, Reagan. I just don't know."

"You *do* know. You know I'm right."

"I'd be endangering your life. I'm your father. I should be protecting you, not subjecting you to such risks."

"I'm a full-grown woman. I ought to be out of the house and married by now—you said so yourself." Her dark eyes met her father's. "I take the risk of my own choosing, just like the others."

Uriah puffed on his pipe. "I suppose I could think about it."

"Oh, yes, Papa!" She grinned. "I knew you'd see it my way. I knew you'd not let our men at Valley Forge suffer in vain."

"I said I would think about it." He picked up a book from the table. "Now I have reading to do and you need to get to bed. It's been a long day."

Reagan leaned over and kissed her father on the cheek. "Thank you, Papa."

"I've agreed to nothing." He waved her away. "The whole idea is foolhardy at best."

"I know, Papa."

He opened his book at the marked page. "My spectacles! Have you seen my spectacles? I just know Nettie's carried them off again."

Reagan chuckled, removing them from a pocket Nettie had sewn on his waistcoat. "These spectacles?"

He took them from her hand and put them on. "Good night, Daughter."

She turned at the door. "Good night, Papa. I love you." She heard him give a grunt as she stepped into the hall and closed the door behind her.

With a smile of satisfaction, Reagan started down

the dark hallway toward the bedchamber she would now be sharing with her sister. Just as she passed her own room, the door swung open and light spilled onto the polished hardwood floor.

Startled, Reagan stopped in midstep.

Sterling's eyes met the young woman's. *God, but she's a beauty,* he thought. *A different time, a different place . . .*

"C-Captain Thayer."

Sterling smiled hesitantly. Firelight from his bedchamber filtered through her thick auburn tresses setting them ablaze with color. Her face was so perfectly formed with porcelain skin and a sprinkling of freckles across her aristocratic nose. And her eyes . . . they were enchanting. "I . . . I really don't think it's necessary for you to address me so, considering the circumstances. Please, call me Grayson."

She moistened her lips. There was something about this redcoat that was unsettling. Something in his eyes. "I don't think that's appropriate."

"Appropriate?" He looked away, thinking of his brother he'd had incarcerated in some jail cell somewhere to the north. Sterling *knew* he had done the right thing, switching places with him for the good of the American Army. Sterling had been assured Grayson would remain safe, but deep in his heart he felt guilty. War forced men to do things they would never do otherwise. "Is there anything *appropriate* about this damned war?" he asked Reagan.

Reagan lifted her chin indignantly. "Odd words coming from a man who earns his keep murdering innocent women and children."

30

Sterling glanced back at her. He could see he was going to have to take more care what he said. This woman was too bright for him to be making careless mistakes in her presence. "I . . . I only meant that everything is so inconvenient. I don't appreciate being lodged with others. I prefer the solace of my own rooms."

The spell of the moment was broken. Reagan chuckled dryly, brushing past him. "You sound as if you think you were invited! Well, I can assure you, sir, that I want you here no more than you wish to be here." She stopped at her sister's bedchamber, resting her hand on the doorknob. "Another house along the street would surely be more *convenient.* Let me know when you go and I'll have our wagon brought around to help you move."

Sterling watched until Reagan disappeared from the hall, closing her door quietly behind her. "Damn," he murmured beneath his breath. "That wench's got spirit. Thank God she's on our side."

The following day Sterling walked down the cobblestone street beside Lieutenant Charles Warrington, who'd been sent to escort Captain Grayson Thayer to their unit headquarters a few blocks away. Sterling strode along, his head bent in concentration as he listened to the lieutenant.

"I can't believe you didn't remember me, Grayson! That night in Marseilles! How could you forget it? That blonde, Antoinette. Christ, how could you forget her?"

Sterling chuckled, giving a slight shrug. "So I was in my cups. What can I say?"

31

"In your cups? You could barely walk, my friend. I was the one who got you back to your room in one piece. Those fellows on the wharf chased us for two blocks. Don't suppose you remember that, either?" The two passed a fellow officer. "Captain." Charles saluted.

Sterling gave a nod. "I'm afraid I don't recall a thing. You certain it was me?"

"I should think there could be only one Captain Grayson Thayer of the King's Army." Charles laughed, giving Sterling a slap on the back. "Unless of course it was that whoreson brother of yours impersonating you."

Sterling came to an abrupt stop. "And what do you know of my brother, Lieutenant?" He prayed the panic he felt in his chest wasn't evident on his face.

Charles's laughter died away. "Uh, very little. Only what you said that night. That he's a Colonial. Of course rumor has it the man's a spy for Washington himself."

Sterling's eyes met his companion's. "Charles, I would take it as a personal affront if you were to mention my brother ever again either to me or anyone else."

Charles gulped. "I . . . I wouldn't think of it, sir. It was only in jest that I—"

"Lieutenant, my brother's treasonous politics are not a jesting matter!"

"No. No, of course they aren't." Charles lifted his hand. "I meant no disrespect."

"And none was taken." Sterling started down the street again. "I haven't seen Sterling in two years. I do not know where he is, nor am I interested in knowing. Any mention of my brother could bring scandal to my career . . . and yours as well," he added meaningfully.

"You can trust me not to say another word, sir," Charles answered weakly.

"Good, now tell me. What was the wench's name again?"

Another block down the street, Sterling heard the sound of men laughing, interspersed with an angry feminine voice. Turning the corner, he and Charles spotted a group of king's soldiers standing in front of a shop doorway.

The redcoats shouted after a man who was hurrying in the opposite direction. "Can't take a joke, tanner?" one called tauntingly.

"You have no right," cried a woman, not visible to Sterling on the street. "That man was our customer!"

A soldier turned toward the door. "Ain't no more, though, is he, missy?" The soldiers laughed, shoving each other playfully.

"I suggest, gentlemen, that you take your games elsewhere."

Sterling stopped on the sidewalk. The woman's voice was familiar. Christ! It was Reagan Llewellyn! The shop ahead had to be her father's printing shop.

"Or what?" The uniformed soldier took a step forward, resting his boot on the shop steps. "What are you gonna do?"

"Look, we've done nothing wrong. What do you want from us?" Reagan reasoned. "You've got no cause to be here."

"Ah, but you're wrong there, missy." The soldier

pushed his way in.

Sterling walked through the group of soldiers and came to halt just outside the door. He peered in.

Reagan took a step back, twisting her hands in her apron. She didn't notice Sterling in the doorway. "We were inspected last week," she explained to the soldier who was harassing her.

"Well, you're being inspected again." He picked up a pile of fresh leaflets and dumped them on the floor.

Uriah hurried into the room from the back. "Reagan, what's going on here?" He stopped. "Good morning, what can we do for you?"

The soldier picked up a tray of type and slowly upended it, sending letters spilling to the floor.

"Stop it!" Reagan ran forward to catch the tray before its entire contents were emptied, but Uriah caught her arm.

"Reagie!" Uriah barked.

"You've got no right!" she fumed at the soldier as she struggled to escape her father's iron grip. "You blackguards have no right to come in here and destroy our property!"

The soldier responded by lifting a salt-glazed jug and yanking out the cork. Slowly he began to drizzle linseed oil onto the planked shop floor.

Unable to let the harassment go any further, Sterling came through the door. "Soldier!" he thundered.

Reagan looked up in surprise.

"Yes?" The soldier laughed, turning around.

"What do you think you're doing, Corporal . . . Corporal . . ."

The soldier grinned. "Sawyer."

34

"Sir?" Sterling intoned.

The smile fell from the soldier's face. "Corporal Sawyer, sir."

Sterling walked to the center of the room, followed by Lieutenant Warrington. "What do you think you're doing, Corporal Sawyer?" Sterling demanded with unmistakable authority.

"D-doing, sir?"

"Cork the jug, Corporal, and come here."

Sawyer set down the container of oil and went to stand before the two officers.

Sterling yanked off his cloak angrily. "Don't you know how to salute a superior officer, Corporal?"

Sawyer came to attention, saluting smartly. "Yes, sir."

"Now tell me, Corporal Sawyer, just what it is you're doing in this printshop." Sterling surveyed the damage. Paper and print letters littered the room, and a puddle of oil was slowly seeping into the floor.

Uriah released his daughter's arm and the two stood watching the British officer in shocked disbelief.

"I . . . I was inspecting, sir."

"Inspecting what?" Sterling's voice was razor-edged.

"T-the shop, sir. Major Burke wants us to keep an eye on all of the Whigs in the city."

"And just what is it you're looking for, Corporal." Sterling's eyes met Reagan's. Was that fear he saw in her face?

"Pamphlets, sir." The corporal shifted his weight from one foot to the other.

"Pamphlets!" Sterling boomed.

"Yes, sir. Somebody in the city's printin' nasty things about the major and he don't like it. We're supposed to be lookin' for anything bein' printed that might be treasonous."

"What in God's name are you talking about, Corporal?"

The corporal trembled. "Pamphlets. Somebody's printin' and then sellin' 'em or givin' 'em away. Pamphlets about these colonists' so-called rights and such."

Sterling swore softly beneath his breath. "So this is how you inspect? You come into this place of business and make a muck of things!"

"Uriah Llewellyn's a known Whig . . ."

"The man is a citizen of the Crown!" Sterling turned to face Uriah. "Master Llewellyn, what is it you're printing?"

Uriah swept a piece of paper off the floor and handed it to Captain Thayer. "It's a bulletin. Mistress Bennett's bondman's run off."

Sterling took the piece of paper and quickly glanced at it. It was indeed a bulletin offering a reward for the return of an eighteen-year-old bondman by the name of Charlie. "Corporal, I take it you can read."

"My mama learnt me."

"Then read this—" Sterling pushed the paper into the soldier's hand—"and tell me what treasonous words appear on the page. Is it the part where Mistress Bennett states her man is five and a half feet tall, or is the only thing treasonous about this bulletin the fact that she's only offering five shillings six for his return!"

The corporal looked from the page in his hand,

36

up at the officer and then back at the page again. "I guess there ain't nothin' wrong with this, but I'm only doin' what I was told."

Sterling tore the paper from the corporal's hand. "I find it hard to believe that you were ordered to harass this man. Now get out of here, soldier, and don't let me catch you bothering these people again. You are dismissed!"

Corporal Sawyer saluted, and then hurried out of the printshop.

For a moment there was silence, and then Reagan walked up to Sterling. There was a hint of a smile on her lips. "Thank you. Captain. It's good to know there is still some sense of right and wrong in the world."

Sterling's eyes met hers and he nearly smiled. This morning she was dressed in a loden-green woolen gown with a white lawn kerchief draped over her shoulders. Her rich auburn hair was tucked beguilingly beneath a starched mobcap, her cheeks rosy.

Taken off guard by Reagan's hesitant smile, he glanced back at his companion standing in the doorway. Had he made another error? Would Captain Grayson Thayer have come to the defense of this woman? After all, the soldier had done no real harm. "Yes, well, I must be going. The lieutenant and I will be late for our engagement." Heading for the door, he called over his shoulder, "I'll be late tonight so don't expect me for the evening meal. Just leave something in the kitchen."

Reagan followed him, intending to say something more, but before she reached the door the captain and his companion had made their exit and were already hurrying down the walk.

Uriah reached past her to close and bar the door. "Willem," he called to his apprentice. "Get out here and start cleaning up this mess."

"I'll help, Father."

Uriah frowned, shaking his head. "No, leave it to us. Best you get on home to your sister. Damned lobsterbacks. That's the third customer they've lost for us in a week."

Reagan laid her hand on his arm. "It could have been worse if it wasn't for Captain—"

"He's no better than the rest, girl." Uriah took her by the shoulders. "He'd see us both hanged, Reagan. Never forget it . . . not for an instant. Captain Thayer is the enemy . . . no less deadly because he hides his mission behind a handsome face."

She rested her head against his chest. "I hear you, Papa," she whispered softly. "I hear you."

Chapter Three

Reagan plucked at the keys of the delicate spinet, repeating the refrain of a favorite song again and again as she struggled to play it correctly. Sharp, resonant chords filtered out of the parlor and through the house. She sang softly, tapping her foot.

"In Freedom we're born and in Freedom we'll live
Our purses are ready,
Steady, Friends, Steady
Not as Slaves, but as Freeman our money we'll
    give."

Drawn to the clear, sweet notes, Sterling couldn't help but stop at the doorway to listen. After a restless night, he had risen early, bathed, broken the fast, and now he was on his way to meet with his commanding officer. The soft, haunting tune Reagan played brought a tightening in his chest. Only a week earlier he had sat around a campfire at Valley Forge with friends, singing *The Liberty Song*.

Without thought, Sterling found himself murmuring the words as Reagan moved on to the second verse.

"Our worthy Forefathers—let's give them a cheer,
To climates unknown did courageously steer;

Thro' Oceans, to deserts, for freedom they came,
And dying bequeath'd us their freedom and
    Fame."

Against his better judgment, Sterling walked into
the parlor and laid his cloak over a chair. How many
hours had he and Grayson spent in their mother's
parlor in Williamsburg, Virginia, playing silly songs,
singing, laughing? But then Grayson had gone to
England and purchased a commission in the King's
Army, Mother had died, and Father had been killed
at Long Island. This damned war had changed everything . . . and nothing would ever be the same.

Reagan stumbled with a chord and began to repeat
it again. Without hesitation Sterling reached over her
shoulder and struck the proper notes again and
again. "Like this," he instructed softly. He inhaled
slowly, breathing in the fresh scent of her clean,
shining hair. "Listen to the notes, relax and let your
fingers be drawn into the music."

Reagan turned her head, her breath catching in her
throat. The sound of the captain's deep tenor voice in
her ear sent a shiver down her spine. The warmth
from his arm seeped into her shoulder, flowing
through her veins.

"Try it again," Sterling urged, foregoing his brother's sharp, grating tone.

Reagan found her fingers gliding over the keys as
the captain nodded. "Good. That's right. You've got
it." He sat down on the corner of the bench. "You
play well. You have a good ear."

Lifting her hands from the keyboard, Reagan
found her voice. "You play?"

"A little." He shrugged his broad shoulders. "Or at

least I did before the war."

"The war, is it?" She smiled. "I thought you Englishmen were still calling it a Colonial Uprising."

Engrossed in his thoughts, Sterling began to play another tune on the spinet. "I've been on the battlefield. I've seen the dead and dying. What else does it take to be a war?"

Flustered by the captain's nearness, Reagan slid off the bench and stepped back. Her gaze lingered on his handsome face. "I . . . I wanted to thank you for what you did yesterday. In the printshop, I mean. Those soldiers have been harassing us for weeks. I can't imagine what we've done to provoke them."

Sterling rose to his feet, his brother's mask falling over his own gentler features. "Yes, well, don't expect me to interfere on your behalf again." His tone was harsher than he'd intended it to be.

Reagan bristled. Whatever that strange tingling in the air between them had been, it was gone. Captain Thayer's voice was raw with authority, his face taut with conceit. "I didn't ask for your help, Captain. You offered of your own free will. I was simply giving thanks."

"Yes, well . . ." Sterling swept his cloak off the chair, unsure what his brother's next response would have been. "I just wanted to make you aware of the fact that I'm not here for you or your father's benefit. In the future you'll have to fend for yourself against the soldiers, right or wrong in their doings."

"I must tell you, Captain Thayer, that I have never in my life met a man so filled with self-importance." Seething, Reagan followed him out of the parlor and toward the front door. "What gave you the idea that my father or I expected any sort of protection from

41

you? What makes you think we haven't been making out just fine without you?"

Sterling threw his cloak over his shoulders, anxious to get out of the house. What was wrong with him, provoking her like that? She was right. There would have been no harm in simply accepting her thanks. In what way would it have undermined his role as a British officer? *I should never have gone into the parlor,* he thought jamming his hat onto his head. "Good day, Mistress Llewellyn," he called, hurrying down the front steps.

Reagan slammed the front door shut, murmuring an oath beneath her breath. "Conceited lout," she shouted to the closed door.

What was wrong with her to have allowed the captain to sit beside her in such an intimate manner? She shook her head. And how in the hell did he know the tune to *The Liberty Song?*

Walking into the kitchen, Reagan found her sister seated on the floor petting her kitten. "Elsa, have you seen Papa?"

"Yes."

"Where is he, Elsa?"

"In the cellar."

"And Nettie?" Reagan asked, noting the half-rolled pie crust on the center worktable.

"In the cellar, too. They said they were getting apples, but that was a long time ago." She lifted her kitten, peering into its face. "Do you think that when the snow is gone I could take Mittens for a walk in the garden?"

"Getting apples?" Reagan frowned. "What are you talking about, getting apples? It takes two of them to bring up a bowl of apples to make a pie?" But then a thought struck her and she smiled. "I'm going to go down and help with the apples. You stay up here and play with Mittens, all right?"

"I don't like it in the cellar. Spiders," Elsa said matter-of-factly. "I think I'll give Mittens some milk." She got to her feet, intent on that thought. "Mittens really likes milk."

Retrieving a candle from the candle-box on the wall, Reagan lit it and pushed it into a candlestick. She then opened a narrow door along the inside paneled wall of the kitchen and started down the steep, railless steps. The warped wood groaned beneath Reagan's weight as she placed one foot carefully in front of the other, the candle's golden aura lighting the way.

Reaching the bottom step, Reagan's feet touched the hard dirt floor of the cellar and she lifted the candle higher. "Papa?" she called softly.

The room was stacked with wooden barrels and broken crates. A spinning wheel missing its spindle lay on its side; a cracked butter churn rested in a corner. The room smelled of seasoned wood, of dust and of passing time. Walking into the next room, the pungent aroma of unwashed potatoes, onions, and apples was overwhelming. Reed baskets hung from the low ceiling and vegetable crates lined the walls. Before the British had invaded the city, the containers had been filled to capacity, now there was barely enough food to last the Llewellyn family the winter.

Reagan's foot touched something on the floor and she stifled a squeal, thrusting the candle out to catch a glimpse of a turnip rolling across the floor.

Chuckling beneath her breath at her skittishness, she lifted a muslin curtain and went into the third and final room. The large, stale-smelling room was void of anything but an old broken rope bed and a myriad of cobwebs. In her grandfather's time the male servants had slept here, but it had been years since the room had been used for anything but storage.

"Papa?" Reagan called. He and Nettie had to be in the secret room below the carriage house, but how to get in? It had been so many years since Reagan had been in the room, and then it had been from the entrance above, in the carriage house. "Papa?" she called again. "Nettie?"

Running her fingers along the brick wall, she wrinkled her forehead in puzzlement. All four walls were brick. How could there possibly be an entrance from here? As if by magic the wall began to separate and part of it swung into the room.

"Reagan?"

Reagan held up her candle. "Papa?"

Uriah came down a narrow passageway. "I thought I heard your voice. Where's your sister?" He was covered from head to foot in dust and his graying beard sported a strand of a spider's web.

Reagan brushed at her father's beard with her fingertips. "Elsa's upstairs with her kitten. She'll be fine." Reagan turned to the door in the wall. "Papa. This is so clever. How did Grandpa do it?"

"Is a bit of handiwork, isn't it?" Uriah leaned on his broom. "Looks simple enough. The trick was to have a master bricklayer. All he did was to knock out part of the wall, make a swinging wooden door and attach the brickwork to the door. With it closed you can barely see the spaces in the mortar between the wall and the door."

44

She nodded, following him through the dugout tunnel and into the secret room. Two lamps hung from the ceiling illuminating the whitewashed walls. A desk, thick with dust, stood in the corner, while a bed and a table rested against the far wall. A wooden ladder descended from the ceiling on the right.

Meticulously, Nettie swung her broom over the packed-dirt floor. "That you, Reagie?" she questioned, not bothering to look up.

Reagan smiled at the old gray-haired woman. Nettie had been her mother's nursemaid in England and had come with her charge when the young woman was married off to Uriah so many years ago. Nettie had lost her vision a good ten years back, but still managed to run the Llewellyn household with miraculous efficiency.

"I thought you were baking a pie, Nettie. Elsa said you came down for apples."

"That I did, that I did," the housekeeper responded. "But you know a man; he just don't know how to sweep a floor proper. There's still dust everywhere. I can smell it!"

Reagan laughed, running her fingers over her grandfather's desk. "If you want to know the truth, Nettie, I think Papa intentionally does a poor job so that you'll sweep it for him."

Uriah lifted his hands in mock innocence. "I stand falsely accused by my own daughter."

Reagan thrust a spare willow broom into his hands. "It seems to me that you've been sweeping your shop for years without Nettie's help."

Caught, Uriah laughed good-naturedly. "That's what I get for having a daughter smarter than myself. I know I should never have paid that tutor! What does a woman need with geography and Latin?" He shook an ink-stained finger. "A dancemaster! Now that's who I should have hired. If you could dance, girl, you'd have caught yourself a husband by now and you'd be out of my hair."

"What hair?" Reagan teased. "That pate's been lacking sorely for years. And you only paid half the tutor's fees. Josh's father paid the rest." She pulled a clean rag from a bucket on the floor and began to dust the desk.

"No respect. What is a man's life coming to when he can get no respect in his own home?"

A sudden knocking came from above, startling all three of them.

"What's that?" Reagan asked in a hushed voice.

The knocking came again in a distinct pattern. Knock, knock-knock, knock.

Uriah went to the ladder and lifted his broom, knocking in reply. The same pattern was repeated, then Uriah climbed up the ladder and released the hatch. Stepping down, Westley descended into the room.

"Reagie!" He smiled. His arms were laden with a massive crate that was covered by a square of oilcloth.

"Here, let me help you." Uriah eased the crate to the floor. "You certain no one saw you?"

"Who's to see me? Since you stabled old Hannah at the smithy's, who'd be in the carriage house?" He turned to Reagan, pushing his dark bangs up off his forehead. "This room is perfect. I knew it had to be your idea, Reagie."

Uriah pulled the oilcloth off the wooden crate and peered inside. "You picked this up in broad daylight?"

"Right in the alley where you told me. Old Friend Goodman's going to lend a hand to the Cause and never know it." Westley looked to Reagan for approval. "After dark I can fetch some of the bigger pieces, but I'll need a horse and wagon."

"Westley's welcome to take Hannah, isn't he, Papa?"

"Of course he is." Uriah lifted the crate and carried it to the far wall. "But I want you to be careful, boy. Those damned soldiers catch you picking up pieces of that printing press and they're bound to ask questions. You can't afford another interrogation like the last one."

Westley nursed his chin, laughing. "No, you've got that. My jaw's still sore from the last!"

Nettie thrust her broom at Westley, and the young man took it. "Now that you're here, Westley, I can get back to my pie." She waved a hand over her head as she maneuvered unhindered across the room and out the secret doorway. "You've got enough hands to finish the cleaning. Will you be staying for dinner, boy?"

"Yes, ma'am. If you've something to spare."

"We haven't," she replied good-naturedly, disappearing into the darkness. "But that ain't never stopped no one in this house before."

Finishing her dusting, Reagan tossed the rag into the bucket on the floor. "So, Westley, how do the ceiling joists look? Papa's afraid the whole thing's going to cave in."

Westley patted a whitewashed wall. "Not in our lifetime. This room will be standing long after Georgie's army's fallen."

47

"Excellent. How long will it take you to get the press pieces down here and put together? I'd like to start printing again as soon as possible."

Uriah frowned. "Daughter, you don't know what's involved. It's going to take time."

"How much time?" she asked shrewdly.

Westley shrugged. "I can have the necessary pieces here by the end of the week."

"But we need ink, paper," Uriah said with exasperation. "I'm short as it is at the shop. We start buying up all of the paper in the city and we're bound to have an investigation on our hands!"

"He's right, Reagan," Westley agreed. "Your father told me about the redcoats you're lodging. This is going to get dangerous."

"And it wasn't before?" She snatched the broom from his hands. "I plan on taking care of the captain and his drunken friend. They'll not be here long to bother us."

Westley caught Reagan's hand, forcing her to look him in the eye. "You be careful. You don't know what you're dealing with. They say Major Burke's got no sense of humor when it comes to treason. They hung Nathan Hale without a trial."

"But he was spying! All we're doing is writing down what we think."

"And then contaminating other minds with it," Westley answered gravely.

"I'm going to do this with or without your help, Westley." She pulled away. "So, you just get the press in working order. I'll take over from there." She began to sweep vigorously. "Now let's get to work. The captain's out for now, but I don't know how long he'll be."

* * *

"Captain."

"Major Burke." Sterling stepped up to the major's desk and snapped to attention, saluting his commanding officer.

The major returned the salute absently and went back to shuffling papers on his desk. "At ease, Captain."

Sterling relaxed slightly, parting his feet and tucking his hands behind his back. Cautiously, he lifted his gaze to study the preoccupied man. The major was middle-aged, rail thin, and sporting an oversized powdered wig. His mouth seemed to be screwed into a perpetual pucker.

"Captain Thayer reporting for duty, sir."

"Yes, yes." Major Burke waved a shriveled hand. "And what am I supposed to do with you?"

"Sir?" Sterling shifted uneasily.

"What am I to do with you?" the major repeated with annoyance. "I've already got three useless captains with this regiment. What in Christ's name am I to do with a fourth?" He dipped a quill into a bottle of ink and scrawled his signature across a document. "You damned blue-bellies. You buy yourself a fancy commission and then we're stuck with you. I'd lay a wager you don't know any more about battle than your wet nurse."

Sterling suppressed an urge to chuckle. The man was right. Too many young men from wealthy families bought commissions and were then foisted upon career military leaders.

Major Burke signed another document and then slammed his quill on the desk. "What did you say your name was, Captain?"

"Thayer, sir. Grayson Thayer."

"The same Thayers of Suffolk?"

"Originally, sir. But I was born in the Colonies. Schooled in Eton and Oxford."

"Well, bloody good for you, boy." The major pushed back in his chair, looking at Sterling for the first time. "And handsome, too," he mocked. "Precisely what I need."

Sterling stared at Burke, an uneasiness coming over him. He didn't like this man. He seemed too shrewd, too calculating. He could be dangerous. "You've no duty for me then, sir?"

The major sighed, crossing his arms over his chest. His scarlet coat was neatly pressed, his white vest immaculate. His fringed gold epaulets swung gently. "I suppose I've got to produce an assignment or you'll most likely spend your time in some tavern gambling away your coin and catching the clap!"

"Yes, sir," Sterling answered, lacking any other response.

A piece of parchment on his desk caught Major Burke's eye and he snapped it up. "I've got it, boy! Have you seen this?" He shook the folded pamphlet.

Sterling took the paper and skimmed it quickly. It was a patriot leaflet expounding individual's rights and the barbarity of monarchism. There was also a satirical piece on Major Burke himself.

"Have you seen it?" the major demanded.

"Not this one, but others like it. They're common enough in the cities. I'm told they're harmless," Sterling answered.

"The bloody hell they're harmless! Treason! That's what it is. These damned Colonists need to be taught

50

a lesson! Someone is printing this trumpery and distributing it. It does nothing but cause unrest among those who are still loyal to their mother country." Major Burke stood. "I want you to investigate this fully. I want to know who this penman is and I want him arrested. Perhaps if we hang the bastard for treason, the other penmen will think again before printing such swill! You may have as many men at your disposal as you deem necessary, but I want this stopped!"

Sterling folded the evidence. "Yes, sir. Consider it done, sir."

"That will be all then, Captain. You're dismissed."

Sterling saluted, turned sharply, and left the room, the patriot pamphlet nestled snugly inside his coat.

Chapter Four

Reagan lifted the hood of her cloak and stepped outside, quietly closing the front door of the Llewellyn residence on Spruce Street. The sun was setting to the west leaving streaks of orange-gold across the dull winter horizon. A lamplighter came around the corner of Fourth Street and touched his torch to a lamp a few feet away. The ragged man nodded ever so slightly to Reagan and she nodded in return as he hurried by.

She tucked her hands beneath her cloak, shivering as much from nervous anticipation as from the cold. Tonight was the night she and Westley would bring home the major components to the printing press. If all was on schedule, he should have already retrieved the Llewellyns' horse and wagon from the smithy's down the street where they boarded the beast; any moment now, he would pick her up.

The front door latch clicked behind Reagan, and Captain Thayer stepped out on the stoop. They glanced up at each other in startled surprise.

"C-Captain."

Sterling gave an agitated grunt. "I thought you said you were retiring early this evening." He meant to take his leave without anyone in the house knowing he was gone. He had an appointment in precisely fifteen minutes with his new contact from Valley

Forge.

Reagan drew her cloak closer, scrutinizing the officer with sharp, dark eyes. "I thought you'd said the same. I distinctly recall you telling Nettie that you were not to be disturbed until morning. A headache, I believe you said you were suffering."

Sterling adjusted his already perfectly placed grenadier cap. "A woman has no business on the streets of Philadelphia after dark."

"There was no danger on our streets before we were infested by the king's rats," she dared.

He studied her perfect mouth, bemused. "You have a sharp tongue. Be thankful your lips are so sweet and that I have a good sense of humor. There are others who would not be so tolerant of your voiced opinions."

Caught off guard by his backhanded compliment, Reagan stepped aside to let Sterling pass. If she intended to go with Westley, she'd have to rid herself of the redcoat quickly. "I suppose you have an engagement. Don't let me keep you."

He stiffened. "An engagement? Certainly not. I just thought that a walk in the night air might clear my head."

Reagan opened the front door. "Then have a good walk, Captain. Good evening."

Sterling waited until she disappeared inside, and then hurried away. If he was late, there would be no contact tonight.

Reagan waited an appropriate amount of time and then stuck her head outside the door. The captain was nowhere in sight. Relieved, she slipped out onto the stoop. A minute later a wagon came rattling down the street and Reagan rushed down the steps and leaped into the wagon. She laid her hand on Westley's arm as the old horse moved forward.

"Ready?" her accomplice whispered.

She smiled in the fading light. "Ready."

Sterling swung open the gate, and the ancient hinges groaned loudly. Looking left and then right to be certain no one had seen him, he slipped into the courtyard and hurried toward the barn that loomed ahead.

The sweet scent of fresh hay and pungent smell of warm horseflesh filled Sterling's nostrils as he slipped into the dark structure. All was silent save for the shifting of horses' hooves and the flapping of a loose shingle.

"Smith," Sterling whispered into the inky blackness. "Smith, are you there?"

A bass chuckle sounded from the darkness. "By the King's cod . . ." The man paused, waiting for the completion of the passwords.

". . . We'll overcome, by God." Sterling finished on cue.

"Welcome, Brother." A huge bear of a man stepped from a horse stall, offering a packet of papers.

Sterling accepted the bundle, glancing up at the bulky figure. In the darkness he could make nothing out of the man, only that he was immensely tall with a rounded belly. *It's safer this way,* he mused. *The fewer identities I'm aware of, the safer it will be for all of us.* He tucked the packet into his coat. "How is our army?"

"Hungry," the voice replied. "Cold. My horses fare

54

better than our men."

Sterling nodded in understanding. A few short days ago he had been among his fellow soldiers, his belly growling with the rest of them. "We'll have to work out a system, Smith. How can I safely contact you?"

The man plucked a stalk of straw from the floor and pushed it into his mouth. "Got a horse?"

"I can get one."

"Trouble with his foot . . . bad shoe. I can take a look at it anytime, day or night. There's more than one redcoat who uses my services."

Sterling smiled, offering his hand. "Thank you."

Smith took the smaller man's hand and clasped it tightly. "We don't want any thanks, soldier, we just want King Gordie's bastards out of our city."

"I think we can do better than that," Sterling boasted. "I think we can chase them across the sea with their red coattails tucked between their legs!"

Smith laughed heartily. "Now there's a sight I'd like to see."

"Well, I'd better be going. I'm lodged with a family; I have to be careful. Good night to you, Brother Smith. I'll be seeing you."

"Good night and Godspeed," the man answered, closing the barn door behind Sterling and locking it.

At the sound of footsteps above in the kitchen, Reagan hurried through the storage room and up the steep stairs, her candle held tightly in her hand. She and Westley had managed to retrieve the main bulk of the printing press from behind John Goodman's old shop and carry it to the room below the carriage house without being noticed. Westley and her father would now have to reassemble the ancient Dutch-made press and see how many vital pieces were missing.

Reagan stepped into the kitchen and closed the door. The fire on the hearth cast long, eerie fingers of light across the sanded plank floor. "Is someone there?" she called softly. She *knew* she'd heard footsteps, but there seemed to be no one about. "Nettie?" She blew out her candle and dropped it into the box on the wall.

All was silent in the house except for the crackle and spit of the banked fire. Walking to the fireplace, Reagan reached for the poker. A hand clasped her shoulder and she jumped, crying out as she spun around.

"Ho, there! Would you strike a unarmed man?" Lieutenant Gardener raised his hands in mock defense.

She looked at the iron poker in her hand, then lowered it. "You scared me," she hedged. "I . . . I thought you'd gone out." She wondered if he'd seen her emerge from the cellar.

Roth Gardener took the fireplace implement from her hand and set it by the hearth. "What need would I have to go out on a cold night when I've a warm house, a fine bottle of whiskey, and a beautiful woman to keep me company?" His speech was thick with drink.

Reagan sidestepped the lieutenant as he tried to take her hand. "It's late. Time I was abed." She turned away, but he lunged forward and grasped her wrist, pulling her against him.

"Why in such a hurry, little lady?" His sour breath

was hot on her cheek.

Suddenly she was afraid. "Let go of me."

"I wouldn't hurt you, just looking for some warmth, a little affection."

She stared directly into his bloodshot eyes. "Lieutenant, if you don't let go of me this instant, I'll report your behavior to your senior officer."

Roth laughed, grasping her around the waist and pushing her back against the wooden worktable that dominated the center of the kitchen. "You think they care? You think anyone does? You're the spoils, Reagie."

She struggled beneath his weight, trying unsuccessfully to shove him backward. His weight was too great for her, his arms too powerful even under the spell of hard liquor. Roth laughed harder, pressing his wet lips to her neck. "That's all right. I like my women with a little fight," he murmured.

"Let go of me, you son of a bitch," she ordered through clenched teeth. She tried to bring her knee up to his groin.

"No, no, no," Roth chided, as he shoved her knee between his legs. "We don't want to damage the goods, now do we?"

Reagan managed to free one of her hands and knocked him square in the ear.

"Ouch!" Roth snatched her hand and pulled it painfully behind her back. "What's say I take you right here in the kitchen?"

She squeezed her eyes shut in pain. *I can't believe this is happening,* she thought dizzily. *Not in my own home.*

Suddenly there were footsteps, but not her father's. Reagan's eyes flew open just in time to see Captain

Thayer grab the lieutenant by his beribboned queue and snap his head back.

"Lieutenant!" Sterling bellowed.

"C-Captain." Roth released his hold on Reagan, taking a step backward. He grasped his hair, trying to relieve the pressure.

"What in the bloody hell are you doing, Lieutenant Gardener?"

Roth gave a loud hiccup. "Sir?"

"Do you speak the king's English, Lieutenant? I asked what you think you're doing?"

"It was just in f-fun," Roth stuttered. "I meant the lady no h-harm."

"Are you so desperate for a woman's company that you'll force yourself upon the unwilling?"

"N-no, certainly not. I can have my choosing of the l-ladies."

"Then I suggest you make your choosing elsewhere!" Sterling released Roth's hair, giving him a boost forward with the sole of his shiny black boot.

The lieutenant fell against the wall, catching himself in the doorway.

"Apologies are in order, Lieutenant," Sterling barked, sweeping his cloak off his broad shoulders.

"S-sorry, mistress." Roth murmured sheepishly. "I meant no harm."

Reagan spun around, presenting her back to the two English officers. Her hands shook as she tried to regain her composure. If it hadn't been for Captain Thayer—for Grayson—she might well have been raped.

Roth Gardener stumbled out of the kitchen.

"Are you all right?" Sterling took her by the shoulders and turned her around to face him. A single tear seeped from the corner of her eye.

Reagan trembled. Her dark eyes met with startling blue. Sterling brushed the tear with his finger and touched its tip to his tongue.

"I . . . I'm all right," she whispered.

"Why didn't you scream? Your father must be upstairs."

"I . . . I didn't want to make a fuss. I thought I could handle him. It's not the first time I've been accosted since—"

"Since the king's men came into your city," he finished for her.

She nodded, squeezing her eyes shut. She was giddy with spent fear. That was why her heart pounded, wasn't it?

Sterling brushed a thick lock of hair off her cheek. "I can't keep coming to your rescue like this, Mistress," he teased.

Reagan laughed, lifting her lashes to return his gaze. "I'm indebted to you again."

"No," he breathed. The scent of her soft, sweet flesh enveloped him. All reason slipped from his head as he watched her rosy lips part with each breath. Before he could stop himself, he lowered his mouth to hers. He had to taste those lips, just once . . .

For one shocking moment, she allowed the captain's mouth to touch hers. He smelled of fine leather, of shaving soap, and of starched linen. Of its own accord, her hand rose and came to rest on the epaulet of his scarlet uniform. She could feel the heat rising in her cheeks. She could feel herself relaxing in his arms.

Suddenly something snapped deep within her—her

59

father's words, the images of dead patriot soldiers, the leering faces of Hessian guards on the street . . . They rose up inside her, making her cry out in anguish.

"Grayson!" She pulled away from him, drawing her hands to her lips.

Sterling reached for her. He couldn't stand the look of horrified guilt on her face. Then he lowered his hands. He knew no way to comfort her. He knew how she must feel. In her own mind she was betraying her beliefs. He was the enemy. "I'm sorry."

"How dare you!" she spit. The color in her cheeks drained to a pasty white. "How dare you! You come in here on the pretense of saving me from the lieutenant's hands!" Her thoughts were coming clearer now, now that he wasn't touching her. "You . . . you're no better than him!"

"Reagan—"

"You're worse, you know that, Captain? Him,"— she pointed to the ceiling, gaining momentum "—he is what he is, it's plain to see, but you, you're deceitful! You take unfair advantage!" She was so damned angry. So angry with him, so angry with herself for not having had enough backbone to resist falling for his game.

For a moment Sterling just stood there, staring at her trembling form. The firelight from behind filtered through her thick, rich hair forming a halo of brilliance. Her face was pale with rage, her eyes dark with bitter resentment. There was something about this woman that made his chest constrict, that made it difficult to gather his thoughts. All reason told him he must walk away. Nothing but doom would come of such a union, but still, for a moment he lingered.

Reagan refused to lift her lashes to meet the captain's gaze. Her shame was hers alone. She didn't look up until she heard him retrieve his cloak and walk out of the room. In frustrated fury she jerked a mug off the mantel and sent it flying across the room. Only the shattering of the clay cup, as it hit the plastered wall, gave her release.

A few mornings later, Reagan came down the front steps and went into the kitchen. "Elsa, are you down here?" Unable to sleep, Reagan had risen early with the intention of baking gingerbread. Making the sweets and selling them to various people was the perfect guise under which she could safely move about the city and distribute her leaflets.

"Elsa?" Reagan stood in the center of the kitchen, perplexed. When she'd woken, Elsa was already dressed and gone. She assumed her sister was downstairs making breakfast. Although Nettie did most to run the household, Elsa was an excellent cook and often made breakfast so that the old woman could sleep later in the morning.

Where could she be? Reagan wondered, panic rising in her chest. She wasn't in the cellar, the latch was hooked on the kitchen side. Reagan hurried through the downstairs rooms; her sister was nowhere to be seen.

Racing up the front staircase, Reagan gave a knock and walked into her father's bedchamber. Uriah stood near the fireplace, shaving. "Papa, have you seen Elsa?" She tried not to sound too concerned.

"Not this morning. Why?"

"Oh . . ."—she lifted her hand "I—just wanted to

tell her something." Before Uriah could speak again, Reagan had made her exit and hurried down the hall.

Without a moment's hesitation she flung open the door to Lieutenant Gardener's bedchamber. "Where is she?"

Roth turned around in surprise. He was dressed in nothing but a nightshirt; in his hand he held a glass of rum. He turned to face her. "Where's who, sweetheart? By all means, do come in."

Her dark eyes narrowed dangerously. "My sister." She glanced around the room. "She's not in here, is she?"

Roth looked around. "Not unless she's under the bed." He lifted his glass. "You can check if you like."

Reagan spun around and ran out the door, slamming it behind her. Other than in the attic, the only room left was Reagan's bedchamber, the one Grayson now occupied. She rested her hand on the polished brass doorknob, then released it. She knocked loudly.

"Yes" came Sterling's voice.

She took a deep breath and entered the room. "Captain, have you seen my sister this morning?" She tried to keep her eyes averted. Sterling was seated on a chair, rolling his stockings. He wore a pair of tight breeches and an immaculate white lawn shirt. His hair was unbound and fell in a golden curtain about his shoulders.

"Seen her? No. Is she missing?" He dropped his stockings and padded barefoot across the hardwood floor.

"No. I mean, I don't think so. It's just that she's not in the house." Reagan ran her fingers through her thick auburn hair. She hadn't tied it back this morning thinking she'd wash it before breakfast.

"Let me dress and I'll go looking. I'm sure she's come to no harm."

"No. I'll find her myself."

Sterling pulled a velvet ribbon off Reagan's dressing table and began to tie back *his* hair. "It'll only take me a minute to saddle my horse."

"I said no, Captain," she snapped. "She's got to be here somewhere." She backed out of the door. "She never leaves the house without one of us."

Taking the front steps two at a time, Reagan ran down the hall and burst into the kitchen intent on retrieving her cloak to go outside.

Elsa was just coming in the back door; a basket swung on her arm.

"Elsa! Where have you been?" Reagan came to a dead halt, her hands dropping to her sides in relief.

"Been?" Elsa shrugged off her red woolen cloak and set the basket on the worktable. "I been out."

"I can see that, Elsa! I mean . . . where? You scared me half to death."

Elsa hung her cloak on a peg near the fireplace and reached for her muslin apron. "I told you, out, Sister. You want cornbread or oatcakes for breakfast?" She knelt in front of the fireplace and began to set up the cooking spider.

Reagan lifted her gaze heavenward in exasperation. Her heart was still pounding beneath her breast. Elsa was her responsibility; if anything ever happened to her, it would be her fault. "Elsa, you know you can't go out without me or Papa or Nettie, now just tell Sister where you've been."

Elsa stuck out her lower lip stubbornly. "I'm not going to tell. You and papa are always going in and

63

out, whispering, scribbling on your little pieces of paper. You don't tell me where you go. Sometimes you don't tell the truth. I don't have to tell you where I went. I'm a full-grown woman."

"Elsa!" Reagan's eyes grew wide with shock. Her sister had never said such a thing in her life. "Who's been filling your head with these things? You don't know what you're saying!" *Dear God,* she thought. *Has one of the soldiers in the house been talking to her? Worse yet, how much does she know of our business with the leaflets? Have I put her life at risk as well?*

Reagan went to her sister and took hold of her shoulders. "You must tell me where you went!"

Fat tears slid down Elsa's porcelain cheeks. She shook her head. "Not telling."

"What's the problem, here?" Sterling came up behind Reagan. "I told you she was here somewhere. Not hurt, are you, Elsa?"

Reagan released her sister and turned to see Grayson handing her little sister his silk handkerchief. "Excuse me, Captain, but this is none of your affair." He'd been so concerned for Elsa's welfare that he hadn't finished dressing. He was still barefoot.

Reagan's eyes locked with his. *Don't do this to me, Grayson,* her mind screamed. *Don't care about us. You're the enemy. I hate you . . . I have to hate you.*

Sterling didn't know what to say. Reagan was right. Elsa's disappearance was not Captain Grayson Thayer's concern. "I only meant to—"

"Meddle," Reagan interrupted fiercely.

Elsa turned and ran from the room, now sobbing.

"No." Sterling sighed, lifting a hand. "But you treat her like a child."

64

"You don't understand." Reagan stood so close to him that she could feel his breath on her face. Her mind was in a jumble. She knew they were discussing Elsa but all she could think of was the last time she and Grayson had stood here in the kitchen. He'd kissed her. She could still taste his breath on her own. She'd enjoyed his kiss and some part of her wanted him to do it again.

"Oh, I do understand." Sterling turned away. He had to stay away from this wench. She was his greatest threat to his cover.

"No, you don't!" Reagan's face was flushed with a mixture of anger, fear and desire. "She's not like us. She's a child. She'll always be one."

"She isn't a child. She's a beautiful young woman."

Reagan shook her head. "She had a fever as a babe. She's not right in the head."

"It just takes her longer to do things," Sterling countered. "Perhaps she'll never read Latin or do figures, but she's a hard worker. She's a good woman."

"I have to protect her."

Sterling poured himself a mug of cider from a jug on the table. "You're smothering her!"

"How the hell do you know so much about this?"

He leaned against the table, crossing his arms over his chest. "I had a cousin, Mary, back in Virginia. She was kicked in the head by a cow when we were ten. She's married now, with eight children. She and her husband have a farm near Williamsburg."

Uncomfortable alone with Grayson, Reagan made herself busy starting breakfast. "She's not like Elsa. Elsa can't take care of herself."

"She was just like Elsa, though maybe not as well off." He paused, knowing he'd already said too much. "You know, sometimes we use people like Elsa as a crutch."

"I don't know what you mean."

"Why haven't you married? You should have your own family, a husband, children."

Reagan whipped around, leaning over a bowl, and broke a precious egg into it. "That's not of your concern, either, Grayson!" *She'd called him by name. It had just slipped off her tongue.*

Sterling drained his mug and put it down. "Don't be a martyr, Reagan. Someday this war is going to be over. Live your life and let Elsa live hers."

She turned back to face him, ready to give him a piece of her mind, but he was gone.

Chapter Five

"You most certainly may not hold a meeting in my parlor!" Reagan lifted squares of gingerbread out of a pan and laid them in a napkin-lined basket.

"I wasn't asking permission." Sterling stated flatly. "I was simply being considerate enough to warn you prior to the event."

He'd scheduled a meeting for tonight with several men who'd been delegated to aid him in investigating the treasonous political leaflets. The sooner he got to work on the assignment, the safer he felt his cover would be. In the meantime, he was compiling his first message to be sent to General Washington at Valley Forge.

In the kitchen, Reagan wiped her damp forehead with her arm. The heat from the oven was oppressive, despite the January chill. "I won't be taken advantage of like this, Captain. Take your drunken Mr. Gardener and have your meeting in the corner tavern. I understand you're quite welcome there."

Sterling leaned against the doorframe. Reagan was utterly beguiling this afternoon with the sleeves of her faded gown pushed up to bare her slim arms, and the damp tendrils of auburn hair clinging to her rosy cheeks. He was only a little surprised that word had already trickled back to Reagan that he frequented the Blue Boar Tavern. His brother was a drinker, a gambler, and a ladies' man. He'd already laid the foundation for the first two of Grayson's vices, it was the last that he hadn't brought himself to conquer. There was something about this red-haired woman that kept him from seeking loose company to warm his bed.

Sterling frowned, forcing his brother's stern expression to take precedence over his own. "If you continue to be difficult, Reagan, I'll just ask that you and your family be removed from these quarters."

She looked up him, her shrewish demeanor crumbling. "You wouldn't, would you? This has been my family's home for seventy years."

"It might just be easier that way." *Easier . . . safer,* Sterling thought, *for both of us.*

"No." She wiped her hands on her apron, approaching him. It wasn't just the family home, it was the printing press. She and Uriah were nearly ready to roll the first publication from their secret hiding place. She had been up half of last night composing an essay on the evils of military trials for the civilian population. "Please don't send us away. It would break my father's heart. Elsa, she'd never adjust to a new home after all these years."

"And what of you, Reagie?" he asked softly. He took her hand and turned it over to study her palm. It was covered in a layer of dusty flour. He raised her knuckles to his lips; she smelled of spiced ginger.

"Me?"

He spoke as Sterling the man, not Grayson the soldier. "You. What are your reasons for wanting to stay?"

She watched, mesmerized, as his lips brushed against her chafed knuckles. English officer, proclaimed womanizer or not, there was no denying that this man made her pulse quicken. "I want to stay here because it's my stability," she answered honestly. "This war, it's turned my life inside out. Friends I was once close to are no longer my friends—"

"Joshua Litheson?"

She nodded, slowly taking her hand from his grasp. "Half of the city has fled, businesses shut down, the blockade keeping food from coming in. Nothing will be right again." She crossed her arms over her chest, staring at the British officer's face. In the depths of his eyes she saw understanding. "This house and my family is all I have left of my life before the war."

"My life's changed, too," he answered softly.

"Please, Captain, don't send us away."

He smiled. "Are you promising to behave yourself?" He couldn't possibly send her away. She was his spark of light in the blackness of this war.

"No. But I won't poison you or your men's drinks."

"Or listen in the keyholes?"

She laughed. "I hadn't thought of that, though I doubt a peon captain like you would have any information General Washington hadn't received a good fortnight ago!"

Sterling's reply was cut off by Roth Gardener's voice. "Captain! Captain!" Roth came down the hall and Reagan returned self-consciously to her gingerbread.

"Yes, Lieutenant?" Sterling glanced up, irritated that he and Reagan had been interrupted.

"You're wanted, sir."

"Where?"

"At the prison down on Third and Market."

"Wanted for what?"

"Witnessing, sir. That spy they captured. They intend to hang him and we're wanted as witnesses."

Reagan paled. "What spy?"

Sterling chose his words carefully. "A boy by the name of Ian St. John was picked up last week."

"Ian? I know him. He's nothing but a child."

"Fourteen," Sterling answered. "It seems he was a drummer in the rebel army. He says his enlistment's up and he just came back to see his ailing mother." Sterling had assumed the boy would just be imprisoned. This was one of the most difficult aspects of his undercover duty—to sit and watch innocents suffer or die and be unable to help them without risk of jeopardizing too many other lives.

"Susan St. John is ill." Reagan's dark eyes met Sterling's. "Surely you don't think General Washington would be using children as spies."

"It isn't up to me to decide, mistress," Sterling answered.

"Well, I don't know about you, sir, but I've got better things to do than stand around in that cold, stinking jail." Roth started back down the hallway. "I'll meet you out front in a few minutes."

"You're going now?" The wheels of Reagan's mind were already turning. Young Ian St. John wouldn't hang, not as long as she still drew breath.

"Yes. I guess I am. My meeting will still be at eight, though." He hesitated for a moment, but when she made no reply, returning her attention to her gingerbread, he left the room.

The moment the captain had gone, Reagan yanked off her apron and went into the lean-to off the back

70

of the kitchen where Nettie slept.

Under the cloak of twilight, Reagan moved along Market Street. A bone-chilling, misty rain fell from the heavens; the street appeared to be deserted. Just to be safe, Reagan walked slowly, her body hunkered over, a walnut cane clutched in her left hand. She wore Nettie's ancient, patched cloak, the hood pulled well over her face. Layers of baggy woolen stockings concealed her trim ankles, with a pair of her father's barnyard boots completing the guise.

Up ahead, the makeshift prison loomed in the shadows. The British had filled the Walnut Street prison to capacity and now used this confiscated building on Third and Market to incarcerate as well.

Hoofbeats came clip-clopping up the street and Reagan slunk against the wall, refusing to look up as two soldiers rode past. When the sound of the horses faded in the distance, she made her way to the door on the street and twisted the knob.

Inside, green-and-red-uniformed officers laughed and chatted. Smoke filled the room, mingling the heady scent of burnt tobacco with the smell of clean leather and starched uniforms. The men smelled of a conquering army.

"What do you want, old woman?"

Frightened, Reagan lowered her head, mumbling. "To see my son." She concealed her youthful voice with the gravelly strain of worn vocal cords.

"What?" the soldier demanded. "Speak up, old woman."

"My son," she whimpered. "Young Ian St. John. They said he was here."

71

The soldier frowned. "I don't think you're supposed to be in here. Out with you." He pushed open the outer door.

Reagan banged her cane on the floor. "My son, Ian, he's my only boy. Please let me see him."

"If you're here to plead his case, it's too late. They're gonna hang him. Treason."

"Please," she begged in her falsetto voice. "Just one last time, let me see my son."

The soldier shifted in his shiny boots. "Wait here," he said finally.

The man walked away, and Reagan dared a quick glance at the open room. Soldiers moved about, laughing and talking. The prisoners were being held somewhere in the rear or upstairs, Reagan surmised.

A moment later the soldier was back. She lowered her head, leaning heavily on the cane.

"All right. But just for a moment. No family members present for the hanging, though. General Howe's orders."

Reagan nodded, following behind him. The soldier wove his way through the room of officers, through a back kitchen, and across a frozen yard. *So the hangings are done in the barn,* Reagan thought. *Better for her and Ian. Once she got the boy loose, it would be easier to get away.*

The soldier pushed open the stable door, pausing until she caught up. "In with you, but be quick about it. The provost marshal's got a dinner party waiting on him."

Reagan hobbled into the dark, dusty barn. Two lanterns illuminated the stark interior. The timbered structure was void of any beasts but still smelled of musty hay and manure. Several officers stood in a line to the left.

The provost marshal in charge of the hanging strutted to and fro. He was a citizen of Philadelphia who'd put the occupation to his own advantage. He was a civilian but one of General Howe's right-hand men. "Look here, young man, your mum's come to give her last farewell!"

Reagan looked up to see Ian's brow furrow in confusion. She only prayed he held his tongue.

"My . . . my mother?" His voice trembled in fear. He stood in a box-stall, his arms at his sides, his back straight with pride. He had been stripped of his coat and shoes and stood shivering in the drafty barn.

"His mother!" a familiar voice commented. "God's teeth, Marshal, is this necessary? You said this would only take a minute. It will have to be postponed, I've a pressing engagement."

Reagan knew that voice. . . . Out of the corner of her eye she spotted Grayson Thayer. She suddenly felt as if the breath had been knocked out of her. She couldn't do this. They'd hang her too! But slowly she hobbled toward the provost marshal and his prisoner.

"Just a moment with my boy," she mumbled. "Please, sir, I beg of you."

"One minute, old hag, and then it's out with you!"

Reagan studied the distance to the rear of the barn as she grew closer to Ian. That was the best way out. "Ian," she cackled. "Ian, my son."

"M-mother," the frightened boy murmured. "You shouldn't have come."

"God's bowels!" the provost marshal exclaimed. "Say your good-byes and be gone!"

Just another step and I'll be able to reach him, Reagan thought. Slowly she moved her cane forward;

73

at the same time, she slipped her right hand into the pocket she wore around her waist beneath her cloak. Her heart pounded in her ears, a dizziness rushing over her . . .

Suddenly, she bolted into action. She slammed the cane hard against the provost marshal's shins, and when he bellowed and jerked forward in pain, she grabbed the lapel of his new coat. "Don't move, Marshal, or I shoot," she managed in the old woman's voice.

The marshal looked up in horror to see the little old woman holding a flintlock pistol square on his temple.

Out of the corner of her eye she caught movement where the soldiers stood. "Tell them to throw down their weapons and not to move again," she ordered, pressing the end of the barrel into the soft flesh of his head.

"Your weapons!" he commanded.

Ian quickly retrieved a pistol and kicked the others into a pile.

Reagan glanced up at the soldiers with a sudden clever idea. She couldn't help but smile to herself. "Strip," she ordered.

"M-ma'am?" Roth Gardener stuttered.

"Strip off them filthy uni-forms. Boots, stockings, all of it. You too, Marshal."

Ian broke into laughter.

Reagan motioned to the boy with her cane. "Get a feedsack and fill it with their belongings. The guns, too." She continued to speak in the same graveled voice. Her face remained concealed beneath the hood.

Reagan kept her eyes averted, but her pistol on

target as the marshal hurriedly shucked off his clothing, revealing layers of milk-white flab.

When Reagan next glanced up, her cheeks reddened. The four young officers stood stark naked, their hands covering their groins. Somehow she managed to keep her gaze from Grayson's form. "Now, Ian, tie the marshal's hands, and leave a good piece of line."

Hastily, the boy did as she bid.

"Good, now get the bags and go ahead, Son. Through that door." She motioned to the rear of the barn with the walnut cane.

Ian leaped forward and ran across the barn, a feed-sack of uniforms and weapons heaved over each shoulder. He threw open the rear door, and a gust of icy wind whipped through the barn sending straw and dust swirling.

Reagan tucked the cane beneath her arm and grabbed the marshal's arm. Cautiously, she began to back up. She watched the naked soldiers while keeping the pistol on the marshal's temple.

When Reagan got to the door, she looked up once at Grayson, standing huddled and vulnerable in the cold, then backed out of the door with the marshal in tow.

The moment they were out, she tied the provost marshal to the door, blocking it.

"You can't leave me like this!" the marshal protested, crouching to cover his nudity. "Hey! Come back here! I've been appointed by General Howe himself! Help! Somebody help me!"

Ignoring him, Reagan grabbed Ian's sleeve and hurried around the barn. The moment they disappeared from the marshal's sight, she and Ian bolted.

Through the yard, out onto the street, and down another street they ran. Down an alley, through a back yard, down another street. The cold air tugged at Reagan's lungs and she labored to breathe. She was too winded to speak as they made their escape, putting more and more distance between themselves and the soldiers she knew were bolting into action.

Another street down, she led Ian through a small garden and ran up to a back stoop. She pounded on the wooden door and was immediately rewarded by a familiar face.

"Yes?" Westley answered.

Reagan threw back her hood. "Westley!" She pushed Ian ahead of her and the two ducked into the house Westley was currently occupying. There were so many empty residences in the city that it was possible for him to move from house to house and keep the redcoats guessing as to his whereabouts.

"Reagan! My God! What are you doing?"

She slumped into a straight-backed chair, lowering her head to her hands. It was a full minute before she could speak. "This is Ian. A friend. He and his family live on Third Street. They were going to hang him for treason. You've got to get him out of the city." There was no need for her to explain who *they* were, Westley knew. "His parents are waiting for him in Frankfort."

"My family?" Ian cried, dumping the feedsacks onto the floor.

"I came by your house on my way to the prison, Ian. They're safe." She yanked off her father's old shoes and began to roll down her lumpy stocking. "You've got to get him some clothes and get him out of here, Westley. They may well search the city tonight. The provost marshal's going to be hopping mad."

"The provost marshal? You broke this boy out of jail?" Westley rocked back on his boot heels in utter amazement. "You and Uriah?"

Reagan pulled off Nettie's cloak and wrapped the extra stockings in it. "My father knows nothing of it and he's not to know. He's got enough things to worry about."

"Reagie, I can't lie to your father."

"Who's asking you to lie? You think he's going to look you straight in the face and say Westley, did Reagan get Ian out of jail?"

Westley scowled.

"I didn't think so." She stood up, her bundle under her arm. "Can you loan me your cloak? I've got to get home before the captain and lieutenant."

"You shouldn't be on the street!"

"No one will suspect me. Besides it's not far. I haven't got time to argue with you. Hurry, Westley!"

He left the tiny kitchen, returning a minute later. He wrapped a flannel robe around Ian's shoulders and then brought his cloak to Reagan. "And what am I supposed to wear?" he asked, already easing it over her shoulders.

"There are pistols, boots, stockings, and uniforms in those feedsacks." She broke into a grin. "Booty."

Westley stared at the redhead in disbelief. "Reagie, you didn't?"

"I'll return your cloak tomorrow. I've got to go."

Ian came to her and offered his hand. "There's no way I can repay you, ma'am."

"Don't be silly. I couldn't let one of General Washington's men hang, could I?"

He blushed boyishly. "Guess not, ma'am."

"Give your mother my love. There's someone in Frankfort already making way for you to Dover. They'll find a place for you to live there where you'll be safe."

Westley opened the door. "Out with you."

She squeezed his arm as she went out the door. "Bless you, Westley. I knew I could count on you."

Once outside, Reagan hurried home through the back streets. Bursting in the Llewellyns' back door, she left Westley's cloak on a peg and kicked off her father's boots. Leaving them in the lean-to, she went into the kitchen.

"That you, Reagan?" Nettie turned from the work table.

"It's me, Nettie."

The old woman's sightless eyes narrowed. "Where you been, child? You've been running."

Reagan tried to breathe easier. "You worry too much, Nettie." She passed the old woman, went to the cellar door and down the steps, the cloak bundle under her arm. She returned a minute later, empty-handed, and latched the door securely.

"You're up to no good," Nettie chided, stirring a pot of stew on the hearth. "I can smell it."

"Nonsense." She snatched the wooden spoon out of Nettie's hand and tasted the rich stew. "You can't smell trouble."

"Hmph!" The gray-haired housekeeper gave a snort. "Who can't?"

"Where's Elsa?"

"In the parlor, I think. Mending." Nettie poured honey into a bowl.

"Make her a tray and send her upstairs. The cap-

78

tain intends to have a meeting here tonight; I want her safely tucked away." Ever since Elsa's disappearance a few mornings ago, she'd been particularly concerned about her sister. She wanted her safely out of reach of any redcoats.

"And what about yourself, missy? You're up to no good. I can smell it sure as livin'."

"Papa home from the printshop yet?"

The housekeeper beat the ingredients of her shortcake. "He was here, but he's gone. Fixin' Widow Carnes's loom. Spindle broke on it."

"Widow Carnes, is it?" Reagan chuckled. "Third time in two weeks her loom's broke, hasn't it?"

Nettie opened her mouth to speak, but an urgent pounding at the front door cut her off.

"Who could that be?" Reagan frowned.

Nettie began to pour the contents of the mixing bowl into a round cake pan. "No way to tell but to answer it."

Reagan dipped her forefinger into the sweet batter and padded down the hall in her stocking feet, licking her finger. "Who is it?" she called to the door.

"Captain Thayer. Let me in."

"Captain Thayer, there's no need to knock. It seems that wanted or not, this is presently your residence," she answered through the closed door.

"Reagan! Someone's locked the damned door! Open it!"

Reagan turned the great key and swung it open but stood barring the captain's entrance. At first sight of him, she burst into laughter. She knew she shouldn't, but it just couldn't be helped. She'd never seen a man look so pathetic.

The arrogant Captain Grayson Thayer shielded his

nakedness with a coarse gray horse blanket. Bare knees and calves, white with cold, were evident beneath the barely adequate covering. On his feet he wore a pair of woman's stilted kitchen clogs.

Reagan leaned on the doorjamb and stuck her finger in her mouth to suck the last of the sweet dough off it. "God sakes, Captain, what's happened to you?"

Chapter Six

"Do you think, perhaps, mistress, that we could discuss this once I'm inside?" Sterling bellowed, slamming the door open and brushing past her.

Reagan dissolved into another fit of giggles as she closed it and turned to face the captain, her hand held tightly over her mouth. He was already stalking up the grand staircase, cursing beneath his breath.

"Bring me hot water to wash," he hollered. "And a drink!"

"We don't have anything left in the house but a little coffee, Captain Thayer," she lied. She had no intention of turning over her father's last keg of Madeira he'd hidden in the cellar.

"Then go down to the Blue Boar and get me a bottle of port. Two bottles! Tell that barkeeper, Jergens, to put it on my bill!" He turned at the top of the landing and disappeared down the hall.

Reagan stood in the entranceway for a moment in indecision. "Go to the tavern, indeed," she muttered. Like hell she was going to a place like that! The Blue Boar Tavern was frequented by English and German soldiers as well as city loyalists. A good patriot wouldn't be caught dead in such an establishment.

But curiosity got the best of Reagan. "Why not," she murmured. Running an errand for the captain, she was in no danger. And it would be wickedly bold to traipse through the English nest after just having broken young Ian out of jail!

Still chuckling, Reagan went down the back hall and into the kitchen.

"Where you goin' now, missy?" Nettie called from the hearth.

"To the tavern. It seems Captain Thayer's met with some trouble. He wants porter."

"You're goin' no such place. You wait for your father to get home and let him go."

Reagan shook her head. "The captain says now. You know he only lets us stay here out of the goodness of his heart," she went on, a tone of sarcasm in her voice. "We shouldn't press our luck."

"Then let me go." The old housekeeper straightened up slowly.

"I'll be fine," Reagan insisted as she went out the back. "Be home before you know it!" She stuck her head back in the kitchen. "You might want to take some hot water up to the captain. He may well have caught a chill."

A minute later, Reagan was walking down the cobblestone walk. Beneath her heavy woolen hood, she smiled to herself. There might be advantages to running an errand or two for the captain, she thought. *If I keep my eyes and ears open, I just might get something for my printings. Wouldn't that be something if I could reveal a bit of confidential information in cold ink!*

Reaching the tavern, Reagan walked right in. Uniformed men turned, and a ripple of sound echoed the men's approval. Tossing back the hood of her cloak, she crossed the smoky public room, going straight to the counter.

"Barkeep!"

A rotund man in a linen apron came to her. "Ma'am?"

She ignored the ribald invitations and low whistles she heard behind her. "Two bottles of good porter, sir, for Captain Thayer."

Jergens reached beneath the counter and brought up two corked bottles. "Here you go, love."

She wrapped her fingers around the necks of the bottles, but the barkeep didn't release them. "I have to hurry," she said with a razor's edge to her voice. "The *captain* waits."

The barkeeper loosened his grip. "So the captain's got himself a feisty piece of female, has he? I hear that man's got a golden touch with a woman. Golden as his hair, they say."

She turned away. "Put it on the captain's bill."

She walked back across the public room. A Hessian soldier caught the hem of her cloak, but put up no resistance when she snatched it from his grasp.

Coming to the door, she reached for the knob, but a pair of hairy fingers beat her to it. She glanced up, and through the dim light saw a swarthy half-breed in buckskins. A leather patch covered one eye, and his hair hung in oily strands to frame a pock-scarred face.

Loyalist scum, Reagan thought to herself. *Traitor.*

The man smiled, baring jagged, rotting teeth. "Where you goin' in sech a hurry? Why not stay and have a drink with Indian John?"

She put her hand on his to turn the doorknob, but his wrist wouldn't budge. "Let me pass."

"What, you got time for the pretty captain but not for me? Why not let a real man give ye a ride? Bet

83

you never had nuthin' like me between your thighs . . ."

Reagan lifted the bottle of porter and brought it down sharply on the man's knuckles. When he howled and released the knob, recoiling with pain, she made her escape.

Ducking onto the street, she ran, praying the filthy creature didn't chase her. When she heard no footsteps, she fell into a walk and glanced over her shoulder. The halfbreed stood on the steps of the tavern, below the sign of the Blue Boar, a lamp illuminating his scarred face. His laughter echoed in the chilly street. "Next time, girlie," he called ominously. "Next time."

Reagan ran the rest of the way home, but this time had the good sense to stop and catch her breath before she went into the kitchen. When she entered the room, both Uriah and Elsa were there, along with Nettie.

"Nettie says you've been to the tavern," Uriah accused.

Reagan stopped in the doorway, Grayson's bottles of porter clutched in her hands. "The captain wanted it straight away. Seems there was some trouble this afternoon. He was pretty angry. I thought it best to do what he said."

Uriah scowled. "Trouble?" He gave a snort. "You don't know the half of it." He turned to his younger daughter, waving with an ink-stained hand. "Go on upstairs now, Elsa, love. Papa will be up in a minute."

"You promised you'd read to me from the Bible." She pouted.

"And that I will." He patted Elsa on the shoulder.

"Now upstairs with you. And if you're dressed for bed when I get there, we'll play a game as well before you turn in."

Elsa grinned, clapping her hands. There was sheer delight on her face. "Oh, Papa, I love you."

Uriah pulled his pipe from his waistcoat. "Go on with you."

Reagan waited until her sister was safely out of hearing range. "Trouble you say?" she commented innocently.

Uriah lowered his voice. "It seems there was a breakout today."

"Breakout? Whatever do you mean?" She set the porter down on the center worktable. "Who broke out of where?"

Uriah went to the fireplace to light his pipe. "You remember the St. John boy who went off to be a drummer in the Army?"

"Ian? Yes, of course. He used to help his papa sell ice."

"Exactly. Well, with the missus being poorly, it seems that Ian came home after his hitch was up. Only the Brits picked him up and accused him of spying."

"Spying! That's ridiculous! He's but a child."

Uriah pressed his fingers to his lips. "Hush, girl. He *was* spying."

Reagan's eyes went wide. "No!"

"Anyway. He kept to his story. They took him down to the jail and meant to hang him this morning. Only it seems somebody, a man they're guessing, came disguised as his mother."

"His mother!" Reagan echoed.

Uriah took a long pull on his pipe. "This impersonator walked straight into the barn where the hanging was to take place, held a pistol to the provost marshal's head, and made him take off his clothes."

"Heaven on earth!" Nettie piped up with a chuckle.

"But it wasn't just the provost marshal. There were some officers there."

"And our Captain Thayer was one of them!" Reagan finished, unable to disguise her delight.

"It's not a laughing matter, Daughter. I don't know who did it," he shook his head, "but the man had nerve!"

"They managed to get away safely?" Reagan asked.

"Ingenious fellow he was. I only wish I'd thought of it. He took the officers' uniforms, boots and all, then forced the provost marshal at gunpoint to go outside, and tied him buck-assed bare to the barn. It's the only thing that saved the two of them. Apparently several minutes passed before Captain Thayer got up the gumption to walk across the yard to the jailhouse." Uriah puffed on his pipe, sending rings of smoke billowing over his head. "This city'll be talking about this stunt a hundred years from now."

"And they don't know who did it?" Reagan picked up the captain's bottles.

"Not only do they not know who did it, but our side doesn't know, either! Ian and his friend just disappeared into the streets."

Reagan shook her head, smiling. "No wonder the captain was worked into a lather. I'd best get this to him before he comes looking for it."

"You want me to take it?" Uriah put out his hand.

"No. I told him I'd do it."

"Watch yourself, Daughter," Uriah called after her.

"He's still the enemy and he'll remember even if you don't."

Reaching her bedchamber door, Reagan paused to smooth the unruly curls at the nape of her neck. She groaned aloud. "What am I doing?" she murmured. *What do I care what I look like?*

She rapped on the door.

"Come in," Sterling called.

"Your porter, Captain." She stepped into the bedchamber that had once been hers.

Various pieces of uniform were draped over two chairs and a bedpost. Reagan's dressing table was littered with Sterling's hair ribbons, silk garters, and stockings. But even with his belongings scattered throughout, staking his claim to her chambers, it somehow still felt like her own room.

"God bless you. Well, come in and shut the door. There's a damnable draft in that hallway."

Reagan closed the door, a half-smile on her face. "Papa says you ran into a bit of trouble at the jailhouse."

Sterling snatched the bottle from her hand. "Trouble, indeed. Damned rebels!" he snapped in his brother's voice. Actually he *was* angry with whoever had run the operation. Had it been necessary to degrade him in such a manner? Why hadn't he been warned of the breakout? He should never have been present!

She tucked her hands behind her back. "I hope you don't catch a chill. Bad season for it. Just last week Jason Gaberdine came down with fever. It took to his lungs and he died before the surgeon ever called. They say he got wet drawing water from his well. It doesn't take much exposure in weather like this to kill a man."

"Thank you for the information. I feel much better now."

She walked to the fireplace and picked up a poker, stirring the red-hot embers. "I could send Nettie up with a poultice if you like."

"No. This will be fine." He poured a draught of porter into a teacup and took a long swallow. The fiery liquid burned a path down his throat, bringing tears to his eyes. He coughed. "Care for a drink?"

She set the poker down on the hearth. "I don't think I'd like it."

"Don't think you'd like it? You mean to tell me that you've never had porter? Where have you been living, beneath a continental plow?"

She shook her head. He was teasing her. She liked that. Josh used to tease her and she missed it. "It's not that Papa ever forbid me." She shrugged. "I just never had the cause to need spirits. I take care of my problems without it."

Sterling stared into his teacup, swirling the amber liquid. "I don't think I've ever met a woman like you, Reagan."

Reagan. She liked the sound of her name on his tongue. Somehow it came out different when he spoke it. It was softer, more delicate. It made her feel more feminine than she'd ever felt before. "It was my grandfather's name."

"Reagan?" Sterling sat on the corner of her bed. "I *thought* it was unusual."

"I was supposed to be a boy, of course, and when I wasn't,"—she smiled—"they named me Reagan anyway."

"I don't think your father is disappointed in you

88

now," he observed thoughtfully. "It seems you're very close."

"You're observant for a man who spends most of his time in the corner tavern." She permitted her gaze to settle on his fine form. He was dressed simply in a pair of navy-blue gabardine breeches and a lawn shirt. His stock hung loosely about his neck. His yellow-gold hair was pulled back in a queue. She wondered vaguely what his hair would feel like beneath her fingertips. Would it be as soft and smooth as it looked?

There was a silence in the room as they regarded each other, he seated on the bed, she standing a few feet away. Her loden-green lutestring gown tugged at her bosom and waist emphasizing her nearly perfect figure. The penumbra of the oil lamp on the table cast a fiery light, illuminating her magical hair.

"A pity we didn't meet before the war," Sterling heard himself say. He didn't know what had made him say it. He could feel himself digging a hole, deeper and deeper with each word she spoke, each slight smile she rewarded him with.

"I was thinking the same," Reagan answered, feeling oddly unembarrassed. "Or at least that you weren't on the wrong side."

He laughed, his rich tenor voice echoing in the paneled chamber. "It's tempting."

She shook her head, her dark eyes narrowing. "That's a red uniform you wear. To . . ." Her cheeks colored. "It would be betraying my country. I couldn't do it."

Sterling came to her, setting his teacup down on the table. She made no advance toward him, but nor did she shun him. She knew it was wrong. She hated

him and all he stood for. He was a drinker, a womanizer . . . but he made her feel good somewhere deep
inside . . . a place Josh had never reached.

"May I kiss you?" Sterling asked. He knew he was
playing with fire, but he couldn't help himself. One
kiss, he told himself, just one.

"If I say no?"

He lifted a heavy lock of auburn hair from her
shoulder and brought it to his lips. "Then I won't."

"Liar. Soldiers, they take what they want." She
lifted her chin, brushing it against his knuckles.
There was something about the forbidden that made
her pulse race. Standing here in the captain's bedchamber, daring him to kiss her, gave her much the
same pounding in her heart that walking into the
Blue Boar Tavern had.

Sterling lowered his mouth to hers as she lifted up
on her toes to meet him. Her hands rose of their own
accord to rest on his broad shoulders. Sterling
gripped her narrow waist with one hand, stroking her
soft cheek with the other. It was a gentle, exploring
kiss that left them both wanting more.

Reagan lifted her dark lashes, still in Sterling's
arms. "I'm not one of your doxies."

"I never thought you were."

She touched her lips as if she could feel his kiss
with her fingertips. "This is wrong."

"For both of us."

"It's dangerous," she whispered. "Nothing but ill
can come of it."

He released her, her words bringing some sense to
his whirling mind. "I apologize." He put up his
hands. "It won't happen again."

She opened the door and stepped into the hallway.

"It can't," she whispered.

An hour later, Reagan tiptoed past the sitting parlor where the Llewellyn family dined together. The door was closed, but inside she could hear men talking. Uriah, Nettie, and Elsa had all turned in early, but Reagan couldn't sleep.

She felt like a traitor! What had possessed her to go into Grayson's room like that? He had kissed her because she'd wanted him to, not because he cared for her, and she was joking herself if she thought otherwise. What man wouldn't have jumped at such a lurid invitation? The man was a known whoremaster, and if she wasn't careful, she'd no doubt find herself, like other innocent women, victim to his manly wiles.

Moving noiselessly down the hall, Reagan went to the candle box in the kitchen and retrieved a fresh stick of tallow. Lighting it in the banked embers of the fire, she went down the cellar steps. *Work,* that was what she needed to keep her mind off the captain and his lips. Work was the perfect solution.

Walking from chamber to chamber, Reagan came to the secret door. She eased it open, closing it behind her before she entered the room beneath the carriage house. Holding the candle high, she found the oil lamp hanging from the ceiling and lit it. Golden rays radiated from the lamp illuminating the small whitewashed room and the printing press that dominated it.

Unable to contain herself, Reagan gave a sigh of delight, running her fingers along its smooth wooden frame. Along the back wall, an angular upright table already held the first typeset page of their new leaflet. She ran her fingertips over the type letters and then lifted them to her nose to smell the ink. The pungent smell of lampblack and varnish was comforting.

With a sigh, she went to her grandfather's desk, lit a second lamp, and bent over the beginnings of a new article on independence.

Sometime later, a distant, muffled voice startled Reagan. She sat straight up, returning her quill to the ink well. There it was again, someone calling her name! She lit her single candle and blew out both lamps. Just as she was closing the secret door, she heard the voice again.

My, God! It's him, she thought.

Panic-stricken, she hurried through the dusty cellar chambers, nearly colliding with Sterling on the steps.

"What are you doing down here in your night clothes?" He lifted his own candle, studying her startled face.

Self-consciously, she tightened the tie on her flannel robe. "H-how did you know I was down here?"

"I met your sister in the kitchen getting a drink of water. She asked me if I'd seen you. She said you weren't in bed." He lifted the candle higher, illuminating the piles of discarded items.

Reagan prayed he didn't see Nettie's cloak balled up and carelessly tossed into the corner near the steps. She'd meant to find a better hiding place, but had forgotten in the confusion of the passing evening. Taking a deep breath, she pushed past him and up the steps. Thankfully, he followed.

Sterling took her candle and put it in the candle box along with his own. "You didn't say what you were doing down there in the middle of the night."

"Um, rats."

He lifted a golden eyebrow suspiciously. "Rats, madame?"

"Yes. I thought I heard a rat." She made herself busy, tending the fire. "There's nothing I hate worse than a rat."

When he made no reply, she glanced up at him. "If you like, I can call *you* next time."

He grimaced. "That won't be necessary. I probably hate a rat worse than you do." He paused, watching her stir the embers and add a log. He wanted to say something about what had happened upstairs earlier, but what was there to say? If he in any way grew entangled with Reagan, he'd be risking his life, risking hers, and many more.

She looked up. "Good night, Captain."

"Good night, Reagan"

She watched him leave the kitchen, then picked up the lamp from the table and started for bed. All the way up the stairs, she swore beneath her breath. "I'll never go downstairs when he's in the house, I'll never take a chance like that again."

Chapter Seven

Sterling entered the dimly lit Blue Boar Tavern and whipped off his cloak with a great deal of pretense. Several patrons turned to see who the officer was, and a murmur of recognition rose among them.

He took a seat at a pine trestle table along the far wall and signaled the barmaid.

A short, buxom brunette hurried over. "Captain! Haven't seen ye in a night or two." She wiped the droplets of perspiration above her bodice with the hem of her apron.

Sterling's gaze lingered over the woman's more-than-adequate breasts. *Play the part,* the survivalist in him warned. "A drink, Annie. The usual." He smiled, and the wench giggled. He couldn't help wondering if Reagan ever giggled so inanely. He doubted it.

"Yes, sir. Anything else? I got me a short break comin' up . . ." She lifted her dimpled chin in the direction of the chambers above the public room . . . rooms the tavern rented by the hour for the soldiers' *relaxation*.

Sterling tugged playfully at her soiled apron. "Not tonight sweetheart." He winked. "But thank you for the offer just the same."

Unoffended, Annie sidled away. "Be right back,

love."

Once the girl returned with his drink, Sterling sipped it, more for appearance sake than to quench his thirst. Inconspicuously, he perused the busy public room. There was a table of rowdy Hessian soldiers to the left, a redcoat and a young woman engrossed in conversation to the right. There were several other clusters of soldiers, but at the far side was a table of eight civilian-dressed men — loyalists no doubt.

In Sterling's eyes these men were the scourge of the city. They had taken advantage of the British occupation of Philadelphia and were reaping the rewards of betrayal. They lined their pockets with coin earned from turning in neighbors as sympathizers, and selling on the blackmarket. The door swung both ways with many of these derelicts. They were just as eager to sell you a forged pass out of the city as they were to turn you over to General Howe as a suspected spy.

Taking care to be certain that no one was watching him, Sterling poured the remainder of his rum beneath the table. "Annie. Another," he ordered, slamming down the glass. It was important that he give the illusion of being a drinking man, but still remain sober.

When the barmaid had brought a second drink, he dropped a half penny on the table. "Those men, who are they, Annie?"

She glanced over "Them? That's Indian John and his bunch." She gave a low whistle. "They say the man would sell his own mother to turn a coin." She lowered her voice. "He's a bad'n if you ask me, Captain."

"But he knows what goes on in the city?"

She laughed. "They say nobody knows more, 'cept maybe the rats."

"Thank you Annie." Sterling added another coin to the table. "You've been a big help."

She scooped up the coins and dropped them into her cleavage. "Just let me know if ye need anything else." She gave a wink.

Sterling smiled. "I'll do that."

Once the girl moved on to the next table, he rose and went over to where the loyalists sat. "Evening, gentlemen."

The man Annie had pointed out as Indian John looked up. "What you want?" He was a half-breed with waist-length black hair pulled into a single braid down his back. He wore a leather patch over one eye.

"Business," Sterling answered evenly.

The half-breed indicated a place on the bench and Sterling took a seat. "Ever seen one of these?" Sterling pulled Reagan's latest leaflet from beneath his coat.

Indian John picked it up, squinting with his good eye. A long, jagged scar ran from beneath his eyepatch to the corner of his mouth. "Yea, seen 'um, or ones like 'em." He tossed the pamphlet onto the table and one of the other men picked it up.

Sterling took his time. These were dangerous men; he could hear it in their voices. "Do you know who's printing them?"

John gave a snort. "That bit of information is locked up tighter'n a Scot whiskey barrel. Who wants to know?"

"I do. Major Burke does."

96

"Whoever it is, they're tearin' the hide off the major, ain't they?"

Sterling picked up the leaflet and returned it to his coat. "Do me a favor, keep your ears open." He stood and reached into his coat. He flipped a coin high in the air and it landed beneath John's nose. "Let me know if you hear anything."

The half-breed snatched up the coin, grinning. "Can do," he called after Sterling.

Sterling returned to his table, and was lifting his whiskey to his lips when a red-coated lieutenant approached the table. "I understand you play a little whist, Captain Thayer."

Sterling took his seat, propping his boot on the table. "I've been known to play a hand," he answered.

"Mind if my friends join us?"

"Be glad to have them"—Sterling tucked his hands behind his head, a cocky grin on his face— "As long as your friends don't mind going home poor."

A week later Sterling rode his brother's horse, Giipa, into the smithy's barnyard. It was a cold, cloudless night; a sliver of a moon hung low in the sky. All was quiet in the blacksmith's yard, but lanternlight poured from the windows of the neat frame house. Sterling tied up his mount and went to the door. He hated to bother the man and his family, but he had a message concerning troop size to be delivered to General Washington. His frequenting the tavern was beginning to pay off. He'd discovered that he could learn more about Howe's army there than he could at the commander in chief's headquarters.

Sterling knocked sharply on the door. A moment later it swung open and the smithy appeared. He was laughing, his cheeks bright with merriment. "Yea?"

"Sorry to bother you, Smith, but I need you to take a look at my horse. I've got a shoe that's just not right."

Smith glanced over his shoulder. "I've got to take a look at this gentleman's horse. Would you mind sitting with them just a minute?"

To Sterling's surprise, Elsa's angelic face appeared from behind the door. She smiled shyly. "Even' to you, Grayson."

The broad grin fell from Ethan Smith's face. "Y-you know the captain, Elsa?"

She nodded, burying her hands in her skirts. "Grayson sleeps in my sister's bedchamber." She giggled. "I think she likes him. She's always saying things about him being a stinking redcoat."

To Sterling's embarrassment, he could feel his cheeks coloring. He scuffed the stone step with his polished boot. "Um . . . you see, I'm lodged with the Llewellyns, me and a lieutenant. I use her sister's bedchamber, she sleeps with Elsa."

The smith's rosy lips twitched. "Certainly none of my business whose chamber you're in, Captain. I'll be just a minute, Elsa," he called over his shoulder. A young boy ducked between his legs and Ethan swung him up into his massive arms. "It's time they were all in bed." The child squealed with laughter as his father passed him to Elsa.

Sterling backed away from the door, waiting for Smith to retrieve his cloak. When the two men were alone, Sterling cleared his throat. "I hope we haven't got a problem here. With Elsa, I mean."

"I see no problem." The blacksmith's breath rose in clouds of white.

"Does Elsa's family know she's here?"

Ethan handed Sterling the lamp he carried and untied his horse. Together the men walked across the frozen barnyard. "Nope. Elsa doesn't want them to know. She says her sister would never let her come."

"So she sneaks out of the house when Reagan's gone."

Ethan opened the barn door and Sterling passed through. "I'm not a deceitful man, but I been lonely since my wife died. My children, they need a woman in the house. Elsa's brought laughter into our home again." The blacksmith took the lamp from Sterling and hung it on an iron hook hanging from a rafter. "I'd take it as a favor if you didn't tell the Llewellyns you saw Elsa here." He patted the horse's flanks. "She's of no threat. She knows nothing of the part I play in this revolution. And even if she did, she'd keep it to herself."

Sterling offered his hand in friendship. "Elsa's a fine young woman. Where she goes is none of my concern."

Ethan clasped his hand. "The name's Ethan."

"This job gets more complicated every day. I'm going to have a hard time remembering who knows what and who isn't supposed to know it."

Ethan laughed. "You're a good man . . ."

"Sterling. We're supposed to keep our identities hidden according to Captain Craig, but sometimes things get tangled, don't they?"

"That they do." The blacksmith pulled a clay pipe from beneath his leather waistcoat. "So what can I do for you?"

"A delivery." Sterling slipped his hand beneath his wool cloak and retrieved an ink quill.

Ethan studied the quill. "You want me to risk my hide getting to Frankfort to send General Washington a quill?"

Sterling laughed. "The message is on tiny strips of paper. I rolled them up and put them inside."

Ethan held the feather up to the light. "I'll be damned. Can't tell."

"A man can't be arrested for carrying an ink quill, can he?"

"I wouldn't think so, but with General Howe, there's no telling."

"Well you be careful, friend"—Sterling patted Ethan's arm, taking his horse's reins from him— "and I'll be seeing you again soon."

Once outside, Sterling mounted his brother's horse and rode off down the street. A few blocks away he turned into the Llewellyn drive and rode around the back of the house to return Giipa to the barn. Just as he was about to dismount, he caught a glimpse of a shadow moving in the darkness.

"Who's there?" he demanded. His hand went to the pistol beneath his cloak and he eased it from his belt.

There was a chuckle, and then the shadow stepped forward. It was Indian John. "Most officer types, I'd be able to slit their throat 'fore they saw me comin'." He nodded. "You got your own tail covered; I like that in a man."

Sterling kept the pistol aimed at John's middle.

100

"What do you want?"

"Not to rob ya! Lower your weapon. I got no firestick."

"Right." Sterling lowered his pistol, but rested it on his thigh. "State your business. I don't appreciate being sneaked up on."

"Those papers you were talkin' about . . ."

"Yes?" Sterling swung out of the saddle.

"Word is, there's a shipment movin' tonight."

"Where?"

"I got to be paid for my troubles."

"Yes, yes, this turns out to be anything and your pay will be more than adequate. Now tell me what you know before I shoot you."

The half-breed took a step back. "Touchy ain't you, fellow?" He opened the barn door. "Step inside and I'll tell you plenty."

A few minutes later, Sterling hurried through the kitchen of the Llewellyn house.

"Evening, Captain," Nettie called from the corner of the room. She sat in her chair, rocking contentedly and smoking her pipe.

The entire house was quiet except for the sound of the old rocker. "Good evening." He stopped in the doorway. "Where is everyone?"

"I don't keep strings on 'em." The old woman continued to rock.

"This is important." If there was going to be any trouble on the street tonight, Sterling would feel better if Reagan was safely at home.

She sighed. "Mister Uriah, he went over to the widow's to check her loom. Miss Elsa, she said she was turnin' in early. Miss Reagan"—she shrugged—"your guess is as good as mine. She don't tell nobody where she's going."

"When Reagan comes in, you tell her to stay in, that I said so."

The old housekeeper waved in acknowledgment and Sterling headed for his bedchamber. Where was Reagan this late in the evening? Did she have a beau she was meeting on the sly like her sister? Was it that Joshua? The thought plagued him as he changed out of his uniform and into woolen breeches and a fresh shirt. Pulling on his riding boots, he slung his cloak over his shoulders and stuffed a cocked hat on his head.

If he could intercept this shipment of pamphlets, perhaps he could find out who was printing them. Whoever it was, he admired him. It took a lot of guts to print and distribute those leaflets right beneath the enemy's nose. And even if he didn't find the penman tonight, at least he would have something to appease Major Burke with. The man was becoming more insistent with each passing day. He wanted the penman found, and he swore that if Sterling couldn't find him, he'd find someone who could.

Mounting his horse, Sterling rode out of the barn and into the frigid night air. Whoever this penman was, he prayed to God he could protect him.

Reagan sat on the cold, hard wagon seat waiting . . . staring into the darkness. Behind her, lantern lights twinkled on Front Street, but the alley she waited in was deserted.

It wasn't her duty to transport the leaflets, and her father would be furious when he found out, but tonight the usual courier couldn't make it. By the time Reagan had received the message, it was too late to cancel the pickup and her father had gone out. There was nothing else to do but make the *meet* herself.

She'd gone to Mistress Claggett's and borrowed her horse and wagon. Then she'd loaded the wooden crate of pamphlets onto the wagon and now she waited. She didn't know who she was supposed to meet, only that it would be here in the alley behind Market Street.

Reagan shifted restlessly on the uncomfortable wagon seat. The lampposts on the street cast only a few murky rays of light down the long, dark alley. She drew her cloak closer as if she could, by sheer will, chase the demons from her mind. Her imagination played tricks on her in the darkness. She heard voices that turned out to be nothing but the wind; she saw shadows of men that were naught but the sway of a skeletal tree branch.

"Where are you?" she whispered to the darkness. "I'll not wait much longer." This was just too chancy being out on the street like this. Only a week before, General Howe had decreed that no pedestrian in Philadelphia was permitted out after dark without a lantern.

Reagan squinted in the darkness watching the street in front of her. Occasionally a horse and rider or a carriage went by, but there was no sign of the horse and wagon meant to retrieve her precious leaflets.

On impulse, she reached behind the seat and took one of the pamphlets from the wooden crate. She fingered the rough paper nervously. It was times like this, times when she was truly frightened, that she wondered if it was all worth it. Did her essays make any impact on the colonists? She told herself they had to, else why would the British be so concerned about them?

Reagan brushed the leaflet against her lips, huddling in the cold. She'd wait five more minutes and if the contact didn't come—she was going home.

Sterling urged Giipa into a trot, leaning forward in the saddle. The frigid night air filled his lungs and mind, giving him a sense of euphoria. This was where he was comfortable, in the saddle, bent on a mission. He wasn't meant for a life of taverns, whores, and endless games of whist. The night air and the thrill of possible danger was what made his blood run hot.

Sterling chuckled beneath his breath. The night air and the sight of Reagan Llewellyn, that was what made his heart pound. Damned, but he'd be glad when the British left the city. Then he'd be able to return to Washington's camp. He needed to get away from Reagan and her clever wit, her fiery hair . . . her rosy lips.

Only a block from the place where Indian John said the leaflets would be waiting, Sterling slowed his brother's horse to a walk. He wasn't quite certain how he was going to handle this. He needed the shipment of leaflets, but he wanted to let the person or persons involved escape without them becoming suspicious of him.

At the sound of hoofbeats behind him, Sterling reined in his mount. He looked over his shoulder.

By the light of the streetlamps he could make out the silhouette of Major Burke and half a dozen mounted soldiers. Beside the major, rode the half-breed, Indian John.

Sterling waited for the major and his soldiers. "Major . . ." he said, his voice even. "What are you doing here?"

"This citizen says that a shipment of those bloody papers is coming through here tonight."

"Yes, sir, I'm investigating it."

"Then why the hell didn't you inform me? If you spent less time in the Blue Boar and more time on duty, you'd have already found the damned penmen."

"I don't know how reliable this man's information is." He glanced up at the smirking half-breed. "And I'm not certain that mounted soldiers is the way to approach this. We'll lose the element of surprise."

"I really couldn't give a rat's ass what you think, Captain. If this man says he can lead me to the penman, then it's worth a few coins to find the whoremonger."

Sterling shifted in his saddle, trying to keep his fear in check. "You paid this man? But I already paid him for the same information."

"Yes, well"—the major indicated Indian John with a gloved hand—"this citizen has agreed to work with me on a permanent basis. I'll be providing a small sum of money each week to have him keep me posted on the goings-on of this city."

Sterling glanced down the street. Now what was he going to do? How could he possibly warn the penman of the trap being set?

Major Burke urged his horse forward, and Sterling fell in beside him. If this man was caught, it would be on his own head. *I should have known better than to deal with scum like that half-breed.*

Major Burke and his men moved slowly up the street, trying to appear unhurried. Half a block farther down, Indian John pointed with the muzzle of his flintlock. Then, tipping his hat to the major, he rode off in the direction they'd come.

The major lifted a hand, and the soldiers drew their weapons. Sterling slipped his hand beneath his cloak and found his own.

The moment Reagan heard the hoofbeats, she stiffened. Soldiers patrolled the street day and night, but these men were moving too slowly — something wasn't right. This group was large and their movement calculated. Instead of riding down the center of the cobblestone road, they rode close to the buildings.

The instant the first horse and rider wheeled around the corner and down the alley, Reagan sprang to her feet. She vaulted over the back of the wagon and Mistress Claggett's horse reared in fright. A voice of authority broke the night air.

"Halt!" Major Burke ordered. "Halt or be shot!"

Chapter Eight

Sterling charged down the alley, pistol held high, and fired once into the air. "Halt!" he shouted. "Halt!"

Reagan heard the musket ball whistle over her head before it buried into the mortar of one of the brick buildings that loomed above. Picking herself up off the bed of the moving wagon, she leaped over the back, her leaflet still crushed in her hand. *They won't take me alive,* she vowed silently. *No one will suffer but me for my own stupidity.*

Reagan hit the ground. She could hear the soldiers . . . their angry muffled voices, the pounding of hoofbeats. One of the soldiers was shouting like a madman as she turned the corner.

"Halt! Halt, you bloody bastard," the voice demanded. Paralyzed with fear, Reagan ran blindly down the sidewalk. From nowhere a hand came out of the darkness, catching her and pulling her through a doorway. The dark-cloaked man held her against his chest, muffling her voice.

"Hush, girl. You're safe now."

Reagan stared up at the man, squinting in the darkness. She could see nothing but the shadow of his face. "Who are you?" she whispered.

"It matters not. Stay silent until they've passed and then someone will see you home."

In shocked relief, Reagan slumped against the cold brick of the interior wall. She still held her leaflet clenched in her hand. Who was this man and why had he helped her?

"I said halt," Sterling demanded, in pursuit. Intentionally, he rode through the narrow passageway between the spooked horse and wagon and the brick wall. Just as the wagon banged to a halt, Sterling threw himself from his brother's horse, adding to the pandemonium.

"For God's sake, Thayer! Get up! You're blocking the alley! He's getting away!" Major Burke reined in his horse and signaled for the soldiers behind him to back up and go the other way.

Dazed, Sterling rested his head against the cold brick. His ploy had been so successful that he'd managed to knock himself nearly senseless in the process.

"Bloody hell, Thayer! You've bungled it!" The major dismounted, offering a gloved hand in assistance. "Can you stand?"

"My apologies, sir." Sterling staggered to his feet, rubbing the back of his head. Warm, sticky blood oozed between his fingers. "I don't know what happened. I thought we had him."

"I'll tell you what happened! You botched it!" Major Burke retrieved Sterling's hat from the ground and hit him in the chest with it. "Who did you think you were, that bastard, Paul Revere? Damn!" He shook his head. "Soldiers like you are the best defense these colonists have!"

"I'm sorry, sir. It won't happen again." Sterling blinked, still trying to get his bearings.

"Damned right it won't happen again or you'll

108

find yourself eating dog meat in some fort on the Ohio River!" He caught the reins of the horse pulling the wagon. "Men like you don't need a commanding officer, they need a wet nurse!"

"Yes, sir." Sterling peered over the side of the wagon. Even in the darkness he could make out the shape of a wooden box beneath the wagon seat. "Sir! I've think we've got some!" Sterling hauled the crate out and lifted its lid. Neatly stacked inside were copies of the penman's latest leaflet.

"Let me see those. You mind the horses." Major Burke pulled a pamphlet from the wooden crate, squinting in an attempt to read it.

A short time later the mounted soldiers came back down the alley. "He got away, sir," called one of the men. "He just disappeared. It just doesn't make any sense; these warehouses are locked up tighter than a drum. I sent some men out to check the taverns nearby. He couldn't have gotten far."

The major tucked the pamphlet beneath his cloak. "All right, gentlemen. I want this wagon brought to my headquarters and the crate of pamphlets left in my office."

One of the soldiers was already dismounting. "Yes, sir."

Major Burke turned to Sterling. "You, Captain, are to return to your quarters and have that gash looked at. I want you in my office first thing in the morning."

Sterling held the major's horse while he mounted and then handed up the reins. "I'll be there." He saluted and the major rode off with the soldiers and confiscated horse and wagon behind him.

* * *

109

Reagan leaned against the counter in the Blue Boar Tavern, waiting on the barkeeper. When the soldiers had passed, Reagan's savior had had a covered coach brought around. The man had given his driver instructions to take her home and then disappeared into the night without ever having revealed his identity.

Frightened by the man and his obvious knowledge of her doings, Reagan had insisted that the driver take her to the Blue Boar. She didn't want the man, whoever he was, to know where she lived . . . if he didn't already know.

Two soldiers had entered right on her heels and asked the barkeeper if any suspicious-looking man had just come in. When the barkeeper said no, the soldiers had glanced about the noisy public room, then taken their leave.

Reagan could still feel her heart pounding. She thought she was safe this time, thanks to the mystery man, but what of the next? Perhaps her father was right. Perhaps this was too dangerous.

The barkeeper, Jergens, set a bottle on the counter in front of her. "Here you are, sweet. Sorry it took so long, but I had to get it out of the cellar."

"P-put it on his bill," Reagan managed. She was still so frightened that she could feel her knees knocking beneath her skirts.

He leaned over the counter, wiping his hands on his apron. "What's the matter with that captain of yours sending you out without a lantern?"

So he's my *Captain now, is that what they all think?* She looked up, taking the bottle. *Let them*

110

think it, then. Maybe there'll be some safety in it. If these men think I'm his, maybe they'll be more likely to let me be. "I just forgot my lantern."

Jergens lowered a burning oil lamp from an iron hook hanging from the ceiling. "Take this one, and bring it back with you the next time. Pretty wench like you don't need any interrogation."

She accepted the lantern gratefully. "Thank you. I guess I'd best be going. The captain'll be looking for this." She raised the hood of her cloak and left the tavern.

A few minutes later, Sterling tied his horse out in front of the Blue Boar and ducked inside. He had to get someone to take a look at his head, but first he needed a drink. This was one night when a pint of rum would do him some good. Besides, he was hoping he'd run into that parasite half-breed.

"Captain Thayer." The barkeeper nodded to Sterling. "Good evening to you. What can I do for ye?" He took notice of the bloodstains across Sterling's cloak but said nothing.

"Rum, and none of that homemade swill!" He leaned on the countertop, glancing about the public room. There was no sign of Indian John or his men.

"I just sent that Llewellyn girl with it."

Sterling turned back. "Reagan was here?"

"Not five minutes ago. She picked up the bottle you wanted and headed for home. She was traveling without a lantern so I loaned her one of mine. I knew you didn't want the wench getting into any trouble on the street."

What was Reagan up to? he wondered numbly. Had she been dallying with that Joshua and was now using him as an alibi? He lifted his eyebrows. "You say just five minutes ago?"

Jergens nodded. "I'm surprised you didn't run into her on the street." He studied Sterling's face. "She's all right, ain't she? I mean, you'll pay the bill?"

"Yes, yes, of course. The end of the month," Sterling called over his shoulder as he went out the door.

When Reagan entered the parlor, Uriah looked up over the rim of his spectacles. "Where the hell have you been?"

Tears stung her eyes. "You're not going to like it, Papa."

Uriah watched her move to the chair opposite his. "There was a problem with the courier?" he whispered harshly. "You know better than to go out of the house on a pickup night. You should have come and found me!"

She wiped her eyes, embarrassed by her tears. "It's not safe to talk now. The lieutenant is upstairs, I don't know where the captain is. We'll talk tomorrow."

Uriah laid down the book he'd been reading and removed his spectacles, rubbing his eyes. This war had come ten years too late; he was too old for this business. "Maybe we should take those passes Westley offered and get out of the city while we still can."

"No." Reagan's eyes met her father's. "Please, Papa. No one was hurt. I just lost part of the shipment." She hung her head.

"You? You what?"

"Shh, someone will hear you."

Uriah stood. "Come upstairs. I want to hear this."

She stroked the arm of the upholstered chair. "I don't think we should take any chances talking in the house when they're here."

Uriah sighed. He knew she was right. He studied his daughter's face. *She's the image of her mother,* he mused. "Reagan."

She looked up. "Papa."

"If anything ever happened to you, I don't know that I could go on living. This isn't worth your life."

"Just wait until I tell you what happened. It really wasn't so bad. Someone helped me."

"Who?"

"I don't know, it was too dark to see his face. He said I didn't need to know his name. He was a wealthy man by the look of his cloak."

"We have many friends out there," Uriah mused. He lifted his gaze to his daughter's dark eyes. "But that doesn't change the fact that you weren't supposed to be out there tonight."

"Tomorrow," she urged quietly. "We can talk about it tomorrow."

"Yes, I suppose tomorrow will be soon enough, Daughter. I'm going to bed and I want you to do the same."

She got up and went to him, kissing his cheek. She smoothed his silver-gray sideburns. "I'll be right up. Good night."

Uriah patted her arm, then left the parlor.

Reagan listened to her father's footsteps as he ascended the stairs. He was right. There was nothing to do tonight but go to bed. She hadn't been caught and there was no way she could be connected to the incident. If the redcoats managed to trace the horse and wagon to Mistress Claggett, the elderly woman would simply say it had been stolen. As for the man who helped her, she would probably never know his name.

Reagan blew out the lamp and went down the hall toward the kitchen. When the front door swung open behind her, she turned in surprise.

"Reagan." Sterling closed the door quietly behind him.

"Grayson. What happened to you?" She rushed to him, helping him with his cloak. His golden-blond hair was stained red, and dried blood caked one cheek. Her heart leaped beneath her breast. There was so much blood!

Sterling frowned. "I fell off my damned horse."

"You certain it wasn't a tavern brawl?" she asked calmly, covering her alarm. She threw his cloak over her arm, pushing all thoughts of the confiscated pamphlets from her mind. If she wanted to protect herself and the ones she loved, she'd have to tread very carefully. "You'll have to come into the kitchen where the light's better. It might need a stitch or two from the way it's been bleeding."

"Oh, no, I'm not letting you get your embroidery needle near me!" He lifted his hands in protest.

"Don't be a baby, Captain." She took his hand, leading him into the kitchen. His hand felt good in hers. "Now sit in that chair by the table and let me get a look at your head. It's at least got to be cleaned."

114

Sterling sat down to watch Reagan bustle about the warm kitchen gathering a clean linen towel, a bowl of heated water, and a tin of ointment. She moved with an unmistakable grace, as if there was a silent, harmonious tune within her, leading her through each step.

Reagan perched herself on the edge of the work-table. "Now let me see this." Her hands shook slightly as she parted his hair to examine the wound. She had never touched a man's hair like this and somehow it seemed very intimate to her. His golden hair was soft and sleek beneath her finger-tips. "You fell off your horse?" She laughed trying to ease the tension she felt in her chest. "Quite a fine soldier the king has here."

"I was on an investigation." *Why not tell her,* Sterling reasoned. *Perhaps through her or her father, word would be filtered down to the penman. He needs to be warned how dangerously close he was to being caught.*

"Investigating the price of ale in some whore-house, no doubt?" She dipped the corner of the towel into the hot water and laid it on his open cut. The rumors she'd heard of the captain's escapades angered her. If he was going to play the whoremonger, why didn't he at least be discreet about it? Grayson Thayer's comings and goings seemed to be more popular dinner talk these days than the war!

"Ouch!" Sterling jumped, laying his hand on his head. "Damn, woman. You murder me here in the kitchen and there's bound to be questions."

She pushed his hand down and began to carefully cut the hair away from the wound with a tiny pair of silver-handled scissors. "Your mission?"

115

"Yes, well, you remember the pamphlets those soldiers were looking for in your father's printshop a few weeks back?"

Reagan froze, the scissors in midair. She suddenly felt as if the wind had been knocked out of her. She couldn't breathe; she was certain she was going to faint. "Y-yes," she managed.

"Well, I confiscated a shipment tonight."

"You did?" She leaned over his blond head, trying to continue to minister to his wound, but her stomach fluttered and her vision blurred.

"I nearly caught whoever was driving the wagon." He paused. "I don't suppose you know anything of these pamphlets or the perpetrators?"

"Certainly not! You think they would go about town identifying themselves?"

"If you happened to hear anything, do you think you could let me know?"

She slammed the scissors on the table. "How dare you!" She began to pace the hardwood floor, shaking her finger, bent on vengeance. "If you think you're going to get any information out of me, you're sadly mistaken, Captain. You know my father is a *Whig*, and you know our opinions on this damned war, and if you think you're going to weasel something out of me with your fancy uniform and smooth tongue, you're dead wrong!"

Sterling leaned back in the chair, surprised by her onslaught. His head was pounding, and suddenly nothing made sense any more. His mission was to portray his brother, the English officer, and to say and do the things his brother would. He'd known from the first day what this job entailed. So why was it suddenly so difficult?

116

Reagan. It was her. He *cared* what she thought about his words and deeds and it was getting in the way of the business at hand. He lifted his hands. If only he could tell her who he really was. If only he could make her understand. "Reagan—"

"Don't you Reagan me! You march into my city, you take over my home, and then you have the nerve to ask me to be your spy!"

"I didn't accuse you of anything. I just asked if you knew anything about these damned pamphlets! It's my duty!" He got to his feet, putting his arms out to her.

Reagan shook her head, backing off. Without his uniform it was so difficult for her to remind herself that Grayson was the enemy. The truth was, even when he wore it, there were times when she forgot. "Don't touch me! Don't you ever touch me! You don't understand what this war is about. You only understand the coin you're paid to wear that damned uniform." Tears formed in her eyes. "What do you think I am, one of those whores at the tavern who'll—"

Sterling grabbed her by the shoulders, pulling her against him. He couldn't stand the disappointment, the shock, the pain in her face. God, what he wouldn't have given to be able to tell her who he really was. But it was out of the question. There were too many people out there, nameless people who gave him aid in his undercover operation. If word leaked out that he was spy, they could all lose their lives . . . the blacksmith and his rosy-cheeked children, the butcher, the girl at the fish market, even Reagan herself.

Reagan struggled against Sterling, trying to escape, but he was kissing her, smoothing her hair, whispering softly in her ear. His mouth crushed against hers and she whimpered in frustration. Her mind told her he was the enemy. It cried, "Run! run!" But all she could do was return his kisses.

Sterling stroked the length of her back as he nibbled at the corner of her quivering mouth. The scent of her soft, sweet hair filled his brain, overwhelming him. Her fingers dug into the flesh of his shoulders as she returned his kisses with equal abandon.

Reagan swayed on her feet as Sterling cupped one breast, his thumb finding her peaked nipple beneath her clothing. She moaned softly, entwining his golden hair in her fingers. Nothing mattered at this moment but the two of them and the spark of light he brought to her soul.

"Grayson," she murmured, stroking the thick cord of his neck. "Grayson." Her tongue delved deep into his mouth, meeting his. She drank from his strength . . . from the forbidden.

Somewhere in the back of his mind, Sterling could hear her murmuring his brother's name. It was the strangest feeling, as it was Grayson who kissed her, who stroked her breasts, not him.

Her hand found his as he slipped it into the bodice of her gown. "No, please, I mustn't," she argued halfheartedly. "You mustn't, else how can I turn back?"

Her words sank slowly to the pit of his conscious mind and his hand grew still. "Oh, Reagan," he whispered huskily. He kissed her eyelids, her cheekbones, the tip of her nose. "I'm sorry. I swore this wouldn't happen."

She lifted her eyelids, stroking his stubbled jaw. Those were not the words of a man of Grayson's tinged character. No matter what he said, or did, she suddenly knew in her heart that he wasn't the man he proclaimed to be. His voice was too broken, too regretful. She knew a man could say anything, but he couldn't feel, not with his heart, not like this.

"Shh." She pressed her finger to his lips. His hand was hot on her breast, making it difficult to speak clearly. "It's my own fault. I've done it again. There's a part of me that can't back off. I know who you are and I hate you for that person, but there's someone else inside you . . ." She sighed, at a loss for words.

"I know. I know," he soothed. "I can't explain it. All I know is that I care for you deeply and that I—"

"Don't say it. Don't say anything else. I don't want to think. I just want to *be* for a minute."

"All right."

She gave him a half-smile, resting her head on his chest. Never in her life had she ever felt this alive, this vibrant. He struck a chord in her no one had ever reached before. Redcoat or not, she was falling in love with this man.

Chapter Nine

Reagan sat at the spinet, playing the same melancholy chords over and over again. Bright morning sunlight reflected off the snowdrifts and poured through the windows of the parlor, but it did nothing to lift her spirits. Last night's revelation had shaken her deeply. With Grayson involved in the investigation of the pamphlets, how could she and her father possibly continue to print them?

This morning she had spoken briefly to Uriah about last night's confiscation of their shipment. Tonight she, Uriah, and Westley, would meet in the secret room to discuss their situation. Today Uriah thought it vital that he remain in his shop and carry on business as usual. The more visible he was, the less likely he would be suspected.

Reagan didn't hear Grayson enter the room and she jumped when he laid his hand on her shoulder. "Oh! You scared me."

"Slide over." Sterling removed his bearskin grenadier cap and set it on the floor.

Reagan moved over, making room for him on the small bench. "Where have you been this morning, starched and bewigged?" She kept her hands clasped on her lap. For the briefest moment she recalled the feel of his hand on her breast, the taste of him, and her cheeks grew warm.

Self-consciously, Sterling touched his powdered wig. He hated the damned thing, but since Grayson always wore his in public, he figured he had to wear it on occasion for appearance' sake. "Yes, well, considering the barbarity of Philadelphia, I see no reason to waste good hair powder, but uh . . . I had an appointment with my commanding officer this morning."

"Major Burke?"

"Yes." Sterling's hand ached to caress the soft curve of her chin. Her face was so pale this morning. It was obvious she was deeply disturbed by last night. Another woman might have seen a few kisses as harmless, but Sterling knew Reagan felt as if she was betraying her country. If only she knew . . .

After a moment of silence, Reagan returned her fingers to the keyboard. She played softly, humming an old ballad her grandmother had taught her. *Just go away,* she thought. *Please, Grayson, leave me be.*

"The major is none too happy with me."

"I don't see why. You said you confiscated those papers." She tried to sound uninterested. It was the only way she knew to protect herself and the others.

"Yes, but I let the penmen get away."

"What makes you think the penman would be idiotic enough to drive his own wagon through the streets after dark?"

Sterling frowned suspiciously. "How did you know there was a wagon?"

121

She never missed a note. "Nothing goes on in this city that everyone doesn't know by nightfall. Everyone's a gossip these days." She continued to play, growing more confident in herself with each passing note. What was she worried about? She was certainly bright enough to outsmart one beribboned dandy of a redcoat! "If I was the penman, I certainly wouldn't be so addlepated as to transport the pamphlets myself!"

He smiled, catching a tendril of bright hair at her temple and twisting it around his finger. "No, I don't suppose you would. You'd be too smart, wouldn't you, my little Continental?"

She couldn't resist a smile. He was teasing her again. "Haven't you got anywhere you've got to be? Some innocent citizen to arrest, mayhap?"

Sterling laid his hand on hers and she stopped playing. "Actually, I have got somewhere to be and you're going with me."

"I am not." She turned to face him, trying to focus on the powdered wig and scarlet uniform. This man stood for what these united states despised. Grayson was England, he was the king's tyranny. If she could just keep these things in mind, she knew she could resist the desire for him she felt building within her.

"I've been invited to go sledding with a friend outside the city. It's a beautiful day out. We could take a picnic."

She shook her head. "Oh, no, I'm not going anywhere with you. I wouldn't be seen on the street with a lobsterback. My neighbors'll be pelting stones at me from their windows."

122

"Come on, don't you ever have any fun?"

"I never thought being stoned to death to be of much *fun*."

"You can meet me on the corner of town. No one would have to know."

"I . . . I couldn't. My father would never—"

"So, we won't tell him. He left for work early, we'll be back before he's home."

"I can't. I won't." I *mustn't,* she thought, feeling her resolve crumble.

"Please?" Sterling cajoled.

Reagan didn't know what to say. How could she even be considering going with him? "Grayson, if any of our friends saw me with you . . ." She sighed. "If . . . if my father . . ."

He lifted her hand to his mouth, kissing one knuckle at a time. "Come on, sweetheart. I won't wear my uniform. You can pretend I'm Joe Feddlebottom, colonial farmer."

She laughed. "Can't you get into trouble? Everyone knows my father's on that list. He still refuses to sign the allegiance document. Aren't you already in enough hot water with that Major Burke?"

"No one will know." He stroked her palm. "And if anyone finds out,"—he shrugged—"I'll tell them I was involved in an interrogation."

He nuzzled a soft spot on her neck and she swatted him. "That's not funny. Word got back to some people in this city that I was carrying tales to the Brits and they'd burn us out."

"Please?"

Her cinnamon eyes sought his. He had the darkest, deepest blue eyes she'd ever seen. She knew she shouldn't go, but it did sound fun, and who could possibly find out? "Outside the city?"

"You can come disguised if you like." He lifted his grenadier cap and dropped it on her head.

"I didn't say I was coming," she stalled. She knew this was a mistake, but she couldn't help herself. There was something about this man that drew her to him. At this moment it seemed as vital to be with him.

He adjusted his cap on her head, excited by the thought of being alone with her away from his duties . . . his fears. "Just this once?" he whispered.

"Oh, all right." She yanked off the hat and tossed it to the floor. "Why not? Elsa and Nettie are going to the mill and then they'll be baking bread. I can make up some story about going to see a friend."

He got up from the spinet, retrieving his cap. "Joshua?" He didn't know what made him say it, it just slipped out. The moment he heard his own words, he regretted them.

"Joshua?" Her brow furrowed. "Why would I see Joshua? Whatever was between us ended when he accepted his commission. Our families don't speak on the street."

Sterling backed out the door. "Yes, well. Dress warmly. We'll go in an hour."

Reagan watched him disappear, smiling to herself. Captain Thayer was jealous!

* * *

Bells jingled merrily as the roan mares pulled the sled over the slick snow, down a gully, and across a frozen field where wheat stood in the summer months. Two red foxes leaped and dove into the snowdrifts along the edge of the woods and Reagan laughed at their antics, pointing them out to Sterling.

She was snuggled in the crook of his arm, a layer of soft woolen blankets and a bearhide tucked over them. He chatted with his friend Lieutenant Charles Warrington and the lieutenant's companion Anne, his breath tickling Reagan's ear with each word.

"I told you this would be fun," Sterling whispered, kissing her rosy cheek.

"You think everything is a game. I'm not kidding, no one must know I came here with you," she warned, straightening the hood of her forest-green wool cloak.

He slipped his hand beneath the blankets, bringing it to rest on the soft flesh of her thigh. "I already warned Charles and Anne, if they reveal a word of this secret mission they'll both be shot."

She sunk her elbow sharply into his side. "You're not taking this seriously." She glanced up at Anne and Charles but saw nothing but the backs of their heads. They were obviously deep in conversation. "My father would send me to my aunt's in Richmond." Her eyes met his. "I can't leave the city, Grayson."

He shrugged. "I just wouldn't allow a pass to be issued. You can't get out of the city without a pass."

"And you think everyone who gets out of the city does it legally?"

Sterling studied her sparkling brown eyes. Damn, but this girl was brazen. He didn't think he'd ever met anyone, male or female, who would dare to be so bold with the enemy . . . no one but himself or his brother. "You'd better keep those sweet lips closed," he warned quietly.

"You'd turn me in if you knew I was doing something illegal?"

"In a heartbeat," he answered against her lips.

Reagan took a deep breath, gazing out over the rolling field. Agreeing to this outing had been a mistake. She should have followed her head instead of her loins. Sterling squeezed her hand beneath the wool coverlets and she smiled bittersweetly. She'd enjoy herself today, but tomorrow she'd make it clear to the captain that she was not interested in his attention. That was the only logical thing to do—before the situation got out of hand.

Lieutenant Warrington brought the sled along a frozen creek and pulled the horses to a halt on a hilly crest above a frozen mill pond. Sterling jumped out and unloaded a picnic basket before he offered Reagan his hand to assist her out of the sled.

Reagan's toes touched the ground and the snow crunched beneath her feet. The countryside here was breathtaking with its rolling hills, jutting rocks, and dense pine foliage. An abandoned mill house was built on the far side of the pond, its miller's wheel silent and still. "This where we're going to eat?"

"And skate." Sterling produced two pairs of iceskates from the sled's floor.

Reagan clapped her mittened hands. "Oh, I haven't skated in ages!"

He patted one of the prancing horses' rumps and the sled slid forward. Retrieving the skates and basket, he started off down the hill toward a fallen log.

"They're not coming?" Reagan followed in his tracks, glancing over her shoulder at the retreating sled. The lieutenant and Anne were locked in an embrace as the horse and vehicle disappeared into the tree line.

"They'll be back later." He gave a wink. "They just wanted some privacy."

"Oh." Suddenly her eyes widened. "Oh! Ooooh." Her cheeks grew hot with embarrassment.

Heartened by Reagan's refreshing innocence, Sterling dropped his hand over her shoulder and kissed the point of her hood. "Sit on the log and I'll put your skates on for you."

She laughed, snatching the iron skates from his hand and ran ahead. "You put your own on!"

A few minutes later they were skating on the small pond. Around and around in circles Reagan skated. The frigid wind on her face was exhilarating as she gained speed, her long legs pushing harder and harder. It felt so good to be out in the fresh air, away from the responsibilities of home.

"You're a daring woman in deed as well as word," Sterling observed. He skated idly in the middle, watching her as she moved faster and faster until it seemed as if she flew over the frozen pond.

"Daring, how?" She skated past him, knocking his wool hat off his head. The sunlight reflected off his golden hair.

"If you hit the bank you could break your neck. Women don't generally take chances."

"So I won't hit the bank," she called over her shoulder. She skated a figure eight and then a bow, closing in on Sterling.

He caught her sleeve and looped his arm through hers. Side by side they skimmed over the ice. "My brother and I used to skate by the hour. We used to stay out on the river until long after dark." He smiled nostalgically.

"You have a brother?"

He licked his dry lips. "Did. But he's dead." He didn't know what made him say it—a love of the dramatic he supposed. "His name was Sterling. We were twins."

Reagan looked at him. What was that she heard in his voice? Pain, she supposed, but something more. "I'm sorry," she said quietly. "I didn't mean to pry."

He released her arm and skated away. "No harm done."

"What did he die of?" It was her turn to stand in the centér and watch him skate circles around her.

"Lead poisoning."

"What do you mean?"

He chuckled, mirroring Grayson's arrogance. "My brother joined the wrong side. He died of

128

lead poisoning, a musket ball through his chest. It was somewhere on Long Island." Actually it was his good friend Luke who had died on that muddy bank on Long Island back in the summer of '76. He'd held Luke's battered body in his arms as his best friend's life's blood had spilled into the mire.

"So he was one of us." She skated over to him, taking both of his gloved hands. "I wish I could have known him. He sounds like the kind of man a woman like me could love."

Sterling pushed forward and Reagan skated backward, guided by his powerful arms. The warmth that shone in her eyes made him jealous, though of what, he wasn't quite certain. His story was fictitious, the brother he spoke of was a mixture of Luke, of Grayson, and of himself. If he and Reagan could have met in a different place, a different time, if she could have known who he truly was, would that warmth in her voice have been directed toward him?

The two skated in silence for a while and then Sterling led her to the bank. "I don't know about you, but I'm starved."

Seated on the fallen log, Reagan watched him build a small crackling fire and then unload the lunch basket. She oohed and ahhed at the delicacies he produced. There was a long loaf of bread from the baker's, a wheel of yellow cheese, slices of ham, polished red apples, and dusty bottles of ale.

Sterling spread out a wool blanket and served her as if she was royalty. The two laughed and

129

chatted about their childhood, about memories of warm kitchens and soft down feather testers . . . even about their first kiss.

"What was her name?" Reagan laughed, her soft, husky voice mingling with the wind.

"Esther, Esther Gunthrie. We were thirteen and it was in the milkhouse behind her father's barn. My brother told me later he had kissed her in the same milkhouse the week before!"

Reagan dissolved into laughter again. "I was fifteen." She looked away, her face softening. "Joshua asked permission. We were supposed to be studying, but he was just watching me. He said he couldn't keep his mind on his books." She blushed, embarrassed. "He said he couldn't think of anything but my lips and he was going to die if I didn't let him kiss me just once."

Sterling was stretched out on the blanket, toying with the hem of her cloak. "So you let him?"

"I was more interested in getting our studies done for the day than kissing so I figured it was the quickest way."

Sterling sat up and pulled her into his arms. "I can see why he would say these lips are irresistible." He leaned to kiss her and she pulled back.

"Grayson, please."

"What? It's just a kiss."

She gazed into his eyes, raising her hand to stroke his clean-shaven cheek. "Why are you doing this? There are so many other women in the city, women far more willing, far less trouble."

"I like you." He brushed his thumb against her lower lip.

130

When his mouth met hers, she gave no resistance. Hot, tingling desire flowed through her chilled limbs as he played her lips in a dance of seduction. A heat spread from Reagan's midsection radiating outward as his warm hand caressed the roundness of her breasts beneath her cloak. She ran her fingers through his soft, golden hair, in awe of the emotions he sparked inside her.

Their tongues met, and she moaned deep in her throat. His taste, his smell, the feel of his hands on her flesh, was intoxicating. He lowered her onto her back, calling her name, whispering sweet words of woo. The sky spun above and Reagan struggled to catch her breath as Sterling lifted her petticoats.

"Grayson, no. Please." She looked up at him, tucking a lock of blond hair that had escaped from his queue behind his ear. "I can't," she whispered. "You mustn't."

Something snapped inside Sterling and he relaxed, burying his face in her sweet-smelling hair. He could feel his heart pounding in his chest, his blood coursing through his veins. What was he thinking? He hadn't let his lust get the best of him since he was seventeen! But it was more than lust with Reagan . . . he could feel it deep within him. Somewhere in the recesses of his mind, he knew he had fallen in love with her.

Reagan lay perfectly still, her arms flung over her head. She stared up at the darkening sky through the leafless branches of the oak tree that loomed above them. She listened to her own breathing becoming more regular. The smell of

Sterling's shaving soap, the weight of his head on her shoulder slowly brought her back to reality. "I'm sorry," she whispered, her voice still raspy.

Sterling pushed himself up on one elbow and smoothed a lock of thick, shining hair that fell over her shoulder. "It's all right."

"I should never have come. This was a terrible mistake. I didn't mean to lead you on."

He stared down at her with those eyes as blue as the heavens. "I know you didn't."

She sighed heavily, looking away, unable to stand his scrutiny. "I don't know what to say. I know who you are, I know what you are, but still, I can't—" She left her sentence unfinished for lack of the right words.

Sterling sat up, offering her his hand. She sat cross-legged beside him, and he brushed the snow off the back of her cloak. He knew no way to comfort her. Silently he chastised himself for having ever brought her along. Every hour they spent together a thread grew stronger between them. She was the forbidden, yet her nearness had become as vital to him as the cause he fought for.

Reagan's voice broke the silence. "You know what I wish?"

He took her cold hand, slipping a woolen mitten over it. "What do you wish?"

"That you were him."

His gaze rested on her dark, penetrating eyes. "Who?"

"Your brother Sterling, because then it would be all right, wouldn't it?"

Sterling stood, brushing the snow from his own

132

cloak. Sleigh bells jingled in the distance. "I cannot change who I am," he said in his brother's voice.

She smiled sadly. "Nor can I, Captain."

Reagan hooked her cloak on a peg and entered the kitchen. The smell of pigeon stew and fresh-baked bread permeated the air. Self-consciously, she smoothed the knot of hair at the nape of her neck, knowing how unruly it had to look after that tumble in the snow with Grayson.

The ride back into the city had been quiet. She had said little to Grayson, leaving the two men to talk among themselves. Her mind was too jumbled for conversation. Nothing seemed to make sense anymore. She had always thought she knew right from wrong. Her life had always been as black as ink, as white as the paper pulp her father ran through his presses. But now—there were a thousand shades of gray.

Grayson was the enemy. He was the conquering army. But Grayson was also kind, he was fun, he was gentle. The man who had held her in his arms today had not been the man who had stood in that cold barn only a few weeks back ready to watch that boy hang. But it *was* the same man! How could she have kissed him with such wild abandon? How could she have let him touch her like that, made her feel that way? She knew she should feel shame, but she didn't. Only utter, bitter confusion.

Seeing no one downstairs, Reagan mounted the

staircase. She'd brush her hair and wash her face; perhaps that would do something to calm the unrest she felt in her heart. She needed her father, her sister. Their presence would chase the demons from her mind, leaving her to think more clearly.

Reagan paused near the tall case clock on the upper landing, thinking she heard Elsa. It was nothing more than a squeak. "Elsa?" She stopped to listen, raising her voice. "Elsa!"

When she heard no reply she ran down the hallway and burst into her sister's bedchamber. To her horror Lieutenant Gardener had Elsa pinned beneath him on her four-poster bed. Her skirts were hiked up and thrown over her head; his breeches were down around his knees.

Reagan snatched the lieutenant's pistol off the cherry sidetable.

Chapter Ten

Reagan brought the weapon down sharply on the back of Roth Gardener's head and he pitched forwards falling unconscious over Elsa's prone body.

"Elsa?" Reagan flung the pistol to the floor and climbed onto the bed, rolling the officer off her sister. "Elsa, are you all right?" She clasped Elsa's face between her palms, her own tears falling onto her sister's pale cheeks.

Elsa's teary gaze met her sister's. "Reagie?"

"Oh, thank God you're all right!" Reagan threw her arms around Elsa's trembling shoulders.

Elsa struggled to sit up, pushing her skirts down. "I told him I wouldn't do it," she said angrily. "Papa would be awful mad if I got in circumstance."

"He didn't—" Reagan couldn't find the right words. ". . . Take liberties?"

Elsa shook her head, climbing off the bed. "He tried but he couldn't. He said something 'bout damned drink." She bent over him. "I hope you didn't kill him. He didn't really hurt me."

Reagan threw the corner of the counterpane over the lieutenant's naked buttocks and bounced up off the bed. She clasped her sister's hand.

"You're certain you're not hurt?" She wondered how her little Elsa knew anything about being in 'circumstance' but decided this wasn't the time to ask.

"No, he didn't hurt me. He brought me a sweet roll from the baker. He wanted me to drink claret"—she wrinkled her delicately upturned nose—"but I don't like claret, so I didn't have any."

The lieutenant moaned and moved slightly and Reagan glanced at him sprawled on her counterpane. "You go down to the kitchen and wait for me. I'll take care of Mr. Gardener."

Elsa walked to the door, then turned back. "Don't be mean to him, Sister. He didn't hurt me. I felt sorry for him. He said he just wanted a little love. He said nobody loved him. Everybody should be loved, and I think it's a sad thing."

"Just go downstairs and wait." When Elsa had gone, Reagan went to the lieutenant and poked his bare calf with the toe of her boot. "Mr. Gardener," she said angrily. "Mr. Gardener, wake up!"

He stirred, but only long enough to turn his face to the other side. He remained lying facedown. Blood oozed from a cut on the back of his head. "Help me," he moaned.

"Lieutenant, if you bleed on my deceased mother's counterpane, I'll kill you for sure! Now get up!"

He stuck out a hairy arm and tried to roll over, but fell back into the goosedown pillows.

Reagan was standing in indecision, her hands perched on her hips, when Sterling entered the room. "Elsa told me what happened. Did you kill him?"

She faced Sterling, her face flushed with anger. "No, I didn't kill him, but only because he wouldn't be worth the powder. That pettifogging bastard tried to rape my sister."

"I know. She told me, but she's all right. You were in time."

"Maybe today, but what about the next time?" Her eyes narrowed dangerously. "Either you get him out of my house tonight, Captain, or I'll kill him. I swear it!"

The tone of her voice told Sterling it wasn't a threat, it was a promise. "All right, Reagan. I'll take care of it." He went to the bed and grasped the lieutenant by the waist, hauling him to his feet.

"How will you do it? He's been assigned here permanently."

"I don't know, but I'll take care of it." Sterling leaned the now semiconscious officer against the bedpost and yanked up his breeches. "Come on, Roth. Up with you."

Gardener's head lolled from side to side as Sterling dragged him out of Elsa's bedchamber. Reagan followed behind, the lieutenant's coat thrown over her arm, his pistol and belt clasped in her hand. She entered the bedchamber Roth Gardener was occupying and dumped his belongings on a mahogany chair near the door. "I'm taking my sister and going to sup with my mother's cousin on Walnut. When I come back, I want him gone, Captain."

Sterling laid Roth none-too-gently on the bed and spun around angrily to face Reagan. "I said I would take care of it," he snapped. "But mind you, this is the last time I cover your attractive little bottom!"

"Cover my—" Reagan's mouth clamped shut. "This is Elsa we're talking about. He tried to rape her! He can't remain in our home."

"I'm in enough trouble over these damned pamphlets, Reagan. Major Burke is not going to like this! He's got better things to do than worry about where his men sleep." *Damn,* Sterling thought. *How am I going to get Roth out of the house without making trouble for myself?*

His position with Major Burke was already precarious. The British officer would not take kindly to Sterling being a troublemaker, and his own commanding officer with the Continentals, Captain Craig, would be even less pleased. His assignment was to infiltrate the British Army at Philadelphia and learn what he could. He was not supposed to become involved with Reagan and her family like this—it was too dangerous. If only Reagan knew what she was asking.

Tears stung Reagan's eyes and she dashed at

138

them with the back of her hand. How could she have so misjudged Grayson Thayer? How could she have allowed the attraction between them to overshadow the true man that he was? She had almost fooled herself into thinking that perhaps he cared for her, for her family. But he didn't care . . . All that mattered to Captain Grayson Thayer was himself. He was nothing more than what he appeared to be. A coin was always face value, nothing more. He was a bloody redcoat.

"Do what you like then, Captain, but I'd advise you to warn Mr. Gardener that if I ever catch him in my home again I'll shoot him right between the legs." She spun around and sailed out the door.

Sterling groaned, turning back to the problem at hand. Roth Gardener was finally coming to. *Now, how the hell was he going to get him out of here?*

Sterling slipped into the Blue Boar Tavern, removed his cloak, and walked to the front counter. "What do I owe you for the month?" he asked Jergens, jingling his month's pay in a leather pouch. "More than I've got, I'll vow."

The barkeeper dried a tankard with the corner of his apron. "Don't owe me a thing, Captain Thayer. Your bill's already been paid."

"What do you mean? I haven't paid you."

"Nope, someone paid the bill for you."

139

"Who?" Sterling frowned. He couldn't believe his captain would have dared send anyone into the city to pay his bills. In fact, Captain Craig had expressed his dissatisfaction with Sterling's exorbitant expenditures in his last message.

"An older gentleman—said he wanted to remain *anon-y-mous*." Jergens shrugged. "What did I care? He paid with good hard coin."

"And you're sure he meant to pay *my* bill?"

The bartender scowled. "You're Captain Thayer, ain't you?"

Sterling paused in thought for a moment, then glanced back at Jergens. *Better not to make a fuss,* he thought. *Grayson certainly wouldn't care who paid his bill.* "A bottle of your best claret, then."

"I'll send it right over, Captain."

When the barmaid, Annie, brought Sterling his wine, he poured himself a draught and sipped it, studying the faces in the public room. He checked his brother's pocket watch. It was nearly ten. By now Reagan would be arriving home to find Roth Gardener had vacated the Llewellyn premises, lock, stock, and barrel. Sterling smiled at his own cleverness, the bar bill forgotten for the moment. A brief conversation with the lieutenant, and the man had packed and hired a wagon to carry his belongings away.

The tavern door swung open and a ragged woman wearing a blanket over her shoulders entered the smoky room. She squinted, pushing the blanket off her head to reveal strings of tangled, thinning hair.

Sterling watched her carefully. She was obviously looking for someone. He cleared his throat. "Excuse me, madame," he said politely. "Might I help you?" Grayson always said treat the whore like a queen and the queen like a whore and you'll have no trouble with the ladies.

The woman looked at Sterling. "A man, a redskin half-breed. They tol' me I could find him here."

Sterling rose, indicating the bench across from him. "Sit a moment. I know who you mean. He must have been detained. I'm certain he'll be along directly."

She glanced at his bottle of claret and licked her cracked lips. Her glazed eyes met Sterling's.

He pushed his glass and the bottle across the table. "A little refreshment while you wait?" The woman sat and reached for the glass. She tipped it, draining it in one breath, then poured another. Sterling signaled a barmaid. "Some bread and soup here."

The wench returned from the kitchen carrying a platter of bread and two bowls of steaming soup. "Anything else, Capt'n?" She fluttered her dark eyelashes. Word was the captain liked the ladies and he tipped well for their favors.

"No, that'll be all, dear." He tugged at her petticoat as she walked by and she burst into giggles.

"You just need call," she told him over her

shoulder as she moved on to the next table.

Sterling watched the haggard woman across from him wolf down two hunks of bread she tore from the loaf with her fingers. She slurped down the bowl of soup and reached for another piece of bread. He eased his own bowl across the table and she lifted her spoon again.

"So you're waiting for Indian John . . ." He folded his arms, leaning on the table. "You have information for him, do you?"

"Maybe." The woman dipped her bread into the soup and stuffed it into her mouth.

Sterling smiled. Lucky guess. "And what might this pertain to?"

"The injun's payin' for information on them papers everybody's readin'."

"Papers? What papers?"

Her spoon froze in midair. "Why you so innerested?"

"Well, it just so happens that I'm investigating those treasonous pamphlets." He poured the remainder of the claret into her glass.

"You are?"

"It looks like Indian John's been detained. Why not tell me? After all, we all want to see justice done here, don't we?"

She sopped up the last of the soup with the heel of the bread loaf and crammed it into her mouth. Soup dribbled down her chin. "All I want's hard money." She took a deep breath and belched.

142

"I've coin."

"Let's see it. Ya soldiers are t'all alike. Ya always want credit."

Sterling laid one coin on the table, then a second. The woman's eyes widened and her hand snaked out to cover the silver.

He placed his hand over the money before she reached it. "Tell me what you know and it's yours, plus another for your trouble."

"It ain't much but they say he's payin' for anything."

"So am I, and I'm paying more."

She slipped a withered hand beneath her ragged clothes and pulled out a sodden bit of paper. She slid it across the table and the moment Sterling reached for it, she snatched up the coins.

He smoothed out the paper. The ink had run so that it was barely visible. Scrawled across it was a list of two items and initials: linseed oil, varnish, "UL." Sterling looked up. "What is this?"

"I cain't read, but my daughter says it's a list for a printer. She knows a gen'lman who brings a wagon or two into the city—black market. She foun' it in his pocket."

Sterling tossed the old woman another coin and she scrambled to catch it before it fell to the floor. "Thank you. You can go." He carefully folded the delicate piece of paper.

When the old hag had gone, Sterling removed a perfumed lace handkerchief and fluttered it under his nose. "By the king's cod, that women stank," he muttered to no one in particular.

When an appropriate amount of time had passed, he took his cloak and hat, leaving coin on the table. Outside the bitter wind blew and snow swirled on the cobblestone walk at his feet. He walked slowly, hunkered down against the cold.

"UL" . . . that could only be one man—Uriah Llewellyn. There was a chance the order was innocent. What harm was there in a man trying to purchase what materials he needed for his livelihood, black market or not? The only problem with that explanation was that Sterling had been in Uriah's shop just last week and along the wall there had been several jars of linseed oil.

Sterling knew little about the printing trade, but he knew enough to be certain that the small bit of printing Uriah was doing legally couldn't demand the need of more linseed oil. It was used to thin down the ink made of lampwick and varnish. Uriah had just been saying how poor business was since the evacuation of many citizens and the occupation of the British. There was no logical explanation other than that Uriah was involved in some illegal printing—most likely the political leaflets.

He smiled in the darkness, crossing Walnut Street and heading down Fourth toward home. It was men like Uriah Llewellyn who had made this revolution possible. It was men like him who were as vital to the cause of freedom as the soldiers at

Valley Forge. Men like Uriah and women like Reagan . . . the little minx. His heart swelled with pride. Surely she knew what her father was doing. Perhaps she had even aided in some small way.

The problem at hand now was to figure how to get Uriah to cease publication without him becoming aware of Sterling's charade. Sterling would write a message to his commanding officer immediately. If Uriah simply stopped writing his treasonous pamphlets, his life would no longer be at risk, and Sterling would no longer be in the position of being expected by Major Burke to locate the penman.

Sterling skipped up the icy steps of the house on Spruce Street and took a deep breath. He hoped Reagan was already asleep. His mind was too filled with urgency on the matter of the pamphlets to deal with her tonight.

The house was silent, the rooms darkened. A single bronze lamp burned on a small mahogany table at the foot of the staircase. Sterling picked up the lamp and climbed the stairs. He passed Uriah's bedchamber, then Reagan's. There was a dim glow of firelight seeping from beneath her door, but no sound. He slipped into the room Roth Gardener had occupied and closed the door. Shedding the distasteful red coat and trappings of his brother's trade, he settled at the small writing desk to print his urgent message.

From the pages of a Bible he produced a "mask" and placed it over a clean sheet of linen paper. The mask was a piece of paper with holes cut in it to form a bell. He wrote his brief message concerning the leaflets, leaving out Uriah's name, in the cut-out spaces. Then, he removed the mask and began to fill in the letter addressed to Cousin Lucy with newsy information on a fictitious family's illnesses. He signed it "Aunt Feddlebottom" and began to sprinkle sand on the paper to dry the ink when a knock came at the door.

Sterling closed up the desk and came to his feet. "Just a moment," he called. He went to the door and opened. It was Reagan, just as he thought it was, but half hoped it was not.

She wore a faded flannel sleeping gown of pale blue with ribbons that tied beneath her chin. Her hair was a glorious mass of curls brushed out and fanned over her shoulders. The anger and bitter disappointment he had seen on her face earlier in the evening was gone.

"May I come in?" Her voice was barely above a whisper.

Sterling stepped back, mesmerized. "Do."

She walked into the bedchamber and closed the door behind her. For a long moment she just stood there staring at him. Finally her lips parted and she spoke. "I don't understand you, Grayson. You're a paradox."

Sterling could feel the heat of the small room closing in on him. Her voice was soft, raspy with a sensuality he knew she was unaware of. "Me?

146

How so?" He walked to a wing chair upholstered in flowered chinz and sat down. He began to remove his boots.

She shrugged. "You're two men, Captain."

He lifted his chin sharply, his eyes meeting hers.

"You wear that despicable uniform." She indicated the red coat hanging from a bed poster. "You attended the would-be hanging of a child."

"He was a spy," Sterling countered.

She went on, ignoring his comment. "You ride your blue-blood horse down our streets while old women walk because their animals have been confiscated. You eat cheese and fruit from a picnic basket while our children go without bread because there's no wheat for flour, then . . ." She paused, studying his striking face. "Then you give me back my room." She fiddled with the ribbons of her sleeping gown. "I just don't understand."

He set aside his expensive calf-hide boots and began to roll down his silk stockings embroidered with clocks. "You make more of it than it is. With Roth gone, I simply saw no reason to occupy a lady's bedchamber when I could have this one."

She took a step closer to him. Her heart was pounding. She didn't know what she was doing in here, but she couldn't help herself. She had tried to sleep, but the image of Grayson's face prevented it.

"No. By giving me back my room, you returned a bit of dignity to me. A conquering army makes no such concessions." She stared into the depths of his heavenly blue eyes. A smile tugged at the corners of her lips. "I sometimes think you joined the wrong side."

Grayson's control slipped from Sterling's grasp. He took Reagan by the waist and brought her down into his lap. His mouth crushed hers and she wrapped her arms around him, pressing her soft breasts into his chest.

"I'm so frightened," she whispered, returning his kisses eagerly.

"Afraid of what?" He kissed the length of her pale neck, tugging at the strings of her nightdress.

"Of myself. I hate you." Her breath came in short gasps. "I hate you, but I need you. I want you."

Sterling kissed her deeply, his tongue delving to explore the cool lining of her mouth. He had never met a woman so uninhibited by her feelings, so aware of her own sexuality. He knew she was inexperienced in the ways of a man and a woman, yet she was eager to love and be loved.

"I would never hurt you," Sterling assured her. His hand slipped beneath the flannel to cup her breast. He tested its weight in his palm, caressing her soft flesh, stroking her nipple.

Reagan sighed, leaning against him, letting him cradle her in his arms as the waves of rising desire washed over her. This man made her feel alive, not just physically, but deep within her

148

soul.

"I want to make love to you," he whispered. His mouth closed down on her nipple, leaving a damp spot on the flannel.

"I want you to," she answered, "but . . ."

"No buts, Reagie. Don't try to think it out. For once, just let it happen."

She threaded her fingers through his magical hair. "You don't understand what you ask. I risk everything, you risk nothing."

He kissed her eyelids, the tip of her nose. "You don't know everything, Reagie."

"You've probably been with a hundred women." She laughed huskily, arching her back as his warm mouth found her nipple again. "A thousand."

"It doesn't matter. Nothing else matters but you, sweetheart. Believe me."

She took a deep breath, clasping his face in her palms. She lifted his chin so that she might look into his eyes. "Don't say things like that. Things you know aren't true. I know what you are, Captain. I hear the rumors at the market."

"Does it matter?" *Something my brother would have said,* Sterling thought as the words fell from his lips.

Her fingertips caressed his lips. "I think not, and that's what scares me the most. I'm loyal to the bone to the cause of freedom, but—"

"I understand," he interrupted.

"How can you understand?" Her dark eyebrows

furrowed as she slipped from his lap. "I just want to be sure, Grayson." She stood unembarrassed before him, her gown open to her waist to reveal the soft curves of her breasts. "There's so much at risk for a few days, a few weeks of pleasure."

Tell her, a voice inside Sterling protested. *Tell her who you are, tell her you love her.* But his sense of duty was too strong. If it was only his own life at risk there would have been no hesitation, but this web was too tangled.

Sterling stood and reached out and began to tie the bows of her gown. "I'll be here should you decide in my favor," he whispered. Finishing the last tie, he kissed her softly, then watched her slip from the room in silence.

Chapter Eleven

"I think it's best, Papa." Reagan nodded gravely. "Westley would take her to Richmond, I'm sure of it."

"The roads are barely passable. Our old carriage would never make it." Uriah pushed back from the dining table in the center of the sitting parlor.

Before the British occupation of Philadelphia, this room had held host to merry dinners. Patriots from all over the city had joined Uriah Llwellyn and his daughter in heated political discussions around the elegant, polished table. There had been a time, when the Continental Congress had been in session, that dozens of calling cards had been left daily. Now, the sitting parlor was left dark, the great oval table and matching chairs covered with oilcloth.

"It's the first of March. There'll be mud but little chance of snow. Send her on horseback if you must, but I think we've got to get her out of the city. It's just not safe. This business with Lieutenant Gardener proved that. Who knows how long the British intend to stay here?" Reagan sipped from a teacup, wrinkling her nose at the bitter taste of the coffee. She preferred good English tea, but had given it up a good two years ago in the name of freedom.

"I knew it was going to come to this." Uriah chewed on the stem of his unlit pipe. "Why not consider going with her?" he added thoughtfully.

Reagan bolted up. "Surely you're not serious? You heard what Westley said." She paced her mother's Brussel carpet. "That last leaflet of ours reached Boston! Papa, someone printed my piece on a bill of rights in one of the gazettes! They said it was intuitive, perspicacious! Imagine, something I wrote being perspicacious!"

Uriah searched his threadbare waistcoat for his tobacco. "You forget you were nearly caught with that shipment. You forget that Captain Thayer is out there on the street at this moment hunting us down."

"Another two weeks and I'll be ready to go to press with the next essay. I'm not abandoning you or my duty." She leaned over him, plucking his pouch of tobacco from between the pages of a book lying on the table, and handed it to him. Her father was so absentminded these days. He seemed to be aging before her eyes. "Besides, this discussion concerns Elsa, not me."

"What about Elsa?" Elsa came into the sitting parlor, her hands clasped delicately in the folds of her skirting.

The episode with the lieutenant had seemed to leave no mark on her. Elsa said it was an "unfortunate happening" but that she was unharmed, and that was the end of the matter. An "unfortunate happening" indeed! Reagan couldn't for the life of her figure out where Elsa was getting such words, such ideas.

Uriah rose from his chair and lit his pipe with an ember from the hearth. "We were just talking, Elsa. Your sister was saying how much you would enjoy visiting Aunt Abby in Richmond."

"No, I wouldn't." Elsa looked at Reagan. "Why would you say that? You know I don't like it at Aunt Abby's."

Reagan came to her sister, placing a hand on her shoulder. "Papa thought it might be good if you had a little holiday."

"I'm not going. I'm not leaving Philadelphia."

"Elsa? What's gotten into you?" Reagan withdrew her hand. "Has Captain Thayer been talking to you again?"

"Captain Thayer is nice to mc. He doesn't treat me like a baby like you and Papa." Elsa lifted her chin. "Philadelphia is my homc and no lobsterbacks are going to chase me from it."

Reagan laughed, glancing at her father. "Where on God's fertile earth does she get these things?"

Uriah puffed on his pipe. "Perhaps she'd be more willing to go if you went with her."

"Papa! I said wasn't going. I can't. You know that!"

Elsa poured herself a china cup of coffee from the pot on the center of the table. "If Reagan doesn't have to go, *I* don't have to go." She sipped her coffee leisurely. Just the other day she

153

had told Reagan that she actually preferred the taste of coffee to tea.

Reagan didn't know what to say. She couldn't imagine where this new sense of independence in Elsa had come from. It had to be Grayson. He had emphatically denied giving her any encouragement, but still, Reagan was suspicious. Who else did she speak with outside the immediate family?

Uriah smiled sadly. "What am I going to do with you girls?" He shook his head. "You're as stubborn as your mother, the both of you."

"I think you should send her, Papa," Reagan said crossly. "I don't know why you didn't send her with the Smiths when they left last fall."

"The truth is that I'm a selfish man, else I would have sent you both to Richmond when we heard the British were marching on us."

"You couldn't do it alone. You can't," she said meaningfully, referring to their printing.

Uriah pulled his pipe from his mouth, drawing himself to his full height of nearly five feet five. His eyes narrowed. "I could, Reagan, and I can. You keep that in mind when you take those chances, because if I decide your safety is really in danger, then you and your sister will be gone from this house. I wouldn't care if I had to tie and gag you both." He picked up his book with an ink-stained finger. "Just keep that in mind, missy."

Reagan watched in stunned silence as her father left the room. She didn't know what on earth had possessed him to rant in such a manner!

Elsa smiled smugly over the rim of her coffee cup. "Guess you better be a good girl, Sister."

The moment Uriah and Reagan heard the splintering of glass in the front room of the printshop, he leaned forward and blew out his lamp on the desk.

They'd been working late tonight in his small office in the rear of the shop. They had been going over the account books trying to figure out where they were going to get money to buy firewood and wheat for flour when their supplies were gone. The white paper money Uriah had was worth nothing in the city under siege. No vendor would take anything but hard coin or bartered goods. Like the other families that had remained in the city, the Llewellyns were nearly destitute.

"Who do you think it is?" Reagan whispered.

"Shh." Uriah eased off his three-legged stool. "Soldiers, I'm sure, looking for evidence."

She could hear the front door latch clicking. The hinges on the door groaned and there were heavy footsteps. At least four men, she surmised. "We can't just stand here in the dark."

"That's exactly what we're going to do," Uriah responded, pressing his ear to the inner door that separated the two rooms. "They'll find no evidence and then they'll go on about their business."

"They've no right!" She took a step, but Uriah's hand shot out in the darkness.

"I said we stay here." He took her by the arm, pulling her back from the door. "We can't afford another confrontation. If they shut me down here, I'll have no way to earn enough money to keep the press going below the carriage house!"

Reagan cringed at the sound of the first chair breaking against the wall. She could hear harsh voices as the men ransacked the front room, obviously in search of something. Pottery shattered and she knew their precious linseed oil was flowing over the floor. A rack of type was knocked over and she heard the letters scattering over the floor.

"Doesn't sound like soldiers to me," she hissed.

Before Uriah could stop her, Reagan's hand was on the doorknob. She flung open the door and burst into the front room. A lamp glowed on the counter near the door. "Can I help you?" she demanded acidly.

A man spun around to face her and she took a step back. It was the half-breed she'd encountered in the Blue Boar Tavern weeks ago.

Indian John's scarred face broke into a crooked smile. Three ruffians turned to stare, but he gave a wave of his hand. "Keep looking," he bellowed. "I'll take care of the captain's whore."

Reagan tasted her fear like ashes. Her judgment had been poor. Her father had been right, they should have remained hidden. Behind her, she

156

could feel the pressure of Uriah's hand on the small of her back.

"What are you doing here?" Uriah demanded. "Get out of my shop or I'll call the soldiers!"

Indian John laughed viciously. "The soldiers is who sent me, old man. Looks like ye're in a bit of trouble." His gaze fell to the bodice of Reagan's serge woolen gown.

"We've done nothing wrong. Please just go," she beseeched, her eyes locked on the half-breed's one good eye. "We want no trouble."

The three men continued to overturn furniture. A man with a tarred pigtail threw a crate of paper onto the floor and began to drizzle black ink over it.

Reagan sidestepped Indian John and snatched the jug of ink from the pigtailed man's hand. "Get out of here," she threatened. "Get out of here or I'll—"

"You'll what?" Indian John caught her by her shoulder, sinking his fingers into her soft flesh. He spun her around, yanking the front bodice panel of her gown.

The sound of tearing material ripped the air and Reagan balled her fist and knocked the half-breed in the ear.

"Reagan!" Uriah shouted.

Indian John's hand went to his injured ear in surprise and Reagan lifted the jug in her other hand and brought it down over the half-breed's skull.

157

Indian John howled with pain as the pottery jug glanced off the back of his head and broke on the floor. "You little bitch!" He pulled back his fist and punched her squarely in the jaw.

Reagan flew backward under the impact. As she picked herself up off the floor, she saw her father swing a chair over his head and knock the half-breed down. A man in a wool cap shoved Uriah against the wall and began to pound him with his fists.

"Papa!" Reagan cried. She hurled herself at her father's attacker, knocking the ruffian off balance. Her starched cap fell from her head and her hair tumbled to her shoulders.

Uriah sank his fist into the man's soft stomach and he doubled over onto the floor.

"Run!" Uriah shouted. "Get help, Daughter."

Indian John scrambled to his feet, swinging the butt of a rifle. Uriah picked up a long, stiff rod used for shifting type and defended himself.

Reagan found the ladder back of a broken chair on the floor and snatched it up, but a third man intercepted her before she could bring it crashing down on the half-breed's head. She screamed and the third man covered her mouth with his hand. She sank her teeth into the dirty flesh of his palm and he gave a yelp.

"Whore!" the man cursed, slapping her soundly across the face. The chair fell from her grasp as her head reeled back under his blow. The man pinned Reagan's hands behind her, but she kicked

158

and bucked so hard that the pigtailed men came to his rescue.

"What's the matter with you, Lenny? The wench too much of a woman for you?"

The pigtailed man approached her and she raised both feet off the ground kicking him in the groin. The man holding her lost his balance and all three fell to the floor. As she struggled to get free of the tangle of arms and legs, she saw Indian John backing Uriah up against the wall.

Uriah swung his stick, ducking and darting like a man half his age. The half-breed was growing angrier by the second as he swung harder and harder with less accuracy each time. Uriah's short legs carried him over a broken stool and Indian John swung his rifle above the front counter, missing Uriah but striking the lamp in the process.

The oil lamp fell to the floor and suddenly the printshop was in flames. The spilled varnish and linseed oil acted like a wick drawing the fire across the floor.

"Run, Reagie, run!" Uriah shouted. His spectacles fell, the fragile glass shattering on the floor, and Indian John pressed his advantage. He slammed the butt of the rifle into Uriah's temple and the gray-haired man went down.

The men who held Reagan pinned to the floor leaped up, freeing her, and she crawled the short distance to her father. "Papa! Papa!" Tears ran down her cheeks as she lifted her father's head.

159

His eyes were closed; there was no blood, but she could detect no rise and fall of his chest.

"You killed him! Murderer!" she screamed. In a rage, she leaped up, taking the pole from beside her father's lifeless body. The printshop was engulfed in flames, but she didn't feel the scorching heat, she didn't see the shooting orange flames. She swung the stick, cracking Indian John in the back. "Turn around," she demanded over the roar of the blaze. Two of the men were already running for the door.

Indian John spun around and Reagan swung the pole over her head. She didn't hear the pigtailed man come from behind. She felt a brief streak of pain as something hit her on the crown of the head and suddenly she was crumpling to the floor. The heat and flames of the room dissolved slowly into a cool blackness.

"Get out of here," Indian John shouted to the pigtailed man. "The roof's gonna come down!"

"The old man's dead, but what about her?" The pigtailed man held his arm across his forehead. He could smell his own hair singeing.

The half-breed John took one look at Reagan and then turned, running for the door. "Leave the bitch!"

Sterling came out of the Blue Boar and looked up. A block north, flames shot into the night sky, filling it with bright light and falling cinders.

160

A fire bell clanged in the distance and a man carrying buckets ran by.

"What's burning?" Sterling shouted after him.

"Printshop on High Street," the man panted. "It's a goner, but we're trying to save the buildings around it."

Sterling raced down the street, turning onto High. "No God, please," he murmured. "Not Reagie. Please." His feet flew over the cobblestones and he passed the man with the buckets. Up ahead he could see a crowd of onlookers huddling across the street from the Llewellyns' printshop.

Sterling came to a halt in front of the crowd. "Anyone in there?"

"Don't know," a woman offered. "Saw a couple of rough men come out, but they ran that way." She pointed toward the harbor.

Sterling swore beneath his breath as he sprinted across the street.

"Hey, Captain. You can't go in there," someone protested from behind. "If there's anybody in there, they're dead by now!"

Sterling pushed through the line of people passing buckets of water. He ripped off his coat and took a bucket from someone's grasp. He doused his scarlet coat with water and threw it over his head.

"Reagan!" he shouted as he ducked into the burning structure. The heat was so intense that it nearly knocked him backward. Sterling dropped

161

on all fours and began to crawl across the floor. Even on the floor the smoke was so thick that it sucked his breath from his body. "Reagan! he shouted hoarsely. "Reagie!"

"Here," came a voice. "I'm here."

"Where? I can't see you." The cinders stung Sterling's face and hands as he crawled toward Reagan's voice.

Out of the inky blackness came a hand, and Sterling clasped it. Tears ran down his sooty cheeks. "Reagie?"

"Grayson! Papa's dead. He's here, but I can't find him!"

Sterling stood, swinging Reagan into his powerful arms. She clung to him, coughing and choking, as he made his way out of the burning building.

Outside, Sterling knelt on the sidewalk, his chest heaving. Reagan clung to him sobbing. "We can't leave him to burn, Grayson." She struggled to escape his grasp. "I have to get him out."

Sterling took one look at the blazing building. Orange and red flames shot high above the crumbling roof. Ceiling joists were beginning to cave in. He straightened, leaving Reagan on the cobblestones.

She watched from the walk as he entered the shop again. Flames shot higher and higher in the air and the citizens hurried to soak the buildings on each side to keep them from catching on fire as well. Seconds passed, and Reagan rose on her knees. A full minute had elapsed, and still there was no sign of Grayson. The center beam of the structure gave a groan and fell and Reagan sank down, burying her face in her hands. Now she had lost both of the men she loved.

Suddenly there was roar from the crowd. Reagan looked up through a veil of tears to see Grayson leaping through the front window of the printshop, Uriah's crumpled body thrown over his shoulder.

Reagan stumbled toward Grayson. He eased Uriah's lifeless body to the ground. Reagan stood before him, sobs wracking her body. He put out his arms and she came to him.

Two men gently lifted Uriah's body and carried him away from the burning building. Sterling's chest burned and his eyes stung. His right forearm had been burned when a timber fell on him as he was bringing Uriah out of the fire, but he felt no pain, only the agony in his heart.

Reagan held tightly to him, her face pressed into the cambric cloth of his shirt. He pushed back her thick auburn hair, wiping the soot from her face. "Shh," he soothed. "It's all right, sweetheart. Cry, it will make both of us feel better."

Reagan clung to Sterling, still disoriented by the smoke. Her knees were so weak that she couldn't stand. Her lungs burned as she gasped for clean night air. When Grayson lifted her into his arms, she made no protest. Suddenly the world was fading again. "Where are you taking me?" she man-

163

aged. Her strained voice was barely a whisper in his ear.

"Home," Sterling answered, kissing her hot, damp brow. He pushed his way through the crowd, oblivious to the freezing rain that had begun to fall. "Home, Continental."

Chapter Twelve

Sterling pushed open the front door of the Lle-wellyn home with the toe of his boot. "Nettie! Elsa!" he hollered. He took the stairs two at a time.

"Grayson?" Elsa called from the front hall. When she saw her sister unconscious in his arms, she gathered her skirts and came running up the steps.

"What's happened? Is she all right?"

Sterling carried Reagan to her bedchamber and laid her gently on the bed, but he was hesitant to let go of her. He cradled her head in his arm, brushing her rain-soaked hair off her face. Her eye had been blackened, by someone's fist. Her upper lip was split. "Elsa! I need some warm water and towels." Violent anger coursed through his veins. He didn't know who had done this to her, but he would find out. He stood up, stripping off his wet cambric shirt. "Where are her sleeping gowns?"

Elsa ran out of the room. "At the foot of the bed," she called from the hallway.

Sterling flung open the cedar chest and removed a soft swanskin gown. He pulled Reagan's shoes off, then her hose. Elsa came in the door carrying a water pitcher, some flannel towels, and a bottle of rum tucked beneath her arm.

"Help me get her clothes off, Elsa." He sat on the corner of the bed and raised Reagan to a seated position, letting her slump against his broad chest.

Elsa climbed over the other side of the bed and began to unlace the bodice of Reagan's gown. Without ceremony, she stripped her sister down, removing her torn bodice, and petticoat, then her corset. When Elsa got to her sister's chemise, she glanced up at Sterling.

"It's wet, take it off."

"My sister—"

"I won't tell if you don't."

She looked up at him, then lowered her head, seeing to the task.

Sterling eased Reagan onto the bed and placed a bolster under her neck. He tried not to stare as Elsa unbuttoned and slipped the linen chemise off Reagan's shoulders. His breath caught in his throat, and he looked away as she drew back the last bit of chemise and threw it into the pile of wet clothing on the floor.

Sterling retrieved the flannel gown and again lifted Reagan, squeezing his eyes shut as Elsa maneuvered to get the gown over her sister's head and her arms in the sleeves.

Reagan's breasts pressed against Sterling's bare chest and he struggled to gain control of his desire. *My God!* he chastised himself. *The girl's father is dead, she was nearly burned to death, and all I can think of is my lust for her.*

"Lay her back," Elsa ordered, and Sterling eased Reagan back, thankful the torture was over.

Elsa pulled the skirt of the flannel gown down and began to tug the coverlets over her sister's now-trembling body.

"What happened?" Elsa asked as she poured warm water into a basin next to the bed. "Where's the fire? Where's Papa?" She took a clean cloth and began to wipe the soot from Reagan's face. "Someone's hit her."

Sterling's voice caught in his throat. How could he tell her her father was dead?

Elsa looked up at Sterling. He was shivering now, too. She grabbed a flannel towel from the bed and threw it to him. "You'd best dry off or you'll be down with the croup." She turned her attention back to her sister. "He's dead, isn't he?" she said softly.

Sterling tightened the towel around his shoulders and lowered his hand to Elsa's. "He is."

A sob escaped Elsa's tightly compressed lips, but she continued to bathe Reagan. "The printshop?"

Sterling took a step back. "There was a fire. I managed to get Reagan out, but your father was already dead. Somebody saw some men running from the shop." He paused, feeling so inadequate. "I'm so sorry, Elsa. But I'll find them. I'll find who did this." His voice cracked and he looked away.

"Go get into something warm and dry, Captain." She wrung out the flannel cloth and stroked Reagan's neck. Black soot rolled off her pale skin soiling the wet cloth.

"Where's Nettie, Elsa? She should help you."

"Sick. I sent her to bed. No need to wake her up."

"Can I . . . Is there something I can do?"

Elsa turned to him. She had shed no tears. He wondered if the girl understood what death was. "Yes. You can get me some ointment from my room. Her leg is burned. It's in a tin on the mantel." He started to go, but she spoke again. "Where is he? Papa's body? Funeral arrangements will have to be made."

So she does understand, Sterling thought sadly. "Someone took him away. I wanted to get Reagan back here as quickly as possible."

Wiping down Reagan's arms, Elsa nodded. "Papa had many friends."

"I'll get that ointment."

Later, Sterling sat beside Reagan on the bed while Elsa attended to the burn on his forearm. He picked up the bottle of rum. "Should we try to give her some?"

Elsa looked up. "The spirits are for you, Captain."

He popped the cork and took a deep swallow, then coughed. The heat of the crude Colonial-made rum brought tears to his eye. "Is she all right?" He took another swallow, then set the bot-

168

tle aside.

"I think she's just sleeping. There seems to be no fever." Elsa wrapped a linen bandage around his arm. "You look tired, Captain. Why not go to sleep? There's nothing more you can do for her tonight." Elsa's voice was soft and pragmatic.

"No. You go on." He pulled his chair up beside Reagan's bed. "I can't sleep. I'll sit with her."

Elsa hesitated. "All right, Captain. Tomorrow will be a busy day."

After Elsa had gone, Sterling leaned over Reagan's sleeping form. He stroked her forehead, kissing her soft cheek. Her lip was swollen, her eyelid and the surrounding area a deep purple. "Oh, Reagie, I'm so sorry," he whispered.

She stirred and he stroked her hair soothingly. "I'll make it all right. I don't know how, but I'll do it. I love you, Reagan."

Somewhere far in the distance Reagan could hear a voice. A soft, husky, soothing voice. It was Grayson. She knew it. But she was so confused. What was he saying? *He loved her? She must have misheard*. She snuggled against the warmth of his arms. She could have sworn she felt his lips on hers.

"Grayson?"

"Shh," he murmured. "Sleep, sweetheart. Just sleep now."

"You won't go?" Suddenly memories came flooding back. The fire . . . the half-breed . . . her papa lying there motionless on the floor. Her

169

eyes flew open but her vision was blurred. "You won't leave me, too?" She tried to sit up, suddenly filled with fright.

"No, no, I won't leave you," Sterling insisted. He slid into the bed beside her, drawing her into his arms.

"He's dead, isn't he?" she asked. Her eyelids grew heavy and she let them slip.

"Yes. He's dead."

Reagan rolled against Sterling, bringing her knee up between his and flinging her arm over him. Her body relaxed and breath came evenly again. He eased his head beside hers on the pillow and tucked the coverlet over them both. "Sleep," he murmured, closing his eyes. "Just sleep."

With the first rays of morning light, Reagan began to stir. A place on her thigh burned and her eyes stung. The left side of her face pounded with pain. Her chest felt heavy and her limbs were slow to move. She remembered the fire and her father's death, but little after that. Her mind was so blurred. Grayson . . . she remembered Grayson carrying her. It was raining . . . then she was warm. He had held her, here, here in her bed. He had told her he loved her.

"Grayson?" Her eyes flew open. She could barely see out of the left one.

"I'm here," he answered quietly.

She squinted. He was dressed immaculately, his hair tied back, his boots polished. She knew the fire was real, she could smell the smoke in her hair, but what of Grayson and his proclamation of love? Had that been a dream?

He pulled up a chair beside her bed. "How do you feel?" He studied her intently.

"My leg hurts."

"You were burned."

She buried her face in her hands, trying to clear her thoughts. "I can't believe he's dead. There was a fight. They burned the place down around us!"

"Who, Reagie?" He clasped her hand. "Tell me who!"

"I don't know his name, but he's a half-breed with a scarred face—a patch over one eye. I've seen him in the Blue Boar before."

Sterling looked away, her hand still held tightly in his. "Son of a bitch," he whispered. He returned his attention to her. "I know him. They call him Indian John." His face was stony with anger. "He'll not get away with it."

She eased her head back onto her pillow. "He said the soldiers sent him."

"What soldiers?"

"I don't know, Grayson!" She closed her eyes against the sunlight that pained her head. "They were looking . . ." she hesitated.

"For what? What were they looking for?" He tightened his grasp on her hand.

Her lower lip trembled as she fought to gain control. "Those stupid pamphlets." *Do I tell him?* she wondered. *It's all over now. There'll be no more pamphlets.*

"The ones Uriah was printing?" he whispered.

"The ones they *thought* he was printing."

Sterling smiled, smoothing back a tendril of hair. He was positive Uriah was the penman. It was etched all over her face. He leaned over and brushed his lips against hers, but before he could withdraw, she caught the back of his head with her hand.

Reagan lifted her dark lashes. "I didn't thank you."

He stared into the depths of her cinnamon eyes, lost in their magic. "I couldn't let you die. Any man would have done the same."

"You're right." She caressed his smooth-shaven cheek. "But no man would be fool enough to risk his life for a man already dead."

Her voice was so soft that Sterling had to lean closer to hear her.

"I'll never forget that, Grayson, no matter where this journey takes us. I'll never forget you or what you did for me." She rose from her pillow, and kissed him.

At first the kiss was hesitant, barely a brush of her lips, but then an urgency grew between them. Sterling lifted her, closing his arms around her. She pressed her mouth against his, kissing him deeply.

172

"I thought I'd lost you," she whispered against his lips. "When you didn't come out of the shop, I thought you were gone, too." She hugged him tightly, laying her head on his shoulder.

For moment Sterling just held her, stroking her thick auburn hair. Nothing was working out the way it was supposed to, but there was no turning back. He loved Reagan more than he had ever loved anyone, but he didn't know what he was going to do about it.

Sterling kissed her cheek. "I have to go now. Business. But when I'm done, I'll take care of the funeral arrangements."

"That's not necessary. I can do it."

He pulled back, but found her hand in the folds of the coverlet. "I know you can, but I want to."

"Christ's Church, down off High Street."

He gave her hand a squeeze and then stood, releasing her. "You just rest today."

"I've got to talk to Elsa." She rubbed her bruised lip. "God, Grayson, how am I going to tell her?"

"She already knows." He slipped his arms into his scarlet coat and she looked away, unable to bear the sight of the enemies' colors.

"You told her, and she's all right?" Reagan's voice was forlorn.

"Elsa's a fine young woman. She's smarter, stronger than you think. She took care of you last night. She bandaged your leg, she washed and dressed you."

"Surely Nettie—"

"Nettie's ill," he intervened. "Nothing serious, but she was asleep last night when I brought you home. Your little Elsa can take command like a general." He smiled. "She's quite a capable woman, just like all the Llewellyn women."

Reagan lay back on her pillow. "Could you send her up?"

He nodded, going to the door as he buttoned his coat. "I will, now I want you to promise you'll stay in bed today."

"I'm fine."

"Promise."

"All right," she answered softly. There just seemed to be no fight left in her. She was empty.

He winked and then he was gone.

In his room, Sterling compiled a quick message to his commanding officer using the bell mask. With coded words he told Captain Craig that Uriah Llewellyn had been the patriot penman, but that now he was dead. He also added a request for more funds. He'd spent so much on wine and bribes that he was nearly broke, despite his mysterious benefactor's occasional payment of his tavern bills. He knew Captain Craig wouldn't be pleased with his request, but the funds were necessary to keep up his undercover operation. He finished up the message by asking for word of his

174

brother Grayson. Did he fare well? Where was he being held? The ink smeared as Sterling quickly added words to the "letter" from Aunt Feddlebottom to hide the true nature of the correspondence. Sealing the letter, he took his hat and hurried out of the house.

When Sterling arrived at Ethan's, the patriot was already waiting for him in the barn.

"I heard," the rotund man told Sterling once they were in the privacy of the closed stable.

"How?"

"Elsa was here early this morning." The blacksmith took a large handkerchief and wiped his red eyes. "Uriah Llewellyn was a damned fine man."

"If only I could have told him we fought for the same cause—that I admired him." Sterling smoothed his horse's haunches.

"The funeral will be tomorrow, Elsa says."

"Yes, I'll be making the arrangements when I'm done here. I got a message this morning that one of the Llewellyns' friends took the body and is preparing it." Sterling slipped his letter from his pocket. "I need this to be passed on immediately. Today."

Ethan took the folded letter, clearing his throat. "Ah, you weren't thinkin' of going to the funeral tomorrow, were you?"

Sterling studied the man's broad facial features. "Of course I was."

The blacksmith ground his boot into the straw. "I wouldn't advise it. Things might get ugly, was

175

there a redcoat there."

"I hadn't thought of that."

"Best you stay home. You can pay your respects there."

Sterling threw his cloak over his shoulders. "I suppose you're right."

"Word is it was redcoats looking for them pamphlets they say Uriah was printin'." Ethan tucked Sterling's letter into his leather waistcoat.

"Word is, he *was* printing them." Sterling's eyes narrowed as he studied Ethan's beefy face.

He shrugged. "I don't rightly know."

"Elsa never said anything?" Sterling pressed.

"No. But that doesn't mean he wasn't or that she didn't know. Elsa's a little slow up here"—the blacksmith tapped his temple—"but she's no fool. She knows when to open her mouth and when to keep it shut."

Sterling sighed, taking up Giipa's reins. "Well, guess I'd better get moving." He started out of the barn. "You'll be certain to get that message on its way today."

Ethan slapped his waistcoat. "Today. I'll start it on its way myself."

"Thank you, friend." Sterling gave a wave, mounted, and rode out of the barn.

Hours later Sterling entered the Llewellyn home. It was still early evening, but everyone in the house had already turned in. He removed his cloak and hat and went into the kitchen. The worktable in the center of the room was laden with loaves of bread, wheels of cheese, and savory baked dishes. A tapped cask of Madeira rested on the end of the table.

Leaving his cloak and hat over a chair, Sterling retrieved a pewter plate and filled it. Seated in front of the hearth, his long legs stretched out, he ate hungrily. Filling his pewter tankard with Madeira a second time, he lounged before the fireplace's flickering flames, sipping the wine. An odd kind of contentment fell over him, seated here in the warm kitchen. He imagined what it would be like to take Reagan as his wife . . . to have their own home, their own warm kitchen. A smile came to his lips as he remembered sleeping with Reagan last night, her warm body snuggled in his arms. His eyes drifted shut as he remembered the feel of her soft breasts pressed against his chest, her light breath on his face. What he would give for an eternity such as that!

But such thoughts were foolery. His life was far too complicated for dreams. He had vowed to defend his new country, to serve her as his commanding officers saw fit. His duty would not allow a wife and a comfortable home. Besides, as long as he remained Captain Grayson Thayer, there wasn't a chance in hell Reagan would agree to marry him. He sighed, tipping his cup. It was too hopeless to even consider.

Sterling was so lost in his thoughts that he

didn't hear Reagan enter the kitchen. It wasn't until she laid her hand on his shoulder that he looked up.

"Grayson." She laughed, her voice low and soft. "Didn't you hear me calling you?"

"Reagan." He felt guilty, foolish even for having been caught daydreaming.

Self-consciously she removed her hand from his shoulder. "Mistress Claggett came by this afternoon. Thank you for making all of the arrangements."

"I hope you don't mind that I didn't bring his body here, but Mistress Claggett offered, and I thought it might be easier this way."

"I think it was wise. I don't know about Elsa, but I don't think that I could stand to have him in the parlor. I want to remember him alive, laughing, arguing, writing, his hands stained with ink." She brought her kerchief around her shoulders, smoothing the linen.

A strange energy hung in the air. Sterling and Reagan could feel it. Both had things to say to the other, but neither dared.

He watched her go to the worktable and cover the cheese with a piece of clean, damp cloth. She was dressed simply in a soft woolen gown the color of sage. Her face was pale save for the purple bruise around her left eye. The swelling had gone down on her lip. It was obvious she had just washed and braided her hair.

Sterling's gaze fell to the oaken tub banded

with copper hoops resting near the door. The wood was still dark with water stains, and he wondered how long ago she'd bathed. He wished he'd come in earlier. He longed to see her standing in the tub letting the warm water run over her breasts and down her long legs. He licked his dry lips.

Reagan sighed. "Grayson."

He was up and at her side in an instant. He held her in his arms, stroking the crown of her damp head. She held him by the shoulders, resting her head on his hard, broad chest. Her heart was beating irregularly. No words were necessary. He felt her pain and she felt his sympathy.

"It's time I turn in," she whispered.

Her warm breath caressed his ear. "Yes. Tomorrow will be a long day."

She held tightly to him another moment and then stepped away. She stopped in the doorway and looked back. Their eyes met and her lower lip trembled. Tonight she needed him. Tonight when all seemed lost she needed to feel loved, to be needed. It was on the tip of her tongue to tell him, but something in the depth of his brilliant blue eyes made her realize no words were necessary. She turned away and went upstairs.

In her own bedchambers, Reagan stoked the fire and threw a sprinkling of herbs to the flames so that it would give a rich aroma to the room. She pulled back the bedcurtains and smoothed the soft flannel sheets of her bed. Driven by some

179

inner force, she went to a chest beneath the window and kneeled, lifting its lid.

It had been a year since she'd studied its contents. The trunk contained the beginnings of the trousseau she had meant to take with her when she married Josh. She laid aside the embroidered table linens, the hand-loomed towels, and down near the bottom she found the sleeping gown she'd meant to wear on her wedding night.

Retrieving the gown she got to her feet and shook it out. It was made of jaconet, a soft, transparent linen. It was bleached a pale white with delicate blue-and-green flowers stitched across the bodice. Pale-green satin ribbons made a closure in the front between her breasts.

Moving dreamlike, Reagan removed her woolen gown and underthings. She hung her dress on a peg and neatly folded the other clothing. When she slipped the gown over her head, it fell over her lithe body like a sheet of silk. She smiled, smoothing the wrinkles set in with time. No matter what happened tomorrow or in the days that followed, she would always have tonight to remember. She loved Grayson as she knew she would never love another man. Tonight she would give of herself, in return for his warmth, his comfort. Tonight she would lay aside the war, her and her father's beliefs. She would lay aside his scarlet coat and they would love as only a man and woman could love.

Sitting at her dressing table, Reagan unbraided

her damp hair and brushed it over her shoulders in a fan of brilliant red and gold highlights. In the reflection of her mother's gilded mirror, she saw her doorknob twist and Grayson enter her room and close the door behind him.

Chapter Thirteen

"You knew I would come," Sterling said hesitantly. He felt like a boy at Eaton again. He stared at his bare feet. He wore only his breeches and an untucked shirt. His palms were damp; his mouth was dry. By God, he had never wanted a woman like he wanted Reagan.

"I knew you would come. I wanted you to." She thought to stand but she was too frightened. Her knees knocked beneath the bridal gown.

Sterling slid the bolt on the door and came to her, his arms outstretched. He kissed her damp temple, breathing in the sweet smell of her freshly washed hair. She no longer smelled of smoke and cinders, but like springtime.

"I love you, Reagan," he whispered.

She lifted her dark lashes, covering his lips with her forefinger. "Shh, don't say what you do not mean. I want no lies. My love for you is enough. I know what you are and what we can never be, but tonight I just want to pretend."

Tears formed in Sterling's eyes and he looked away. There was a lump in his throat that kept him from speaking. She loved him! But that only made their situation all the more desperate. He felt like the scoundrel his brother truly was. How could he deceive this woman who had been so honest with him? She hid nothing, baring her soul, laying her heart out to him, yet he faced her with lies, one piled on the other.

Sterling closed his eyes, nuzzling the soft spot on her neck. "I've dreamed of this, Reagan."

She smiled hesitantly. "So have I," she admitted against his lips.

They kissed deeply, exchanging a bittersweet token of their desire. She looped her arms around his neck, pressing her breasts into his chest. Sterling lifted her in his arms and carried her to the bed. He laid her down and sat back on the edge of the bed to gaze at her. The firelight poured through the tapestry bedcurtains, setting her hair aflame with bright color. Her face was pale and her mouth quivered.

He leaned, kissing her brow as if he could kiss away her fears. "There is nothing more beautiful than the love between a man and a woman," he assured her huskily.

She closed her eyes as his fingers brushed over the mounds of her breasts. Every nerve was raw within her as he stroked her body through the thin weave of her sleeping gown. He kissed her softly again and again until she rolled toward him, pressing her lips hard against his.

Cautiously Sterling untied each satin bow of her gown. Inside he raged with desire and the need to seek fulfillment, but he forced himself to move slowly, to give her time to adjust to each new sensation.

183

A soft moan escaped Reagan's lips as he slipped his hand beneath the filmy swanskin and his fingers touched her bare breast.

"Ohh, that's wonderful." Her voice rose like a sigh.

He smiled. "You're easy to please," he whispered as he lowered his mouth to her nipple.

Reagan arched her back in surprise, catching his head with her hands. She ran her fingers through his thick blond hair, in awe of the power of his caress. Her entire body quaked with feelings never experienced before. Her eyes drifted shut as he suckled her, taunting her breast to an erect peak.

He lifted his own shirt over his head and let it drift to the floor. It was madness, the feel of her hesitant fingers exploring his bare shoulders and chest, finding his own hardened nipples.

Sterling stroked her gently, feeling his way to the hollow of her stomach beneath her rib cage. His fingers traced an intricate pattern as he teased her flesh until she quivered with want. When his hand found the down between her thighs, she half sat up with surprise. He whispered soft, sweet words of assurance and she relaxed in utter trust.

"I've never felt like this before," she told him, her breath coming in short gasps. "I didn't know."

He lifted her gown over her head to admire her breathtaking form, and color diffused through her cheeks. Sterling could feel his own heart pounding as if it would burst from his chest. He wanted to take it slowly this first time with Reagan, but his

184

own desire was burgeoning beneath his breeches. His hands went to the leather ties and she watched through heavy-lidded lashes. Self-consciously, Sterling slipped from the confining fabric and stretched out beside her.

Reagan lay back on the pillow, her eyes closed, letting the waves of pleasure wash over her as he stroked her naked flesh. When he rolled onto her, she arched her hips instinctively, wanting to feel his male hardness against her.

Sterling sprinkled her face with kisses, holding the bulk of his weight off her with his powerful arms. She moved against him, her hips already rising and falling in an ancient rhythm. He touched her gently with his fingers, stroking her damp, moist flesh. She moaned softly.

He lowered his head, to whisper in her ear. "It will hurt, but only for a moment, my love, and then never again."

She nodded but didn't lift her lashes. Her head was thrown back on the pillow, her thick hair falling partially across her cheek.

Unable to hold back another moment, Sterling eased his shaft into her. She rose up, and a small gasp escaped her lips. Sterling held completely still, trying to slow his breathing. He had dreamed of her for so long that it was impossible to hold back. He began to move, slowly at first, until she rose and fell with him.

She clung to him, digging her nails into his shoulders. "Grayson," she murmured. "Grayson."

Sterling squeezed his eyes shut. He couldn't bear to hear her call his brother's name. "Reagan," he whispered. "Reagan, my love."

She raised her hips against him, again and again becoming one with him as her body strained for what she did not know. She cried out, in utter agony . . . in sweet jubilation as he brought her closer and closer to the threshold of full womanhood.

Suddenly there was a burst of bright light and Reagan gasped as every muscle in her body tensed. She was filled with the white light of fulfillment.

Sterling broke stride in shocked surprise. No woman was supposed to gain such pleasure with her first encounter with a man. He held her tightly, kissing her perspiration-soaked face as she trembled, slowly falling back to earth. Then Sterling began to move again, faster, stroking harder as he sought his own release. Reagan wrapped her legs around his, moving with him again, and he arched his back, groaning with pleasure as he finally found peace. Sterling collapsed in relief and she laughed, deep in her throat, her voice still blurred with passion.

"Grayson, I can't breathe!" She pushed at his damp chest and he rolled onto the bed. He still struggled to catch his breath as he buried his face in her hair. A damp and musty smell of pleasure clung to her, making him want her all over again.

"Reagan," he managed.

She stroked his back. "It's gotten rather warm in

186

here, hasn't it?"

He laughed at her joke, rolling onto his side to gaze at her lovely, flushed face. "You certain you haven't done this before?"

Playfully, she grasped a handful of his hair and pulled his head up. "You know very well I haven't! My sheets will be proof of that."

His kissed her love-bruised mouth. "I know. You've given me the greatest gift a woman can give a man."

Reagan sobered. "I don't understand myself. You're still a red—"

He pressed his mouth to hers, cutting off her last words. "Not tonight, love. Let's not talk about it tonight."

She brushed back a lock of his blond hair, returning his kiss. "All right," she answered quietly. "Just so long as you know—"

He kissed her again. "I know, I know, but like you said, we can pretend." He lowered his head to her breast, snuggling against their warmth.

Reagan sighed, stroking the corded muscles of his shoulders. *All right,* she thought. *I won't think about it, not tonight, but tomorrow I must. This changes nothing, yet it changes everything.*

For a long time they lay in peace. Sterling forced himself to remain still as she explored his body with her light touch. The fire crackled and spit, dying down low until the embers glowed red. Reagan rested in Sterling's arms and he grew drowsy.

"Grayson." Reagan suddenly sat up, pushing him aside.

He pushed up on one elbow, his brows furrowed. She was always so intense. "What?"

"That song. How did you know that song?"

"What song?" He brought the counterpane over them to ward off the chill in the room.

"The song I was playing that morning on the spinet. *The Liberty Song*. How did you know the tune?"

Sterling paled. She had caught him off guard. He tugged at the counterpane, trying to stall for time. Then he looked up at her, smiling with a shrug. "God's bowels, Reagan! You don't think the tune was original, do you? You don't think that Dickenson fellow wrote it on his own?"

Her eyes narrowed suspiciously. "What do you mean?"

He laughed, his brother's voice parting his lips. "He stole the music from an old *English* song. Only the words were original." *What a liar I've become,* Sterling thought dismally. *Falsehoods roll off my tongue as easily as truths these days!*

Reagan lay back. "Oh." She wasn't quite convinced. Something just didn't seem right about the tone of his voice.

"How did you possibly think I would have known it?"

She pulled the covers up to her chin. "I don't know." She turned to him, studying his face intently. "You're not one of those counterspies are

188

you?"

He swallowed hard against his rising fear. If she knew, how could he protect her? "Madam?" He stared back quizzically.

"You haven't been in General Washington's camp, pretending to be one of us. It would be easy enough. You said yourself your brother had been a patriot. He could have inadvertently given you all sorts of information you could use to work under cover." Her dark gaze bore down on him. "If you were a spy, I'd turn you in—that or kill you myself."

He chuckled. She was perfectly serious! He could tell by the look in her eyes that she'd not hesitate to turn in a man she thought to be betraying his fellow soldiers, even if he was her lover.

"Don't be ridiculous, Reagan," Sterling answered, relieved that she didn't suspect his true identity. "Me in a Colonial camp? Where in heaven's name would I get a proper palm toddy?" She frowned, and he leaned to kiss one pert breast. "Now come here and warm me, it's grown cold in here."

Giving in to Sterling's charm, she settled in his arms, letting the sensation of his tongue on her nipple drown out her thoughts. Tomorrow the war would come tumbling down on them again, but tonight was theirs to savor.

Snow fell from the heavens, covering the cobblestone walk, and Sterling hurried down the street.

189

He had returned to Uriah's printshop, but had been unable to find evidence to prove Uriah had been the penman he sought. Any proof had gone to the grave with the courageous patriot.

After picking his way through the charred timbers of the printshop, Sterling had walked to Major Burke's headquarters and spoken with him. He presented his evidence, and the major seemed to be satisfied that the case was closed. He was, however, annoyed that Indian John had reached the conclusion first and had reported it yesterday. Sterling made no mention that the half-breed was responsible for the fire. He intended to take care of the bastard on his own.

Major Burke said he would think on Sterling's next assignment, and in the meantime he was to stand duty at the Walnut Street prison. Once dismissed, Sterling had made his way immediately in the direction of the Blue Boar Tavern.

The wind howled, and he walked faster, passing Christ's Church. In the distance he could see the mourners huddled together over the shallow gravesite of Uriah Llewellyn. The churchyard was filled with friends and relatives of the family and Sterling longed to join them. He wanted to say farewell; he wanted to stand at Reagan's side but he didn't dare.

Keeping his head down, Sterling hastened by, trying not to think of Reagan and the glorious night they had spent together. He had left her bedchamber before dawn and had not spoken to her. He wasn't purposely avoiding her . . . Actually he was. He wanted to hold on to those memories just a little longer. He wanted to pretend, just for a few hours, that everything was perfect between them. He wanted to think he would sleep beside her tonight, but he knew he was just fantasizing. Reagan had made it clear that only for one night could she lay aside his scarlet coat and forget the man that he was.

Reaching the Blue Boar, he went in. His eyes adjusted to the dim light as he perused the busy public room. Spotting the half-breed Indian across the room, he strode over. "John?"

The half-breed turned, laughing. "Yea? What'cha want?"

Sterling grabbed him by the shoulders and lifted him out of his chair. "You bastard! You burned that printshop!"

Indian John's feet dangled above the floor. "So what if I did?"

Sterling slammed his body against the wall. "You hit her." He held him with one hand, knocking him in the jaw with his fist.

Indian John's head reeled back, ramming into plastered wall. The buzz of conversation dwindled as men stood to see what was happening.

"That's enough, Captain," someone called from the crowd. "You'll be on report."

Sterling gritted his teeth, his attention focused on Indian John's scarred face. "You ever touch her again and I'll kill you, you understand me, you

191

slimy son of a whore?"

The half-breed gave a crooked grin and Sterling caught a flash of light out of the corner of his eye. Instantly he sidestepped the Indian's blade and slammed his wrist against the wall, knocking the hunting knife from his fingers. Kicking the knife backward into the center of the room, Sterling threw several well-aimed punches. "You're messing with the wrong man this time, redskin!"

Indian John gave a muffled groan as Sterling released him and he slid to the floor. Sterling turned away, ignoring everyone's stares. He went straight to the door.

"This isn't over, you arrogant bastard," Indian John called after Sterling as he disappeared into the night.

Reagan pushed her way through the crowd of friends and neighbors that filled her sitting parlor. She moved numbly, offering food and drink, responding appropriately when someone offered a word of condolence. Several friends had suggested she sit and rest, but she felt better with something to do with her hands.

"Reagan." Elderly Mistress Claggett came slowly toward her, a gentle smile on her wrinkled face.

When she offered her ringed hand, Reagan accepted it warmly. "Thank you so much for taking care of Papa. I don't know that I could have done it."

"Of course you could have." Mistress Claggett smiled. "But I wanted to do it for you."

Reagan helped her into a chair near the fireplace. "Is there anything I can get you? Something more to eat? Our friends have been so generous. It will take us months to eat all of this food."

"Certainly not, child. But I wanted to speak to you." She settled on the chair and set her cane aside, arranging her fashionable petticoats.

"What about?"

The old patriot lowered her graveled voice. "There's been talk, Reagan, even before your father died and now"—she shrugged her withered shoulders—"now it will be worse. Why not come and live with me?"

"Talk? Whatever do you mean. I can't leave here, This is my home. Elsa is comfortable here. She could never adjust elsewhere."

"You and the captain," Mistress Claggett said gently. "It's just not seemly."

Reagan paled. "Grayson? What are they saying about me and Grayson?"

"That you're his demirep," she answered honestly.

Reagan kneeled on the blue Turkey carpet. "Who calls me a whore?" she asked fiercely.

"There, there," Mistress Claggett soothed. "It's just idle talk. No one has anything better to do with their time than deface the character of their neighbors."

"I'm no whore!" she insisted. *I love Grayson. A woman can't be a whore to the man she loves!* she

193

screamed from within.

"Of course you aren't, dear. I know you would never do anything to dishonor yourself or your father's name. But maybe it would be better if you and your sister didn't remain alone with the captain."

"No." Reagan stood. "This is my home and here I'll stay." She bit her lower lip. "But thank you for warning me."

"I mean to carry no tales." Mistress Claggett blotted her dry lips with a lace handkerchief. "I just don't want you to be hurt."

"I know." Reagan managed a smile. "Thank you. And now I had best return to the other guests."

Hours later, Reagan, Nettie, and Elsa worked in the kitchen, washing dishes and storing leftover food goods. They were all tired and filled with the empty feeling one has when they've lost a loved one. Nettie was the first to give in.

"Well, girlies," she said, stripping off her apron. "I'm going to bed. You leave the rest and I'll take care of it in the morning."

Reagan put out her arms, embracing the old friend. "Thank you," she whispered, resting her head on the housekeeper's shoulder. She smelled of flour and arthritis tonic.

"There, there. You're worn clean out. Go on with you."

Reagan sniffed, stepping back. "You . . . you could move upstairs now if you like. You could take Papa's room."

194

"Nonsense." She waved a withered hand, headed for the lean-to she slept in. "I been laying my weary head in this room for forty odd years. I ain't about to change nuthin' now."

Reagan chuckled, having known that would be Nettie's answer. "Good night to you then." When Nettie had gone, she turned to Elsa who was kneeling on the hearth to pet her kitten. Mittens was half grown now, fat and sleek from a diet of mice and milk.

"Nettie's right. To bed, Sister. Put the cat out."

"Oh, Reagie. It's raining outside. Let him stay." Elsa petted the black cat and it arched its back, purring loudly.

"Cats sleep out. He can get into the barn if he wants to."

Elsa sighed, scooping up the animal. "Someday I'm going to have my own house and them I'm going to have a cat in the house. I'm going to have two cats," she said under her breath as she went out the back door.

Reagan frowned, tossing a flannel towel onto the table. That was the second time in a week that Elsa had made mention of having her own home. How could she make Elsa understand that she could never have her own home, that she would always live with Reagan? Reagie sighed. Better to just let it pass, she reasoned. By next week she'll have forgotten about it entirely.

* * *

Reagan was stoking the fire when she heard Grayson come in. The hair bristled on the back of her neck and her hand trembled as she lay the poker down. She could feel his hot hands on her as images of last night raced through her head. She remembered the taste of him and the feel of his manhood deep within her. Not trusting herself to speak, she went about her business, preparing to go to bed.

Sterling stood in the doorway for several minutes watching Reagan as she moved about the room. Her cheeks were as pale as flour paste. "Reagan," he finally offered in a half-whisper.

She spun around, holding up her hands as if to ward off some evil spirit. "Please, don't say it. Don't say anything. They're calling me your whore already," she flung bitterly.

Sterling's arms ached to hold her, but he stood his ground. "It's just gossip."

She shook her head. "A redcoat whore. That's what they're saying."

"Is there anything I can do?" He felt so damned inadequate.

"Yes. Don't ever come to my room again. Just let me be!" She snatched up a lantern and brushed past him, leaving him in darkness.

Chapter Fourteen

Sterling walked to the rear of the house where he found Reagan on her hands and knees pulling weeds from an herb bed. "I'm leaving."

"Godspeed," she answered tonelessly.

Sterling sighed. He was off for a night or two to carry a message to a band of patriots outside the city. He had told Reagan he was on business for Major Burke but that it was a delicate matter so she was not to tell anyone, not even a fellow officer. She had asked if the mission was dangerous, but when he'd replied yes, she'd only nodded and gone back to sorting a pile of buttons.

A silence yawned between them as he watched her pluck weeds from the muddy bed. It had been six weeks since Uriah's funeral and still Reagan's constitution had not faltered. She treated him with a cool arrogance that infuriated him. Neither sweet talk nor angry words would sway her. She wanted nothing to do with him, and her behavior was so convincing that Sterling was beginning to believe her. That night she had lain in his arms was nothing but a wisp of a memory he conjured again and again. Twice he'd gotten the nerve to go to her chamber and turn the knob, but both times it had been locked.

Sterling watched her continue to weed, down on

197

her hands and knees, the sleeves of her faded woolen gown pushed back to her elbows. A simple muslin mobcap covered her mass of red hair, but tendrils sneaked from beneath the covering to taunt him. No matter what she said, what she did, he believed she still cared for him. He had to believe it. He'd seen her watching him, though she always turned away when he lifted his eyes to return her smoldering gaze.

"Reagan we can't go on like this forever."

"Whatever do you mean, Captain?"

He groaned aloud. "Damnation, woman! I have a name, use it! How can you treat me like this? I held you in my arms, I—"

"Captain, kindly lower your voice before someone hears you."

He crouched down beside her, removing his grenadier cap. The fresh, clean scent of her carried on the chilly spring breeze. "I've done nothing to deserve being treated like this."

"I don't know what you mean. I do your laundering, I see that you have fresh linens and three meals a day. What else do you expect?" She struggled to keep up the facade she had so carefully constructed. Grayson couldn't know how badly she for yearned him, not just physically but emotionally. In the days since her father had died, she had wept until she couldn't shed another tear. She was lonely, and without the work she and her father had done together, she was lost.

Agitated, Sterling stood, striking his hat on his

198

knee. He'd done everything he possibly could, short of revealing his undercover operation, and nothing would bring Reagan around. He loved her more than he'd ever loved, ever hoped to love, but he'd reached the end of his patience. He was sick to death of her sharp tongue and shrewish tone of voice. Maybe that woman he'd held in his arms had never truly existed. Maybe he'd formed an image in his mind of her because he needed her so badly.

Sterling spun around, placing his hat on his head, striding away. He was so angry with Reagan and himself that he didn't hear her call his name.

Walking down the cobblestone street toward the blacksmith's, Sterling breathed deeply, filling his lungs with the sharp mid-March air. Though it was still early morning, the streets of Philadelphia were alive with activity. A young woman yelled up to another on a second story, and the two argued over the price of fresh milk. A whore stood on the street corner, enticing customers. Sterling wondered if she was out early or working late.

He turned the corner onto Third Street, shaking his head. Tories from all over the Colonies had flocked to the city in the winter months filling it to capacity with citizens drawn to the superficial tinsel-gaudy days of the occupation. Just as in Boston in '76, the Tories came to Philadelphia seeking refuge from the patriots as well as favors from the Crown. In one winter, the dignified city had become a sewer of filth and ugliness. Refuse was thrown into the streets, citizens' homes were broken into, inhabited, and then abandoned when the windows were shattered and the furniture broken. Trees were cut down in every yard and along the streets and burned for firewood, their jutting trunks left in stark evidence.

The soldiers and Tories alike wallowed in homemade rums, drinking in the decadence and debauchery that idleness produced. Sterling tipped his hat to a fellow officer who passed with a doxy on his arm. *If the entire British Army doesn't come down with a case of the running clap, it will be a miracle,* Sterling mused sardonically.

The city of Philadelphia danced and whored into the wee hours of the winter mornings while General Washington and his men starved at Valley Forge. Only the early run of shad in the Schuylkill River had saved the ragtag army.

With food in their bellies and Baron Von Stueben driving the soldiers into some semblance of order, Sterling was told, the Patriot Army was evolving. With General Howe of the British Army being replaced with General Clinton, the patriots would be ready when the new commander-in-chief made his move from Philadelphia.

How Sterling yearned to join his fellow soldiers at Valley Forge, but his own commanding officer, Captain Craig, had denied his request. He would have to be satisfied with getting as far as General Sullivan's lines near the Schuylkill. There, among his fellow patriots, his friends, perhaps he could clear his mind of Reagan Llewellyn and concentrate on his mission. So far, the intelligence reports he had made were minimal and he was becoming anxious. His position was too dangerous. Too many people were risking their lives to protect his cover for a few bits of information on secret shipments of wine and smoked partridge for the new general and his officers.

Turning into Ethan's yard, Sterling headed directly for the barn. He spotted Elsa behind the blacksmith's house hanging out laundry and he waved to her, wondering if Reagan knew where her sister was this morning.

"Good morning, Elsa," he called to her.

She waved shyly and then turned back to a flannel sheet in her arms. Two of Ethan's young children ran beneath the clothesline, laughing when Elsa threw the sheet over their heads.

"Beautiful children you have there," Sterling told Ethan with envy as he entered the barn where Giipa was stabled.

Ethan nodded. "Children who need a mother."

Sterling lifted a blond eyebrow. "Reagan still doesn't know?"

The blacksmith shook his head, tossing the polished saddle onto Giipa's back. "My Elsa says it's not time." He shrugged his massive shoulders. "So for now it's not time."

Sterling fit the bit into his brother's horse's mouth. "I don't envy you the task of telling her, friend. Reagan's nothing like Elsa. The woman's

201

got a nasty streak in her." With Giipa saddled and ready, he mounted.

Ethan pushed open the stable doors. "I thank you for the warning. Good luck with your ride and Godspeed."

Sterling tipped his hat and leaned forward in the saddle, racing out of the muddy barnyard and down the cobblestone street.

Sterling stretched out on the hard, damp ground, tucking his hands behind his head. The campfire at his feet spit and sputtered as a fellow soldier added another piece of wet wood. Long fingers of firelight cast shadows over the huddle of men, distorting their features. Laughter rose from the group and Sterling smiled, wiggling his toes to warm them inside his wet boots. Damn but it felt good to be among friends again.

"Christ, Sterling, you smell like rose water," Zacharia Boggs complained good-naturedly. "When you join us again, there won't be a soul willing to share your pallet. It'll take weeks to rid you of the stench."

Sterling sat up, drawing nearer to the fire. "I don't want to hear it, Zach! I'm out there risking my life dining on roast turkey and drinking good rum while you scolds enjoy a life of luxury, fishing on the banks of the Schuylkill."

"Aye," Robert Finnigan joined in. "We lie about drinking our tea and nibbling at our salted fish

202

while you rut with every maid in the city."

Sterling broke into a grin. "A falsehood, my friends! I stand innocent against your accusations." He took a warm tankard of mulled wine someone offered and sipped it, passing it on. He had brought what provisions he could manage without raising suspicion, a small keg of Madeira, some salt, fatty pork, dried beans and some of Reagan's gingerbread.

"Don't give us that horseshit," Zach bellowed. "You're beginning to get quite the reputation."

Sterling's cheeks reddened. "It's my brother they speak of, not me, fact or fiction. A whisper in this direction or that and suddenly a man has a reputation."

Robert, a flaming redhead, gave his friend a playful shove with a bandaged hand. Five years their elder, he had known the Thayer boys since they were children. "I know Grayson, 'tis all true. Sterling may be the elder of the two but most certainly the lesser with the ladies."

"Speaking of my brother . . ." Sterling changed the subject. "Does anyone have any word? I haven't been able to find where he's being held." He squatted by the fire, poking at it with a charred stick.

John Marble accepted the tankard of mulled wine from Robert and sipped deeply. "A fellow by the name of Creckle came by here a fortnight ago —"

"Tim Creckle?" Sterling pushed a lock of chin-length blond hair behind his ear. "Tim's seen Gray-

203

son?"

"And said he was white-hot mad. Said to tell his brother he'd get even. They got him locked up in some fort we took from the Brits and the Iroquois up in New York."

The other men broke into laughter, and Sterling grinned. He was certain there were no palm toddies being served in any wilderness fort. "He's all right, then?"

John's eyes met Sterling's. "Hell, yeah, he's all right, but what do you care? He's a bloody red-coat."

Sterling turned his gaze back to the blazing fire. "He's still my brother," he answered evenly. "I wouldn't see him harmed."

The group sobered, growing silent, lost in their own thoughts for the moment. They all had friends, if not relatives, who were now considered the enemy. No matter what each man said, they all knew the divided loyalties, the heart-wrenching pain this war had brought.

Zach belched loudly, breaking the silence. "We don't mean to give ye such a hard time, Sterling. We know it can't be easy living among rodents like that. We might have been hungry once or twice out here, but at least we had each other." He pushed the tankard of wine into his comrade's hand.

"It's not so bad." Sterling shrugged. "I've got my own bed, a lady to cook for me . . ."

"Ah hah! Now it comes out. Got yourself a little Tory piece of fluff, do you?" Isaac Warren tossed a stone and Sterling ducked.

"Not hardly."

Robert got to his feet, laughing with the others. "The lot of you sound like a gaggle of geese. I'm turning in."

Sterling rose. "Me, too. You, John?"

"Nah, goin' to finish up this Madeira, with Isaac and Zach. Never tasted anything so damned good, 'cept maybe a tit."

Sterling raised a hand good night, ignoring their bawdy banter. "I'll see you tomorrow before I go."

"Tomorrow?" Isaac frowned. "Thought you were staying till Sunday."

Sterling shook his head, leaving the circle of light. "The war goes on, gentleman. The general can't make a move without me."

"Right." John laughed, lifting the keg of Madeira over his head. Dark wine drizzled into his mouth. "Last we heard, you were standin' duty in a goat barn!"

The men's laughter died away behind them as Robert and Sterling walked side by side. A comfortable silence stretched between the two men. A quarter moon hung low in the clear dark sky, illuminating the path that led to the lines of tents and crude cabins.

Robert stopped near a rotting oak tree. "All right, my friend, out with it." He dug beneath his tattered blue coat and brought out a clay pipe and the leather pouch of precious tobacco Sterling had brought him.

205

Sterling crossed his arms over his chest, shivering. "Out with what? It's cold out here. I left my cloak back at the campfire."

"Who is she?"

"Who's who?"

"Don't play your clever games with me, Sterling Onassis Thayer. I'm the man who brought you your first wench."

"She wasn't just for me, I had to share her with Grayson." Sterling tugged at a leafless branch that hung over his head.

"A Tory girl, is that the problem?" When Sterling made no reply, Robert began to tamp down his pipe with the fingers of his bandaged hand. "You might as well be out with it. I can spot those cow eyes a mile away."

"She's not a Tory," Sterling flared.

"Ah, so it *is* a wench."

Sterling exhaled irritably. "If she was a damned Tory it would be easier."

Robert nodded. "She hates your guts."

"I can't think. I've lost my sense of reasoning."

"You've got it bad."

"She's a damned redhead."

"That makes it worse."

Sterling rubbed his arms for warmth "They've got me housed with her family. Her father was the man printing the pamphlets coming out of the city."

"I have one. Damned perceptive man." Robert struck a spark with his flint and steel, attempting to light his pipe. "You say her father *was* the man."

"It's long story, but he's dead. They burned him out."

"So what's the problem?" Robert struck his flint again and this time was rewarded with a glow in the bowl of his pipe. "When Clinton makes his move, you'll be transferred. Take her with you. Marry the wench if you've got your heart set on it."

"You forget she hates me."

"I have faith in you, Sterling. Just don't be doing anything stupid. You can't tell her who you are if that's what you're getting around to."

"You know I wouldn't jeopardize myself or the others." Sterling twisted the toe of his boot in the soggy ground. "Robert, I'm afraid . . . I'm afraid I won't be able to protect her."

"As long as you keep your cover, she's perfectly safe."

"I'm afraid she's going to figure it out. She's a smart woman."

Robert puffed on his pipe, enjoying it immensely. "I hadn't thought the words to be synonymous."

Sterling snatched the pipe from Robert's hand and drew on it, choked, and then began to cough as he pulled the stem from his mouth. Robert pounded his friend on the back.

"You were never a man for vices," he teased when Sterling was breathing again. "You can't drink, you bed a girl once and you feel responsible for the rest of your life, you—"

"I can play a mean game of whist."

"Only because I taught you."

Sterling passed the pipe back to Robert. "Grayson plays better."

Robert grinned. "Grayson cheats."

Sterling gave a nod. "Thanks, Robert. You're a good friend." He was already walking away.

"Thanks? Thanks for what?" he called after him. "I didn't do anything."

"For listening." Sterling waved a hand as he disappeared into the grove of trees. "Good night."

Robert leaned against the old oak, sighing. Smoke rose above his head, filtering through the skeletal branches of the dying tree. "Good luck, old friend," he murmured. "You're going to need it."

Sterling paced the small front office that had been some housewife's sitting parlor before the occupation of the city. Like most higher ranking officers, Major Burke had taken up residence in a home the owners had vacated when the British Army had marched on their fair city. Only two blocks away, General Howe was quartered on Second Street, just below Spruce.

Behind the paneled door, Sterling could hear the murmur of voices; one of them he recognized as Major Burke's. The major's secretary, some young ensign, shuffled papers at a small writing desk.

"You're welcome to have a seat," the ensign offered. "I don't know how long the major will be."

"Who's in there?" Sterling studied his own reflection in a small mirror hanging on the wall near the window.

"Not at liberty to say," the ensign responded, removing a pocket watch from inside his rumpled coat.

Sterling adjusted his grenadier cap, studying the major's door with interest. "Famished. How 'bout you?" He smiled at the young man.

"I haven't had anything since dawn. The major had me running up and down the streets between here and the Walnut Street prison."

Sterling shrugged, perching himself on the corner of a damask-upholstered settle. "The ale house around the corner serves a good biscuit and baked pigeon pie."

The ensign licked his lips. "I'm supposed to stay here and wait until the major's done with the Indian."

"The Indian? He's in there?" *Who else,* Sterling mused. *I hear three voices.*

The ensign nodded, glancing toward the window. "My mother always made a good pigeon pie."

"Go on, then," Sterling urged, buffing his fingernails on the knee of his pristine breeches. "If the major asks where you've gone, I'll tell him you went to fetch his dinner."

The young man glanced longingly out the window. "I'm really not supposed to leave my post."

"I have an account there. Just ask the proprietor to put it on my bill."

At that, the ensign popped up off his stool. "I'll only be gone a minute."

"It's just around the corner," Sterling urged, watching him scoop up his hat and hurry out the front door. "You'll be back before the major knows you're gone."

Sterling watched from the window until the boy disappeared down the street, then moved to the major's paneled door.

Sterling listened as Major Burke's voice rose in anger. "Impossible!"

"Makes sense to me," Indian John offered.

"Keep your mouth shut or you'll be out of here," the major snapped.

Sterling's muscles tensed involuntarily. "Who was the third man? What was Major Burke talking about? What was impossible?"

"My sources are rarely wrong, sir," came the third voice.

"Then why the hell didn't you come sooner?"

"Waiting for a confirmation."

Sterling heard something slam to the floor. "You need confirmation before you report that I've got a bloody spy among my men?" Major Burke roared.

Sterling suddenly felt dizzy, and he squeezed his eyes shut in defense. *Holy Mother Mary,* he thought, *I've been caught!*

Chapter Fifteen

A thick, suffocating fear filled Sterling. His first instinct was to run. He lowered his head, swallowing the bile that rose in his throat. They were still talking behind the door; he forced himself to remain there and listen.

". . . know yet, but we'll find out," the third voice assured Major Burke.

"You could let me take a look into it, Major," Indian John offered. "You have to admit I did right well with them pamphlets."

"And you were well paid," the major snapped. A chair scraped the floor and there was silence.

The third voice cleared his throat once, then again. "Ahh, you want me to carry on, Major?"

"You think you can manage it without getting yourself hanged, Murray?"

Murray. The spy's name is Murray, Sterling thought. His breath was coming easier now. They didn't know who the spy was, only that he was one of Major Burke's men.

". . . sir," Murray went on in reassurance. "I've had no problem getting in and out of the city."

"When can you report again?"

"A week, sir. I should know the identity of the spy by then."

"You had damned straight better know or you'll

be sitting out on one of those prison ships in the New York harbor!"

Sterling could hear the major shuffling papers. He was about to dismiss the man called Murray. Sterling stepped away from the door, taking a seat on the settle. He was just removing one of his brother's lace handkerchiefs from his coat when the major's door swung open.

"Yes, sir, you can count on me, sir." A man of average height backed out of the office, saluting as he made his retreat. He wore a wrinkled red uniform coat, but from the rear Sterling couldn't make out what unit he was from.

"Dismissed," Major Burke bellowed.

The spy spun around and rushed out the door. Sterling only caught a brief glance of the side of his face as he hurried past. There was nothing unusual about the man — brown hair, dark eyes, medium build. It was going to be hard to track him down.

"What the hell do you want, Thayer?"

Sterling turned, startled to see the major standing in the doorway. Sterling stood, wiping his brow with the handkerchief. "Well, sir, I need to speak to you about my duty at the prison . . ."

"I don't want to hear any more of your pansy-ass excuses, Thayer. I got another complaint the other day from some tavern down by the dock. You're still starting brawls, Thayer!"

"It's not my fault, sir."

"Of course it isn't! It's never your fault, is it, Thayer?"

212

Sterling tucked his handkerchief back into his coat. His brother's words formed on the tip of his tongue. "When a man accuses another man of cheating, a gentleman must defend himself."

"Spare me the dissertations." He waved his hand, glancing at the desk. "Where, for Christ's sake, is my secretary?"

"Went out to get you dinner, sir."

The major shook his fist, the fringe of his epaulets shaking vigorously. "How the bloody hell are we supposed to win a war with no one for soldiers but Mama's boys and goat-futtering Germans! If we don't get out of this damned city, the whole bunch of you are going to eat, drink, and whore yourselves to death."

"Yes, sir."

"Now get out of my office, Thayer."

"Yes, sir." Sterling saluted as Major Burke spun around, marching back into his office.

"And Thayer . . ."

"Sir?"

"I hear about you fighting anymore and you'll be cleaning horse stalls on Walnut Street!"

"Yes, sir."

Major Burke slammed his door so hard that a small portrait of someone's grandfather flew off the wall. Sterling gave a heavy sigh of relief, making a quick exit. He had to get back to Reagan's and compose a message immediately. He would request that he be removed from this assignment.

* * *

"Elsa? Elsa, where are you?" Reagan hurried from room to room. Elsa was nowhere. In the kitchen, Reagan sought out Nettie. The old woman was dipping candles at the center table.

"Nettie, where's Elsa?"

"Thought she was with you." Nettie sat perched on a tall cane stool, content with the methodical work.

"She isn't with me. She hasn't been with me all day. I've been at Mistress Claggett's. I thought she was with you. She told me she was going to help you with the candles."

"She left the same time you did this morning."

"Nettie, I said she didn't go with me," Reagan repeated. "Where could she be?"

"She's been missin' a lot lately. An hour here, an hour there."

"How can you be so calm, Nettie? She could be hurt or lost."

"That or found herself a beau."

Reagan gasped. Such a thought had never occurred to her, not until that instant. "Oh my God," she murmured. It would be so easy for some nefarious redcoat to take advantage of her little Elsa.

"It's what young girls do, you know," Nettie offered philosophically. "You had a beau once. That Joshua boy. He was right nice—thought you were going to marry him and then came this war fuss."

"Nettie!" Reagan wrung her hands. "I don't know where to start looking for her."

"Looking for who?" Sterling swept into the room, making a beeline for the cast-iron pot that

214

hung on the hearth. Tucked safely beneath his coat was his message requesting that he be transferred immediately.

"Elsa. She's missing." Reagan was so frightened for her sister that for the moment she forgot her animosity toward him. "You've got to help me find her, Grayson."

"She can't be *missing*." He dipped a wooden ladle into the soup and sipped it loudly. "She's got to be here somewhere."

Reagan snatched the dipper from his hand, dropping it into the pot. "She's been gone for hours. She could be anywhere."

Reagan's face was so taut with fear that Sterling gave her shoulder a reassuring squeeze. "Calm down, honey. I'm certain there's logical explanation here."

"That's what I said," Nettie piped up.

Reagan stared up into Sterling's face. "We're afraid there might be a man involved."

The look of horror on her face that was so great that Sterling smiled tenderly. "I'll find her." He caught a wisp of Reagan's red hair on his finger and twirled it. It felt so good to be so near her. He could smell the fresh, clean scent of her skin. His mind filled with the memories of that one night they'd shared and he felt his loins quicken with need.

Reagan laid her hand on his arm. "I'll go with you."

"No."

"Yes. I can't just sit here and do nothing."

"No, you stay here in case she comes home before I get back."

Reagan exhaled slowly. "I suppose you're right." Her eyes narrowed suspiciously. "What do you know about this?"

"Just stay here." Sterling stole another sip of the warm broth in the pot and then went out the door.

Reagan stood in the center of the kitchen in indecision for a moment. Something wasn't right here. For weeks she'd suspected that Grayson had something to do with the subtle changes in her sister, her demand for increased independence.

Nettie's head popped up at the sound of Reagan's shoes tapping on the hardwood floor. "Where are you going?"

"I'll be right back. You stay here and wait for Elsa."

Reagan waited until Sterling turned the corner and then she went down the street after him. She seethed angrily as she picked her way down the muddy street. She didn't know what Grayson had to do with all of this, but she was damned mad. How dare he keep something from her that concerned her sister! *Oh, God*, Reagan thought suddenly. *What if she's pregnant?*

"Reagan, where the hell do you think you're going?"

She stopped short, nearly colliding with Grayson's tall, broad-shouldered frame. "G-Grayson." She had been so caught up with her thoughts that

216

she hadn't seen him standing at the corner.

"I told you to stay put."

"She's my sister. She could be in danger."

"She's not in any danger." Sterling found it difficult to keep his hands at his sides. He wanted so badly to stroke the line of her jawbone, to trace the arch of her eyebrows.

She was dressed in a faded blue cotton gown with a kerchief thrown over her shoulders and tucked into her apron. Her mobcap had slipped to the back of her head so that a mass of bright red curls tumbled onto her shoulders. Her dress was so simple that she might have been mistaken for some serving wench out to do her mistress's bidding, but she held herself like a queen.

It would be so hard for Sterling to leave her; it would be the most difficult thing he'd ever had to do.

Reagan held her ground stubbornly. "I said I'm going."

Sterling groaned aloud. He didn't want to cause trouble for Ethan, but they had known that sooner or later this would happen. He only wished he could have warned Elsa and Ethan first.

"All right," Sterling finally agreed. "But I want you to promise to stay calm. It's not what it seems."

"What isn't what it seems?"

Two passersby in green Hessian uniforms glanced over their shoulders with interest as they passed Sterling and Reagan on the street.

"Shh!" Sterling pressed a finger to her soft lips.

"Everyone for a block will hear you."

"I don't care! Where's my sister? She's my responsibility!" she cried hysterically. "I promised Papa I'd take care of her!"

On impulse, Sterling pulled Reagan into his arms, smoothing her unruly hair. "It's all right," he soothed, kissing her forehead. "It's all right, sweetheart. I'll take you to her."

Reagan melted into Grayson's strong arms, feeling a relief of tension surge through her. How many nights had she wanted to come to him since Papa had died? How many times had she made it to his door before she turned and ran, retreating to the lonesome safety of her own bedchamber?

"Grayson," she whispered, her voice raspy. She had to tell him that she *did* love him. She had to tell him that she didn't care if they called her whore. She needed him, she wanted him.

"Not now, Reagie," he answered, feeling his throat constrict. "One thing at a time." He brushed his lips over her damp brow and then released her. "People are watching," he murmured.

Reagan stood for a moment, her eyes half closed as she composed herself. "Let's go."

"You certain you don't just want me to bring her home?"

She shook her head, taking his arm. Let people look. She'd lost her father, she wasn't going to lose Grayson, not yet. She was never going to love a man as much as she loved her arrogant Captain Thayer. General Clinton wouldn't remain in the city much longer, so she would make the best of the

218

time she and Grayson had left. Reagan wasn't sure what had brought on this revelation, but she felt as if a burden had been lifted from her shoulders. "Lead the way."

It was a short walk to the blacksmith's house, and Reagan and Sterling made it in silence. There was so much to say, yet nothing to say. They both knew that no matter what transpired with Elsa today, no matter how angry she was with him, tonight he would come to her bedchamber. Tonight she would lie in his arms again.

"The smithy's? Why are we going here? This is where we keep our horse."

"You know Ethan?" Sterling led her across the yard. There was a fresh coat of whitewash on a picket fence in the front yard. Someone had cultivated a flowerbed just beneath the windows of the neat frame house.

"The blacksmith? Not really. Only in passing." She frowned. "Elsa's here?"

"Ethan's wife died. He has small children."

"What's that got to do with little Elsa?"

Sterling walked up to the front door and gave a knock. Somewhere behind the house a dog barked. "Reagan, she's not your little Elsa. It's time you faced up to it."

The door swung open and Ethan appeared, red-faced from laughing. He wore a napkin tucked into his rough linen shirt. His face was freshly shaved, his hair wet and slicked back. "Captain!" Ethan's eyes widened. "Miss Reagan . . . Mistress Llewellyn."

The sound of Elsa's laughter floated from the house, followed by a chorus of gleeful children.

"Elsa? Is that you?" Reagan pushed her way past Grayson and the blacksmith, into the great room of the cozy house.

Elsa looked up from the trestle table, where she stood over a towheaded child, dishing him out a portion of meat pie. "Reagan," she answered guiltily. The pie slid off the spoon and plopped onto the floor.

The children giggled.

"Elsa, what are you doing here?" Reagan glanced about the room, taking in the utterly domestic scene. It looked as if she had just walked in on a family's dinner hour. There was a place set at the head of the table with a plate heaped with pie and slices of bread. On the opposite end of the table was a place setting with a delicate portion dished out—obviously Elsa's. Reagan surmised immediately that this was *not* the first time Elsa had had dinner with this man and his children.

"Having rabbit pie," Elsa answered in a small voice.

"M-Mistress Llewellyn," Ethan stammered.

Sterling stepped inside and closed the door. "Reagan."

"I want to know what the meaning of this is mister . . . Mr. . . ."

"Cannon . . . Ethan Cannon, ma'am." Ethan went to offer his hand, but then thought better of it. He snatched his napkin from his shirt.

"Mr. Cannon, what are you doing with my sister?"

"Wouldn't you like to sit down?" Ethan indicated a chair.

"No, I don't want to sit down! Elsa! Get your cloak and come with me!"

Elsa set the pie on the table and wiped her hands on her apron. "Don't you tell me what to do, Sister," she answered fiercely.

Reagan opened her mouth to shout back at her sister, but everyone was staring at her—Grayson, the blacksmith, even the children. "Elsa," she said finally, in a calm, collected voice. "We can talk about this when we get home. *Get your things.*"

"I don't have to if I don't want to!"

Ethan went to Elsa, touching her arm gently. "Go ahead, Elsa. Everyone is upset. We can talk tomorrow."

"I don't think that will be necessary," Reagan answered.

Elsa lifted her dark lashes, looking up at Ethan in a manner that made Reagan uncomfortable. What was that she saw in her sister's eyes? The poor girl worshipped the red-faced blacksmith!

Ethan patted Elsa again, giving her a little push toward the door. "Go on with you," he said gently.

"I'll be back," she told him, glancing at the children.

"I know you will."

Sterling stood at the door, opening it for Reagan and Elsa. "You go on," he told Reagan. "I'll be along right behind you. I want to speak with this man for a moment."

221

Reagan looked up at him gratefully. "I think that's a good idea." She lowered her voice. "Tell him that he is not to see my sister ever again, and if she comes up in the family way, I'll have him arrested."

Sterling ushered the two women out of the house, with Ethan following behind. Sterling waited until Reagan and Elsa were on the street and then he turned back to Ethan. "I'm so sorry. I didn't mean for this to happen, but Elsa was gone all day. Reagan was afraid something had happened to her sister. I couldn't calm her down."

The blacksmith stroked his chin. "It's not your fault," he answered dismally, watching his Elsa disappear around the corner. "It's gone on too long like this. I'll just have to tell Miss Reagan my intentions."

"Those being?"

The blacksmith stared at Sterling with his hooded dark eyes. "To marry her of course!"

Sterling grinned. "Damn, then you've got your work cut out for you."

"I'll just come to the house tomorrow and lay it out on the table for Miss Reagan. Elsa is a full-grown woman. She can do what she pleases under the law."

Sterling frowned. "Maybe it would be better if you waited a few days, a week or two. Let things calm down. Reagan's been under a lot of stress since her father died."

Ethan nodded. "If you say so, all right. You've been a good friend through all of this. I'll trust your opinions."

Sterling patted the man's arm. "Give it a while and I'll let you know when I think it's safe to show your face. She can't be mad forever."

Ethan nodded. "Well, guess I'd better get back to my colts. We hadn't meant for Elsa to be away so long, time just got away from us today. She wanted to stay for dinner, then she was going straight home."

Sterling pushed his hand into his coat, feeling the smooth parchment of the letter he'd just composed. For the briefest moment, he considered not sending the message. How could he leave Reagan now? But if he was found out, there were so many who would suffer. Reagan would certainly be arrested, and probably Elsa and old Nettie as well.

"Ethan, I've another message."

Ethan looked to be sure no one was passing the house and then reached out to take it. Slowly Sterling removed the letter from his coat and handed it to the patriot blacksmith. "It looks like I'm going to have to be transferred. We've got a real mess here."

"Sorry to hear that, friend. Anything I can do?"

"No, just pass the letter and keep an eye on your back." Sterling gave a wave and started for the Blue Boar Tavern. He'd let the dust settle back at the Llewellyn house and then he'd go home.

When Sterling entered the front hall, all was quiet. Reagan was waiting for him in the parlor. She sat at the spinet playing a nameless tune.

"You took care of it?"

"Reagan."

She lifted her hands from the keyboard. "Did you take care of it or didn't you?"

He leaned on the doorframe. "I told him to let things settle down and then come talk to you."

"Why did you say that? There's nothing to talk about. Elsa says he didn't touch her. I believe her."

Sterling sighed. "Do we have to talk about this tonight?" He tossed his cap on a chair and came up behind her. He lifted her mane of heavy hair off her neck and kissed her nape.

Reagan shivered. "You knew about the blacksmith. Why didn't you tell me?" Her voice sounded breathy to her.

Sterling kissed her again and again, slowly making his way to her ear. "I'll tell you anything you want . . . later."

"Grayson," she whispered, letting her eyes close. "Not here. Not now."

"When?" He nibbled at the lobe of her ear, sending a flood of goosebumps down her back.

"We have to be discreet." He was removing the kerchief that served as a modesty piece. He slid one hand into the bodice of her gown and she leaned against him. "No one must know."

Sterling pulled her to her feet burying his face in the valley between her breasts. He could feel her heart beating wildly beneath his lips. "Oh, God, I've missed you."

"Grayson." She struggled weakly. Not here, not in her father's parlor. What decent woman made love to a man on the floor of her father's parlor.

224

Chapter Sixteen

Long after Sterling slept, Reagan lay on her side, awake, resting her head on his shoulder. They had made love here in his bedchamber a second time, then a third. He had taken her beyond the limits of sweet, searing rapture. He had lifted her to a pinnacle of all-encompassing pleasure until together they'd shattered into a million shards of bright light and fell back to earth.

Reagan stared up at the damask curtains that framed Sterling's bed. She could feel his breath on her cheek as his chest rose and fell rhythmically. His hand rested comfortably on her waist. She was still in awe of the feelings he aroused in her, not just physically, but emotionally. Since Papa had died, she thought she had lost her ability to feel . . . to care.

For the past month she hadn't permitted herself to think of Grayson or the feelings he stirred in her. He was the enemy. *He* was responsible for her father's death and the cessation of publication of their leaflets, just as every red and green coat in the city was responsible. But no matter how strongly she believed in her new country, she knew deep in her heart of hearts that the love she had for Grayson transcended sides in a war.

She knew she should feel sad that theirs

wouldn't be a permanent relationship. They would never marry, have children, and live here in her grandfather's home with Elsa. The British Army would move on and Grayson would be gone from her life forever. But he was *here, now,* and that was what mattered, tomorrow be damned. He said he loved her, and she believed him. She knew he was a man with a talent for wooing women, but this was something he couldn't lie about. She could see it in his eyes when they made love. She could also see that he, too, knew the futility of their love.

Sterling stirred beneath Reagan, sighing in his sleep, and she turned to study his angular face. A lock of blond hair brushed the corner of his mouth. Carefully, so as not to wake him, she pushed it back. "Thank you," she whispered. "Thank you for loving me, for making me realize that life goes on . . . for making me realize what I have to do."

Kissing him lightly on his parted lips, she slipped from beneath the counterpane. She gathered her petticoats, her stockings and underthings, and slipped silently out of the room. In her own bedchamber she dressed in a soft flannel gown and wrapper and slipped a pair of cotton mules on her feet. Taking a lamp she went down the hall, pausing at Grayson's door. Hearing no movement, she went downstairs and into the kitchen.

Turning up the lamp's wick, she opened the door to the stairs, and descended into the cellar.

Driven with purpose, she walked through the damp, musty chambers, coming to stop at the secret door. A lump rose in Reagan's throat as she recalled the afternoon she'd spent here with Papa cleaning out the secret room. Tears welled in her eyes as she walked down the passageway and entered the printing room. She hadn't been here in over a month . . . not since the fire.

Closing the door behind her, she lit the lamp that hung overhead. Bright light illuminated all but the far corners of the small room. The printing press sat silent, sheets of paper scattered on the floor; crocks of mixed ink sat congealed. It looked as if her father had just stepped out of the room for a moment . . . except for the cobwebs that stretched across the press.

"Papa," Reagan whispered. "Papa, can you hear me?" Her voice grew stronger with each word. "Papa, your death won't be for naught. Your work won't come to an end just because you've been taken from us."

Purposefully she moved to her grandfather's old desk and set down her lamp. Pulling up a stool, she took a quill and uncorked a small bottle of ink. She slipped a sheet of foolscap from the drawer, a smile on her lips. "Tell me what to say, Papa," she whispered.

She sat for a moment, her eyes half closed, and then she began to write. In her mind she heard her father's voice. She heard him arguing with men, she heard heated discussions from years

229

past. Until the wee hours of the morning she wrote. When her quill broke from the pressure of her hand, she found another.

Sometime before dawn, Reagan rose stiffly from her stool and blew out the overhead lamp. Taking the light from her bedchamber, she closed the secret door and made her way upstairs. She was exhausted, physically and emotionally, but her heart swelled with pride. In only a few short hours she had composed the penman's next leaflet.

"Good morning." When Reagan came into the kitchen for a late breakfast, both Sterling and Elsa were there. The two crouched near the fireplace, admiring Elsa's cat.

Sterling looked up. "Morning."

Reagan blushed, looking away. She remembered his lips on hers, the feel of his touch, and she wanted him all over again.

Elsa was silent. She scooped up Mittens and retreated to the far side of the kitchen, glaring at her sister.

Sterling glanced back at Reagan, offering her a hint of a smile. With Grayson's reassurance she chose just to ignore Elsa's unforgiving behavior. In a few days she knew her sister would completely forget about Ethan the blacksmith.

"I think I'll start whitewashing the barn and carriage house today. It's been needing it for a good two years." Reagan retrieved a muffin from a plate on the table and bit into it.

"I could help," Sterling offered. "I have some business this morning, but I'll be back by one or two." He watched Reagan's tongue dart out to lick the crumbs from the corner of her precious mouth. Memories of their lovemaking floated through his mind. This morning, seeing her bright eyes, her teasing smile, he didn't know how he would tell her he was leaving. He didn't know how he could go.

"I don't know how that would look, Captain. A man of King George's Army aiding the enemy."

Sterling lifted a blond eyebrow. He knew she was teasing him. "As you like, madame." He spread his arms. "I only thought to offer help to a defenseless woman."

"Well, I know how you can help *this* defenseless woman." She took another muffin, eyeing him.

"How? Ask and I shall do all in my power to grant you your wish."

She watched Sterling demonstrate with a dramatic sweep of his hands. He was more handsome this morning than she'd ever seen him. Very rarely did she see him in his wig these days. His golden-blond hair was pulled back into a neat queue and tied with a black velvet ribbon. His blue eyes twinkled with a secret only the two of them shared. She pointedly ignored the scarlet uniform. "I was thinking about going back to selling my gingerbread, but I'm nearly our of gin-

231

gerspice as well as sugar."

"I could see what I could do," he offered honestly.

"There's not much money, and now without Papa to provide—" The words caught in her throat. ". . . so we could use the money from my gingerbread." It wasn't a lie—not entirely. They could use the money. Of course the gingerbread would also provide her with a reason to come and go freely about the city without the soldiers becoming suspicious.

"There'd be plenty of men in the barracks willing to buy it if you'd be willing to have redcoats eating your gingerbread."

"I'll have to think about it."

"Fair enough." Sterling winked, turning to Elsa. "Why don't you help your sister with the whitewashing. It's supposed to be a beauty of a day."

Elsa shot Reagan an evil glance and swept out of the kitchen, her cat clutched in her arms.

Reagan sighed, leaning against the table. "What am I going to do with her? Papa and I had talked about sending her to Richmond to stay with family, but I don't think she could go without me."

Sterling froze. "You're leaving?"

Reagan arched an eyebrow. "No, but what if I was? When your new commander takes over, *you'll* be moving out, won't you? Wouldn't be much of a war if you just sat in this city while Washington waits on the other side of the river."

Sterling came to her, putting a hand on each side of her and leaning forward so that he had her trapped. "Methinks I hear a bit of hostility in my lady's voice."

"Damn right you do! What have you to offer me, Captain?"

Sterling flinched. She was right. What *did* he have to offer her? Marriage? Security? Honesty? He could offer her nothing. He stared at her lovely face, his blue-eyed gaze settling on her dark, pleading eyes. "My love . . ." he whispered. "For now all I can offer you is my love."

Reagan's voice caught in her throat as she threw her arms around him. "Oh, Grayson, I'm sorry. I knew what I was getting into. I knew every step of the way." She rested her head on his shoulder. "I had no right to say that."

"It's all right, sweet." He kissed her cheek, smoothing her fiery hair.

"It's just that it's all so futile," she murmured. "My beliefs are what make me who I am and I'll not change that. I can't, not even for you." She lifted her head, taking in his steady gaze. "And you can't shed your uniform for me, can you, Grayson?" She knew what his answer would be, but somewhere deep in her heart, she prayed she was wrong.

"No," he whispered. "I cannot." It was the hardest thing he'd ever had to say. "So what are we to do?"

Reagan's eyes drifted shut as she squeezed him

tightly. *"Do?* We live for today, that's what we do. Who knows if there'll be any tomorrow."

"Oh, Reagan, my little Reagan, women aren't supposed to be so sensible!" He held her against him, feeling the pounding of her heart against his chest. "Just remember that no matter what happens, I love you. I always will."

Reagan accepted his kiss and then stepped back, smoothing his clean-shaven cheek with the tips of her fingers. "You'd best go on. We both have work to do." With a bittersweet smile, she lifted her skirts and turned away, leaving Sterling behind to wipe his misty eyes.

Sterling hurried up the cobblestone walk on to Spruce Street, the message he'd been waiting for, the message he'd been dreading, tucked safely beneath his coat. This letter from Captain Craig had been a week in coming. It was his new orders.

Reaching the steps of the Llewellyn home, Sterling stopped to pick up a wooden crate resting on the bottom brick step. Lifting the canvas cover, inside he saw cloth bags of varying sizes, obviously foodstuffs. The pungent aroma of ginger rose from the crate.

Carrying the crate into the house and down the hall, he found Reagan in the kitchen, kneeling on the hearth.

"You left this sugar on the front stoop. You'd

234

better be careful or someone's going to walk off with it." He set the crate on the table.

"What are you talking about?" Reagan came to him. She lifted the canvas cover and gave a squeal of delight. "I thought you said you couldn't find any ginger. You said you would have to find a way to order some."

"It's not mine. I told you it was on the step. I thought you'd left it out there." He pressed a kiss to her warm lips, but she pushed him away, anxious to dig into her treasure box.

She removed a small sack of sugar and a crock of honey. A frown creased her forehead. "If you stole it, I don't care. Blasted redcoats stole everything in our larder the week they came to Philadelphia."

"I didn't steal it. When I couldn't find any ginger in the market, I asked Jergens at the Blue Boar about it. He said he could get me some, but the price was steep. Too steep for a captain's pay."

"Mmm. Someone just left it on the step then— a gift." An image of the mysterious man who had aided her the night she'd nearly been caught by the redcoats entered her mind. "Maybe the blacksmith left it, trying to bribe me."

Sterling laughed. "I've a feeling you're not a woman to be bribed."

"No. I'm not. But I'll take the sugar and the honey, and the ginger just the same." She dug into the crate. "Oh, look . . . and sewing needles!

We were down to one to share among us, and Nettie keeps forgetting where she's left it."

Sterling glanced into the box. "And tea, Reagie." He picked up a small tin, waving it in front of her face. He lifted the lid and sniffed. "English tea." Mischievously, his eyes met hers. "How long has it been since you had a cup of good tea?"

"I won't allow that tin in my house! Give it to me! I'll burn it!" She took it from him, but he snatched it back.

"Oh, no you don't. Come on, what would it hurt? One tiny cup? I won't tell if you don't," he coaxed.

She looked at the tin. The truth was that she had dearly loved her tea before the war like any other Englishwoman. "I couldn't. Now give it to me."

"It was a gift, Reagan. You didn't buy it. You've committed no sin against God and country."

"It doesn't matter." She began to put away her bags of precious baking supplies. Tonight she'd bake her gingerbread. The first printing of her new leaflet was ready to be distributed.

"I think I'll just take this for safekeeping then." He shook the can over his shoulder as he left the room.

Upstairs, Sterling took his time removing his uniform. He slipped on a pair of his own breeches and a simple cotton shirt. In his stocking

236

feet he went to the desk and sat down. His hands trembled as he held the message from Captain Craig. With a sigh of regret, he retrieved his bell mask from his belongings and opened the letter.

Hesitantly, he laid the deciphering mask over the message. "Request for transfer denied?" he read aloud. "Son of a bitch!"

"Where's he going?" Westley whispered. He stood beside Reagan in the shadows of the carriage house, watching Sterling ride away. It was twilight, and the streets were coming alive. Carriages rumbled over the cobblestones and soldiers, on foot, hurried to their evening meal.

"I don't know," she whispered. *No whorehouse if he knows what's good for him.*

He was dressed in civilian clothes, a dark cloak thrown over his shoulders. That seemed odd to Reagan. Why would an English officer want to conceal his identity?

Earlier, he'd come into the kitchen where Reagan was baking her gingerbread. He'd been agitated, his voice edged with controlled anger. But she sensed an emotion stronger than anger. Fear? Relief? She wasn't sure. He had said he was going out and that he didn't know when he'd be back. If anyone came looking for him, she was to say she knew nothing. She'd not seen him all day.

Reagan watched him as he rode out of sight down the lamplit street. Something wasn't right here. Despite their happiness in the past week, Grayson had been acting oddly — as if he had something to tell her.

Westley laid his hand gently on Reagan's shoulder. "The driver will be along shortly. If this shipment's to go out tonight, we'll have to get moving."

"Then let's do it."

"Reagan." Westley's voice penetrated the darkness. "Are you certain you want to do this? You know the danger."

"I know the danger," she answered, slamming the carriage house doors shut.

"When the pamphlets surface, that Major Burke'll start the investigation up all over again. You'll be their first suspect."

"A woman?" She laughed, scrutinizing him in the darkness. "That's the ingeniousness of it. No one will suspect me. It's been assumed from the beginning that a man was writing those essays. Women don't have opinions on political issues, and if they have, they certainly could never express themselves on paper."

Westley sighed. "I just don't like it, not with that lobsterback still in your house. You're playing with fire."

"Westley . . ." — Reagan dropped her hands to her hips — "are you with me or not? I'll do it with or without your help."

He exhaled slowly, scratching his head. "Hell, yeah, I'm with you, but I warn you, if they hang you by your pretty little neck, I'll have no sympathy for you. You don't have to do this. You've done more this winter for our army than most w—"

"Women!" Reagan grabbed the iron ring handle of the trapdoor that led to the secret room below and gave a hearty tug. The hinges groaned and the door swung open like a great yawning mouth. Lamplight poured into the carriage house. "Westley, you say you're different, but you're just like the rest. You don't think I can do it, do you?"

"I didn't say that, Reagan. I'm only concerned for your safety. Uriah—"

"Uriah, is it? Now tell me, if it was me who'd been killed in that fire, would Papa have gone on printing without me?"

"Uh, well, yeah, I guess so."

"So there's your answer."

"It's not the same thing, Reagie."

"It's precisely the same thing. End of discussion." She hiked up her skirts and started down the ladder into the secret room. "Now are you going to help me bring those damned pamphlets up or am I going to have to do it myself?"

Chapter Seventeen

"Captain, you denied my transfer." Sterling stood at ease, his hands tucked behind his back. Captain Craig's headquarters were a small frame farmhouse in Frankfort, just outside the Philadelphia city limits.

"That I did, Lieutenant." His superior officer gave a nod. He sat on a bench at a trestle table in the center of a large, cozy kitchen. In this unimposing room he trained the American Army's finest spies.

"I don't understand, sir. I'm about to be found out. It's no longer safe for me to remain Captain Grayson Thayer."

"Have you revealed to anyone your true identity?"

"No, sir."

"Not even to the woman?"

"No, sir," Sterling answered, his voice lowering in pitch. "You know me better than that, Captain."

Charles Craig sighed. "I'm sorry, Sterling, but I had to ask. Have a seat." He indicated the bench across the table from him. "And cut the captain crap. You and I have known each other too long for that."

Sterling sat down and leaned his elbows on the table. The suspended oil lamp above cast streaks of golden light over the table illuminating his face. "It's not me I'm worried about, and you know it, Charlie. It's the others who support me there in the city. If I'm caught, it won't only be me who goes down."

"Burke doesn't have any idea who the spy is, right?"

"Thank God, no. Not yet." Sterling looked up to see a young woman entering the kitchen through a back door. Captain Craig gave an easy nod, and Sterling went on with what he was saying. "But there aren't that many officers beneath Burke's command. Twenty maybe. By process of elimination . . ."

"You won't be in the city that long. Once Clinton gets his shoes on straight, he'll be moving. It's vital that General Washington know in what direction, north or south. You're too close to the action for us to let you go now, Sterling."

Sterling accepted a mug of spiced, mulled wine from the dark-haired woman. He glanced up at her; she was pretty in an earthy way, but lacked the sophistication or Reagan's form. It was funny how he compared every woman he saw to Reagan these days.

Sterling turned his steady gaze to his commanding officer. "I'm scared, Charlie," he said honestly. "It's gotten to the point where I don't know who I am anymore. I'm afraid I'm going to make a blunder. So many lies." He stared into his tankard. "I can't keep it straight in my head when I'm Sterling and when I'm Grayson."

"You knew this was going to be difficult when you took the job. You knew the chances you were taking." The captain waved to the woman and she exited the room as quietly and inconspicuously as she had entered it.

"True enough. But you said you'd take me out if things got too tight." Sterling leaned forward, his blond hair brushing his shoulders. "Charlie, I'm squeaking."

Charles shook his head. "We take you out now and Burke'll know for sure it's you. You'll be of no good to us the remainder of the war. Besides, we'd have to move the woman and her family at the Army's expense. She'd be held accountable. They'd never believe she didn't know who you were."

"Burke's still got that half-breed working for him. He's got it in for me. I think he's already suspicious." He paused. "But you're right, I'd best stay put."

"You're doing fine, Sterling. Captain Grayson Thayer's the talk of the city. Your exploits are what keep people chuckling at the supper table."

Sterling grinned wryly. "I see now how a man can gain a false reputation. I spread a few coins, tipped a few jacks of ale, pinched a few asses, and suddenly I'm a legend."

"Which is exactly what we counted on. It's the perfect guise. How can you be a threat when no one takes you seriously?"

"Yes, well there was one thing I hadn't counted on." Sterling took a deep swallow of the warm, spicy concoction.

"The woman?"

Sterling gazed at the burning embers stoked in the deep fireplace. "Does a man have no secrets in this Army?"

Charlie laughed, his rich voice filling the warm chamber. "I make it my business to know what my men are about."

"She's very clever, Charlie. She could probably be of some help to us." Sterling glanced up hopefully. "You recall it was her father who was responsible for those damned fine leaflets. Her heart's certainly in the right place."

Charlie began to shake his head before Sterling was finished. "You can't let your emotions control you, friend. It is imperative that you keep your true identity a secret. There'll be time enough for courting when we beat these pettifogging redcoats."

Sterling drained his tankard in silence. *Not with this girl there won't be,* he thought. *There'll not be another chance with Reagan.*

Charlie watched Sterling rise and stretch his long legs. "I'm sorry I had to deny your request for transfer. I'd do it if I could, but this comes from the top. I'll be keeping a close eye on you. We'll get you out if things blow."

Sterling nodded. "All right. Now, what of the spy, Murray? Any clues to his identity?"

"No." Captain Craig rose to see Sterling out. "But we're going to find him, I promise you."

He laughed. "Before he finds me, I should hope."

Charlie patted Sterling on the back. "Someday,

243

we're going to sit our grandchildren on our knees and tell them what a great hero you were."

Sterling's blue eyes met his commanding officer's. "I don't want to be a hero, Charlie. I just want to get out with my neck. I don't want anyone dying for my sake. I want to go home to Virginia, prop my boots on the veranda rail, and watch my tobacco grow. I want to get old."

"We all do," Charlie answered as Sterling walked out the door. "We all do, my friend."

Reagan tapped softly on Sterling's bedchamber door with the toe of her shoe, a pitcher of water in her hands. It had been well past three in the morning when she had finally heard him come in last night. She had wanted to go to him, but she was afraid to. She was afraid she would smell the scent of cheap perfume on his fresh, clean skin. She was afraid his clothes would be rumpled, the taste of hard rum on his lips. Though she'd never seen him drunk, she heard the tales passed from citizen to citizen down at the market. They said he knew every whore's petticoat in the city and a few respectable ladies' as well.

That didn't sound like her Grayson. The man she loved was thoughtful, responsible, kind. He loved her, she knew he did. He had promised there'd be no whoring as long as she shared his bed. Reagan tapped again. "Grayson?"

When she heard him reply, she entered his bedchamber. His clothes were thrown haphazardly on the floor. She picked them up, one item at a time, thinking how odd it was. Grayson was always so fastidious.

"You were out late last night," she remarked. She hadn't intended to be so forthright. She didn't want to be accused of being an old fishmonger's wife. After all, what claim did she have to him? The words had just slipped out before she had time to check them.

Sterling squinted as she pulled open the heavy drapes, letting the sunshine pour into the room. "Business," he murmured, pulling the counterpane over his head. The truth was that after he'd left Captain Craig he'd gone to the Blue Boar and overindulged in claret. He didn't know what time it was when he'd stumbled home.

"Business, is it?" She poured fresh water from the pitcher into his washbowl. "Funny how you lobster-backs think a roll in the hay is business," she accused tartly.

Sterling pushed up on one elbow. "Reagan, I told you I'd not do that and I've kept my promise."

"That's not what I hear down by the wharf." She shook a slender finger at him. "I swear, Grayson Thayer, if I come down with some disease, I'll blow your head right off your shoulders."

Sterling sat up, swinging his feet onto the floor. "What's made you so vicious this morning?"

She shrugged, leaning over a cane-bottom chair as she watched him pad across the floor nude. She felt a familiar twinge deep in the base of her stomach as she admired his striking form. His shoulders

245

were broad and rounded, his chest muscular with a sprinkling of blond curls across it. His stomach was flat; a trail of hair led from his navel to his groin. She stood unabashed, watching as he turned to splash cool water on his face. She had never imagined a man's body could be so beautiful . . . so tempting.

Sterling turned to her, drying his face with a flannel towel. "What are you staring at?" He glanced down at himself, throwing his towel over his shoulder. "Am I missing a vital part?"

She laughed, coming to him. "I was just thinking how happy you've made me. How sad I'm going to be when you go."

Sterling took her in his arms, stroking the back of her head. Her hair was pulled back girlishly over the crown of her head and tied with a ribbon so that it hung in a heavy curtain down her back. "Don't think about it. No one's going anywhere yet."

"But you will and soon, I think. The Army's getting restless." She stroked the corded muscles of his arm. "Do you know when yet?"

He nibbled the lobe of her ear. "What are you, a lady spy now?" He pressed a kiss to a soft spot on her neck and felt the goosebumps rise beneath his lips. "You know I'm not privy to such information and if I was, I certainly wouldn't tell you, Continental."

She laughed, pulling away. "Just trying to keep you on your toes." She patted the damp spot on the bodice of her lutestring gown. "You got

246

me all wet."

He snatched her hand, pulling her roughly against him. "I can make you wetter."

She took the flannel towel off his shoulder and hit him with it.

"Ouch! That stings!" He rubbed his chest where she'd left a red welt.

"That's what you get for taking liberties with an innocent!" she snapped, feigning injury. "And before breakfast," she finished in a low, sensual voice.

"What time is it?" Sterling stepped out to capture her again, but she darted behind a worn upholstered chair.

"Time to get dressed. You left a note on the table saying you had an appointment. You asked me to wake you up so you wouldn't be late."

Leaning over the chair, he traced her breast through the material of her gown with his finger.

"And that"—she smacked at his hand—"will make you late, soldier."

Both of them laughed and Sterling gave in, sitting down to roll on his stockings. "You make a man want to give up his life as a soldier, Reagie, my sweet. You make him think of a wife, children, and other such silliness," he dared tentatively.

Casually, she crossed her arms beneath her breasts. "Not me. I have no desire for a husband—not anymore at least." *How could I marry,* she thought. *Now that I've known your love, life is spoiled for matrimony. No man could ever meet my expectations, not after you, Grayson.*

He looked up. "No husband? No children?"

"I can't very well have children with no husband, now can I?" She offered him a freshly pressed shirt and he pulled it over his head.

"What if . . . what if you were to become pregnant?" he asked, his voice muffled by the folds of the shirt.

"Have no fear, Captain. I'll not strap you down with a bastard." She watched him push his head through the shirt and smooth the soft linen. "I had an illness as a young woman. My father's physician said I was probably barren," she lied. Reagan *had* considered what she would do if she became pregnant, and she had decided that she'd just have the baby. Grayson, wherever he might be, need never know. She'd deal with the social repercussions as best she could.

Sterling took that bit of information in, chewing it slowly. He knew he should be relieved to know she ran no risk of getting with child, but a small part of him ached at the thought. How sad to know that she would never have a babe, that they could never have had one, even if circumstances had been different . . . or they changed.

Reagan wondered what had brought on Grayson's silence. Relief, she supposed. "Where are you going this morning?" She changed the subject not wanting to dwell on unhappiness this morning.

"Major Burke's. Why?"

"I was thinking about what you said about the gingerbread. I have some made and I thought maybe you could escort me to one of the barracks so that I could see it."

248

"You'd be seen with me on the street? A stinking redcoat" he imitated.

"I need the money, Grayson, and it's barely safe for women to walk the street unattended. I just thought that if you were going in the same direction . . ."

He pulled up his white breeches. "You'll have to wait for me outside Major Burke's office, but then we could go."

She smiled, handing him his vest. What better way to safely distribute her leaflets than with a uniformed British escort? Certainly, she'd sell the bloody redcoats her gingerbread, but she'd make a few stops at *patriot* homes on the way!

Reagan eyed the private home that served as Major Burke's headquarters. Friends of Mistress Clagget, the Rolands, owned the stately brick home, but they had fled like so many other patriot families and now resided in York with the Continental Congress. "I think I'll just wait outside," Reagan told Sterling quietly.

"Nonsense. Come in and wait in the parlor. I'll only be a minute." He hurried up the front steps and opened the door for her. "It'll look worse, you standing there."

She looked up and down the street. People hurried along, bent on their own errands. No one seemed to notice her and her redcoat. "All right, she conceded. Clutching her basket of gingerbread, she went up and into the front hall.

Sterling closed the door behind her. "This way." He rested his hand on her hip, steering her into the parlor.

"Thayer!" Major Burke's voice boomed from his inner office.

"Sir," Sterling answered. He pointed to the damask settle near the window, and Reagan nodded.

"You're late! Get in here!"

"Yes, sir." Sterling winked at Reagan and disappeared into his commanding officer's office, closing the paneled door behind him.

Reagan set her basket on the floor and took a deep breath. Somehow it seemed sacrilegious to sit here in Mistress Roland's parlor and wait on her lover, the British officer.

Sighing uncomfortably, she smoothed her blue-green silk taffeta gown. Glancing out the window, she fiddled with the fine lace of the neck handkerchief tucked modestly into her bodice. She could hear Grayson's voice and that of the major.

The echo of footsteps sounded on the front step and she rose off the settle to see who was entering the major's offices.

Terror rose in Reagan's throat.

It was him. The half-breed who had murdered her father.

Indian John strolled into the parlor, coming to a halt inside the door. He removed his battered three-cornered hat and bowed stiffly. He was dressed in a tattered pair of buckskins and a torn brocade vest. "I don't believe we've had the pleasure of meeting, ma'am."

Finding her voice, Reagan half rose in anger. "I believe we have, sir." Grayson had said there was nothing that could be done about the man. He was Major Burke's pet. Even if the major could have been convinced that the half-breed had burned Uriah Llewellyn out, it wouldn't have made a difference. Justice was a funny thing to an occupying army.

He tossed his hat onto the secretary's desk. "Nope, don't believe we have. I'd remember a face like yours." He reached out to touch her cheek.

Reagan slapped his hand as hard as she could and he pulled back, rubbing his hand to ease the sting. "You shouldn't've done that, wench."

Tears pooled in the corners of her dark eyes as she came to her feet. "You killed my father."

"You're mistaken. Must've been another man who looked like me." His scarred face turned up a jeering smile.

"You can't get away with murder."

He was so close that she could feel his sour, hot breath on her lips. "Looks like I did, girlie." Catching the scent of her gingerbread, he kicked at her basket on the floor with the tip of his leather boot. "What you got in there?"

She reached for the basket but he was too fast for her. She lifted her gaze to stare at his eyepatch. Beneath the layers of gingerbread were two piles of leaflets. "Give them to me," she managed, tight-lipped.

He lifted the clean cloth cover, inhaling deeply. "Pretty face and the lady can cook, too." He raised

251

his head. "I could use some woman-flesh like you."

Reagan's cheeks burned. "Give it to me!" She grasped the basket, but he held it fast, refusing to give it up.

"Gingerbread. I want me a piece."

"Over my dead body, you bloody redskin," she hissed.

"Can talk dirty, too," Indian John quipped.

Reagan held her breath as he slipped his hand beneath the cloth. The moment he brought out a chunk of the fragrant cake, she snatched the basket from his hands. Slowly, she began to back out of the room.

"Where you goin', little lady?" He stalked her, stuffing the gingerbread into his mouth.

"If I were you, I'd mind my back," she said vehemently.

He tipped back his head in laughter.

At that moment Reagan turned and ran out into the hall, through the door, and down the front steps. She ran as fast as her legs could carry her, her basket clutched to her chest. Behind her she could hear her name being called, but she ran, still frightened.

"Reagan! Slow down! Wait for me!" Sterling called.

Recognizing Grayson's voice, she slowed to a walk. Her breasts rose and fell rapidly as she struggled to catch her breath.

"Are you all right?" He spun her around, holding her by the shoulders.

Reagan nodded. She trembled, more from anger

252

than from fear. "Son of a bitch," she whispered beneath her breath. "Bastard. He killed my father and there's nothing I can do about it. He *knows* there's nothing I can do!"

"I'm sorry, sweetheart. I didn't expect him to come in."

"He killed my father!"

"Shh, it's all right now," he soothed, wrapping his arm around her waist. "Let's get a drink. You'll feel better."

"I don't want a drink! I want to kill that man!"

"No you don't, darlin'." *I want to kill him for you,* Sterling thought. "People are beginning to stare. Let's go into the Blue Boar." He led her down the street.

"I don't care! I don't care!" she repeated. "I never wanted anyone dead before, but I want *him* dead and I want it to be painful."

When they reached the Blue Boar he took her to a table in the rear and ordered a bottle of claret. He offered his hands across the table. "Are you sure you're all right?"

She nodded. "How can your army allow men like that to go free?" she questioned bitterly. "How can you stand to be a part of this?"

Sterling crossed his arms over his chest, choosing his words carefully. "Not every loyal man is a murderer. I've killed no one."

She looked up at him. "Never?"

"No." *Liar! Liar!* images of the Hessian soldiers that fell at the Battle of Long Island cried out in his head.

"Oh, Grayson." She looked away, staring out into the busy public room. "I used to be proud that I was born when I was. I was proud that I was part of this revolution, but now . . ." Her voice faded into nothingness.

Sterling's heart wept for her as he took her cold hand and pressed it to his lips. "Have a sip, it will make you feel better."

He pushed the claret into her hand, and she accepted it. The sharp bite of the alcohol tasted good. It jolted her back to the reality of her world. She finished her claret and then stood. "I'm ready. Let's go."

"Home?" Sterling pitched a penny onto the table.

"Certainly not. I've already been seen with you by half of Philadelphia. We might as well go on to the barracks."

"You're sure?"

She pushed her basket onto her elbow and linked her arm through his. "I'm sure. I've business to attend to." She patted the underside of her basket as they stepped out onto the street.

Chapter Eighteen

Reagan walked down Spruce and onto Fourth Street, a merry skip in her step. The March breezes had turned warm with the coming of April, and for once all seemed to be going well in Reagan's life. At least as well as could be expected, considering her circumstances.

In the last few weeks, she and Grayson had shared a warmth she had never known could exist between a man and a woman. It wasn't just the passionate nights that brought a smile to her lips, but the days as well. When Grayson wasn't on duty, he spent most of his time with her. They played the spinet, they laughed and talked while she baked her gingerbread, they rolled in the hay in the barn and laughed like schoolchildren.

The longer Reagan knew Grayson, the odder he seemed to her. It was as if there were two men in his one lean, muscular body. The man in the uniform who reported to Major Burke seemed without purpose. He was late to guard duty and lax with his paperwork. He seemed to take nothing seriously but his biweekly card games at the Blue Boar and his never-ending supply of porter and claret.

Yet, when Grayson returned home to the privacy of the Llewellyn home on Spruce Street, he transformed. Nowadays he was taking to wearing civilian clothes as he sat for long hours in the parlor, reading aloud while Reagan mended. Perhaps it was for her that he had laid aside his red coat in the evenings; he knew how torn she felt inside. But Reagan wasn't sure. It was as if when he shed the coat, he shed the rogue, revealing beneath a man of respectability . . . the man she loved.

An old friend of the family passed Reagan on the street, bringing her out of her reverie. "Afternoon, Mistress Morgan." She bobbed her head, conscious of the new flat straw hat covered with cream silk and gauze Grayson had produced as a gift.

Mistress Morgan made ceremony of lifting her pointed chin in the air and hurrying past without so much as a word.

Reagan ignored her, going on her way. It was a strange situation she was in these days. With Grayson's involuntary aid she was managing to get more pamphlets out than she had when her father was living. She was doing more for the cause than she had ever hoped; her leaflets were reaching beyond the city as far as New York and Richmond. Some coin was even filtering back to aid in the cost of printing. But as her essays became more popular, her friends in the city began to shun her, not knowing it was she who produced the lively, intuitive political pamphlets. All her patriot neighbors saw was her being escorted by Captain Thayer. She began appearing at small informal parties given by the British officers. In her friends' eyes she had become another bloody Tory.

The thought stung Reagan, but she knew she was

behaving wisely. The more she appeared to have bent to the Crown's will, the safer she would be. Though Westley and the others in the network that helped her didn't like Grayson, they all agreed that she had created a brilliant cover. No one asked what she had had to do to gain the British officer's protection, and she didn't offer the information. She didn't reveal to them that she was in love with the man. As far as they knew, it was all part of the ploy.

"Afternoon, Mistress Llewellyn." A tall man in a fashionably feathered cocked hat stopped on the corner, waving his silver-tipped walking cane.

"Afternoon, Mr. Baxter." He was one of the Tory sympathizers who had brought his family to Philadelphia to take advantage of the occupation. He had broken into a large, airy house down by the wharf and made it his own. Last night she and Grayson had attended a reception there.

"And how are you? Lovely crowd last night, wasn't it?" He removed a gold toothpick from his coat and stabbed it between his teeth. "I was so pleased that Major Burke and Major Durgen were able to come. The food was quite exquisite, wasn't it?"

"Quite," Reagan responded, forcing a smile. The thought that this man was serving smoked duck stuffed with oysters and orange cake while Washington and his men lived on half-raw shad make her furious.

"Fabulous man, that Thayer boy. He'd make a perfect suitor for my dear little Constance." Baxter lifted a powdered eyebrow. The toothpick moved up and down as he spoke. "I take it you intend to hang on to him?"

"Captain Thayer and I have no formal agreement." She smiled sweetly, already creating a political cartoon in her head, featuring the effeminate Mr. Baxter.

"No, no, of course you don't." He smiled, a jealous twinkle in his eye.

"Well, I have to get to the market, but it was good seeing you. Give Mistress Baxter and dear little Constance my best." A giggle rose in Reagan's throat as he passed by, tipping his hat. Dear little Constance needed all of the help her father could give her in finding a husband. The poor girl had a face like a heifer and the brains of a bottle fly.

Reaching the busy market, Reagan made her way through the crowd. Fishmongers and dairy men called out their wares. Fat geese hung from a wooden frame above the poulterer's booth. An old woman with herbs chanted her plants' medicinal purposes, guaranteeing she could cure anything from women's ailments to gout. Just about anything could be purchased here at the market for a price—and the price was exorbitant.

A group of red-and-green-coated soldiers wandered through the market, laughing as they drained bottles of cheap ale bought at a booth down the street. A covey of young women stood near a weaver's stand giggling behind their paper fans as the soldiers passed singing a bawdy song.

Reagan rolled her eyes heavenward. Had she ever

been that young? She took in their pink cheeks and rosy mouths. These girls still dreamed of falling in love, being swept off their feet, and carried off to a wedding bed of chaste kisses and sweet wooing. Yes, Reagan decided she *had* been that young, a very long time ago—before the war. She had dreamed she would marry Joshua and they would fill her grandfather's home with children. She had known nothing of love and its bittersweet sorrows.

"Nothing ever turns out the way you expect it to," she murmured.

"What, girl?"

Reagan looked up, realizing she'd spoken out loud. A pinch-faced farmer stared at her. "You want the turnips or no?"

"How much?" she asked, flustered.

"Tuppence."

"For turnips?" She laughed, brushing past his stand. "I think not, sir."

Turning and walking back in the direction she'd come, Reagan purchased a small bag of dried beans, a slab of pork, and a handful of dried spices sealed in a paper packet. Her purchases made, she decided to start for home.

Just before she reached Fourth Street, she encountered a shopgirl, displaying a card of grosgrain ribbons. Tentatively, Reagan reached out to stroke one of forest green.

"Two tuppence," the shopgirl spoke up. "Came from It-taly. Purty, ain't they?"

Reagan chewed her bottom lip pensively. It was beautiful. It would look so pretty in her hair. And there was a red one for Elsa.

"A tuppence for them both and you've got a deal," she finally told the young girl.

"Sorry, ma'am, but my mistress she said no dickerin'. The price is the price. If you don't buy 'em, the next one will."

Impulsively, Reagan snatched the red ribbon off the card. "I'll just take this one then."

"If ye don't mind me sayin' so, ma'am, the green'd be better for that hair of yers."

"No." She fished the precious coin from her pocket. "It's a gift." A peace offering, Reagan thought. Elsa had been cool to her a good month now. She went about her business at home, spending long hours at church on Sundays. She had said nothing of the blacksmith, so Reagan assumed that though she was still angry, she saw the wisdom of her sister's decision.

Paying the shopgirl the precious coins, Reagan tucked the scarlet ribbon into her market basket. Elsa had always liked pretty things. Perhaps the gift would bring her around. Reagan missed her sister's sweet disposition. She missed the little Elsa she had known before the incident with the blacksmith.

"Hey, you, Tory wench!"

A voice from behind startled Reagan. She spun around.

"Yes, you!" A slender woman in a graying mobcap and heavy wool petticoats stood a few feet behind Reagan.

"Me?" Reagan didn't know what to say.

"What? You stupid? Me and the old man saw

you struttin' up and down the street with that man of yours."

"And we don't like it," a man shouted from behind the woman.

"You oughta be ashamed of yerself, your papa weren't hardly cold in the grave and you were offerin' your tail to the Brits!"

To Reagan's horror, a crowd was beginning to gather around her. "Leave me be! It's none of your business!"

"Our moppets live on bread and scraps of cheese and ye're wearin' pretty bonnets and marchin' up and down the street to them parties," another woman accused.

"You don't understand," Reagan protested. The crowd was pressing closer. Someone reached out and knocked her new hat off her head.

Reagan gave a cry of fright, backing up into the arms of a short, foul-smelling man. "Not so fast, we ain't done with you yet, redcoat whore!"

Reagan stumbled forward. *Won't anyone come to my aid?* she wondered wildly.

Hands reached out to tug at her sleeves and someone tried to yank her market basket from her arms. "Stop it. Stop it!" she demanded. People pushed and shoved her, shouting obscenities.

"Whore!" a high, shrill voice accused.

"You know what we do with Tory whores in other cities, don't you?"

"Yes! We tar and feather the wenches!"

A hand reached out, wrenching Reagan's new neck-handkerchief from her bodice.

261

With a frightened scream, she knocked a woman to the ground and pushed her way through the crowd. A sob rose in her throat as she darted down an alley, heading for Spruce Street and the safety of home. To her horror she could hear footsteps behind as the agitated crowd pursued her.

Running as fast as she could, her basket clutched in her arms, she turned another corner, weaving around a building hoping to lose them.

But the angry voices and the drumming of feet did not fade away. Reagan had heard of these crowds of disgruntled patriots attacking Tories, but she had been told by her network of friends that they were harmless. *This* was not harmless!

Reagan cut a sharp corner onto Spruce Street, but when she did, her quilted petticoat caught on the rusty hoop of a rain barrel. She cried out as she buckled to her knees. Footsteps pounded on the cobblestones behind her as she grasped her new petticoat and gave a yank, tearing it asunder. Freed, she stumbled to her feet, her eyes fixed on the front steps of her home.

"There she is!" someone cried from behind. "There's the little pettifogging trollop!"

Something round and hard smacked her in the back as she took the brick steps two at a time. Running into the front hall, she dropped her basket, slammed the door shut, and threw the iron bolt home.

Elsa came running down the hallway from the back of the house, her petticoats bunched in her hands. "Sister! What's wrong?"

Reagan gasped for breath, too angry for tears. She heard something hit the door with a thud and a splatter.

Voices came from the street as the crowd shouted and pelted their ammunition of rocks and rotten vegetables.

"Where's your soldier now, slut?"

"Come on out here, little lady! Show us what ye're showin' every redcoat in the city!"

Something else struck the door and a pane of glass shattered in the sitting parlor.

"What are they saying?" Elsa demanded. She ran to the window, but Reagan pulled her away from the crowd's view.

"Just let it be, Elsa. They'll go away."

Elsa stood for a moment, listening. "A Tory! They're calling my sister a Tory!"

"Elsa . . ."

Elsa gathered her skirts and raced up the grand staircase.

"Where are you going?" Reagan ran after her sister, afraid of what she might do.

"Nobody calls my sister a stinking Tory!"

"Elsa! Come back here!"

Reagan chased her up the steps and into Elsa's bedchamber at the front of the house. Reagan watched in horror as her sister threw open the window.

"No, Elsa! You mustn't!"

"Who you callin' a Tory?" Elsa demanded from the window.

The woman in the mobcap who had started it all

at the market looked up, squinting. "That red-headed dropdrawers, that's who!"

"That's my sister you're talkin' about, and I don't like it!" Elsa shouted, her hands perched on her hips. "Now you get out of here and you leave my sister alone!"

The others in the crowd began to laugh. Someone pelted a potato and it flew through the open window, landing on Elsa's bed.

"You stop throwin' that stuff right now!" Elsa shouted.

"You gonna make me?" the woman below screeched.

"Yeah!"

"Then come down here and try it, sister of a trollop!"

"Elsa, please," Reagan begged. "You'll only make it worse!"

Elsa turned around, her jaw set with determination. "Nobody calls my sister a dropdrawers and gets away with it!" She strode across the room and opened a small cabinet, extracting a chamber pot.

"Elsa!" Reagan breathed. "What in heaven's name are you doing?"

"Nobody calls my sister names!" Elsa pushed Reagan aside, sticking her head back out the window.

"I thought you was gonna come down here!" the woman called from below.

"Are you leavin' or not?"

"Hell no, we're not leavin'," the woman's husband shouted, coming to stand on the steps beside his foul-mouthed wife. "Things is just gettin' fun."

Reagan watched in stupefied horror as Elsa leaned out the window and turned the chamber pot upside down, spilling its contents. "Take that, slattern!"

Screams and bellows came from below as Elsa closed the window and marched across the room, returning the chamber pot to its proper place. A smug smile dominated her angelic face.

"Elsa!" was all Reagan could manage as she stared in disbelief at her little Elsa. She couldn't believe her dear sister could have done such a thing.

Closing the cabinet door, Elsa slapped her hands together with pride. "Won't be coming around here anymore, will they?"

Reagan stared stricken at her sister, and then burst into laughter.

Elsa looked at Reagan and began to giggle.

Reagan laughed louder, then harder, clutching her stomach as tears of merriment formed in her eyes. "S-slattern! Elsa! Where did you learn to use such language?"

Elsa giggled, running to the window. "They're gone," she managed.

Still laughing, Reagan plopped herself on the floor. She rolled on the braided rag rug, pounding the floor with her fists. "Did you see the look on her face?"

Elsa snickered, coming to sit on the floor beside Reagan. "You've torn your new petticoats!" She sniffed, breaking into another fit of giggles. "They're ruined!"

"My new lace neckerchief is gone, too." Reagan laughed harder.

A minute or two passed as the two sisters tried to gain control of themselves, but each time they looked at each other they burst into laughter again.

Finally Reagan sobered. She lay on her side, cradling her head on her arm. It had been years since she had lain on the floor with Elsa.

"Reagan! Elsa!" Sterling called from the hallway.

"In here," Reagan answered. "In Elsa's room."

Sterling stuck his head in the doorway. "What's happened? Did you know the front stoop is covered with rotten vegetables and filth?"

Reagan took one look at Elsa and the two burst into laughter.

Sterling looked from one to the other in total confusion. "What's gotten into you two?" He shook his head, backing out of the room to leave the women to their merriment.

Hours later Reagan and Sterling lay in the afterglow of lovemaking. Reagan teased the blond hair on his chest with her fingertips.

"Reagan."

"Mmm?" She leaned over, touching his nipple with the tip of her tongue.

"Reagan, do you know anything of these pamphlets?"

She had known this was coming. She was only surprised it had taken this long for Grayson to ask. "Pamphlets?" she responded innocently.

266

"Don't play coy with me." He nipped at the lobe of her ear and she laughed deep in her throat. "Those damned pamphlets are popping up everywhere again, and Major Burke is on my tail." He rolled onto his side and reached over her. From the table next to the bed he extracted one of Reagan's leaflets. He placed it between the full globes of her breasts. "Well?"

"Well, what?" She tossed it aside with disinterest. "I told you Papa wasn't your culprit," she said in a singsong voice.

"I know what you told me, but when they stopped after he died, I was so sure—" He cut himself off.

Reagan lifted her head to study his face. It was taut with concentration. "Major Burke is hellbent on catching this man and stringing him up by a noose."

"Why are you telling me?" She rolled on top of him, sitting up. She caressed his broad shoulders, reveling in the feel of his skin beneath her fingertips. "I told you I don't know anything about them, and even if I did—"

"You wouldn't tell me?"

"Are you going to tell me when the Army's moving? Where they're going?"

Wish to hell I knew, he mused. His eyes met hers. She had the most heavenly dark eyes. He could never tell what she was thinking. "Certainly not, Continental!" He raised up, taking her nipple between his lips. No matter how many times they made love, he could never get enough of her. She gave to him from her heart.

"Grayson," she breathed, pressing her lips into his sweet-smelling hair.

Sterling ached to hear her call him by his true name rather than his brother's. "Reagan," he cajoled.

She rolled into his arms, stroking his thigh. Their lips met, and she moaned softly.

"Reagan, this is serious business. You have to tell them it's gotten too dangerous." He *knew* she knew who the penman was. "Major Burke's got the half-breed on it. If he catches them, there'll never be a trial."

Reagan ran her fingertips over the corded muscles of his chest, down his flat stomach to the apex between his thighs. "No more talk," she murmured. "Not now."

Sterling sank back into the pillows as she stroked his burgeoning shaft. His thoughts scattered to the winds as she brought her mouth down to kiss the tender flesh of his manhood.

"Oh, Reagan," he cried, entwining his fingers in her rich auburn hair. "The things you do to a man . . ."

She teased and taunted him with her tongue and mouth, her own desire rising to match his. Her ability to please him the way he pleased her made her heart sing. Here between the sheets she felt no animosity between them. Without his scarlet coat she could love him as she wanted to be loved.

His resistance waning, Sterling rolled Reagan over onto the discarded pamphlet. She twisted in ecstasy as he lowered his body over hers and flesh met flesh.

"Now, Grayson," she cried. "Love me now."

"No, not yet." He kissed her damp neck, cupping her breast with his hand.

She caught his head, threading her fingers through his golden hair as she led his mouth to the throbbing nipple. "You torture me" she protested weakly.

"That's not torture," he teased huskily. "This is." He lowered his mouth to the triangle of bright red curls between her thighs, and she cried out in delight.

Reagan's breath came faster and faster. The room spun until she was delirious with want.

"Now, Grayson," she told him.

He slipped his hand beneath her buttocks and lifted her. She raised her hips in aid, parting her thighs in reception of his first thrust.

Reagan sank into the bed in utter relief, and then slowly began to rise and fall, meeting his rhythm as her drive for fulfillment overpowered all reason. The two rose and fell in unison until they reached the heavens, burst into shards of feathery light, and drifted back to the soft down of Sterling's feather tick.

"Oh, Reagan, why can't it be like this forever?" Sterling asked when he found his voice. He rested on his side, his arms draped over her middle, still unwilling to let her go.

"You ask too many questions," she whispered sleepily. "You want what cannot be. I love you, isn't that enough?"

He caressed her flushed cheek, pressing a kiss to her lips. "You're too sensible for a woman, my sweet. Your father was right in giving you such a masculine name."

"Shh." She brought his head to her breasts. "Sleep. I'll have to go back to my room soon."

"I don't know why you insist on leaving, why you won't let me sleep in your bed."

"I told you." She lifted her dark lashes. Her eyes still smoldered with the passion they'd spent. "Elsa mustn't know. *Besides,* she thought, *I have to be able to sneak downstairs. I have to be able to work on my essays while you sleep, my love.*

Sterling shook his head. He knew there was no sense in getting into this discussion about Elsa. Reagan was so stubborn, so hardheaded when it came to discussing her sister. "Wake me when you go." He kissed her again and then closed his eyes.

For a long time Reagan lay listening to his breathing, stroking his broad back and corded muscular shoulders. With her head clear again, her thoughts raced. Why had Grayson asked her about the pamphlets? Why had he told her she had to warn the penman? It just didn't make sense. A redcoat didn't warn the enemy. There were a lot of things about *Captain* Grayson Thayer that didn't make sense.

Chapter Nineteen

"You're going to get yourself into trouble spending so much time in the Blue Boar." Reagan stood in the front hall watching Sterling adjust his grenadier cap. "Soldiers shot and killed someone in there last week."

He ran his hands over his immaculate, pressed uniform coat. "We don't shoot our own—at least not on purpose."

"It's not safe for a man to take a pint of ale in this city these days without worrying about being murdered."

"He was a thief. He tried to slice up one of the barmaids with a butchering knife."

"You go right ahead and play your cards, but if you get shot, don't come home here asking me to tend your wounds and kiss your brow."

"So tender-hearted." Sterling brushed a kiss against her lips. She tasted of gingerbread.

Reagan swung open the front door and stepped back to let him pass. She hated it when he left the house, transforming into the enemy she knew she must despise. At home she could pretend he was just a man, but when he left the confines of Spruce Street he was once again a redcoat.

"Just don't say I didn't warn you."

Sterling turned on the front step to face her. She

was dressed in cotton petticoats with a spotted bodice and an apron. A mobcap was perched precariously on the back of her head, her mass of firelit curls thrust under it. Her cheeks were rosy from the warmth of the kitchen and her dark eyes sparkled.

These past few weeks she seemed so happy, and that made him happy. Her gingerbread sales had increased twofold in the last fortnight, and she was busy day and night keeping up with the orders. Not only were there a lot of soldiers purchasing the sweet cake, but also quite a few private citizens. Thanks to the anonymous benefactor, she always had a supply of the necessary ingredients. When she got low, the dry goods miraculously appeared on the front stoop.

"You going to be baking all afternoon?"

Reagan dimpled mischievously. She already had a new pamphlet going to press. There was a good two hours of work to be done in the secret room. "All afternoon."

"I love you." He kissed his finger and touched the tip of her nose.

"I told you, I don't want to hear your sweet talk. Lies, it's nothing but lies."

"Say it." He stood on the lower step looking up at her.

"You're causing a scene. Look, carriages are stopping out front," she lied. "You'll be getting beaned with a rotten turnip any minute."

"Say it," he cajoled.

"It's not true," she playing the now-familiar game.

"Say it anyway. Lie to me."

She chuckled. "All right, but it's only to make you leave. You're letting flies in the house."

He grasped her hand, white with flour, and began to kiss her knuckles one at a time. "Say it or I'll really embarrass you."

"I love you," she whispered, snatching her hand from his grasp.

"Louder."

He's so handsome she thought, *even in his scarlet coat.* "I love you," she repeated.

"That's better." Giving her a wink, Sterling turned on the cobblestone walk and headed for the Blue Boar.

Reagan watched him until he disappeared from sight and then went back into the house. In the kitchen she poured a batch of gingerbread mixture into a rectangular baking pan and set it on the hearth.

Elsa sat on the floor beside Nettie in her rocking chair. The old woman darned a wool stocking, her sightless eyes no hindrance, while Elsa rolled a ball of yarn across the hardwood floor for her kitten.

"You going downstairs to get apples now that the captain is gone?" Elsa asked Reagan.

Reagan had to smile. Elsa had decided that all of the time Reagan spent in the cellar, when Grayson was out of the house, she was getting apples for apple pie. Elsa didn't seem to notice that they rarely had apple pie, but since her sister didn't question it, Reagan saw no need to come up with a better alibi.

"Yes, I think I will. What are you going to do?"

Elsa stroked Mittens, and the cat arched its back purring audibly. "If you think it would be all right, I want to take some of your gingerbread to Reverend Marboro. Mistress Corby said he was feeling poorly."

"Oh, I don't know, Elsa. I don't like you on the street alone."

"I'll go just the way I go to church, through the Smythes' grape arbor, around Henderson's, and then through Joshua's garden. His mama told me it was fine as long as I didn't step on her baby boxwoods she's growing near the fountain."

"I don't know, Elsa." Reagan busied herself putting away the flour and sugar. "You're always gone so long when you run an errand for the reverend."

Elsa twisted the scarlet ribbon in her hair that Reagan had bought as the peace offering. "That's because the Smythes' gray cat has a new bunch of kittens. I always stop to visit them."

Reagan sighed. Since the incident at the market, she and Elsa had become friends again. There had been no more talk of the blacksmith nor had Elsa spoken of any notions of living on her own. She had *almost* returned to herself again, and for that, Reagan was thankful. With Grayson and the pamphlets to think about, she didn't have the time or energy for any other complications in her life right now.

Reagan watched Elsa bounce up and down on the tips of her toes anxiously. "Please, Sister. I'll be back before you come up out of the cellar."

Reagan knew Elsa couldn't tell time, and yet

lately she seemed to have developed an uncanny knack for knowing how long Reagan would be in the cellar, or how long she and Grayson would be gone on their route to deliver gingerbread and pamphlets. "Well, all right. But don't stay long. One cup of Mistress Corby's chamomile tea and then you come home. No talking to strangers, and stay off the street."

Elsa gave a squeal of delight. She ran to Reagan and pressed a kiss to her cheek before she dashed off down the hall.

"Grown into a young woman, that girl has," Nettie offered, rocking rhythmically.

Reagan watched her petite, dark-haired sister disappear around the corner. "That she has, and it scares me."

"That she might not need you?"

Reagan turned to the old woman. "Whatever do you mean? Elsa will always need me."

Nettie went on rocking, her wrinkled face breaking into a smile. "Things happen that ye'd never expect, that's what I like 'bout life."

"I'm going downstairs to work. Could you watch my gingerbread?"

"Just leave it to old Nettie. She can smell done gingerbread a mile away."

Reagan laughed, lighting a candle before she started down the steps. "My gingerbread will never be as good as yours."

"Oh, I reckon it will when you've been bakin' it seventy-odd years."

Nodding in agreement, Reagan went through the

275

cellar door and closed it behind her. Once she was in the secret room, she lit her oil lamps and went to work on setting her type for the next leaflet. With Westley's help, she figured they'd be printing by next week.

Some time later Reagan reached through the slit in her petticoats and into the pocket she wore tied around her waist and extricated Uriah's old silver pocket watch. An hour had passed. She wiped her damp brow with the corner of her apron. Without air circulation, it was stifling down here.

Wistfully, Reagan looked up at the trapdoor that led into the carriage house. The air that the door brought in when open was magnificently refreshing . . . but of course Papa had told her to always keep it fastened from the inside. She looked up at it again. What harm could it do if she just left it open for a few minutes?

Reagan scrambled up the ladder rungs, unlatched the door, and heaved it upward. The fresh, cool spring air hit her like a splash of well water. Sighing with pleasure, she brushed back her damp locks and then went back down the ladder and returned to her typesetting.

Reagan wasn't sure how much time had passed when she realized she was so thirsty that she'd have to go up for a drink of water. Blowing out the lamp for safety's sake, she took her candle and went out of the room, through the cellar, and up the ladder into the kitchen. Out in the sitting parlor she could hear Nettie humming as the old woman dusted the keys on the spinet. Reagan took a long sip from the ladle left in the water bucket near the door, and then poured herself a full tankard to take back downstairs.

"Elsa back?"

"Not yet," Nettie answered.

Reagan checked her father's pocketwatch again. She'd been in the cellar two hours. It was time Elsa was home. Nervously, Reagan went to the front window in the parlor. "You think I should go looking for her, Nettie?"

Nettie went on dusting, sounding each note as she dusted the keys. "Give her a little time. She didn't go right after you went downstairs."

Reagan sipped her tankard of water, tapping her foot. "I don't know. It would only take me a few minutes to walk over to the church." She pushed back the drapes to get a better look at the street.

"Holy Mary!" Reagan breathed.

Nettie lifted her dustrag, startled by the tone of Reagan's voice. "What is it, child?"

"Soldiers!" She stood frozen by the window, watching a Hessian officer come up the front steps. "And they've got that bastard half-breed with them!"

An immediate pounding sounded at the door.

"What do they want?" Reagan gripped her tankard, her knuckles turning white from the pressure.

"I don't know, but you'd best go answer that door before they break it in."

Reagan nodded, setting down her water. Her heart beat loudly in her chest as she crossed the short distance to the front hall. Taking a deep

277

breath, she swung the door open. "What do you want?"

"Ve are of sa Corps of Feldjager of Hesse-Cassel." The burly German pushed past her into the front hall, his muddy boots leaving a trail behind him. "Major Burke has sent us fur de search of sis home."

Stricken, Reagan stared at the pock-faced officer. "Search? What do you mean? You have no cause to search!" Stoic soldiers filed past her, fanning into different rooms.

"Yes, ve do haf cause." The leader shook a piece of foolscap in front of her nose. "Sis is cause. A varrant fur see search of any home see major sees fit to search."

Reagan's eyes narrowed to slits as the half-breed, Indian John, stepped into her front hall and closed the door behind him.

He swept off his battered felt cocked hat. His clothes were cleaner than the last time she had seen him, but his one good eye had not lost that evil glint that had frightened her so.

"You! What are you doing here? Get out!" To her dismay, she could hear the soldiers stomping through her house, scraping furniture across the polished floors and opening drawers. Upstairs, Nettie fussed with someone as he searched Grayson's room.

"It's like the greencoat told ya. We're here to search." He reached out to touch her and she jerked back.

"Search for what?"

"Suspicious evidence." His scarred face turned up in a lopsided grin. It seems that captain of yours is too busy futterin' to do his job. Somebody's writin' them papers again, and the major wants to know who."

Color diffused through Reagan's cheeks. "My father's dead. He can't very well be printing from the grave, can he?"

"You vant us to go downstairs?" a soldier shouted from down the hall.

The German officer glanced at Reagan. "Vhat is downstairs?"

Reagan's throat constricted so that she thought she'd not be able to speak. "N-nothing. Nothing really. Storage. It was where we kept our food before your army hauled it all off."

The German watched her facial expressions. "Take mine man downstairs."

"But—"

"Now!" he shouted, his face growing red.

Reagan glanced at the half-breed, then hurried down the hall. The young soldier who had been ordered to take into the cellar fell into step behind her.

"We'll have to take a light. It's dark down there." She chose a candle rather than a lantern, which would produce more light, and lit it. Lifting the latch on the cellar door, she started down the steep, rickety steps.

The soldier remained directly behind her.

"You see, nothing but junk." She lifted the candle to illuminate the piles of clutter. The cracked

279

butterchurn still lay on its side on the dirt floor; her mother's broken spindle stood covered with cobwebs.

"Vhere does dis lead?" The soldier pointed into the next small room.

"More storage. That's where we kept our food, but there's not much left."

"You vill take me."

Her hand trembling, Reagan lifted the candle. "Come on then, but don't blame me if you get bit by a rat!"

"R—rat? You haf rats here?" The soldier glanced uneasily at the floor.

Noting his fear, Reagan took the advantage. "Big rats. Can't keep a cat down here because the rats are bigger than they are," she explained as she took him into the next chamber.

"I sink I haf seen enuf. Dere is no-sing suspicious here."

"I told you, nothing but junk and a few rats." She stood with her back against the secret door.

The soldier turned and started for the stairs. "Bring sat candle here so I can see where I valk."

A triumphant smile on her face, Reagan led the young German back up into the kitchen.

"Sere is no-sing down sare but junk and rats," the soldier reported to his commanding officer.

The German gave a harrumph, crossing his arms over his chest. "I told sa major sat sis was a waste of time," he told Indian John. "Next time you want men, you get your own. I haf better sings to do than bother innocent vomen."

Indian John leaned against the doorframe of the kitchen, his eyes fastened to Reagan's face. "You're right, Hans. I don't see nothin'. But then that don't mean there ain't anything here, does it?"

Reagan looked away. *He knows something,* she thought numbly. *Someone's tipped off the half-breed.* She turned back to him, knowing that the guiltier she was, the more innocent she had to act. "Anything else you want to see? Because if not, I'd like to get a broom and mop and get to work. You and your men have made a mess of my house."

The German officer looked at Indian John. "I sink ve are done here. I vill send two men to see outbuildings and sen ve vill go."

"I think I'll go, too," Indian John offered.

Reagan went numb with fear, and for a moment her face reflected it before she had the good sense to hide her emotions. *I left the hatch open!* she thought with horror. She swallowed hard and looked up at the half-breed.

He hadn't missed a thing. He broke into a grin. "You want to show us outside or you wanna just stay here?"

"I . . . I'll go with you, of course." *All's lost,* she thought dizzily. *They're going to find the printing press, the pamphlets. I'm going to hang. Oh, Elsa, Grayson. They'll accuse you, too.*

"Vell, vhat do you vait for? Lead the vay," the German ordered.

Soldiers were already filing out of the house. Indian John lifted a hand in mockery, allowing her to go before him.

281

Reagan's feet felt like leaden weights as she led the men out through the lean-to and into the back garden.

"Vhat is sis?" The German officer waved a hand, telling the two green-coated soldiers to open the door.

"A shed for gardening tools. That's the privy there. A two-seater." She lifted her dark eyelashes angrily. She had too many things left to do in her life to die now. "You want to inspect the privy, too?"

Indian John scowled. "Watch your mouth, wench. I don't like a woman with a smart mouth."

"And sis?"

"The stable. One old sway-backed horse. You took my father's gelding just before Christmas." Reagan watched from outside as a soldier entered the small stable and came out a minute later shaking his head.

There was nothing left but the carriage house now.

Reagan walked right up to the door. She was no coward. She'd done all she could for her new country; no man could fault her. Setting her jaw, she flung open the door. A soldier marched by, followed by Indian John.

She held her breath, waiting. Seconds passed. She could hear them walking around. The wagon was rolled forward, then back.

In confusion, Reagan stuck her head in the door. To her startled relief, there was no evidence of the secret hatch. It was closed, a pile of old feedsacks

282

Reagan nearly laughed as she felt Sterling lowering her to the wool carpet. What decent woman made love to the enemy?

Reagan ran her fingers through Sterling's hair, returning his kisses with a fierce wanting. Suddenly everything bottled inside her was spilling forth. She pushed off his coat and clawed at the opening of his white shirt, tugging it over his head. She pressed kisses to his hard, bare chest as he tugged at the strings of her bodice.

Reagan moaned with delight as he released her breasts, catching one already-hard nipple with his teeth. She fumbled with the flat pewter buttons of his breeches. This was no maid's thought of a romantic interlude with her love. Reagan needed him, hard and deep within her.

"Grayson," she whispered, nipping at the flesh of his shoulders. "Grayson, love."

Sterling had never experienced such desperation, such utter abandon in a woman. He had never had a woman want him so badly, he had never wanted a woman so badly.

"Reagan." He lifted her petticoats, laying his face on her bare breasts as he released his manhood from its confines.

"Please, Grayson," she begged, pulling him down on her. She lifted her hips in reception of his first thrust, crying out and biting down on the soft flesh of her hand.

He pushed into her again and again, and they both rocked and bucked in wild fury. It was over in a minute as first Reagan, then Sterling cried out.

Sterling collapsed on Reagan, buried in her pile of petticoats. She squeezed her eyes shut.

"I'm so embarrassed," she said when she finally found her voice.

He rolled off her, still panting. He kissed her damp brow. "Why?" he breathed.

She covered her face with her hands. "No woman should behave like that." Her breath still came in short gasps.

"It's a man's dream to be wanted like that," he whispered softly.

"We're not animals."

He smiled, lifting up on an elbow as he pushed down her petticoats. "Sometimes we are." He kissed her lips, gently, lovingly. "Give me a little time and we'll do it the right way," he teased. "Slow. Painfully slow."

Reagan sat, scooting out from under him. A smile teased her love-bruised lips as she fumbled to tie up her bodice. "Please put your clothes on, Grayson."

He sat up, pulling his shirt over his head. "But you just ripped them off me."

Her flushed face grew redder as she backed out the door. "Upstairs, Captain. You can take it up with me in your chamber."

"That a promise?" he called after her.

She stuck her head around the doorway. "A promise."

thrown haphazardly over it.

Indian John gave one of the feedsacks a kick, and a billow of dust rose in the air. "Damn it to hell," he muttered, coming out of the carriage house. He pushed a dirty finger beneath Reagan's nose. "I don't know what you and that dandy captain got goin' here, but I'm gonna find out, and then ye're gonna pay. You might think this is some game, but let me tell ya, I'm gonna eat you alive."

Reagan stood ramrod straight. "Are you quite finished?"

The Hessian soldiers were already retreating through the garden, stepping on her herb seedlings, taking shortcuts through her newly cultivated vegetable beds.

The German officer waved a hand over his head. "Come," he told Indian John. "You vill report to see Major. I vill be at see Blue Boar if he vants me."

Indian John backed off. "This ain't the last you'll see of me," he warned. "I ain't a man who likes to be made a fool of. You just keep it up and I'll catch you. I'll bring you down and Thayer, too!"

A tremor of ominous fear slithered down Reagan's back as she watched the half-breed cut through the garden and leap over her front picket fence. If she hadn't made an enemy of Indian John before, she had now. She would have to cover her tracks very carefully if she was going to continue to print her essays.

"Reagan! Reagan," Nettie called. "Are you all right?" The old woman hurried dawn the path as

283

fast as her cane would lead her.

"I'm here, Nettie. I'm fine. No harm done." She decided not to tell Nettie about the trapdoor being closed by someone. She didn't want the old woman to worry any more than she already did. "They just poked around and went on their merry way."

"What do you think they wanted?"

Reagan led Nettie back up the path and into the kitchen. "I don't know," she answered. "Looking for something to steal, no doubt."

"That soldier didn't see anything suspicious down in the cellar?"

Reagan smiled. "Nope. Grandpapa's door in the wall is practically invisible."

Elsa came bursting in the back door behind them. "I saw the soldiers. What did they want?"

Reagan turned to her sister, thankful she was safe. "Elsa, you mustn't be gone so long. I'm not going to let you leave on your own if you're going to stay away for hours at a time."

"I'm sorry, Sister." Elsa tugged at the ribbons of her pale-blue calash bonnet. "I won't do it again. It was just such a pretty day and the kittens were so frisky. I just forgot to come home."

"Just as well she weren't here," Nettie offered.

Reagan sighed. "I suppose you're right." She looked at Nettie. "I'd best go downstairs and see to the apples. I'll be right up."

"I'll make supper." Eisa produced a cloth sack from behind her back. "I got a piece of beef."

"Beef? We can't afford beef. Where did you get it?"

Elsa bit down on her lower lip. "Don't remember."

Reagan eyed her sister suspiciously. "You don't remember?"

"Not exactly," she responded with childlike innocence. "Maybe I found it on the step."

"On the step?" Reagan echoed. "Like the flour, and the honey, and the ginger? I didn't see a sack on the front steps."

"Ummm . . . fell in the flowerbed." Elsa broke into a smile. "Yeah. It was in the flowerbed."

"Let me see. It could have been lying there since the last time stuff was left. It's probably not any good." Reagan took the bag and slid the piece of beef onto the table. To her surprise the excellent cut of beef was still cool.

"It's all right, isn't it?" Elsa grinned. "I can make stew if it's all right."

"Yes, it's all right." Reagan studied her sister's angelic face. "You haven't seen that blacksmith, have you?"

"You told me not to," Elsa responded, turning to her task.

With an exasperated sigh, Reagan lit a fresh candle and went down into the cellar. Her head was spinning with all that had taken place today. Who could possibly have closed the hatch door in the carriage house? It just didn't make sense. Westley was out of the city today.

Reagan straightened the secret room, taking care to lock the latch on the door from the inside.

Grayson. It came to her like a strike of bright

lightning.

She stopped in midstep, clasping her trembling hands. Grayson *wasn't* who he said he was! Her heart swelled and a smile turned up her rosy lips. It had to be Grayson who had closed the hatch! That's why he acted so differently among his fellow officers from the way he did with her. Months ago when she'd nearly gotten caught with the wagon of pamphlets, *he* had saved her as much as the mysterious man, only he hadn't known who he was saving. The song, the *Liberty Song*, that's why he knew it so well. That's why he had told her she must warn the penman. Grayson Thayer was a patriot spy!

Chapter Twenty

Thick, suffocating smoke filled the crude log prison cell as Grayson Thayer worked the iron bars of the window back and forth. Timbers crumbled above as the fire spread rapidly, fed by the dry bark left attached to the log walls. A bone-chilling war whoop sounded somewhere in the fort as one of the Mohawk Indians took his first kill.

Just before dawn the British soldiers and their Iroquois accomplices had attacked the fort that lay somewhere in the wilderness of New York. An occasional cannon ball thundered as Grayson worked faster. His eyes stung from the acrid smoke, and cinders floated through the air, burning his exposed limbs. If he didn't free this last bar soon, he would die before anyone found him.

Choking, he thrust his head out the window, sucking in great gulps of the cool morning air. The sun was just beginning to rise on the horizon. He could see the bursts of orange and gold over the battlement of the log fort. He brought his head back in, releasing the bar. It was too hot to touch anymore; blisters were rising on his palms.

"By the king's cod," Grayson muttered. "I can't believe I've survived all these months in this hellhole to be fried now!" He tore a strip from his tattered shirt and tied it around the bar to make a good hand-hold.

Spitting on his hands, he grasped the bar and threw the weight of his body against it. To his relief, the wood splintered and gave way and the bar came free.

"Saints in hell!" he chuckled, heaving himself up and out of the window. It was a tight squeeze but he managed to get himself through.

Falling onto the hard ground, Grayson picked himself up and dusted himself off, taking in the melee around him. The Iroquois had scaled the fort walls and were fighting in hand-to-hand combat with the patriot soldiers. Horses screamed and men moaned in the final throes of death. The fort's doors strained under the impact as the British rammed it from the outside. From the look of the fighting, the British, or rather the Indians, were winning by a long shot.

Grayson looked down at his clothing, brushing back a singed lock of golden-blond hair. "They're liable to take me for a Colonial," he murmured, hurrying along the edge of the wall. "Best I get myself out of here before they lift my scalp!"

Running in a crouched position, Grayson made it around the back of the log prison building and then began to scale the outer wall of the fort. Once he was on the other side, he knew he'd be safe. All he thought of as he clambered up the wall was Sterling and the look of shock that would be on his face when he found him. All of these months Grayson had spent in confinement he had imagined the revenge he would wreak. The thought was so sweet that he could taste it on the tip of his tongue.

Grayson's hands turned bloody as splinters embedded in his palms, but he kept climbing. He laughed as he reached the top and hurled himself over the wall, falling the twelve feet to the ground. Freedom! It burned in his lungs.

Sprinting through the dense forest, he spotted horses tied to trees. Seeing no one in sight, he untied the best of the lot and swung into the saddle. He sank his heels into the horse's sides and rode away—bound for Philadelphia.

"Grayson."

"Hmm?" Sterling turned his head and his voice was lost in the folds of Reagan's quilted blue petticoats.

She sat on the floor, mending a pair of his silk clock stockings while he lay stretched out, his head resting comfortably in her lap.

"Where did you go yesterday?"

"The Boar. I told you I had a card game with Warrington and some friends of his."

"You were there the whole time?"

"What is this with the interrogation?" He moved his head, finding a more comfortable position. "You're getting awfully nosy these days. I told you I've steered clear of the whorehouses." Reagan had been digging for information these last few weeks, and it concerned Sterling. Why was she suddenly so interested in the goings-on of the British Army? She wanted to know what was said at meetings, who said it, and what the higher ranked officers had replied. She was careful with her prodding. She caught him off guard with seemingly innocent questions, and he found himself answering truthfully before he realized what he was saying.

The more he thought about it, the more suspicious he became of her. She had changed since the night they'd made love the month following her father's death. She seemed spirited by some unknown force. There was a twinkle in her eyes that bore evidence of a secret she kept from him. She was fueled by some event or information he wasn't privy to and it frightened him. If Reagan was involved in some patriot plot, he wasn't certain he could save her if she got into trouble.

Reagan laid aside her sewing. She was tempted just to blurt out that she knew who he was, and to confess that she was the penman he sought. But she held her tongue. Prudence told her to wait just a little longer. There had to be reasons why he was keeping his true identity a secret. Still, the thought that they *weren't* enemies thrilled her. Suddenly there seemed to be possibilities in her life. The war couldn't last forever.

"You tell me you're not whoring, but there are still rumors at the market." She stroked his head absently. Firelight from the oil lamp on the table played against the highlights in his hair, turning it to spun gold beneath her fingertips.

"There are also rumors that the king himself has come to oversee General Clinton take command of the Army. Do you believe that, too, wench?"

She giggled. She'd heard the same rumor only last week and it *was* utterly ridiculous. She leaned and kissed his soft, clean hair. "I was just asking."

The tall case clock struck the hour and Sterling pushed up on his elbow. "Give us a kiss. I have to be going."

"Going? Going where?"

His blue eyes met hers. "I told you," he said seriously, "you ask too many questions. You're going to get us both into trouble."

She pressed her mouth to his, but he pushed her away. He was suddenly in no mood for play. He was afraid for her. "Reagan, this is no jest." He stood, putting his hand out to help her to her feet. "I don't know what you're keeping from me, but I'll find out."

"I don't know what you're talking about." She giggled. She was so happy. Grayson loved her and he wasn't a stinking redcoat.

He strode out of the room and down the hall to retrieve his cloak. She met him in the front hall.

"You've a meeting, I suppose? Dressed like that? Who are you seeing?"

Sterling looked down at his simple civilian garb. He was wearing a pair of tan breeches, a muslin shirt, and a long blue vest with pewter buttons. "You stay inside tonight, do you understand me? I hear you sneaking around at night. I hear doors closing. You think I don't realize that Westley is dodging in and out day and night?" He pointed a finger at her, and she bit down on it gently. He pulled back, flinging his cloak over his shoulders.

"If I didn't know better, I'd say you were dallying with him."

She laughed. Nothing Grayson could say would dampen her spirits tonight. He knew damned well he was the only man she had ever made love with. "Good night. Wake me when you come in and I'll warm your chilled bones," she told him, a saucy smile on her lips.

Sterling frowned, leaning to peck her on the cheek. "Good night."

"Godspeed," she called after him as he went into the night.

Elsa stood at the end of the brick walk leading to Ethan's house. Light from the streetlamp illuminated her hair. She clasped Ethan's hand, staring up at his beefy red face.

"I have to go, Ethan," she whispered. "Sister will be angry if she knows I went out the window and shimmied down the drainpipe."

Ethan chuckled low in his throat. When he had never thought he would know laughter again, Elsa had come into his life. They had met in church just before the occupation of the city. They had taken an immediate liking to each other, and Elsa had soon begun to appear at his doorstep offering to help with the children, mend a shirt, or bake a few loaves of bread. Their friendship had begun as a bud of hope in Ethan's life and had blossomed into love.

"I told you, Elsa, you shouldn't climb over that

292

roof." He caressed her tiny hand. "You'll break yer pretty neck and then where will the children and I be?"

Elsa smiled shyly. "I don't want to go home but I have to."

He pulled his pocketwatch from beneath his leather vest. "Let's see what time it is."

"No, let me." She took the watch from him, lifting it so that the light struck its face. She pursed her lips with great concentration. "It's . . . it's ten minutes after ten o'clock in the night!"

Ethan pulled her into his massive arms. "You did it again! I told you I could teach you!"

Elsa squealed with delight. "You told me I could do it! Sister wouldn't teach me because she said it would only upset me, but I *can* do it, can't I, Ethan?"

The blacksmith smoothed her cap of dark hair, closing his eyes as he rested his chin against her forehead. "Oh, my Elsa, what are we going to do? How will we ever be able to be together?"

She looked up at him. "I'm going to marry you, of course," she answered innocently.

"Marry me? You would marry a big, ugly blacksmith, Elsa?"

She laughed, wrapping her arms around his round middle, the watch still clutched in her hands. "I love you and we're going to get married."

"What about your sister?"

"She'll change her mind. She always does. She said I couldn't have a kitten because I'd forget to feed it, but then she got Westley to get me one for

293

Christmas, only she told Westley to tell me it was from him."

"Elsa, I'm not a cat."

"It's the same thing. She didn't think I could take care of my kitty, but I do. She doesn't want me to get married because she thinks I'll be sad if I can't be a good wife."

Ethan took her by the arms, looking into her blue eyes. "All the children and I want is your love. All I ask of you as my wife is to love me and my children."

She nodded her head, smiling. "I can do that, Ethan. But I can take care of your house, too. I'm gonna make a good wife for you."

"Marry me now, then. We'll just do it. We won't tell Reagan until it's too late for her to stop us."

Elsa shook her head. "That wouldn't be right. I have to get her permission. I would ask Papa, but he's dead."

"She'll never give you permission to marry me, buttercup. She's forbid you to see me."

"Sister's got a lot on her mind. These redcoats are gonna go soon and then things will be better. We just have to wait until she's thinkin' clear."

Ethan sighed. Elsa's outlook on life was so beautifully naive, so unscarred by the destruction and hate around her. "All right, we'll wait a little longer, but you just tell me and we'll get married."

"I'll still come to see you and the children. Reagan's so busy with things that she doesn't know what I do." Elsa reached out to stroke Ethan's wiry beard. "I have to go, Ethan, or she'll catch me."

294

He released her and leaned over the picket fence. Out of the darkness he came up with a sprig of yellow jasmine. He pressed it into her hand and then kissed her rosy lips ever so gently. Elsa laid her hands on his broad shoulders and the kiss deepened.

Sterling watched sheepishly from the shadows of the street. He hadn't wanted to intrude on such an intimate moment between Elsa and Ethan, yet he couldn't turn back. It was necessary that he see the blacksmith *tonight*. Turning discreetly away, a smile came to his lips. He had suspected that they had continued to see each other, yet neither had spoken of it to him. Reagan was sure going to be furious when she found out. He turned back to the lovers who were parting in farewell. If only Reagan could see them together like this, she could never deny her sister this happiness.

Elsa hurried past Sterling. "Evening, Captain," she said as she passed him. "You and Ethan have a good meet." She didn't appear to be surprised that he was hiding in the shadows of the street.

Sterling frowned, his forehead creasing. "God sakes, Ethan, you haven't said anything to Elsa, have you?" He walked through the blacksmith's front gate.

"You know I wouldn't do that. Elsa don't ask questions and I don't tell her anything." He watched her disappear into a neighbor's back garden. "But Elsa, she's got smarts where others don't. She always knows what's going on, even when we don't."

Sterling shook his head. "Sometimes I think the

little lady's got more upstairs than that pigheaded sister of hers."

The two men laughed, starting for the barn. "So tell me," Ethan said, touching Sterling's shoulder. "What have you got for me? Another message?"

"Yes. But it will have to be passed on by word of mouth. With that spy among us, I'm afraid to write anything. I think I've got some clues to his identity."

Ethan pushed open the barn door. "Then step right in, friend, and tell me what you've got. The word'll be to Captain Craig before dawn."

After Sterling was gone, Reagan had returned to the parlor. She had intended to finish her mending, but she'd been too restless. All she could think of was Grayson and his true identity. The cards just didn't fall into place. She was beginning to wonder if she had wanted it to be true so badly that she had warped the facts in her own mind to suit her needs. She knew full well that she was allowing her feelings to eat at her logic, and that was dangerous. Westley said she was on the edge and that she'd better take care. He'd even accused her of sympathizing with the British. Was her love for Grayson coloring her beliefs? The thought frightened her.

Staring out the window, Reagan watched people walk down Spruce Street. A carriage rattled by. Two greencoats carrying a third sang a German ditty in drunken voices as they passed by. Then Reagan spotted two redcoats. She leaned closer, pressing her nose to the thick glass. Was that Lieutenant Warrington? It was! Hadn't Grayson told her he'd been playing cards at the Blue Boar all afternoon and into the night with Warrington?

She ran down the hall and out the front door, not taking time to get a wrap. "Lieutenant Warrington!" she called.

The two men stopped and turned toward her. Reagan's face fell as she realized that it was Joshua standing beside the lieutenant.

"Reagan!" The lieutenant smiled with a familiarity that made her uncomfortable. He draped an arm over her shoulder. "Reagan dear, this is Lieutenant Joshua Litheson."

Reagan lifted her dark lashes. She had spurned Josh because he was a Tory, because he'd joined the king's troops, and now she was a redcoat's lover. She knew he knew. It seemed everyone did.

Joshua returned her gaze, and in his eyes she saw pain . . . anger. "Mistress Llewellyn and I already know each other, Charles." His voice was cool.

How could she explain it to him? How could she tell him why she had turned down his respectable offer of marriage and now slept with the British soldier who took quarters in her home? How could she tell him that she had never loved him, never could have come to love him? How could she tell Josh that she loved Grayson beyond reason no matter who he was?

"What can I do for you, sweetness?" Charles rubbed her shoulder briskly. "It's cool out here. We're headed for the Blue Boar. Want to come?"

297

Reagan was slow to answer. Joshua held her attention with those dark, accusing eyes. "Um, sure. The Blue Boar it is. We could use a bottle of port. You know how Grayson likes his port." Guiltily, she glanced over at Joshua.

"It's late for you to be on the street, Mistress Llewellyn," Joshua intoned.

"She's safe enough. The men on this street and the next know she's Thayer's. They'll keep their hands to themselves."

Reagan was beginning to think that going to the Blue Boar was a bad idea. She should have stayed at home and held onto the hope that Grayson was not a British officer instead of sticking her nose into it. But she was her father's daughter and lived by the truth, not by fantasies, however badly she needed them.

Charles and Reagan chatted as they walked to the tavern two streets over, while Joshua took up the rear in silence. Inside the tavern the three chose a table near the front. Charles said he liked to see who was coming and going. It wasn't until Reagan had sipped half of her claret that she got up the nerve to ask Charles about yesterday.

"Charles."

The officer lifted an eyebrow, watching a barmaid sashay by. He tugged at her sleeve as she passed and she squealed with laughter.

"Charles, you played cards with Grayson yesterday, didn't you?"

"Beat the breeches off me, he did. I'm surprised you're not decked out in a new gown and bonnet."

298

"He was here all afternoon?"

Charles took a drink of his rum. "That he was." He looked at her. "Lord, sweetheart. You don't think he'd be seeing another wench, not with a face like yours."

Reagan blushed, but her insides tumbled, her heart fell. Perhaps it *hadn't* been Grayson who'd closed the hatch on the secret room. Perhaps she'd been wrong, perhaps he was nothing but what he appeared to be—a redcoat.

Joshua tipped his cup, shadowing the anger on his face.

Reagan swallowed against her rising fear and pressed forward, taking Charles's lead. "He says he isn't, but I hear tales."

"Christ, Reagan. He got here about three and we left him by your house after midnight. You happy now?"

She leaned over the table, offering her prettiest smile. She had to know the truth even if the truth wasn't what she wanted to hear. "You wouldn't lie to me, would you, Charlie, not even for an old friend?"

"Hell no, because if he doesn't treat you right, I'm going to take you for my own!" He glanced up at Joshua sitting off to the side of the table. "Josh was here all night, weren't you, old boy?" He snickered. "Except of course that half an hour while you were upstairs with Molly Loosedrawers—"

"Your captain was here all night," Joshua interrupted.

Numb, Reagan stumbled to her feet. They were

telling the truth. She could see it in their eyes. "I . . . I have to get home."

"So soon?" Charles stood, but she was already heading for the door. "Hey, you forgot Grayson's port!"

Reagan ignored the lieutenant calling her name. She didn't see the man rise from his seat in the corner of the tavern and start for the door behind her. She had to get out of that tavern before she was suffocated by those soldiers' presence. Grayson was no patriot spy! Was she mad?

She stepped out onto the street and started for home. She felt light-headed . . . disoriented. She tried to remember all of the reasons she had thought Grayson might not be a Brit, but she couldn't think of one, not one. She had built this entire foolish hope on one silly unexplained incident. She had almost told Grayson she was the penman. Months ago she remembered him telling her he would turn her in for any wrongdoings. She didn't think he could possibly do such a thing — but she wasn't sure. The thought that she almost risked so many lives with her schoolgirl dreams was shattering. How had her love for Grayson made her so blind?

From nowhere came a hand. Reagan had heard no footsteps, but suddenly she was being pushed back against a brick wall. She opened her mouth to scream, but his hand clamped down so sharply on her lips that it knocked the wind out of her.

You! she thought wildly. It was the half-breed.

"Y'ere real smart for a wench, you know that?"

300

Indian John brought his face inches from hers. The scarred tissue of his flesh moved up and down as he spoke. "But you ain't as smart as I am"—he pulled her toward him and then slammed her against the wall—"bitch!"

Reagan squeezed her eyes shut, her head spinning from the force of hitting the wall.

" 'Tween followin' you and that captain of yers these days, I can't hardly get time for a drink and a screw."

Reagan lifted a knee and shoved it hard into his groin. He gave a groan, cursing foully, but didn't release his iron grip on her.

"I don't know what you two are up to, but I'm workin' on it. I told you before, I don't like being bested!"

Reagan trembled, her eyes fixed on the half-breed's leather eyepatch. When he moved quickly, pulling a knife from his belt, she stiffened but kept her gaze locked on his. She'd not give him the satisfaction of seeing her fear. Determinedly, she narrowed her eyes, clenching her jaw beneath his hand.

Indian John held her pinned against the wall with his knee while keeping his hand over her mouth. Slowly, he took the tip of his knife and pressed it to the rise of one of her breasts. Reagan flinched as the steel bit into her. Blood stained her pale skin.

"You know, I could kill you now and be done with it." He licked the blood from the tip of his knife. "But see, I look at this as kind of a challenge. I won't be outsmarted by a pair of tits." He slowly began to loosen his hold on her. "So you

301

go—"

The moment Reagan felt him let up on her, she dodged beneath his arm and took off down the empty street. Her heart pounded in her ears as she ran. Behind her she could hear the half-breed shouting.

"You go," he hollered after her. "But I'm gonna have yer ass if it's the last thing I do, woman!"

Chapter Twenty-one

Reagan pressed her cheek to the damp leather wall of the covered carriage. Grayson's deep tenor voice echoed in her ears as he called good night to a fellow officer. Rain fell rhythmically, drowning out the man's reply.

Sterling leaped into the carriage and closed the door with a resounding bump, sliding onto the narrow seat beside her. He gave a tap on the roof and the carriage lurched forward. His hand found hers in the folds of her brocaded gown and she turned to him, unable to resist a smile. "I thought you were never coming."

He kissed her bare shoulder and then covered it with the soft wool of her evening cloak. "I'm sorry. I know I told you we'd make it a short evening, but you know how that goes."

They'd attended a party given by the officers of the Grenadier Company, 64th Regiment of Foot, in honor of Major Burke's birthday. It had been a lavish event with imported delicacies, expensive French wines, and soft chamber music. It had also been a profitable evening—the flow of wine had loosened more than one tongue. Tonight Sterling had found himself only inches from discovery when General Clinton intended to move his troops out of Philadelphia and where they were bound.

Reagan sighed, holding tightly to Sterling's hand. She still couldn't believe she had almost given herself away to Grayson. She had wanted so badly to believe he was not who he appeared to be that she'd fabricated a story. She nearly laughed aloud. Imagine! Grayson a patriot spy!

Sterling lifted Reagan's hand to his lips, kissing her fingertips. The thought that he would soon be forced to leave her was nearly more than he could bear. Without her there seemed to be no reason to go on. But he had given his word to his father, to his comrades who'd died on the lonely dirt banks of the Long Island Sound. He had given his pledge; his personal life was of no consequence.

"I watched you tonight." Sterling's voice grew husky. The closer their inevitable separation became, the more obsessed he became. He couldn't get enough of Reagan and the sweet things she did to him.

"Oh?" She lifted her dark lashes. In the darkness, she *felt* rather than saw his smoldering gaze. Theirs was a love born on the wings of hopelessness. Each day, each hour, each moment that passed brought them closer to the end. They could sense it in each other's touch, they could taste it with each kiss.

"You're an intimidating woman, Reagan Llewellyn."

"Intimidating? How so?" Her eyes drifted shut. Enemy or not, she couldn't deny the feelings he aroused in her.

"There you stand in a circle of men," he kissed

304

her eyelids, "speaking your mind, while the women stand back tittering behind their fans."

"My father taught me to say what I think." She lifted her chin, allowing him to kiss the soft spot on her throat.

"Yes, but in front of the enemy?" He laughed deep in his throat. "Major Burke tells me you're a dangerous woman."

Her eyes flickered open. "Dangerous how?" She smoothed his clean-shaven cheek. With Captain Thayer as her escort she'd become dangerously bold. Her essays were being read far and wide. Her words were making an impact on the Colonies, fueling the revolution. The more obsessed Major Burke became with discovering the pamphlets, the more she produced and distributed.

"I don't know. He told me, and I quote, 'Tits and brains can be a dangerous combination'."

Their laughter filled the cramped carriage.

"Do I seem *dangerous* to you, Captain?"

He studied her face in the darkness. "Quite."

She brought his head down to the valley between her breasts. "Let's go home," she whispered, "and make love."

"Why wait?" Sterling dared, tugging on the strings of her brocaded bodice.

Reagan laughed. "Not in the major's carriage!"

"Why not?" With one swift motion, he lifted her into his lap, cradling her in his arms. He slid his warm hand beneath her bodice, cupping one full breast.

"Because," she breathed in his ear, "Major

Burke's expecting his carriage. He only let you take me home because it was raining."

Sterling set Reagan down on the leather bench and leaned to stick his head out the door. "Driver! A tour of the city!"

Reagan pulled Sterling back in beside her. God, but she'd miss his spontaneity when he was gone. "The major will have your head," she warned, unbuttoning his uniform coat. The thought of making love in the major's carriage sent a thrill down her spine.

"Witch!" He took her mouth with his, pressing her roughly against the the leather wall of the carriage. She could taste the desperation of their love on his lips. He slipped his hand beneath her skirts and she curled instinctively against him.

He brushed the velvety flesh of her thighs and she moaned softly in his ear. She tugged at the velvet ribbon that held back his hair, releasing it in a golden curtain about his face.

"Oh, Reagie, my sweet Reagie," he whispered, stroking her. She was soft and damp and pliant beneath his fingertips. He lowered himself to his knees and lifted her yards of starched petticoats.

Reagan gave a gasp, stiffening as his mouth touched that secret place, and then she sighed, melting against the wall of the carriage. Her hands found his head and she guided him, crying out with pleasure.

When she could take no more of his silken torture, she took him by the shoulders. "Sit," she heard herself tell him.

Sterling moved to the opposite bench seat, watching through half-closed lids as he saw Reagan lower herself to the floor. She stroked the confining pristine cloth of his breeches and then began to unlace him. A moan escaped his lips as she slipped her hands over his tumescent shaft.

"Reagan," he managed. "You ask too much of a man."

She smiled wickedly, raising up. With his hands resting on her hips, she allowed him to guide her. She straddled him and then sank down, accepting the evidence of his love deep within in her. The sound of the carriage wheels died away as she began to rock with the sway of the rolling vehicle.

Sterling and Reagan moved as one, their passion for each other hard and driving. The desperate hopelessness of their love fueled them as they strove for ultimate fulfillment while still sharing in the give and take of mutual pleasure. Higher and higher they climbed until with one great shudder of ultimate ecstasy, they fell back to earth. Tears of fulfillment rolled down Reagan's cheeks as she slumped against him, burying him in her mountains of petticoats.

"In the major's carriage," she whispered when she finally found her voice.

Sterling slid her off his lap and onto the bench beside him. His breath still came in short gasps. "I'm beginning to think you had this planned all along."

She laughed, fumbling with the ties of her bodice. "Let's go home," she whispered through the

307

darkness. "And do it again."

When the carriage pulled up at the Llewellyn house on Spruce Street, Sterling emerged, handing down Reagan. He flipped a coin to the major's driver. He and Reagan stood in the lamplight, watching the carriage roll down the street.

He stroked her hair, brushing an auburn lock behind her ear. Though she'd straightened her clothing as best she could, she was still gloriously disheveled. Bright pink spots burned on her pale cheeks, the afterglow of their lovemaking.

"Let's go in," she urged. "I'm tired." She was weary and wanted nothing more than to climb into bed with Grayson, but tonight she had a delivery to make with Westley. He was expecting her at three. She had to get her captain to bed and asleep so that she could sneak out.

Sterling raised her hand to his lips, kissing her knuckles. *Odd,* he thought, turning her hand in his so that the golden light of the oil lamp touched it. He'd never noticed those dark stains on Reagan's fingers before, but they seemed familiar. He kissed her fingers one at a time. What would stain her fingers black? What *was* that odd smell?

Reagan suddenly pulled her hand from his and hurried up the steps. "Are you coming to bed or aren't you?"

He looked up at her and smiled, feeling that familiar tightening in his groin. Her stained fingers forgotten, he took the steps two at a time. "I'll

308

race you," he dared.

Indian John crept noiselessly along the cold brick wall of the warehouse, the steel blade of his hunting knife clenched in his teeth. Somewhere in the distance a watchman called the time in a haunting, singsong voice, "Two o'clock and all is well."

A horse nickered softly and the half-breed slunk into the shadows.

An old man lifted the harness over his mare's head, smoothing her neck as he slipped it on. He soothed her with soft words of reassurance. " 'Nother hour and we'll be out of this blasted city, Bessie. We make this meet, and then you and me are out of here." The thought of his cozy brick home in Baltimore and the new great-grandson who awaited him there made him smile in the darkness.

"Got us a pass stamped and signed, I do, all legal-like," he told the nag. "We get them pamphlets and we're home free. I told Martha we could do it. I ain't too old to do something for them boys at Valley Forge."

The horse gave a snort and the old man looked up, squinting into the darkness. "Oh, hush, ain't nothin' out there, old girl," he murmured.

Indian John moved without warning, his blade flashing in the moonlight. Nothing more than a bubbled groan parted the old man's lips as he slumped to the ground, his life's blood pouring from his neck onto the rough cobblestones.

Indian John gave a sinister chuckle as he wiped his blade on his greasy blue durant breeches. He finished harnessing the swayback mare and then jumped into the wagon, heading toward Dock Street.

Sterling bolted upright in stark horror. His body was covered in a thin sheen of sweat, his muscles coiled to strike. He struggled to catch his breath as he fought the terror that consumed him. "Oh, God," he breathed. It had come to him in a instant. "Ink," he choked. "Ink!"

He threw back the bedsheets and leaped out of bed. The stains on Reagie's hands, he knew he'd seen them before. Uriah's hands had been stained. It was printer's ink! *Reagan Llewellyn was the penman Sterling sought!*

"Reagan! Reagan!" he shouted, racing down the dark hallway. He flung open her bedchamber, but she was gone."

Sterling ran back down the hallway to retrieve his breeches. A moment later, Elsa appeared at the door.

"Captain, what is it?" She rubbed her eyes sleepily.

"You have to tell where she's gone." Sterling grasped Elsa by the shoulders. "Where is she?"

"I . . . I don't know." Elsa stared up at him with round, frightened eyes. "Out. She goes out, but I'm not supposed to know."

Sterling thrust his balled fists into a shirt and scooped up his boots off the floor. "She's in danger, Elsa. I've got to find her."

"Danger? How do you know?" She held up the lamp so that its light reflected off his ashen face.

"I don't know." He thrust one foot into a boot and then the other. "I don't know how I know, I just do." He grabbed a cloak off a chair and reached into the drawer of his desk. He retrieved two primed flintlock pistols and tucked them into the waistband of his breeches. "Go get Nettie up. See if she knows where she's gone."

Moments later Sterling met Nettie and Elsa in the kitchen. The old woman stared at him with her sightless eyes. "In danger you say she is? How do I know you aren't up to no good, Captain? That *is* a red coat you sport." She shook her cane.

"I love her, Nettie."

"That I believe." She nodded, contemplating her choices. They were slim. "All right," she said finally. "I'm gonna tell you where she's gone, because I trust you, Captain, but I warn you, if anybody harms a hair on her head because of you, I'll kill you myself."

Sterling threw his cloak over his shoulders and reached for Uriah's flintlock rifle standing in the corner of the room. "Where, Nettie? Tell me where she's gone!"

"There he is." Reagan pointed down the alley. "Right on time, Westley. I told you he was reliable."

Westley looked both ways and then guided the wagon down the alley off the deserted dock street. "I don't like it, Reagan. You're gettin' too big for your petticoats. You feed on this danger. You're going to get us both killed."

Reagan gave a sigh, climbing over the seat as the wagon rolled to a stop. "I told you I'd come alone. It couldn't be helped. The shipment had to go out tonight if it was going to make it to Baltimore before week's end." She swung to the ground, a small crate of pamphlets cradled in her arms.

"Good even' to you," she called to the huddled driver of the other wagon. When the man didn't speak immediately, she stiffened, the hair rising on the back of her neck. She saw Westley slip his hand beneath his coat to grasp his pistol.

"I said, good even' to you," she repeated evenly.

"Nice night," the driver replied. "Peepers out early this year, ain't they?"

Reagan gave a visible sigh of relief. "Peepers," that was the password. She climbed into the back of the wagon and set down the crate of pamphlets. She heard Westley walk toward her, and she turned to take the second crate of pamphlets.

Out of the corner of her eye, Reagan saw the flash of the gun barrel as the man pulled it from beneath his cloak. "Westley!" she heard herself scream. "He's got a gun!"

The driver turned swiftly, smacking her in the side of the face with the handle of the flintlock.

She reeled backward under the brutal impact, falling to the bed of the wagon as the pistol sounded.

The acrid smell of blackpowder and burnt flesh assailed Reagan as she scrambled to get to her feet. Using the side of the wagon to push herself up, she peered over the side. On the ground lay Westley's motionless body. The cobblestones were littered with pamphlets.

Reagan swung around in stark horror to see the driver coming at her. She fell backward, crying out as he threw back the hood of his tattered cloak.

It was Indian John!

"You!" she raged, stumbling to her feet. "You son of a bitch, you killed him!"

Indian John's scarred face twisted into a crooked grin. "I told you I'd catch you, didn't I?" He waved a knife at her, its steel blade glimmering in the moonlight. "Wanted you and that pretty boy Thayer, but I guess I'll have to settle for you."

Reagan shook her head. "Why? Why me?" Her gaze fell to Westley's lifeless body. The half-breed had fired his pistol, but not reloaded. If she could just reach Westley! The primed pistol he still wore tucked beneath his coat was her only chance. "What have I done to you?"

"You made a fool of me in front of the major."

He took a step closer, and Reagan took a final step back. He stalked her like some crazed predator. She was trapped by the tailgate of the wagon. "You made a fool of yourself," she flung as she judged the distance she would have to leap to reach Westley.

"Hey there, girlie," Indian John dove for Reagan, grasping her hand as she tried to hurl herself out of the wagon. "Where you think you're goin'?" He twisted her arm behind her back so that she cried out with pain.

He laughed, loud and hard, his voice bouncing off the brick walls of the warehouses that loomed above them.

Reagan trembled violently as he brought his knife to her chin and cut the tie of her hood. Her wool cloak fell in a heap on the wagonbed. She thought to scream, but who would she scream for? Soldiers? With her pamphlets strewn across the cobblestones for evidence, she'd be swinging by a hangman's noose by dawn. No, her only chance was to kill Indian John herself. It was murder or be murdered.

Reagan lifted her lashes to stare defiantly into the half-breed's one good eye. "Whatever Major Burke's paying you, I'll pay you more."

He shook her so hard that her teeth rattled. "It ain't a question of coin, bitch! I told you, you made a fool outta me!"

She blinked to clear her head. Her senses were reeling. She could smell the scent of horseflesh and cheap whore's perfume on him. She could feel his long jagged fingernails burying into the soft flesh of her forearm. "So kill me."

He brought his face so close to hers that she squeezed her eyes shut. His breath reeked of whiskey and sour mutton. "I'm gettin' to it, but it seems a shame not to have a little fun first, don't

314

it?" He squinted, staring at the bodice of her gown. "I been meanin' to get a taste of you for some time now." He twisted Reagan's arm, bringing his face down the curves of her breasts that heaved above her laced bodice, and then he bit down on her tender flesh.

With a shriek, she brought her knee up sharply to his groin, but Indian John blocked her blow with his own knee. "That's it, girlie, that's how how I like it. Rough!"

The horse grew skittish from the movement in the wagonbed and the wagon rolled forward a foot or two.

"Whoa there," Indian John cried, trying to get his footing.

Realizing that she might be able to knock Indian John off balance if she could get the horse moving, Reagan began to struggle violently.

With a sweep of his hands, the half-breed lifted her into his arms and leaped to the ground. She pummeled his face with her fists, and he threw her against the cold brick of the warehouse wall.

A scream tore from her lips and suddenly there was the sound of hoofbeats. Startled, Indian John swung around. A cloaked rider came racing down the alley, full speed, a flintlock rifle raised in the air.

Indian John gave a foul curse as the rifle belched fire and smoke. Reagan heard the whiz of the musket ball as it flew over their heads and buried in a mortared wall.

The half-breed turned and ran in the opposite

direction and Reagan flung herself to the ground, fumbling for the flintlock in Westley's coat. Her fingers closed over the cold oak pistol grip as the rider dismounted.

Without hesitation she pulled back the hammer and swung to face her new assailant.

"Christ, Reagan, don't shoot me!" Sterling cried, throwing his hands up in the air.

For a moment her hand was frozen on the trigger. She *heard* Grayson's voice, she *saw* his golden hair falling from beneath the dark hood of his wool cloak, but nothing registered. All she saw was the enemy's face.

"Reagan!" Sterling shouted, kicking one of her pamphlets. "You've got to get out of here, this place is going to be crawling with redcoats in a minute!"

Slowly, she lowered the pistol.

Sterling grasped her by the shoulders, giving her a vicious shake. "Go, I tell you! I can't save you if they find you here."

"Indian John," she managed as she stumbled to her feet.

"I'll take care of him!" Sterling was already remounting. "Now you get the hell out of here!"

Reagan stared at Westley's body . . . at the pamphlets that littered the ground. She was caught. Grayson knew who she was. All was lost . . . if he turned her in.

The sound of hoofbeats and shouting soldiers suddenly echoed in the streets.

"Westley can't be helped, Reagan, you can only

save yourself!"

The harsh reality of Sterling's voice suddenly penetrated her stupor.

"Go! Damn it!" he shouted.

She looked up at Sterling's volatile face and was suddenly more frightened of him than she had been of Indian John. With a cry of anguish she turned and ran.

Chapter Twenty-two

Sterling sank his heels into Giipa's flanks and galloped down the alley and onto Dock Street. The thought of leaving Reagan behind to find her own way home was terrifying, but he had no choice. If Indian John reached Major Burke, he and Reagan would both lose their lives, along with a score of other patriots.

Sterling leaned forward in the saddle, reloading his rifle as he raced down the street. Only minutes had passed; the half-breed couldn't have gotten far. Passing a line of empty fish stalls, he caught sight of movement. Turning onto Walnut Street, headed for the docks, he spotted the half-breed.

Indian John scrambled over a pile of wooden crates left along the street, scattering them as he went. Sterling rode his brother's mount through the crates and flung himself out of the saddle, his rifle in hand, knocking Indian John over. The two men hit the ground, rolling over and over, making a horrendous noise as the wooden crates splintered beneath their weight. Indian John swiped Sterling's arm with his knife, slicing through his cloak and staining it crimson.

With a groan, Sterling threw himself backward out of the half-breed's reach, dropping his rifle in the process. The musket sounded off as it hit the street's surface. With a piercing scream Indian John hurled himself at Sterling. Sterling just had time to slip a pistol from the waistband of his breeches and pull back the trigger. In a split-second decision, he slammed the butt of the pistol against the Indian's skull instead of firing.

Indian John pitched forward, his knife flying from his hand. He landed, pinning Sterling's legs, and Sterling scrambled to get out from under him.

Sterling stood panting, the flintlock aimed at the half-breed's head as he waited for signs of movement. When he was certain Indian John was unconscious, he whipped a length of rope and a sash from his saddlebag and quickly bound and gagged him.

A few moments later Sterling was headed out of town toward Frankfort and his commanding officer's headquarters with Indian John tied across Giipa's back. Sterling's first instinct had been to kill the half-breed and feed him to the fishes in the harbor, but then he'd realized that Indian John might be of some good to the patriot cause. He knew the spy Murray, who was searching for Sterling. Sterling would take Indian John to Captain Craig and let him use him as he saw fit. With his duty done, Sterling could then make it back to the Llewellyn house and be certain Reagan was safe.

Reagan inked a block of letters and mechanically began to turn the roller to print her next page. Her ink-stained hand trembled as she turned the wooden bar, feeding blank sheets of paper into the press. It was midmorning and still Grayson hadn't returned. She had paced the kitchen floor until well after dawn, half expecting soldiers to appear at the door to take her away.

Grayson had once told her he would turn her in if he ever caught her doing something illegal. But that was a long time ago . . . before they had fallen in love. The question was, what was more important to him, his country and his king, or her? Reagan turned the handle of the press around and around, tears slipping down her flushed cheeks. She was so scared, so damned scared. What if Grayson hadn't caught Indian John? What if Indian John had made it to Major Burke and given a full report? What if Grayson was dead? A sob escaped her lips.

But where were the soldiers?

Grayson must have caught up with the half-breed. She had to believe it. But where was her Captain Thayer? He had told her to go home. He *knew* she was here. Why didn't he come?

Upstairs, Sterling burst through the back door of the kitchen. His cloak and breeches were splattered with mud. He held his flintlock rifle clutched tightly in his hands. "Where is she?" he bellowed, flinging his cloak to the floor.

Elsa's eyes widened. "C-Captain. Sister's safe, but we were afraid you were dead."

"Yea, well, I'm alive, no thanks to her."

"You didn't turn her in, Captain," Nettie said. "You kept your word."

He turned to the old housekeeper who sat rocking in her chair. "Where is she, damn it?" he boomed, his voice bouncing off the walls of the cozy kitchen.

Nettie paused and then pointed to the cellar door.

In four long strides Sterling was at the door. He threw it open and ran down the steps, taking them two at a time. "Reagan!" he shouted. "Reagan, goddamnit! Where are you?" He ran from chamber to chamber, through the darkness, until he reached the far side of the cellar.

The secret brick door was open. Light spilled through the dirt tunnel that led to the printing room.

Reagan's hand gripped the handle of the roller so tightly that her knuckles went white. Slowly she lifted her dark lashes to see Sterling standing in the doorway.

His golden hair fell about his shoulders in tangled disarray. His heavenly blue eyes, filled with rage, rested on her ashen face.

He turned his gaze to the room in disbelief, setting his rifle by the door. *Damn,* he thought as he took in the printing press, the crocks of ink and linseed oil, the crates of blank paper. *Right under my nose! How could I have been so stupid?*

Reagan took a step back in fright. She had never witnessed such anger, such volatility in her life. He looked so furious that, for a moment, she thought he might lift his flintlock rifle and shoot her.

He kicked a wooden crate of paper, and it went flying into the air. Paper sailed across the room.

"All of these months I've been busting my tail looking for the penman and it was you!"

Reagan cringed, tears running down her face "You don't understand. I was committed to this long before you came. It was Papa's way of helping. It was my way."

"All this time you've been risking your life, your sister's! Nettie's!" He shook a fist at her. *God, but he was relieved she had made it home safely.* "Do you know what you've done here? Westley's dead, Reagan! He's dead and no one can even claim the body! He'll never even get a decent burial!"

Reagan came from around the press, her shock beginning to wear off. How dare he! How dare he speak to her like this! Westley had been her friend! Didn't Grayson think she wept for him! Didn't he know her heart ached for what she couldn't help! But this was a revolution! There was no stopping it now!

"You don't understand!" Reagan shouted back at Sterling. "You don't know what it is to believe in something—to fight to the death for what you love! Captain in King George's Army or not, the only loyalties you've ever known were to a bottle of porter, a game of whist, and a good whore!"

Sterling grabbed a rack of type and threw it across the room hitting the far whitewashed wall. The tiny tin letters rained from the ceiling. "You never cared for me, you just found me convenient! How could you do this?" he cried with anguish. "You told me you loved me!" He grabbed a jar of linseed oil, but she snatched it out of his hands

322

before he could break it across the floor.

"Stop it!" she shouted. "Stop it now!"

"It was all a game to you from the beginning, wasn't it? The moment I stepped foot in this house, you set out to play it to your advantage! You sold yourself to keep your precious printing press turning!"

"No!" Reagan shook her head in horror. Her auburn hair had come loose from her wooden hairpins to fall in a thick mane down her back. "It wasn't like that!"

His face was suddenly wrought with the pain of betrayal. "You figured you'd keep me busy in your bed while you printed your damned pamphlets."

Reagan balled her fist and slammed him in the jaw so hard that she knocked him backward. "How dare you!" she shouted. "You think I planned all of this? You think I meant to fall in love with a card-cheating, womanizing, drunken redcoat?"

Sterling nursed his jaw, staring at Reagan in shock. She'd hit him! Goddamnit! she'd nearly knocked him over!

Gaining momentum, Reagan slammed her palms against his chest, pushing him backward. "You don't think it tore me up inside to know that I was betraying my father, my friends, my new country by sleeping with you . . . by loving you. But I couldn't help it, you worthless son of a bitch. I couldn't help it! I loved you!" Tears ran down her cheeks, falling to dampen the torn bodice of her gown. "I hate myself for it, but by God I love you!" she cried.

Reagan's breasts heaved breathlessly up and down

as she stared into Sterling's blue eyes. Suddenly her lower lip began to tremble and, against her iron will, she burst into tears again. Embarrassed, she turned and ran, up the ladder that led to the carriage house.

Sterling stood stunned for a moment, watching her shimmy up the ladder. It wasn't until she disappeared through the hatch that he started after her. "Reagan! Reagan!" he shouted. He climbed up the ladder, amazed to find himself in the carriage house.

Spotting Reagan running for the door, he took off after her. "Wait!" he cried. "Christ, will you wait, Reagan?"

She ran like a frightened animal, scrambling for the door. He caught her around the waist and she screamed, pounding him with her fists. "I hate you," she shouted. "I hate you for saying those things!"

Sterling ducked, trying to avoid her blows. She kicked and clawed at him until he lifted her off her feet and dropped her into a pile of straw on the floor and threw himself on top of her.

"Let me go!" she shouted, her struggle starting anew.

Sterling pinned her wrists to the ground above her head, amazed by her strength. "I'm sorry, Reagan," he whispered, burying his face in the crook of her neck. "I'm sorry. I didn't mean those things." He wanted so badly to tell her who he was, but he didn't dare. Not after tonight. After the hornet's nest they stirred up tonight he'd be lucky if he lived to get out of Philadelphia. He couldn't risk telling her, not now. "I was so damned scared for you."

Reagan ceased to struggle. She squeezed her eyes shut, fighting the tears that still ran down her cheeks. "I didn't mean for any of this to happen. I didn't mean to love you," she cried.

"Shh," he soothed, kissing her neck. "I know you didn't, sweetheart."

"I didn't want to love you. You're the enemy. Papa told me you were the enemy. I knew it. I just couldn't help it." She lifted her wet lashes. "No man has ever made me feel inside the way you make me feel."

Sterling drew her into his arms, his own eyes beginning to water. "I'm so sorry, sweetheart. I understand."

"No." She clung to him. "You don't understand what it's like to be torn in two like this. I love you, I love you more than life, but I was committed."

Commitment, Sterling closed his eyes, burying his face in her sweet, damp hair. If only she knew. Because of his commitment to the patriot cause, he couldn't give her, his beloved, any commitment, no promise of happiness, or even a future together. His days ahead were too uncertain.

"He didn't hurt you, did he," Sterling crooned, smoothing her hair against her cheek. "Tell me Indian John didn't hurt you."

"He didn't hurt me." She closed her eyes against the flood of memories . . . the sight of the half-breed's leering scarred face . . . the smell of his ran-

325

cid breath on her cheek. "You caught him, I guess. He's dead, isn't he?"

Sterling brushed his lips against her trembling ones. "He's dead, sweetheart," he lied. "He can never harm you again." At least that was the truth. Captain Craig had promised he'd be imprisoned somewhere far from Philadelphia, far from Reagan. But Sterling couldn't tell her that he'd taken him to his commanding officer . . . one of General Washington's own.

Reagan reached out to stroke Sterling's stubbled chin. "I hit you hard," she said quietly.

"That doesn't sound like an apology." He kissed her gently, bringing a hand up to caress the soft curve of her breast. How could he have accused her of scheming like that? How could he have accused her of not loving him? No one had ever looked at him with such love in her eyes.

"That's because it wasn't." She stirred under him, brushing her hips against his. This was madness! This man was the enemy! He held her life in his hands and all she could think of was touching him, being touched. "You deserved it," she went on, her voice growing husky. "You called me a whore."

"No," he whispered in her ear. "Never that."

"Are you going to turn me in?" she asked, finally gaining the courage.

"For hitting me?" he teased, tickling the lobe of her ear with his tongue. "No, I don't think so."

She grasped a handful of his blond hair. "Don't make this any harder for me. For the pamphlets. Are you going to tell Major Burke that I'm the pen-

326

man."

He slipped his hand beneath her petticoats. "No."

"Why not?"

"What kind of animal do you think I am?" He left a trail of kisses down her throat to the swell of her breasts. He kissed the reddened spot where Indian John's teeth had marred her skin. "He did this to you," Sterling asked angrily.

"I'm all right." She held his face between her palms. "Why aren't you going to turn me in?" she whispered.

"Hush your mouth and love me," he crooned. "I came too close to losing you last night. Love me, Reagie."

Later, when their passion was spent, the two sat on the floor of the carriage house, one across from the other, regarding each other speculatively. Their relationship had taken a new turn, one that would take some time to adjust to. "I've got to get to the Blue Boar," he told her, plucking a piece of straw from her hair. "That'll be the best place to hear what's happened to Westley's body. If anyone knows what happened after you got away last night, it'll be somebody at the Blue Boar."

She shook her mane of bright, tangled curls, running her fingers through it. "I'll go with you. It'll only take me a minute to get ready."

"No." He shook his head. "Absolutely not."

She narrowed her dark eyes. "Don't be a fool. Everyone is used to seeing us together. Nothing will look out of place. I have to hear for myself."

"Reagie," he clasped her hand, "this is no child's

game. We're talking about the hangman's noose here—you and I both if the major finds out I aided your escape."

She stood, brushing the straw from her striped petticoats. "I can be ready in ten minutes. We'll have dinner so that we can sit and listen a while."

He laughed, getting up. "You're the most pig-headed woman I've ever met. I said you're staying here."

"And I said I'm going, with you—or alone. It's up to you. I just thought we'd be safer going to-gether. That way nothing will appear out of the or-dinary."

"It's too dangerous."

"I can't just sit here and wait for the red-and greencoats to come knocking on my door." She went to the hatch in the floor of the carriage house and went down the ladder. A moment later her head popped out again. "Are you coming?"

Sterling gave an exasperated groan and followed her back into the printing-press room. He closed the door overhead and locked it soundly. She had already taken the lamp and was hurrying down the narrow passageway that led into the cellar. He grabbed his rifle and ran to catch up. He stepped into the cellar and watched her close the door be-hind him. "Amazing," he murmured. He ran his fingers over the cracks in the mortared wall. "If I didn't know what I was looking for, I'd never have found it."

"Let's go, Grayson." Reagan lifted the lamp and stepped back to let him lead the way.

328

"As soon as it looks safe, we'll get down here and start dismantling the press and carry it off."

Reagan gave a snigger, falling into step behind him. "Dismantle it, hell," she murmured under her breath. As long as he wasn't going to turn her in, she was going to keep printing her pamphlets!

An hour later, Sterling entered the Blue Boar tavern with Reagan on his arm. She'd changed into her green lutestring gown and added a honey-colored caraco jacket. Sterling had bathed and allowed her to tend the wound on his arm. He was dressed immaculately as always, sporting his scarlet uniform coat, white breeches and vest, and impressive grenadier cap.

Sterling led her to a far table and she sat on the far bench, her back to the wall so that she could see who came and went. He slid in beside her, and made an event of placing his cap on the trestle table.

A moment later a barmaid came to the table. She looked at Sterling, seeming to recognize him. "What can I get fer ye, Captain?" She ignored Reagan, grinning shyly.

Intent on watching the public room, Sterling didn't even look up. "Just a bottle of port for now."

The girl gave a nod, but remained at the tableside, squirming. "I . . . I wanted to thank ye fer the coin, sir."

Sterling frowned, growing annoyed. The girl was blocking his view of the steps that led to the second floor. "What coin are you talking about?"

She blushed. "You know, from the other night. I'm Sally Morris. It weren't here." She leaned forward, baring her pockmarked breasts as she lowered her voice. "I jest work at Miss Kate's on Saturday nights. I got a man an' three babes to feed. You was so nice to pay even though I couldn't do exactly what you wanted."

Reagan turned to watch Sterling's reaction, listening intently for his reply.

"I don't have the foggiest idea what you speak of, girl. You obviously have me confused with another fellow. Now could you get the port?"

The barmaid chewed her lip in indecision, then looking up at Reagan, she bobbed a curtsy and scurried off.

Reagan laid her hand on Sterling's arm. "What was that all about?" She kept her voice even.

He glanced at her. "I said I don't know. She obviously has me confused with someone else. There are a few of us here in the city, you know."

Reagan arched an eyebrow. "You swore you'd not whore on me, Grayson Thayer."

He took her hand, rubbing it and then kissing her palm. "And I haven't. Look at these eyes. Are these the eyes of a lying man?"

Reagan studied his face. If he was lying, he was damned good at it. She pulled her hand from his. "All right, Captain. I'll take your word on it, but I swear, I catch you, and I'll cut off that bit of anatomy of yours that we're both rather fond of."

Sterling threw back his head in laughter. The funniest thing was that he believed her! He draped an arm over her shoulder. What would his days be like when she was gone? He couldn't bring himself to think about it.

The barmaid appeared again with a bottle of port and two glasses. Setting them on the table, she glanced cautiously about the room and then slid a piece of foolscap across the table. "For you, Captain?"

Sterling took the paper, turning it in his hand. It was sealed with an unfamiliar family coat of arms pressed into the wax. "From whom?"

The girl shrugged. "Don't know, sir. The barkeep tol' me to deliver it."

Sterling pressed a half penny into the maid's hand and she curtsied, took a step back, and then curtsied again before she turned away. The moment she was gone, he broke the seal on the message. He read it quickly and then tucked it into his coat.

Reagan's stomach knotted. "What? What does it say? Who is it from?"

Sterling shook his head, his face grave. "I don't know. All it says is for me to lay low for the next few days." He didn't tell her that it also said that Murray was close. Murray the British spy.

"And you don't know who it's from?"

"No. It's signed with a 'C.' Nothing more."

Reagan reached for the open bottle of port and poured him a healthy dose. "Drink up and then we'll go. Everything's quiet here. I've not heard a word about Westley's body or the pamphlets. If there's anything to hear it will be in Major Burke's

331

office tomorrow morning." Her eyes sought his. "I think we're safe enough. The axe would have fallen by now."

Sterling lifted his glass to his lips, taking her hand in his. "I hope so, sweet," he whispered. "I sure as hell hope so."

Chapter Twenty-three

"Thayer!" Major Burke bellowed from inside his office. "Get in here, boy!"

Sterling bounced up off the settle in the parlor and hurried through the door. He saluted smartly. "Yes, sir. I'm here, sir."

Major Burke pushed back from his oak desk. "Shut the door," he ordered, returning the salute.

"Yes, sir." Sterling closed it, returning his gaze to the major. If possible, he seemed thinner than he had been a few months ago when Sterling had first come to Philadelphia. His oversize powdered wig now dominated his painfully narrow face and sunken cheeks. Duty this winter in the confines of the city had obviously taken a toll on his health. "What can I do for you, sir? Those reports are almost done."

The major slapped two sheets of paper on his desk. "Bills, Thayer! God damn it to hell, can't you keep out of trouble?"

"Bills, sir?"

"It seems there's an establishment by the name of Miss Kate's over off Vine and Fourth. According to the lady, and I use that term lightly, who owns the place, you got into a brawl with a sailor over some little 'poxbox' and broke," he began to read off the list, "two twelve-paned windows, a caned chair, a

Venetian beveled mirror, and two glass oil lamps, and you apparently stained a Turkey carpet with blood before being tossed out on your ear." He tossed the slip of paper, letting it sail through the air.

Sterling caught it in midair.

"And this one," the major went on, "is from some whorehouse down by the docks. "Mattilda's, I believe. Only one window, which I must say is commendable, but two tables, a bedstead, and a vase from the Orient. Before that brawl, you and your companions apparently consumed five roasted ducks, four pails of oysters, three pigeon pies, and twelve bottles of port!" He looked up. "All of which must be paid for!"

Sterling caught the second paper, glancing over it in disbelief. "Major," Sterling shook the second slip of foolscap. "I stand falsely accused. Look, sir. This is dated the night of your birthday party. It says ten o'clock. If recall correctly, sir, I was rolling dice at your birthday fete."

The major frowned, crossing his arms over his pressed coat. "That you were, weren't you? So what do you make of it?"

"I . . . I don't know, sir. I just know it wasn't me."

"Some ambitious tavernkeeper trying to cash in on your reputation, I suppose. Which reminds me. Where the blast did you take my carriage? I stood in the rain for fifteen minutes waiting to be taken home!"

"I just returned the lady to her residence, sir, as

you instructed."

Major Burke sighed, running a hand over his wig. White hair powder rose in clouds above his head. "All right, Thayer, onto the next matter." He snatched a folded sheet of paper off his desk and thrust it in Sterling's hand. Sterling immediately recognized it as one of Reagan's political pamphlets. "We had a mess on Dock Street two nights ago. Two wagons found, a dead body, and two crates of this confounded triteness. We found the body of an old man a few blocks away. No identification on them of course."

Sterling lifted a blond eyebrow.

"I thought you were on this, boy! You told me that Llewellyn man was printing this trumpery. What's he done, Thayer, come back from the dead?"

"No witnesses, sir?"

"I had men question up and down the street, but it's mostly warehouses. No one saw or heard a thing." He slammed his fist on the desk. "No one ever hears or sees anything!"

Sterling treaded carefully. "The horses and wagons couldn't be traced?"

"I haven't got that far. I was going to put the half-breed on it, but so far he hasn't shown up. You think you can take a little time from your busy social calendar to look into it?"

Sterling never flinched at the mention of Indian John. "Yes, sir. I can take care of that. I'll check all of the livery stables first."

"You do that and then report back to me. I'll

free you from your other duties if you swear to me you'll get on this right away. I want to see you by the week's end with some solid information. The general's breathing down my back on this, Thayer. I want the penman found before we move out of the city!"

Sterling rested his hand on the doorframe. "So you think we'll be moving out soon?"

Major Burke lifted a goose quill pen from an inkwell and began to scrawl across a document. "General Clinton has already got ships on the way," he said absently. "We've got to do something with the citizens who want out of the city before we turn it back over to the rebels."

Sterling nodded. "I'll see you by the week's end, sir." He saluted and then strode out of the office heaving a heavy sigh of relief. *A miracle,* he mused. *He and Reagan were safe . . . at least for the time being.*

Reagan hurried down the street, her arm wrapped around Sterling's. On the other arm swung a basket of fragrant gingerbread. A mockingbird soared overhead, screeching as it dove for a scrap of apple on the street. "So turn me in," Reagan said calmly. She nodded to two green-coated Hessian officers passing by.

"Reagan, you're not being reasonable." Sterling tried to keep his voice low. "You can't expect me to be able to protect you."

"I don't want you to protect me. All I ask is that

336

you keep quiet and pretend you know nothing more than you knew a week ago."

"You make it sound so simple." They stopped for a passing carriage and then crossed the street. "But it's not. Major Burke wants to know who the penman is. He wants answers and I've got to come up with some."

She bunched her quilted yellow petticoats to step over an open drain that ran sewage into the street. "Stall. Give him a few nibbles. Identify Westley if you have to. He had no family. He had no place of residence. Major Burke won't be able to find any evidence against anyone else."

"He must have lived *somewhere*."

"Lived somewhere, of course," she admitted. She glanced up at him from beneath her straw bonnet, secured under her chin with a yellow grosgrain bow. "But he was never in one place very long. He liked to keep the authorities guessing."

"Just what did Westley do for you Continentals?"

She tightened her grip on Sterling's arm thinking that she would never get used to the sight of the scarlet coat he wore. "He dabbled in this and that."

"You've done it again."

"Done what?"

She smiled at him, but he resisted the urge to smile back. This was all a game to her! The danger didn't seem to daunt Reagan. God, but he admired her. Few men would have had the guts to do what she'd been doing on her own these past months. If possible, he loved her even more for it. But it had to stop. The pamphlets weren't worth losing her life over. He tightened his grip on her arm. "Changed the subject of course. You've been doing it all week."

"No, we'd finished with the subject of my leaflets. I told you, I have to keep printing, just like you have to continue reporting to Major Burke."

"It's not the same thing and you know it." Sterling forced a smile as two Tory women passing them on the cobblestone walk admired his good looks.

"It's precisely the same. Nothing has changed between us, Grayson. I love you, you love me, but we're on opposite sides here, and unless you're willing to shed your red coat for a blue one, there's really no need for us to go on about this."

Sterling's voice caught in his throat. Now that he knew that Reagan was the courageous penman, he felt as if he was betraying her by not revealing his true identity. They were on the same side for God's sake! But he'd given his word to Captain Craig, and the word of a commanding officer was the word of God in General Washington's Army. It had to be that way. It was the only way they could possibly beat the greatest military power in the world.

"Reagan . . ." Sterling opened his mouth to speak and then closed it again. He was so frightened for her. If she was caught printing and distributing the pamphlets, he didn't have a chance of saving her. His position was too precarious right now. And by the time he could get help from Captain Craig, it would be too late.

She smiled at him sweetly. "Here we are." She stopped at a brick stoop. "Mistress Claggett's. I'll only be a minute." She skipped up the steps and knocked.

A few minutes later Reagan and Sterling were headed back up the street, her empty basket swinging on her arm. She had delivered a batch of gingerbread to Mistress Claggett, as well as a stack of her latest pamphlets.

She had resigned herself to the fact that there was no turning back now. She had a responsibility to the cause to continue printing her essays now that they were making an impact. Soon the British Army would be gone and much of the pressure would be lifted. Reagan wiped at the moisture that gathered in the corner of her eye. Of course, then Grayson would be gone, too.

Grayson Thayer gave a cackle as he snatched the nearest wench off the table. The dark-haired woman was barefoot, a striped tick petticoat tied around her waist. Her breasts hung bare, her dark nipples the size of silver coins.

"Criminy, Capt'n, go easy on a girl!" She lifted a leather jack of ale off the table and took a great gulp.

Grayson spun her around in his arms, taking one nipple in his mouth. She laughed, spewing ale over the both of them. "You got a appetite that just won't quit, don't ya?"

John, a privateer with a gold earring in his ear, joined in their laughter as he caught a barmaid by the hem of her skirts. She was the only woman in the private room at Miss Kate's that was fully clothed.

"Keep yer hands off," Sally Morris cried, slapping the man hard on the hand with a wooden trecher. "I'm just servin' up the meal, not the dessert!"

Grayson spun around, the dark-haired woman still in his arms. "I told you about that, John." He laughed, his golden-blond hair brushing his shoulders. "Miss Sally here's been promoted, haven't you, girl?"

The barmaid blushed, turning away from a blond doxy still dancing on the table to the sound of music from below. "Thanks ta you, sir."

"Now why don't you go down and see about my palm toddie. Old Kate said she got the arrack in today." Grayson dropped the whore he held into John's arms, and the girl gave a squeal of delight.

"Yes, sir." Sally bobbed a curtsy and turned to go.

"Oh . . . and, Sally. Could you check and see about a package for me. I'm expecting my uniform."

"Yes, Capt'n Thayer."

Grayson smiled, closing the door behind her. He had to report soon, but first he was going to have a little fun with that dear brother of his. Sterling Thayer was going to pay for the months Grayson spent in that hellhole of a fort in New York!

Reagan lifted the light flannel of her nightgown and knelt on Sterling's feather tick. "Grayson." She shook him roughly. "Grayson, wake up!"

Sterling bolted upright, his hand flying instinctively to the primed pistol resting on the table beside his bed.

Reagan pulled back.

Since he'd discovered she was the penman, he barely slept, and when he did, it was a light, fitful sleep. "What? What is it?" The bedchamber was pitch-black except for the malodorous beef-tallow candle she'd left on the desk.

"Where is it?"

He pulled the goosedown pillow over his face. "Where's what?" came his muffled voice. It was low and husky from lack of sleep.

"You know very well what. The ink. Not only is my last jug gone, but I can't find an inkwell in the house," she shouted angrily.

Sterling groaned, rolling onto his stomach, the pillow still over his head. "Can we talk about this tomorrow. It must be three in the morning." He'd stayed up until two writing a message to Captain Craig. It was now folded and tucked safely inside a flat pewter coat button.

"No, we can't talk about this tomorrow. Do you know how hard it is to get ink into the city? You can't sabotage me like this, Grayson!" She yanked the pillow off his head and hurled it across the room.

He rolled back over, opening one eye and then the other. "I can and I will. If you haven't got enough sense to stop this nonsense, then I have to."

"Why? Why are you doing this?" She leaned over

him, her mass of auburn hair falling on his bare chest. "You don't care about Mother England, or the Army, or any of this flummery!"

Anger seized Sterling and he sat upright, snatching her wrist so that he could draw her closer. She struggled against him, her eyes bright with fire and brimstone. "I care about you, damn it!"

She scrambled off the bed. That wasn't the kind of answer she wanted — it wasn't one she could deal with. She had to think rationally, and there was nothing rational about their love. "I'm not going to let you do this to me." She shook her head, backing out of the room. "Do you hear me, Grayson Thayer? I won't let my father die in vain."

Sterling ran a hand through his shoulder-length hair "Reagie, your father never expected you to carry on after him. It's not what he would have wanted."

"I know, a woman's safety and all of that," she answered sarcastically.

He clenched his fist. "It's not worth dying for."

She took the candle and went out the door. "To me it is," he heard her say as she left him alone in the dark room.

Sometime later in the night, Sterling felt Reagan shaking him again.

"Reagie, no more tonight," he told her sleepily irritable.

She clasped his bare arm. There was a tremble in her barely audible voice. "Grayson you've got to

342

help me. She's gone."

"Who? Who's gone?" He rubbed his eyes, looking up at her stricken face.

"Elsa. She went to bed early with a headache. I couldn't sleep so I went to her room." She gave a nervous laugh. "When we were little girls and I couldn't sleep, I always got into bed with Elsa. But she wasn't there, Grayson."

"She's not anywhere in the house?"

She shook her head. "Her bed was never slept in."

Sterling heaved a sigh, swinging his legs over the side of the bed. It seemed he wasn't meant to get any sleep tonight. "Reagie . . ." His guess was that she was with Ethan.

"I know. The blacksmith, but she wouldn't do that. Not spend the night with him. She doesn't know anything about what goes on between a man and a woman."

Sterling nearly laughed out loud. How could Reagan be so blind? What would it take for her to accept Elsa as a woman? "I'm sure she's all right."

"No. Something's happened. I just know it."

He reached for a pair of breeches and stepped into them. "I'll find her, Reagie."

"I'll go with you!"

"No." He shook his head. Dawn was beginning to break in the east, bursting with the colors of a new day. "We shouldn't be seen this time of morning walking the street. I can travel faster alone. If someone stops me, I can just say I've been playing cards at the Boar all night." He pulled his shirt over

343

his head.

Reagan knew he was right, but it was difficult to concede to him. She twisted her hands in her pale-blue sleeping gown. "I don't know how she got out of the house. I was in the parlor all evening. She never went by."

"The window, maybe?"

Her eyes widened. "It's the second story! Little Elsa—"

"Little Elsa isn't little anymore, and the sooner you face it, the better." He pulled on a brown serge vest, the pewter button with the message inside tucked safely in the pocket. "Now you wait here for me. Can you do that?"

She watched him check his flintlock pistol and then slide it into the waistband of his breeches. She nodded. "I'll wait."

"I'm not kidding with you about this. You can't be seen on the street anytime you shouldn't be there. I've appeased Major Burke by identifying Westley, but I don't know for how long."

"Just find Elsa," she whispered, clutching the bedpost. "Just find her and bring her home, Grayson."

A short time later, Sterling tapped on the front door of Ethan's cozy frame house. Lights burned inside; something was wrong. This was too early to be up, even for a blacksmith.

Ethan came to the door, his dark, sleek hair mussed, his clean muslin shirt untucked. "Captain." He pushed back a lock of hair off his forehead. "Elsa's here, isn't she?"

344

The blacksmith nodded, motioning for Sterling to come in. "I told her to go home, but my Elsa refused. The bobbins are sick, all four of them. Some kind of fever. She's been up with them all night."

"I thought it might be something like that." Sterling laid a hand on Ethan's shoulder. "Is there something I can do for you, friend?"

He shook his head. "My Elsa says the worst is over. She's broken the fevers. The bobbins just need rest now." He led Sterling through the main room of the house and into a smaller one off the side. Two beds lined opposite walls with Elsa seated between them on a kitchen chair. Two small figures lay curled up in each bed with quilts tucked tightly around them.

Elsa looked up. "Captain," she said in a tired voice.

"Reagan was worried about you," Sterling said quietly so as not to disturb the sleeping children.

Elsa turned down the lamp and tiptoed past the two men. Sterling and Ethan followed her back into the main room of the house. "Tell Sister I'm fine, but I can't come home until the children are better."

"Elsa, she was afraid something had happened to you. You can't keep climbing out windows."

Gently, Ethan took her hand. "It's all right. Go home with the captain. You tell me what to do and I'll take care of the children."

"Don't be silly!" She went to the fireplace and swung a kettle of water over the flame. "Sick children are women's work. I'm not leaving them until I

345

know they're all right. Fever can do funny things."

Sterling went to the door. One sister was as obstinate as the other. "Reagan's not going to like it, Elsa."

She shrugged. "So she won't like it. Tell her I'll be home before it gets dark. She can holler at me then."

Ethan followed Sterling to the door and stepped outside with him into the early morning sunlight. "I'm sorry to cause trouble, friend, but she can't be stopped when she sets her mind." He laughed proudly. "Like a bull, she is."

"I know precisely what you mean, Ethan. I know someone else just like her." He slipped his hand into his vest pocket and brought out the pewter button that contained his message. "While I'm here, I might as well give you this, to be delivered as soon as possible."

"That I can do." He gave a wave as Sterling went past the white picket fence and through the gate.

Out on the street, Sterling hurried home. Reagan was waiting for him in the front hall.

"I found Elsa," he told her, closing the front door behind him.

"You found her?" She spread her hands. "Then where is she?" Reagan had thrown a dressing gown over her nightclothes and had tied back her hair with a satin ribbon. She was an angel in the early-morning sunlight.

"Ethan's little ones are sick. Elsa stayed to get them through the fever." He took Reagan by the hand, leading her up the grand staircase.

"I don't understand. How did she know they were sick?" She allowed herself to be led upstairs. She'd had no sleep all night and was so tired that her vision was blurred.

"Because she was there when they got sick."

"She was there? But I forbade her to see the blacksmith."

Sterling led her into his room and to his bed, and began to unbutton her dressing gown. "It looks to me like your sister's got a mind of her own."

Reagan gave no resistance as he pulled her gown over her head, leaving her naked. "But I have to go get her."

"No, you're not going to get her. I told you, she's taking care of sick babies." Sterling lifted Reagan and tucked her into his bed. In a moment he was nude and sliding in beside her. He took her in his arms and kissed her bare neck. "Go to sleep, Reagie, and we'll fight about it in the morning."

Chapter Twenty-four

"Elsa, I'm just trying to protect you."

Elsa stroked her cat's head. "You don't understand, Sister," she answered stubbornly. "The children were sick. They could have died!"

Reagan gripped the broom in her hand, struggling to find patience. "Elsa, you shouldn't have been at the blacksmith's house to begin with. You could have killed yourself climbing out that window."

"Could not." She opened her arms and the cat leaped to the plank kitchen floor. "I use a rope."

"Elsa, how can I make you understand? The blacksmith's just taking advantage of your kind nature. You're there cooking and cleaning for him like some maidservant."

Elsa crossed her arms over her chest. "His name's Ethan."

Reagan frowned, looking up from her sweeping. "What?"

"Ethan's not 'the blacksmith,' he's Ethan and I want you to call him Ethan."

Reagan exhaled slowly. "All right. Ethan is just using you rather than paying a maid. I forbid you to go back to his house. Nothing but ill can come of it. You don't understand the dangers involved. You don't know how he could hurt you." She stopped to stroke her sister's ivory cheek. "You're so beautiful, Elsa. You don't understand how a man can take advantage of a girl as pretty as you."

Elsa pushed Reagan's hand away. "He's not going to get me in *circumstance,* if that's what you mean."

Reagan's eyes widened in shock. "In *circumstance!* Elsa!"

"Me and Ethan talked about that and we decided we wouldn't do it until after we were married."

Reagan could barely speak. "What do you know about *that?*"

Elsa smiled, giggling. "Same as you and Captain Thayer."

Reagan gasped.

Elsa went on, twisting her hands in her apron. "I like it when Ethan kisses me. He makes me feel soft and squishy inside. But we're not going to do the rest, even though I wanted to. Not until we're married."

Reagan laid aside her broom. She couldn't believe she was having this conversation with her little Elsa. What did she know about her and Grayson? She was afraid to ask. "Married. You're not getting married!"

"Don't yell at me." Elsa went to the fireplace and unfolded an iron spider. "If you yell, I won't listen." She covered her ears with her hands. "I won't listen to a thing you say."

Tears stung Reagan's eyes, and she wiped at them hastily. It seemed like she'd cried more this week than she'd cried in her entire life. How could she make Elsa understand that she wasn't capable of being married, of having a family? The fever she'd had as a baby had left her incapable of a normal life. Their physician had said so himself. Reagan took a deep breath. She went to her sister, taking her hands away from her ears. "I won't yell," she said quietly. "But you have to promise me that you won't see the blacksmith anymore. I'm only doing this for your own good."

Elsa opened her mouth and then snapped it shut. She lowered her eyelids submissively, and reached for the fireplace poker. "Yes, Sister. I won't see him anymore."

"It's for the best, Elsa," Reagan soothed, stroking her sister's dark cap of hair.

"It's for the best," Elsa echoed obediently.

Reagan pressed a kiss to her head. "Thank you. Sister's got enough to think about without having to worry about you."

Elsa lifted Mittens into her arms, watching Reagan leave the kitchen. She kissed the cat between the ears, brushing its soft fur against her cheek. "Sometimes you just have to agree with her," she told the cat quietly. "Then you just go ahead and do what you want anyway."

"No." Reagan bolted upright in bed, clutching the bedsheets. She gasped for breath. She was hot all over, but shivering with cold. "No! No!" she shouted, grasping her throat in stark horror.

"Reagie, wake up." Sterling shook her trembling

shoulders. "Reagie it's just a dream! Wake up, sweetheart."

Her eyes flew open and she grasped his arms, her eyes dilated with fear. "No! He was there! He's going to kill me! He knows everything!"

"Who? Who knows everything? Who's going to kill you?" Sterling pulled her into his arms, covering her bare shoulders with the counterpane.

She trembled with fright in his arms. She was bathed in perspiration, her heart still thudding wildly. "Indian John."

Sterling's breath caught in his throat. "Indian John?"

"He was there. I could hear him. I could smell him. That knife." She rested her head on Sterling's shoulder. "He was going to cut me with that knife."

Sterling took a deep breath. "He's dead, Reagie. He can't hurt you."

"I know," she breathed, finally beginning to calm down. "I know he's dead. You killed him. But it seemed so real!"

Sterling settled back on the goosedown pillow, holding Reagan in his arms. "Go to sleep now," he whispered. He kissed her soft, flushed cheek. "There's nothing to be afraid of. No one's going to hurt you."

She nodded, snuggling down in the bed beside him. Wrapped in Grayson's arms, she knew she was safe. He had killed Indian John. She knew her fears were unfounded. Slowly she drifted off to sleep again, determined to dream of pleasanter things.

For a long time Sterling lay awake, listening to

351

Reagan breathe evenly. There was something about her anguish that sent a chill down his spine. Tomorrow he would send a message to Captain Craig in Frankfort—just to be certain Indian John was safely imprisoned.

"Cheat? God's bowels, Carter!" Sterling pushed back from the trestle table in the rear of the Blue Boar. The tavern was busy with the late-afternoon crowd. Voices buzzed in the background. The smell of cloves, lemon peel, rum, and sweat mingled with the pungent smoke of soldiers' pipes. "A man doesn't have to cheat to beat a pitiful card player like you!"

Rum clouded the middle-aged officer's vision. "You son of a bitch of a pretty boy! They told me you were a cheat. I should never have played you!" He leaped up from the table, thrusting a fist beneath Sterling's nose. "You're talking about a month's wages here!"

Sterling took a step back. The truth was, he *had* cheated. Just like Grayson had taught him. It was the only way to beat the man, and he had a reputation to uphold. He just wasn't as good at cheating as his brother was. "Now look, Edward, there's no need to get hot with me. If you haven't the coin, you can pay me later."

The burly Carter took a step forward and Sterling took a step back. He had no desire to get into a brawl with this man . . . he'd been too helpful. This afternoon, Sterling had managed to glean several

352

worthy tidbits of information from the drunken man. Edward Carter had recently been assigned to General Clinton's headquarters and was well informed of what the British Army was planning.

"Coin! I'll tell you what I'll give you!" The red-faced man swung his fist, but Sterling ducked.

"Come on, Carter, my major'll have me jailed for fighting."

Several chuckles rose from the patrons of the tavern. One or two redcoats stood to get a better look at what was happening.

"Can always count on Thayer for a little entertainment," someone shouted.

Sterling held up his hands, backing up toward the door. "You've had too much to drink, Edward. I shouldn't have taken advantage of that."

Carter swung again, but he was so intoxicated that he missed Sterling completely, his fist connected with the wall. "Ouch!" he hollered, shaking his hand.

Sterling turned to make a quick escape.

"You better get out of here!" Carter roared. "And I'd better not see your pretty face again tonight!"

Sterling made it out the door, and headed down the street. He had a new informant to meet at a tavern on Vine Street in ten minutes and then he'd head home. He'd promised Reagan a quiet night of reading in the parlor, a night they were both looking forward to.

Grayson Thayer stood in a silversmith's shop and watched Sterling pass by. When his brother disappeared around the corner, Grayson slipped out of the shop and sauntered across the street. The faded Blue Boar Tavern sign creaked as it swung over the doorway.

The Blue Boar, this is where John said Sterling spent much of his time. Grayson smiled, smoothing his scarlet coat. Now it was time to have a little fun with that dear brother of his. By the time Sterling made it all the way over to Vine and waited for the informant that didn't exist, Grayson would have had a little time to cause a ruckus. The thought of Sterling being accused of things he hadn't committed made Grayson chuckle. A few days of Grayson being seen here and there and Sterling wouldn't know which way was up. Then there would be that red-haired woman to deal with. Grayson loved redheads.

Running a hand over his tight blond queue, Grayson walked into the Blue Boar.

"You! Edward Carter bellowed from across the public room as he came toward the door. "I thought I told you I didn't want to see your face in here again tonight!"

Grayson cracked that handsome grin he was so well known for. "Surely, sir—"

"Surely, sir, hell!" Edward cocked back his fist and slammed it into Grayson's flat stomach.

Grayson doubled over in surprise and the man hit him over the back of the head, knocking his grenadier hat off his head.

"God's bowels, man," Grayson muttered. "Must you force me to knock you senseless?" With that, he straightened, placing a well-aimed fist square

354

across Edward Carter's jaw.

Carter fell straight back, his head banging on the plank floor. Grayson stepped over his unconscious body, ignoring the other soldiers who had gathered around. He retrieved his cap, placed it on his head, and gave a nod as he went out the door. "Have a good evening, gentlemen," he called as he adjusted his cap.

Outside, Grayson grinned. *Well, that certainly didn't take long!* Whistling beneath his breath, he headed back toward Miss Kate's for an evening of futtering and cards.

Reagan hurried down Vine Street, trying to keep her petticoats out of the muck of the street. Over the winter the city she loved so dearly had become a cesspool of filth and ugliness. Trees had been cut down for firewood on every block. Windows were broken out of abandoned shops and houses, homeless dogs and cats roamed the street, starving to death. Everywhere she looked, she saw the desecration of the city that was the seat of her new country.

Purposefully, Reagan shifted her thoughts. Tucked inside her gingerbread basket was a small jug of ink. A friend on the far side of the city had managed to acquire the ink and promised to get lampblack and varnish for Reagan to make her own again. With that business taken care of, she was bound for home.

Grayson had promised to be in early tonight.

They were going to have supper and then retire to the parlor for music some games, and a little reading. A quiet, domestic evening was just what they both needed.

Reagan rubbed an aching temple, crossing the street. The weight of the world seemed to resting on her shoulders these last few days. Nothing was going right. She was concerned about Elsa. She was mad as hell with Grayson over the confiscation of her ink, but she feared to make too much fuss. He had said he wouldn't turn her in, but nothing seemed to be a given lately. She wasn't sure about anything anymore.

With surprise, Reagan lifted her head. Was that Grayson up ahead? It had to be. There was no one else in the city with hair that beautiful. She smiled, watching the way his thick queue glimmered in the sunlight. Spun gold, she mused. She lifted her hand to wave to him and call out but came to a halt. Her hand fell to her hip. Her lower lip quivered, but the pain she felt in her heart was quickly replaced with white-hot anger. "How could you?" she whispered beneath her breath.

Her Captain Thayer had just walked into Miss Kate's, the most infamous whorehouse in all of occupied Philadelphia.

Reagan's first impulse was to run in after him and drag him out by his ear. But her heart was shattering beneath her breast. He had sworn he loved her and that he could never make love to another woman. But there it was, four o'clock in the afternoon. He'd stopped by for a quick tumble with

356

some looseskirt before he came home to her!

By the time Reagan reached her house, she was so angry she was spitting fire. She was furious with Grayson, but even more furious with herself. How could she have set herself up to fall like this? She had known from the first day what kind of man Captain Grayson Thayer was. He had made no attempts to hide it. She had only imagined that he was a different man here at home with her than he was to the rest of Philadelphia. She'd fooled herself into believing that the real Grayson was the man she knew, the tender, humorous, intelligent man. She'd tricked herself into believing that when he put on his uniform to leave the house, he put on an act. He became Captain Thayer, the pretty boy who drank too much and gambled too heavily.

How could she have been so stupid? Grayson was one man. It was as clear as the black of her ink, the white of her paper. There had never been any shades of gray; she had imagined it because she had wanted it so badly.

Reagan took the front steps two at a time. She set her basket inside the door, and marched up the grand staircase and into Grayson's room. Carefully, she removed her bonnet and set it on the bed, then she went to the window and flung it open.

The first thing she picked was a pair of polished black riding boots. *No man's boots should be that shiny!* She hurled them out the window and stuck out her head in time to see them hit the cobblestones of the street and hear the satisfying thumps.

"Hey!" a milk girl called from below. "Watch it!

357

Ye nearly clobbered me!"

Reagan ducked back into Grayson's bedchamber. Next went three starched linen shirts and two stocks. They floated to the street below, one stock sailing on the wind until it caught on a neighbor's fence. That was followed by a handful of hair ribbons, a lump of shaving soap, and a new razor.

"Hey up there!" came Sterling's voice. "What are you doing?"

Reagan snatched up a pair of emerald-brocaded breeches and threw them out the window.

Sterling caught a glimpse of her head as she ducked back in the room. "Reagan? Reagan, have you gone addlepated?" Sterling began to retrieve his belongings. A crowd was beginning to gather behind him across the street.

"Guess you've really done it now, Captain," someone shouted.

"In hot water, are you?" a man asked good-naturedly. "Glad it's you and not me!"

Embarrassed, Sterling snatched up two shirts, now stained with mud. Another pair of breeches sailed out the window. "Reagan!" he shouted. "For God's sake, what are you doing, woman?" He picked up the breeches.

Reagan leaned out the window, tossing down his new mulberry velvet coat. It landed on the rail of the front stoop and Sterling grabbed it, in the process dropping his armful of clothing.

Anger rose from the tip of his polished boots upward until his face grew red with rage. First the near-brawl with Edward, then his informant hadn't showed up, and now this. What did she think she was doing? He couldn't take much more of her temper! A pair of French gabardine breeches floated by him.

"Reagan!"

She tossed out a full bottle of port and he dove to catch it. The toe of his boot caught on a cobblestone and he went down on one knee. The bottle burst on the street, sending shards of glass flying.

Sterling threw down his armful of shirts and breeches and the mulberry coat and raced up the stoop steps. He burst through the front door and ran up the staircase. "Reagan Llewellyn," he shouted. His bedchamber door was closed. He turned the doorknob. Locked.

"Reagan! Open this door!"

"Get out of my house!"

"You're embarrassing me in front of my colleagues. I'll be a laughingstock. Now open this door and tell me what the hell you're so fired up about now!"

"I said get out." Her tone was frigid. "You're no longer welcome here!"

"Reagan, this is where I live," he told her, tight-lipped. "Now let me in and tell me what's wrong."

"Go away!" she shouted. "You swore to me!"

"Swore to you what?" When she didn't answer, he took a deep, cleansing breath. "Reagan, I don't have time for games. If you don't open this damned door, I'm going to break it in."

"I don't ever want to look at your face again. Turn me in if you want. I'll not have vermin like you in my house."

Sterling was so angry that his balled fists shook at his sides. With one hard kick to the door, it splintered at the lock and he burst inside. *She's picked up every stitch of my clothing and thrown it out the window for God sakes!* he seethed.

"Reagan!"

She stood at the window, throwing out a handful of worsted stockings and garters. He pulled her from the window, and a cheer rose from the crowd down on the street.

"That a boy, Capt'n!" someone cried from below.

Sterling slammed the window shut. He lifted an accusing finger. "Tell me what's going on here, now, before I really get angry."

She crossed her arms over her chest protectively, swearing to herself that she wouldn't cry. "You lied to me," she flung bitterly. "I gave you the only thing I had to give, myself, and you deceived me."

What was she talking about? Sterling didn't have the foggiest notion. He rubbed his temple, he had a pounding headache. "You've got to tell me what we're talking about here."

Her throat was so constricted that she could barely speak. "I saw you there."

Losing all patience, he shouted, "Saw me where?"

She looked away, biting down on her lower lip. "Miss Kate's," she said finally.

"The whorehouse on Vine?" he asked in disbelief. *Wasn't that where one of those bills had come from?* "I've never stepped foot on the premises in my life."

She threw back her head in bitter laughter. "I can't believe you'd stand here and deny it. I *saw* you. You're as guilty as sin."

He was flabbergasted. "Reagan, I swear to you I've never been in Miss Kate's. I can account for every place I've been today."

She dropped her hand to her hip. "Oh, well then, tell me, Captain. Where were you an hour ago? I was on Vine."

He looked away. Everything was falling apart. Reagan was the one good thing in his life, and he could feel her slipping from his grasp. "I can't tell you," he said quietly.

Her eyes went wide. "Can't tell me? You can't tell me because I know where you were. I saw you walk into that whorehouse!"

"It was business, but not there." He tried to reach for her, but she pushed him away. "Just trust me, sweetheart. I wasn't in any whorehouse. Something isn't right here, but I don't know what it is. Major Burke got a bill from Miss Kate's a few days ago, saying I'd been there the night of the birthday party." He saw a light flicker in her cinnamon eyes.

"Grayson, I don't want to hear any more lies." *I want to believe you,* she thought. *But I've been so stupid. I've let my heart lead me instead of my head since the day you stepped foot in the house.*

"I'm telling you," he said slowly, evenly, trying to make his words sink in, "that it wasn't me. What can I say to make you believe me, give me the benefit of the doubt?"

"There's nothing you can say," she snapped, sailing through the doorway into the hall, her skirts raised well above her ankles. "Unless of course you can tell me there's *two* Captain Grayson Thayers in Philadelphia."

It came to Sterling like a flash of lightning in a storm-darkened sky. Grayson.

Chapter Twenty-five

"You shouldn't have come here, Sterling." Captain Craig let him in the back door. "It's four o'clock in the morning! You weren't spotted leaving the city, were you?"

Sterling walked into the lantern-lit kitchen. "It couldn't wait, Charles." His eyes met his commanding officer's. "My brother, where is he?"

Captain Craig tucked his linen shirt into his breeches. "You agreed that it was best you didn't know."

"Where is he, Charles?"

He studied Sterling's face for a long moment. "New York, a fort. He's been well taken care of."

Sterling shook his head grimly. "He's not there."

"I've gotten no word of an escape. He's still there."

"He's not there because he's here. He's in Philadelphia, Charles."

Captain Craig gave a snort. "Impossible." But then his eyes narrowed. "What makes you say so?"

"There've been inexplicable happenings all over the city. I've been accused of getting into brawls, stealing horses, and taking on whores two at time. Witnesses everywhere . . . except that it's not me, Charles." He took a ragged breath. "Who else could it be but Grayson?"

"That's absurd! No man could get away with it. Surely your brother wouldn't—"

"You don't know Grayson." Sterling sat down on a bench, running a hand through his thick blond hair. "My brother has a sick sense of humor."

"You honestly think it's him?"

Sterling nodded, and Captain Craig slammed his fist on the trestle table. "Damn! You were so close. But I guess this is where we pull you out, friend."

"No. I'm this far"—he spread his thumb and his forefinger—"from finding out when the Brits move and where they're going. I've found an excellent source, a man who's assigned to General Clinton's headquarters. They're going to move *soon*. General Washington needs to know if the troops are going to move north or south, and when. I can't bail out now."

"Sterling, it's too dangerous. Grayson catches up with you and you'll be swinging from a rope before we can get to you."

Sterling leaned across the table. "I don't think so, Charlie." He lifted a finger. "It's not Grayson's way. If he was coming for me, he'd have come by now with a full regiment behind him. No, this is some sort of revenge for me, having him kidnapped and locked up in that fort."

"You're too good a man for us to lose, it's not worth it."

"I have no intentions of getting into trouble this late in the game. All of these months I've spent in that city and I'm inches from getting that information we need." He got up off the bench. "Charlie,

364

I've got to go back in." *I have to say good-bye to Reagie,* he thought.

Charles heaved a sigh. "I don't like it, Sterling."

"Give me another week, just one week." *I can't leave her like this, not with the way things are between us.* "I swear to you, I'll be out in a week."

"What do we do about this brother of yours, if it is him?"

"I don't know," Sterling answered honestly. "I won't know until I talk to him. We may have to capture him again, although it won't be as easy a second time. I may just let him go."

"Let him go! We can't do that! He could come after you anytime!"

"Opposite sides of this war or not, we're still brothers. Grayson might play with my head a bit, but I don't think he'd intentionally scc me hang."

"You don't *think?* Seems to me the bct's awfully steep." Charles followed Sterling to the door. "Are you sure you don't just want to call it quits? I've got a good, safe assignment coming up in Williamsburg. You deserve it."

"I'll be all right, Charlie." Sterling gave him a squeeze on the shoulder as he ducked out the door and into the night. "Oh, by the way, you haven't got any other information for me, have you?"

Captain Craig held up the lantern, letting the lamplight illuminate Sterling's face. "No. What do you mean?"

I can't tell him Reagan dreamed about Indian John . . . that somehow, somewhere deep in her mind, she knows he's not dead, Sterling reasoned to himself. He swung into Giipa's saddle. "Never mind, it was nothing important. I'll be back before the week's end, *with* the information on that troop movement."

"It's not worth getting killed over, Sterling," Captain Craig called after his friend as he rode away.

"Sure it is," Sterling muttered, his voice lost in the wind.

Elsa's scream pierced the early-morning air. Reagan froze. In an instant she was running down the grand staircase. "Elsa! Elsa, what is it?" She could hear her little sister sobbing uncontrollably.

Reagan came to a halt just inside the kitchen. Elsa's cat, Mittens, was hanging from a ceiling beam, a rope around his neck. It stared lifelessly. "Oh, God, Elsa." Reagan ran to her sister who sat on the plank floor, sobbing into her hands.

"My kitty!" Elsa cried. "Who would do such a terrible thing to my kitty? Oh, he's dead! He's dead!"

Reagan went down on one knee, flinging her arms around her sister's quivering shoulders.

Sterling came running in the back door. "What in the heavens—oh, hell!" He grabbed a knife off the worktable and cut the cat down. He carried it outside and then came back into the kitchen.

"What happened, Reagan? Tell me what happened." He took her by the hand, raising her to her feet.

After stopping at Ethan's with Giipa, he'd hurried home this morning. He needed to talk to Reagan. He needed to tell her he was leaving. He needed to tell her that he wanted her to go with him. Somewhere between Frankfort and Reagan's home here on Spruce Street, he'd realized he couldn't leave her behind. She was his life's breath. Once they were safely in Williamsburg, he would tell her who he really was. Then he would make her his wife.

"I don't know. Elsa came down ahead of me." She stared into Sterling's blue eyes. "The cat was just hanging there."

"Where's Nettie? Maybe she heard something."

"She hasn't been here. She spent the night with her niece across town."

He held her hand in his. "The doors were locked?"

"Yes. But the window's open." She pointed to the far wall, lowering her voice. "Who would do such a thing, Grayson?" She knew who . . . a man who would kill an old printer, a man without an ounce of pity or human kindness. But that was impossible! "You killed him, didn't you, Sterling? You're certain Indian John is dead?"

Sterling brushed the back of his hand against her pale cheek. He hated lying to her like this. God, but he hated the lies. "Yes. He's dead, I told you."

"Well, whoever did this, they were just trying to scare us." Reagan looked down at her sister still seated on the floor. She was crying softly now. "If they'd wanted to hurt us, they had the opportunity." An image of Indian John's leering, scarred face flashed before her eyes and she shuddered. She knew she was being irrational.

"You're right, someone was trying to scare you." Sterling glanced at Elsa. "Look, I have to report to Major Burke this morning, but then I'll be back. I'll bury Mittens then. Right now I want both of you to get ready, and let me take you to Mistress Claggett's. I don't want you here alone."

"Grayson, this is our home." Reagan pressed a hand to her forehead. She was feeling light-headed again. It had started a few days ago, an odd queasiness in the pit of her stomach, a spinning dizziness. All of the excitement, she supposed. She turned her attention back to Grayson. "I'll not run scared. Elsa needs to be tucked into bed. We're not going anywhere."

Elsa came to her feet, and Sterling and Reagan turned to her. Her face was bright red from crying.

"Elsa, where are you going?" Reagan followed her sister down the hall.

"I want Ethan," Elsa cried.

"Elsa, you're overwrought, let's go upstairs. Grayson has some tea. Some real tea. Wouldn't it be wonderful to have a cup of real tea and a biscuit?"

Elsa shook her head emphatically as she put on her straw bonnet. "I want Ethan, and I want him now. I don't want tea and a biscuit. He said to come if I need him. I need him now."

Reagan stepped in front of the door. "Elsa . . ." she said quietly. "Remember, we agreed you wouldn't see the blacksmith anymore."

"Get out of my way, or I'll bust you!" Elsa stuck

368

out her lip in determination.

Reagan opened her mouth to speak, but Sterling caught her hand and pulled her away from the door. "Let her go," he whispered in Reagan's ear. "I'll follow her to be sure she gets there safely."

"Grayson, I—"

"For once in your life, listen to me. Ethan's who she needs right now, whether you approve or not."

Reagan watched her dark-haired sister run down the front steps and onto the street. She was losing Elsa, she could feel it in her bones, and it hurt.

Sterling went out the door behind Elsa. "I have something very important to talk to you about, Reagie," he said, pulling her along. "I have to be at Major Durgen's tonight, it's a important affair, a ball, and I want you to go with me. Have you a gown?"

"Grayson, this isn't working anymore. Shouldn't we just say good-bye?" Her dark eyes met his. God, but she loved him, redcoat or not.

"Reagie"—he spoke haltingly—"I'm in trouble. I may need your help." He pressed a kiss to the center of her palm.

She watched him intently. His striking face was etched with fear . . . she could smell the danger. He wasn't lying. "That really wasn't you at Miss Kate's, was it?" she half whispered. The sights and sounds of the busy city street faded. Suddenly nothing existed but the two of them.

He hung his head. "No. There's a lot to tell you. I've deceived you." He felt her stiffen and he looked up. "But not the way you think. We'll go to the

369

party and then we'll go somewhere and talk."

"I really should stay home with Elsa tonight."

"I'll get Nettie from her niece's and I'll bring Elsa home, too, tonight, before we go." He leaned for a kiss and she offered him her trembling lips. His kiss was hard and demanding. He tasted of ale and desperation.

When Sterling pulled away, Reagan was breathless. "Go after Elsa and see that's she's safe," she told him, pressing her hand to her abdomen.

"Tonight? You'll go with me tonight?"

She knew she should say no. Captain Grayson Thayer had been nothing but trouble since that Christmas night they first met. But she wanted to know what he had to confess. He had deceived her? How? Why was he choosing to tell her now? What kind of trouble was he in? She leaned against the wooden rail of the front stoop watching him disappear down the street. She was anxious to hear him out. She went into the front hall and closed the paneled door, heading upstairs to her bedchamber. She already knew what gown she would wear; it was one tucked away, having never been worn. If tonight was to be her last with her captain, she would make it a memorable one.

"Reagie!" Sterling burst into her bedchamber and she turned from the mirror.

He inhaled sharply. Reagan was a beautiful woman, but he'd never seen her like this. She took his breath away. She was dressed in a gown of

370

cream silk brocaded in metallic gold gilt. Her stomacher was sewn from gold gilt lace, paper, and floss silk. Her petticoat was of green satin, quilted in running stitches. Her glossy auburn hair was twisted fashionably on her head with strands of metallic gilt threaded through it. Around her neck she wore a heavy gold necklace.

Reagan laughed, self-consciously. "What? I look ridiculous, don't I?" It was her wedding gown she wore, the one she'd intended to wear the day she and Josh married.

"No, you . . . you look beautiful." He came to her, kissing the soft, silky flesh of her bare neck.

"It's not too fancy for the ball?"

"No, certainly not." He was so taken aback by her fairy-princess transformation, that he had forgotten for a moment why he'd come to her. "Reagan, we have to hurry. I'm going to leave you at the major's—"

"I don't want to go alone!"

He put up his hands. "Please. It's almost over. Just trust me a little longer. I won't be gone long. I'll come back to the ball, we'll dance, we'll drink a little of the major's wine, we'll make conversation, and then we'll go."

"What's so important that it can't wait?"

Sterling touched his hand to his scarlet uniform coat. Under his white vest was a message he'd just written to Captain Craig. His mission was complete. Beneath his coat he carried the official date of the British evacuation of Philadelphia and the direction they were moving. His earlier sources had been wrong! It wasn't south! It was north! On June 18, only a little more than two weeks from today, in the wee hours of the morning, General Clinton would be taking his army across the Delaware river to the Jersey shore.

General Washington was going to get his chance. It was a commander-in-chief's dream come true. He would be able to hit the strung-out enemy line from the flank with his compact force. The question was, would the councils of war agree to the chancy maneuver or would they advise Washington to sit tight in Valley Forge?

"Grayson?" Reagan waved a hand in front of his face. "Grayson, are you all right?"

Sterling looked up at Reagan. He wanted so badly to share the information he'd just gleaned from the drunken Edward who'd heard it accidentally in Clinton's headquarters only yesterday. But he couldn't, not yet. Not until the information reached General Washington safely, not until he had Reagan out of the city.

"I'm sorry, sweetheart." He smiled. "I've got a lot on my mind. I'm fine. It's just that I have to make a quick stop before I go to the ball."

"I'll go with you then."

"No." He smoothed his powdered wig. "You can't, but I swear, love, I won't be long."

"You promise, tonight is it." Her cinnamon eyes met his. "Tonight you'll tell me what's going on — why you're in so much trouble."

He kissed her gently. "Tonight. I promise."

* * *

372

"Captain, glad to see you." Ethan came down the walk to meet Sterling in front of his home. He watched the hired carriage that had brought Sterling pull onto the street and head west. "I was on my way to find you."

Sterling's eyes narrowed. "That important, is it?"

Ethan gave a nod, but neither man spoke again until they were safely cloaked in the privacy of the barn.

"So what is it you needed me for?" Sterling pulled out the message he'd written with the bell mask, disguising it as another letter to Cousin Lucy from Aunt Feddlebottom. A duplicate letter followed. One was meant for Captain Craig, the other was bound for General Washington himself.

Ethan accepted both letters. "This business first."

"One goes the usual route." Sterling lowered his gaze to the blacksmith's beefy face. "When can you get the other to Valley Forge?"

"When you need it to be there?"

"Yesterday."

"That important?"

"As important as any message the general's ever received."

Ethan patted his waistcoat. "Then I'll start it on its way myself. It'll be there just after midnight."

Sterling broke into a grin, grasping Ethan's hand. "I knew I could count on you."

Ethan returned the smile. "Listen, what I was coming to tell you was that I was contacted and told that you were to meet a party at 8:30 on Front

373

and Water Streets. An alley to the left of the store-house."

"Meet who? About what?"

"A young boy came here not more than half an hour ago. He said the message was for Captain Thayer to be on Front and Water if he wanted his man Murray."

"Murray, is it?" Sterling couldn't believe his luck! He pulled out his brother's pocketwatch. "I'll have to hurry to make it."

Ethan immediately went to Sterling's saddle. "You want me to take you in my wagon? It might be safer."

Sterling shook his head. "Just saddle up Giipa. I can't pass this up. I haven't been able to identify the man—a spy—and he's looking for me."

"I don't know how you keep this all straight, friend." Ethan pulled the bridle over Giipa's head.

"I wonder the same myself sometimes." Sterling laughed as he cinched the saddle. Suddenly everything was falling into place! He'd make this meet, find out what the contact had to say about Murray, and he'd put someone on it right away. Then he'd be off to join Reagan. He'd ask her to go away with him to Williamsburg.

Sterling cleared his throat, glancing over the horses back at Ethan. "I wanted to tell you I'd be leaving."

"I figured as much. With the Army pulling up stakes, I knew they'd want you."

"Ethan, I want Reagan to go with me."

The blacksmith glanced down at the clean straw

at his feet and then raised his gaze to meet Sterling's. "You don't mean to take Elsa from me?"

"If she wants to come, she's welcome." Sterling chose his words carefully. "She'll always be welcome in our home, but she's a grown woman, free to make her own choices as far as I'm concerned, Ethan."

"If her sister goes with you, she'll try to force Elsa to go, too." Ethan looked away, wiping at his eyes with the back of his thick hand. "I don't know what I'd do without her."

"You're the best thing that could have happened to her, Ethan. The way you took care of her this morning when that business with her cat happened."

Ethan sniffed. "I don't know why people do such horrible things. Why would anyone want to hurt Elsa? Her heart's golden. I don't do half as much for her as she does for me and the bobbins." He looked at the barn. "This was my papa's barn before mine. Born and raised here I was, but I guess I could pick up and move. Just wouldn't mean anything without Elsa." He checked a strap on the bridle and then pulled up the reins, looping them over the saddle horn. "Mind if I ask where you're bound?"

"Williamsburg."

Ethan nodded. "Never heard much good about a Virginian, but I guess I could get used to them."

Sterling came around Ethan's side of the horse. "I don't want to tell you what to do, but maybe you ought to sit down and talk to Elsa about all of this.

375

I'm not even sure Reagan'll go with me."

"She'll go. Elsa says she loves you madly." Ethan smirked.

His smile was contagious. Sterling took Ethan's hand, then on impulse, swung his arms around the man's massive shoulders. "I hate to force Elsa into it, but she may have to make some choices."

"Thanks for lettin' me know." Ethan patted his back. "You're a good man, whatever your name might really be." He backed off, swinging open the barn doors. "So good luck to you, friend. Good luck and Godspeed."

Sterling tipped his hat and then rode out of the barn and headed for the docks.

Chapter Twenty-six

Reagan sipped champagne from a Venetian glass, watching the doorway. Thousands of fragrant beeswax candles glittered in the crystal chandeliers above, reflecting light off the etched mirrors that lined the walls. Heavenly music filled the grand ballroom.

Where was Grayson? She had been here well over an hour and she was beginning to get restless. She offered the red-faced Hessian officer standing beside her a smile. She hadn't heard a word he'd said in fifteen minutes, but he hadn't seemed to notice.

Lieutenant Roth Gardener strode by, bowing slightly but didn't stop to speak. He'd steered clear of her and Elsa since that night Grayson had kicked him out of the Llewellyn home. Reagan still didn't know to this day how Grayson had managed it.

The Hessian laughed and she laughed with him, not having the foggiest idea what he'd said that amused him. She wondered if he had a wife somewhere on German soil. She sidestepped him as he attempted again to fondle her buttocks through the yards of brocaded silk of her gown. "God's teeth," she murmured. "Where are you, Grayson?"

As if she was able to conjure him up by magic, he appeared in the far doorway. He was stopped by a handful of women fluttering lace fans, and they burst into laughter when he made some reply.

Across the wide expanse of the crowded room, their eyes met. He lifted a blond eyebrow and she covered her smile by sipping from her glass. She was suddenly warm from the tips of her toes to the top of her head. She could feel her cheeks burning. He could be so irresistible when he wanted to be. The trouble was that she wanted to resist. Tonight was not the night for charm. Tonight she wanted truths.

Slowly Grayson made his way toward her, stopping to speak with this officer or that. His immaculate scarlet coat, faced in black, complemented his striking form. The gold lace of his buttonholes, the gold of his buttons, gorget, and epaulets sparkled in the candlelight. The crimson net silk sash he wore over his white vest was tied precisely, his black shoes buffed until they shone.

Reagan gave a sigh. Handsome, he was.

Captain Grayson Thayer walked over to Reagan and nodded to the Hessian officer. "Good evening to you." He caught her hand and pressed a hot kiss to the back of her hands.

She offered him the barest smile. "I thought you'd never get here, Captain. Henrich has been kind enough to keep me entertained while I waited."

Grayson took the glass from her hand and sipped from it, nodding approvingly. "I must thank you then, Henrich."

Reagan didn't know what had gotten into Grayson. That insolent grin on his face, though utterly captivating to her, certainly wasn't appropriate. It was obvious he'd been drinking; an unfamiliar aroma clung to him.

"Excuse us, Henrich," Reagan said, taking Grayson's arm.

The German stepped back, bowing stiffly. "A goot night to you, mistress. It hass been a pleasure."

Reagan gave a nod and lifted her skirt, allowing Grayson to lead her away. "I trust your business went well," she murmured when they were a safe distance from the Hessian.

"Well enough."

Reagan nodded to Lieutenant Warrington as they passed him.

"Captain Thayer, I need to talk to you," the lieutenant called after them.

Boldly, Grayson rubbed Reagan's bare arm. "Later, Lieutenant."

"Where are you taking me." she asked as he whisked her through the doorway and out onto a patio illuminated by soft candlelight.

"Out," he whispered in her ear.

His tongue darted out to touch her lobe, and she shivered. "I thought we were going to make an appearance and then go home. I thought you had something important to tell me. The trouble you're in, how you might need me . . ." She closed her eyes, savoring the feel of his touch.

He took her around the waist, guiding her until her back pressed against a whitewashed rail.

Her eyes fluttered open. "You remember, Grayson, the part about you deceiving me."

He chuckled. "Not now, sweet." He kissed the pulse at her throat. "Watching you from across the room, I wanted to lift you into my arms and take you there on the ballroom floor."

Reagan knitted her brows. "What have you been drinking?" *He's acting so odd,* she thought. "You smell like you've been doused in it."

He clasped her hands, bringing them around his waist. "A kiss, my love, before I shatter."

She pulled back, studying his familiarly handsome face. Something wasn't right. "Are you certain everything went all right?"

His breath was hot in her ear. "Enough talk. Kiss me."

Hesitantly, Reagan rested her hands on his broad chest and leaned to kiss him. The moment their lips touched she stiffened; her head spun in utter confusion. *Holy saints in hell! This isn't Grayson!*

Sterling pulled up on the reins, easing Giipa into a trot. It was twilight, that eerie time between day and night when sounds and shadows deceived even the most observant of men.

Two red-coated patrolmen rode by, saluting as they passed. Sterling returned the salute and rode on. Front Street was deserted now save for a stray cat or two and a few sailors here and there. It was Saturday night and men with a spare coin were either playing their luck at cards at a corner tavern or trying their luck with a lady. The city was buzzing with a strange energy. Everyone knew the British Army would soon evacuate Philadelphia, but only a chosen few knew when.

Sterling smiled in the semidarkness. This afternoon he'd become one of the chosen. All of these months of work had finally paid off. Now, if this contact could identify the spy, Murray, then the threat of being caught would be gone . . . or nearly gone. In his excitement, Sterling had forgotten his brother.

Yes, there was still Grayson to contend with. What was his purpose in tantalizing him like this? Playing this deadly cat-and-mouse game? If the British caught on, both of them would most likely be hanged. They would never believe that Grayson had been kidnapped and held prisoner.

No, Sterling didn't have things wrapped up here in Philadelphia. There was still Reagan. Would she come with him? The thought of having to ask made him want to reach for a stiff drink . . . a palm toddie even! He laughed to himself. Everything was going to be all right. He just knew it. He could feel it in his bones.

Sterling turned the corner at the storehouse and stared into the long, dark alley. It was wide, with an assortment of wagons, carts, and wooden crates lining the brick building walls. A lone man stood, waiting.

Sterling urged Giipa off the street and into the alley. He stopped a good distance back. "By the king's cod," he called, then waited for the password.

"We'll overcome by God," answered the man in a

381

low gravelly voice.

Sterling gave a nod and rode in. "You wanted to see me?"

The gray-whiskered man with a bulbous red nose shook his head. "Not me, him." He pointed to an overturned wagon.

Before Sterling could reach for the pistol in his coat, a man popped up from behind the wagon aiming two loaded matchlocks. It was the man who had been in Captain Craig's office. It was Murray.

At the same instant the barrel of a rifle pressed into Sterling's side. The man who had lured him into the alley ran off. A familiar cackle rose on the night air and Sterling turned to see Indian John. "You son of a bitch," Sterling muttered. "How did you get away?"

"A little help from me," Murray said, coming to Sterling, his pistols still aimed. He was dressed in the blue coat of one of the New England regiments. "Liberty or Death" was emblazoned across his cap. "I was asked to transport him, a few others, and myself. A pity we ran into that patrol of Hessians. We never had a chance."

Sterling rested his hands on the saddle horn, forcing them not to shake as Murray snatched Sterling's pistol from beneath his uniform coat. "How dare you wear that uniform!"

Murray laughed, throwing back his head. "How dare *you* wear *that* uniform, Captain Thayer." He tucked Sterling's pistol into the waistband of his own breeches.

Sterling glanced over his shoulder wondering how

much they knew. It sounded as if they believed he was Grayson. He knew he only had moments to live; his only regret was that he would never grow old with Reagan at his side. "So why isn't Major Burke here? No trumpets? No fanfare?"

Murray signaled to Indian John to bring Sterling down off his horse, and Indian John grasped his arm, pulling him roughly off Giipa. Sterling tumbled, his head hitting the ground, but he rolled up into a sitting position.

"We didn't know for sure who it was," Murray said, staring down at Sterling. "The major swore you were innocent. He said you were too busy trying to catch the French pox to be a spy."

Indian John lifted Sterling's cap and wig off his head with the barrel of the rifle he held. "Me, I knew you was up to something, you and that Llewellyn bitch." He threw the cap and wig into a pile of wooden crates.

Sterling flinched. "She doesn't know anything about me."

"Right. I'd sure believe anything you had to say, Capt'n. Couldn't catch her at it, but I guess she was printin' them pamphlets all along. Mighty cozy the two of you, writin' your little essays."

Sterling glanced over his shoulder at Indian John. "You and Murray are quite a pair. Where do you get your facts? Both of you are off the mark."

"We caught you, Thayer," Murray said. "We tracked you down by way of a baker, then the blacksmith. We knew that whoever came to get information on me was the spy." He grinned. "Now

383

all of you are going to fall and I'm going to get myself a promotion."

Sterling felt his hands tremble. *Not Reagan, not Ethan! Dear God, no!* he thought. He lifted his gaze, eyeing the pistols Murray held on him. "So no one knows but the two of you that it's me?"

"Not yet they don't . . . know soon enough, though." Indian John caught Sterling by the collar of his coat and jerked him to his feet.

"So what you're telling me is that if I kill the both of you, I'll be safe. No one will ever know."

"Bold bastard for a man who's about to turn belly-up, ain't he, Murray?"

"That he is." Murray lifted his foot and kicked Sterling in the groin.

Sterling gave a groan, stumbling backward. Only the hold Indian John had on his coat kept him on his feet.

Indian John cackled. "You hold him now and give me chance."

"No." Murray shook his head. "We need to get him over to the prison."

"The prison? I thought we were going to take care of him ourselves. I figured we'd get the Llewellyn bitch with him for bait. Two dogs with one stone."

"I'm not getting involved in any personal vendettas." Murray shifted his weight. "We take him in now."

Sterling lifted his head, blinking to clear his mind. It seemed that Murray and Indian John didn't quite agree on what was to be done with him.

Just the advantage Sterling could use to make an escape!

Indian John tightened his grip on the back of Sterling's scarlet coat. He was quiet for a long moment. "Nope, sorry, but that ain't what I planned," he said finally.

Sterling watched Murray's eyes narrow. "What you planned is of no interest to me, half-breed! You came along to assist, and your assistance is no longer needed. I'll take the prisoner now. Captain Burke wants his spy alive so he can have the pleasure of seeing him hang." He waved one of his pistols.

Indian John took a step back, dragging Sterling with him. Sterling thought to try and make a break for it, but with both of them aiming primed firearms, it would be a stupid risk.

Indian John gave a grunt. "So we just tell the major that we had to kill him — got right violent, he did." He gave Sterling a vicious shake. "Sure looks violent to me!"

"I said, release the prisoner," Murray ordered through clenched teeth.

"He's mine!"

"If you don't back off right this minute, redskin, it'll be you strung up right next to him. You understand that?"

"I understand this . . ."

Before Sterling knew what was happening, Indian John raised his rifle and fired point-blank at the spy. Simultaneously Murray fired his flintlocks.

Sterling saw a flash of light, and suddenly he was

reeling backward. His left temple seared as he felt himself hit the ground. In front of him he saw Murray lying in a pool of blood, his head blown off his shoulders.

An eerie cloud of confusion settled on Sterling's mind. Beneath him he could feel the half-breed struggling to get up. Sterling willed his own limbs to bend. He knew he had to make his escape, but his legs refused to obey. He heard the shout of a man, but it wasn't Indian John.

Then there was pounding of horses hooves. Soldiers! They were coming down the street!

Sterling felt the half-breed shove him aside and then heard him scramble to his feet. A pistol or a rifle fired again and Sterling heard the half-breed howl. Sterling blinked. He was losing focus. Time seemed to stretch on endlessly.

Suddenly there was an older gentleman leaning over him. "Grayson." The man felt for Sterling's pulse. "Grayson, can you hear me? We've got to get you the hell out of here!"

Sterling tried to speak but no sound rose from his vocal cords. *Who is this gray-haired man?* he wondered, feeling oddly at peace. Somewhere in the distance he could hear gunfire and men shouting. Who was firing on the soldiers?

"Grayson! Listen to me! Hold on, boy, we'll get you to a surgeon!"

"No," a soft feminine voice said.

Sterling tried to focus. Was that Reagan? Reagie? No, this woman was dark-haired with a heart-shaped face. An angel sent from heaven to retrieve

386

him? No, it was Elsa!

"No," Elsa repeated firmly. "No surgeon, sir."

Sterling could feel her lifting him by the shoulders. "You've got to help me get him into the wagon. Ethan and Jeremiah can't hold the soldiers off much longer."

Sterling felt himself being raised and then lowered again. He smelled damp wood and horseflesh. He could feel Elsa's soft touch on his cheek as the wagon bounced forward, and then slowly he sank into a comforting blackness.

Chapter Twenty-seven

The wheels of Reagan's mind churned as she withdrew from the stranger's kiss. If this wasn't Grayson, who was he? She looked up at him through a veil of dark lashes; her fingertips went instinctively to her lips. The man who held her in his arms was a mirror image of her Grayson. He had the same striking blue eyes, the same perfect form, and she knew that beneath his powdered wig, his hair was a glorious golden-blond. But he didn't kiss like Grayson. When Grayson's lips met hers, she felt his love radiate through her. This man tasted of pure lust.

She lowered her gaze, not wanting the imposter to realize he'd been found out. A conversation she had with Grayson months ago while ice-skating replayed in her mind. A brother. He'd said he had a brother . . . a *patriot* brother. What was his name?

The stranger caressed her cheek.

Sterling! That's what Grayson had said his name was! She met the stranger's gaze. Was this Sterling? It had to be. Why hadn't Grayson told her he and his brother were twins? *Because his brother hadn't died at Long Island! That was why!*

She smiled at Sterling. "I'm ready to go home if you are," she whispered huskily. She didn't know what game Sterling and Grayson played, but this was not the place to find out.

Grayson's mouth turned up in a handsome smile. "Sounds like an invitation I couldn't possibly turn down. Let me just say a few hallos and then we'll be on our way, lover."

"Now," she said softly, covering her fear with the sound of desire in her voice. "I want to go home now."

His grin turned to a smirk. "If you insist." *Lusty wench,* he thought to himself. It seemed he was in for a treat. Not only would he take his revenge on Sterling, but he'd get a good lay in the process!

"Let's go out the back way."

"Out the back?" He lifted a blond eyebrow. "How will we call a rig?"

"Let's walk," she insisted, leading him down a set of stairs off the balcony and into the garden behind the major's residence.

"Walk!" He scoffed. "It'll ruin the finish on my new shoes!"

That sounded like something Grayson might say. But Reagan always had the feeling that Grayson was putting on a show when he made such silly comments. This man who walked beside her was serious!

She laughed aloud, knowing she mustn't let "Sterling" know she knew who he was, not yet. "Oh, come on. The exercise will do us good." She smoothed his coat sleeve. "It'll give us energy."

Grayson gave a chuckle. "Sounds like I have quite a night ahead of me." His voice was low and filled with sensual overtones.

"Quite a night, indeed. I can promise you that, Captain!"

Once they reached Reagan's home, she led him in the front hall. The house was quiet and dark.

Grayson grabbed her around the waist, kissing her bare neck, but she managed to maneuver away from him. "You go upstairs and I'll get a lamp," she whispered.

"Up-upstairs?"

She smiled in the semidarkness. He was so much like Grayson, yet so different. "To your room, of course."

Grayson found the thought of bumbling around in the dark looking for his brother's room rather unappealing. "Why . . . why don't you come with me, sugar?"

She chuckled to herself. Just how *would* he find the right room in the dark? "No, you go first and get things ready. You know the way I like it." She paused and then looked up at him. The yellow-white light of the streetlamp shadowed his face. "Be sure and take everything off—except the cap."

Grayson cleared his throat. "The cap?" His hand went to the fur-trimmed grenadier cap perched on his head. What kind of woman had Sterling hooked up with?

She smiled seductively. "The cap, of course." Giving a wink, she went down the hallway, leaving him to find his way upstairs alone.

In the kitchen Reagan lit an oil lamp. She didn't know what was going on here, and though she felt she was in control of the situation, she was frightened. Where was Grayson? Captured? A pang of sympathy flowed through her veins. She prayed he hadn't been hurt.

The question was, what was Sterling up to? Did he mean to trade places and infiltrate the British Army? That had to be it! He meant to step in and take Grayson's place as a captain in the British Army and in her bed as well! How dare he! If this was a decision made by the Continental Army, then she should have been informed!

She glanced at the flintlock rifle that leaned in the corner of the kitchen. That wouldn't do, too obvious. After a moment's hesitation, she slipped into Nettie's room in the lean-to off the kitchen. Locating the old housekeeper's sewing box, she dug through the fabric scraps to the bottom and was rewarded by the feel of cold metal. She lifted the ancient matchlock pistol out of the box. It was primed and ready to fire.

Minutes later, Reagan stood outside Sterling's bedchamber door, the lamp in one hand, the pistol in the other. Taking a deep breath, she stepped inside. She set the lamp on the table near the door, tucking the hand she held the pistol in behind her back.

A smile rose on her lips when she caught sight of Grayson. He was standing stark-naked in the corner of the room . . . save for the bearskin grenadier cap on his blond head.

"This is what you wanted?" He spread his arms, offering his most seductive smile.

Reagan's eyes narrowed. "More or less." She

pulled the pistol from behind her back and waved it toward the chair. "Now have a seat."

He laughed uncomfortably, eyeing the pistol. She was kidding, right? "This . . . this is how you like it?"

"I said, sit down!"

Grayson took the seat quickly, crossing his legs as if he protect his vital parts. He'd never realized his brother had a taste for this sort of thing! The girl played the part well, though. She actually had him rattled! He wondered if she intended to tie him to the bedposts. "Now what?" He tried to sound causal as if he always made love to fully clothed women while they held a gun on him.

"Now start talking."

"Talking, madame?"

She came to stand a few feet from him. "Yes, talking." Anger rose in her voice. "And it had better be fast and good because I'm not a good shot. Instead of hitting you in the head or the chest, I might accidentally hit lower. You catch my meaning?"

Grayson blinked. He looked at her face, then the pistol, then her face again. Slowly he reached for his cap on his head and lowered it to his lap. "Yes, I catch your meaning there. What I don't catch is the rest. What should I talk about?"

"Don't play coy with me! I want to know what's going on here! I want to know where the hell Grayson is!"

So she didn't know Sterling's true identity! A lazy smile worked its way across his face. Damn, but his redhead was a ball of fire! She was obviously too much of a woman for Sterling . . . definitely more his own type. "How did you know I wasn't Grayson?"

"Because you're a lousy kisser!"

His smile fell. "Gads, love, no one's ever complained before!"

She shook the pistol. "I want to know what you've done with Grayson. If you've hurt him, so help me, I'll string you up! I should have been notified you were making some sort of exchange! You had no right to try and take advantage of me like this!"

"It was all in jest." He spread his hands, then catching sight of the pistol lowered them to the grenadier cap on his lap again. "But I don't know where my dear brother, Grayson is. I thought he was supposed to be at the ball. I was hoping to meet up with him there."

Reagan's eyes went round. "You mean you didn't have him picked up?" Her hand fell to her side. "Oh, God, he said he was in trouble, you don't suppose something could have happened to him?"

Grayson moved slightly, and she lifted the pistol again.

He threw up his hands. "Easy, easy, girl. Where was he going when you dropped him off at the blacksmith's?"

"You followed us?"

"Where was he going?"

"I . . . I don't know." Her dark eyes met his. It was such a strange feeling to stand there looking at

Grayson, knowing it wasn't him. "He said it was business. It's what he always says."

Grayson started to stand up and she stepped back, taking aim.

"Look, Reagan, can I at least put my breeches on? It's difficult for a man to think clearly exposed like this."

She hesitated, sizing him up. "You meant to take advantage of me."

"My apologies." He stood cautiously. "I meant you no harm. This is between Sterling and me."

"Sterling?" Her brow creased. "I thought you were Sterling."

He took a deep breath, slowly reaching for his white uniform breeches folded neatly over the back of the chair. "I hadn't meant for things to get this sticky."

"Sticky!" Reagan exploded.

A sudden bang of the front door downstairs drew both of their attentions.

"Reagie!" Elsa cried frantically from below. "Reagie! Come quick."

"Elsa?" She turned and ran out of the bedchamber. Her breath caught in her throat as she reached the upper staircase landing. Below, Ethan, the blacksmith was carrying Grayson into the house. Both men were covered in blood. Elsa led the way. A middle-aged, gray-haired gentleman followed, closing the door behind them. Reagan recognized him in an instant. It was the man who'd saved her from the redcoats so many months ago!

Breaking from her daze, Reagan flew down the

steps. Grayson followed behind, barefoot and bare-chested, tugging on his breeches. Ethan and the gray-haired man stared at Grayson, then at the unconscious Sterling, then back at Grayson again.

"Oh, is he still alive?" She laid her hand on Sterling's ashen cheek.

His eyelids fluttered. "Reagie," he breathed.

She pressed her lips to his. "You stinking redcoat, what have you done to yourself?" she demanded softly.

Sterling looked up at Ethan, fighting against a black void. "The message, did you send it?"

Ethan nodded. "Our commander-in-chief will have it in hours."

Elsa grabbed Reagie's arm. "We've got to get him downstairs, Sister." She glanced up at Grayson, just noticing him. "Look at him, he looks just like the captain." Her gaze went back to Reagan's stricken face. "The soldiers'll probably not be far behind, we've got to hurry."

"Elsa, you're moving too fast for me! What happened? What do you mean downstairs? What soldiers?"

"Your secret room, Sister. We'll take him there. The redcoats, of course, you didn't really think he was on their side, did you?"

Reagan was so light-headed that for a moment she thought she might faint. But Elsa pushed her way down the hall and everyone followed her into the kitchen, including Reagan, not daring to question Elsa's authority. Elsa snatched a lamp, lit it, and started for the cellar door. "Ethan. You have to get rid of the wagon. Give the captain to him, he can carry him." She pointed to Grayson.

"I have to talk to *him*," the gray-haired man said.

"Your business will have to wait, Mr. Carleton."

Reagan watched the exchange between the two men, dumbfounded.

Grayson turned to the middle-aged gentleman. "So you're Carleton!"

"That I am, but who's—"

Elsa lifted a finger, interrupting the two men. "Right now, you get me hot water and clean cloths to bind the wound, Mr. Carleton. You can talk later when the captain's been taken care of."

Ethan passed Sterling into his brother's arms and gave a wave. "I'll hide the wagon and be back as soon as it's safe."

Elsa was already starting down the steep wooden steps. "And Mr. Carleton . . ." she called over her shoulder.

"Yes."

"Liquor, sir. Rum, whiskey, whatever you can find in the captain's room upstairs. The wound's going to have to be stitched."

Carleton removed his cloak and tossed it onto a kitchen chair. "I'll bring blankets to lay him on."

Giving a nod, Elsa led Grayson down the steps and through the dark chambers. Reagan followed numbly behind. When they reached the far back wall, Elsa stepped aside. "You'll have to open it, Sister, I don't know how."

Reagan swung open the door. "I . . . I didn't know you knew this was here, Elsa."

"You never asked me." She stepped past Reagan. "Bring him this way, sir," she told Grayson.

Inside, Elsa lit the lamp that hung from the ceiling, filling the small whitewashed room with bright light.

Grayson knelt, lowering his brother to the floor. "Sterling," he murmured, his face etched with concern. "You hanging in there, old boy?"

Sterling opened his eyes, then smiled. "You son of a bitch," he managed good-naturedly. His speech was slightly slurred. "What are you doing here?"

Reagan fell to her knees. "I don't understand what's happening here." She looked at Sterling. "Your name's not Grayson?"

Sterling licked his dry lips. "No"—he managed to lift a hand—"he is. I . . . I'm Sterling."

Reagan wiped his face with the corner of her green silk petticoat. "If you weren't already half dead, I think I'd kill you."

He laughed weakly. It felt so good to hear Reagan's voice, to feel her touch. He had thought sure he was a dead man. "I suppose you're going to want an explanation."

She sat down, lifting his head so that it rested on her thigh. "Damned straight." She held her cream silk skirting against the wound on the side of his head. His beautiful blond hair was stained red with blood. "But right now, I just want you to shut your mouth while we clean you up." Her words were harsh, but her voice was soft and soothing.

The man called Carleton appeared and Elsa moved about busily. When she knelt beside Sterling's head, she held a needle and thread and a bottle of whiskey.

"Captain . . ." Elsa said quietly. "You have a bad head wound. The bullet went along your skull and cut the skin. You've got a big piece here that has to be sewn."

Sterling nodded. "Sew, then."

"First have a good drink." Elsa touched his lips with the rim of the whiskey bottle and he took a sip.

Reagan looked at Elsa. "You want me to do it?"

Elsa shook her head. "No. You just sit there, Sister. You don't look like you feel good."

Reagan nodded, taking Sterling's sticky hand. She was amazed that the head wound could have caused so much blood.

With the first stitch, Sterling stiffened, Reagan went green. With the second, he relaxed slightly, but kept his jaw tense. Reagan swayed. On the third stitch, she jumped up and ran from the room.

Reagan rested her head on the cool wall of the cellar chamber. When Grayson walked up behind her, she barely glanced up. She thought sure she was going to be sick.

"Are you all right?" He laid a hand on her shoulder, then withdrew it awkwardly. It was obvious to him in the other room that this brave young woman and his brother were deeply in love.

"I'm fine," Reagan managed.

"Did you tell him?"

"Tell him what?"

"That you're breeding?"

She took another deep breath, holding her stomach. "Don't be silly. Women are supposed to faint at the sight of blood."

Grayson chuckled, his voice reverberating in the small, dark chamber. "Not women who tell men to strip their drawers and then hold guns on them."

Reagan closed her eyes. "I really don't want to have this conversation with you, whatever your name is." It wasn't until this moment that she'd finally admitted to herself that she might be carrying Grayson . . . Sterling's child.

"Grayson."

She looked up. "What?"

"My name is Grayson."

She crossed her arms over her chest, lifting her gaze to meet his. Light from the printing room shone across his face. "So who's *actually* Captain Thayer of the Grenadier Company, Grayson or Sterling?"

Grayson took a deep breath. "Actually, neither of us, madame."

Chapter Twenty-eight

Reagan looked up at Grayson. "Now I'm really confused," she said softly.

"You think it's safe to tell her?" The gray-haired gentleman intervened from the doorway.

Grayson twisted his bare foot on the dirt floor. "Christ, I don't see why not, Carleton. She's into it up to her teeth. I'd say she's been damned good about the whole thing."

Reagan looked from one man to the other. Her nausea had passed and her head was clearer. "I'd say I deserve an explanation. A *full* explanation. Everyone seems to know what's going on but me!"

Grayson eyed Carleton, and the man shrugged. "Be my guest, Grayson. You *are* Grayson, the man I hired?"

Grayson broke into a grin, nodding formally. "That I am, sir, and it's good to finally meet you. I'm just sorry my brother made such a mess of things." He clasped the gentlemen's hand.

Reagan gave a snort, dropping her hands to her hips. "Can we make introductions later? I'm waiting for my explanation. What do you mean, neither of you is Grayson Thayer? You just said you *were* him."

"No, what I said, madame, was that neither of us was actually Captain Grayson Thayer of the Grenadier Company."

She lifted her hands, shaking her head in utter confusion. "I'm still lost."

"I am Grayson Thayer, but I'm not—"

A loud, insistent pounding upstairs startled them.

"Oh, God, soldiers," Reagan breathed. "They've come to get him!" She lifted her petticoats and ran through the dark cellar, headed for the stairs.

"You stay here, Carleton, and keep them quiet," Grayson ordered over his shoulder as he ran after Reagan.

Reagan stepped into the kitchen and Grayson slammed the door behind them, throwing the lock. The pounding continued on the front door.

"Open up," a man shouted. "Open now or we break in the door!"

Reagan's hands flew to her cheeks. "What do I do?"

Grayson grabbed her hands. "Calm down, love. Now listen to me. They're looking for a man with a head wound." He touched his forehead. "I've no wound. Just play along with me."

"All right. I can do that. I just pretend you're Grayson." She looked up at him anxiously. "Of course you are, but I have to pretend you're—"

Grayson laughed. "You've got it, love." He caught her hands, studying her attire. But this won't do. You've got entirely too many clothes on."

Reagan's eyes widened. "I beg your pardon, sir!"

The pounding on the front door started again.

"Look at me." He spread his arms. "I've nothing but my breeches on. We have to be able to convince

401

these knaves that we've been too *busy* to be participating in any kind of ruckus."

Reagan's cheeks colored, but already she was turning around to let him unlace her bodice. "Oh, thank God you thought of this," she murmured as she stood while he pulled her gown over her head. "My skirting is covered in blood!"

Grayson balled up the heavy cream silk gown and flung it through the door to the lean-to. Then he grabbed her hand and pulled her down the hall. "God's bowels," he shouted as they passed the front door. "Can you hold a moment?"

He stopped at the staircase and began to unbutton his breeches. "Run up to the landing and just peek around the corner," he ordered.

Reagan obeyed. When she reached the polished case clock on the landing, she looked back at Grayson. He was running a hand through his blond hair to tousle it as he slid the bolt on the front door. "Saints in hell!" he cried. "What is it you want?" He swung open the door.

It was Major Burke himself, still dressed for the ball. "Thayer?" The major took a step back, startled.

Grayson lifted a blond eyebrow. It was obvious this officer knew him . . . knew Sterling. "Sir?"

The major glanced over his shoulder. There were six uniformed soldiers standing behind him, weapons drawn. Another ten were mounted out on the street. "Good God, Nellers! I thought you said this was our man!"

A young soldier stepped forward, blinking as his

eyes grew accustomed to the lamplight in the front hall.

"I . . . I thought sure it was, sir."

"I thought you said he had a massive head wound!"

The young man stared at Grayson. "He . . . he did, sir. I saw him in the alley just before I went for reinforcements."

The major caught a glimpse of Reagan standing on the landing, half hidden by the railing. He slipped his pistol back into the red sash of his uniform. "Does that look like a man with a futtering head wound, Nellers?"

"No, no, sir, it doesn't. But there was a woman, too."

The major exhaled slowly, rubbing his forehead. "Mayhap *that* woman, Nellers?" He pointed to Reagan on the staircase.

The man squinted. "No, no sir. I don't think so. This woman was dressed and she had dark hair. I don't remember exactly what she looked like, but that's not her."

Grayson leaned on the polished doorknob, taking in the conversation. "Obviously a mistaken identity," he glanced at Burke's insignia, "Major. You were looking for one of your own men?"

"Goddamn you all straight to hell! I'm sick of your incompetence!" The major glanced up at Grayson. "Well, don't just stand there. Get out of the doorway before I have you arrested for indecency!"

"Does that mean you're through with me?"

Reagan nearly giggled. This was just how Grayson . . . *Sterling* acted with the major. She wondered who was copying whom.

"Yes, I'm through, but I want you in my office tomorrow morning by seven."

"It's Sunday, sir. I've church to attend."

"Don't give me that horseshit, Thayer. You be there tomorrow. I lost a man tonight who supposedly had some damned important information for me. I guess I'll have to put you on it. You're the least incompetent in a sea of incompetence."

"Yes, sir. Tomorrow then."

The major turned and went down the stoop steps, the soldiers following behind him. The front door closed, and Reagan gave a squeal of delight as she came racing down the stairs. She threw herself into Grayson's arms, hugging him. "You did it," she breathed. "He's safe!"

Grayson laughed. "Now let's get you a wrap and go see how that brother of mine is faring."

Downstairs, Reagan and Grayson found Sterling resting comfortably on a makeshift bed on the floor.

Elsa rose when they entered the secret room. "Is it all safe?"

Reagan smiled. "Grayson took care of the soldiers. They'll not be back tonight."

"Well, I'm going to make the captain some tea. Just make sure he lies still."

Reagan watched her sister gather some bloody rags off the printing press and then leave the room. When she was gone, Reagan knelt. "Hey, there," she whispered, brushing back a lock of Sterling's damp hair. Elsa had cleansed and sewn the wound, then bound it with clean strips of flannel.

"Hey there," Sterling answered weakly. "I'd get up, but I think I'd fall flat on my face."

She took his hand, rubbing it between hers. "If you got up, I'd knock you on your face."

Grayson chuckled, kneeling beside her. "Tough wench you've got here. She just scared off a regiment of redcoats."

Sterling raised a hand to rub his eyes. "I'm surprised you didn't invite them in." He blinked, suddenly aware that Grayson was bare-chested and wearing nothing but his breeches. Reagan was in her nightrobe, but it was obvious she was wearing her shift and corset beneath it. "What the hell are you doing, Grayson? Where're your clothes?" He looked at Reagan. "And where are yours?"

Reagan looked at Grayson, then back at Sterling. "Can you blame me? I thought he was you."

Sterling's mouth dropped open. "Jesus, Grayson, you didn't."

Grayson went along with Reagan's little game. "You shouldn't have had me locked up in that fort." He waggled a finger. "I had nothing but cornpone and bad ale to sustain me for months! I never thought I'd lay eyes on a palm toddy again!"

Sterling squeezed his eyes shut in disbelief. "I never meant for all of this to get so complicated. I just wanted to do the right thing for the country."

"Heroism is terrific, Sterling, I just wish you'd checked to be sure which side I was on first."

Sterling's eyes widened "What?" He looked at Reagan. "What's he talking about?"

She shrugged. "I'm the last person to ask." She added sarcastically, "But Elsa probably knows. She's figured everything else out."

Sterling raised up from his bed on the floor. His gaze met his brother's and he saw his own eyes looking back at him. "What are you talking about, Grayson? You're going to have to go slow. My head's in a muddle."

Grayson glanced over his shoulder at Mr. Carleton, who stood in the far corner of the room examining a page of Reagan's proofs. He gave a nod of approval.

Grayson turned his attention back to his brother. "I'd made my choice before you had, you fool. Some solicitors representing Mr. Carleton, a merchant here in Philadelphia, approached me way back in '74 when I was in London."

"Four years ago? I was working the fields with Father."

Grayson helped Sterling into a sitting position, propping him against the whitewashed wall. "Mr. Carleton, would you like to take over?" Grayson gave a sweep of his hand.

The gray-haired man walked toward them. "A group of merchants here in Philadelphia were concerned how a war would affect us. We needed to know what was happening, what military decisions were being made. After all, our business was trade . . . though our hearts were with the Colonies. So, we hired a young man, Grayson Thayer."

"They bought my commission and paid me a healthy salary," Grayson offered.

Reagan sat back on the floor, listening in awe as the story unfolded.

"As a captain in the army, Grayson was to report any pertinent information to us. When the war broke out, we all agreed to continue the charade." Carleton smoothed his finely embroidered sleeveless waistcoat. "Only we decided to let Thayer pass the information onto us, to *our* men, and we would then pass it to the Continental Army."

Grayson grinned boyishly. "We decided I'd be safer that way."

"Only what you didn't count on," Reagan joined in, remembering what Elsa had said upstairs, "was that Sterling, a patriot, had become a spy, too."

Sterling rested his head against the wall in shock. "And that I'd come up with this clever idea of trading places with Grayson when he was transferred to Philadelphia."

Grayson took a swig from the whiskey bottle. "Doesn't sound confusing to me."

"But if you were one of us, Grayson, why didn't our Army rescue you?" Reagan asked.

"Because we didn't realize he'd been captured and held in an American prison," Mr. Carleton answered for him. "Grayson arrived in Philadelphia on schedule."

"But he didn't report to you."

"No. We got word that he was reporting directly to Captain Craig of the Continental Army in Frankfurt. My associates and I assumed that the military had taken over the operation. We didn't want them to know that information had been coming from us. We had families to consider, you know, so we didn't say anything."

Reagan turned to Grayson. "Why didn't you tell the men who were holding you imprisoned who you really were?"

Grayson chuckled. "The story was too ridiculous. Who'd have believed such a tale?"

"Besides, I was the only man who knew it was Grayson Thayer we'd hired," Carleton added, "and I'd have to have denied any knowledge of it if I'd been contacted by the Army."

She nodded. "All right, so back to this business here in Philadelphia. You thought Sterling was Grayson so you just kept an eye on him. And you helped *me*."

Sterling looked at the well-dressed merchant. "You paid my bar bills."

"And left the ginger spice," Reagan added.

"And left the note at the Blue Boar warning me that Murray was hot on my heels. You signed it 'C.' "

Carleton smiled. "I also closed the hatch." He pointed upward. "Though that was clearly by accident. I'd heard, by way of one of my informants, that soldiers were being sent. I came to check on things, inconspicuously, of course, and saw the hatch open in the carriage house. When I spotted the printing press, I knew immediately that the woman was the penman every Briton in the city was looking for. What I didn't know was why our Grayson would be taking such a chance being involved in it . . . allowing it."

Reagan smiled proudly. "He didn't know."

Grayson looked over at Reagan. "Now I'm confused. What pamphlets?"

"Never mind," Sterling told him. "I'll explain it to you later. Right now, if you'll excuse us, I'd like to talk to Reagan alone."

"I must be on my way," Carleton said. "I shouldn't be seen here. Walk me out, Grayson. We'll see what we're to do here."

When both Grayson and Mr. Carleton had left the room, Reagan lifted her dark lashes to study Sterling's ashen face. He was sitting upright, but barely. She knew this wasn't the time or the place to confront him, but she couldn't help herself. "How could you have deceived me like this," she asked bitterly. "We were on the same side all these months and I didn't know it. I *hated* myself for loving you because you were the enemy."

Sterling tried to take her hand but she pulled away. "Reagan . . ." he drew a ragged breath. "I wanted to tell you, God knows I wanted to tell you, but I couldn't. There were so many lives at stake that I couldn't tell *anyone* who I was. They find out you know I'm a spy and they'll hang you too, sweetheart."

"Oh, so you did it to protect me?" Her voice was laced with sarcasm. "Well, it was wrong. I felt dirty, ashamed of myself. You *knew* that. How could you stand there and tell me you loved me and then lie to me?"

Sterling gazed into her cinnamon eyes. They were streaked with resentment and anger. "It was an order."

"I don't know who you are now." She got to her feet and began to pace. "The person I knew, was he Grayson? Was he Sterling going by the name of Grayson? Who did I make love to? You, or him?" She hooked her thumb upward, referring to Grayson.

"Me. It was me."

She shook her head, tightening her arms around her waist. She had never felt so alone in her life. "Lies. It was all lies. I loved a man who didn't exist." *And now I may carry his child,* she thought.

Sterling's head was throbbing. "You have a right to be angry," he told her quietly. "But what was I supposed to do?"

"If you had a mission to fulfill, then you should have done it. You shouldn't have seduced me," she snapped.

"I didn't seduce you! I fell in love with you!"

"Don't shout at me, Grayson . . ." She took a deep breath ". . . Sterling."

A heavy silence hung in the air.

Sterling studied her face. He loved her so much. He hadn't meant to hurt her, but the pain he'd caused was etched deeply in her face. He closed his eyes. "Reagie, can we talk about this later? I'm hurting something awful."

She bit down on her lower lip. Why was everything so wrong? Her suspicions had been right. He *was* a patriot. Everything she had wanted was being

410

handed to her. So why did she feel this ache in her heart? Could she forgive this man *Sterling* for his lies? She didn't know.

"You're right," Reagan said softly when she found her voice. She ran her hand along the cool wood of the printing press. "Let's get you upstairs and into bed. Tomorrow will be soon enough to sort this out between you and me."

Grayson sat in a chair he'd pulled up to Sterling's four-poster bed. His booted feet rested on the bedframe. In his hand he held a glass of porter. He glanced about the bedchamber with interest. "Heavens, Sterling, you've made a mess of my clothing."

Sterling managed a smile. He was feeling better now. Elsa's tea had given him some strength. He was dead tired but he and Grayson had to talk before they slept. "I can't believe you didn't tell me you weren't a bloody redcoat!"

Grayson shrugged. "It was part of the agreement with Carleton. Besides. I figured you'd be safer that way."

Sterling snatched the glass from Grayson and took a deep swallow. The liquor burned a path to his stomach. "We were all so busy protecting each other that the left foot never knew what the right was doing!"

"Water over the dam now, Brother." Grayson took back his glass and refilled it with wine.

"The question is, what do we do tomorrow? How do we get out of here with our heads still connected to our shoulders?"

"We?" Grayson laughed. "We're not going anywhere. You take the redhead and hightail out the minute you can sit straight on a horse. I'm staying."

"Staying?"

"Carleton's making the arrangements at this very moment. Once my identity is confirmed with your Captain Craig, I'll be taking your place." He chuckled, sipping from his glass. "Or my place as the case may be."

"No. Captain Craig will never go for it."

"He'd be a fool not to!" Grayson leaned back, crossing his ankles on the edge of the bed. "The only man who knew who you were, Murray, is dead."

"No. There's the half-breed. His name's Indian John. Unless he was lying there dead in that alley, he could ruin us all."

Grayson waved his hand. "I don't know if he's dead or not yet. I'll find out tomorrow."

"If he isn't?"

"A minor detail. Carleton told me all about him. I'll take care of him."

"You won't know where to find him."

"Carleton's got people all over the city. If he's not already dead, we'll find and dispose of the half-breed nuisance before you can say 'King Georgie's got the clap.' "

"I don't like it, Grayson."

"Who cares what you like, big brother?" Grayson drained his glass and stood, stretching his legs. "Now tell me, what are you going to do when you

412

leave? Where are you going to go?"

"I've got a new assignment in Williamsburg. I'll be able to go home." Sterling paused. "I was going to ask Reagan to marry me."

Grayson gave a snort. "The woman who stomped by here a few minutes ago didn't seem to be in the marrying mood."

Sterling rubbed his temple. "She said I lied to her, that I deceived her."

"You did."

Sterling's eyes flew open. "Whose side are you on, anyway?"

Grayson toyed with a hair ribbon thrown over the back of a chair. "She has a right to be mad. The woman's got brains. She'd never have blown your cover. You should have told her the truth when you fell for her."

"It wasn't up to me, Grayson. It was a direct order." He paused. "Besides, I thought I was sparing her. I thought I was protecting her."

"So what do you do now?"

Sterling slid down in the bed. It was lonely there without Reagan at his side. *"Do?* I wait until the steam blows and then I try to discuss it with her."

"Discuss, hell! I'd bed her. That's the quickest way to end a tiff if you ask me."

Sterling grabbed a pillow and flung it at Grayson, hitting him in the chest. "You're talking about the woman I love, so you'd better take care."

Grayson picked up the pillow and tossed it back onto the bed. "Go to sleep, your brain's turning to Christmas pudding. I've got to report in the morning so I'll want to get you up early. I'll need some information about Major Burke if I'm going to pull this off."

"All right. Elsa showed you your room?"

Grayson was already at the door. "Yeah. Good night. Some sleep and things will look better in the morning."

"Good night." Sterling blew out the candle beside his bed. "And Grayson . . ."

"Yes?" his voice came in the darkness.

"Thanks Brother."

Grayson paused. "For what?"

"For being here when I needed help. I'll never forget it."

Sterling heard the door close, then footsteps as Grayson went down the hall, and then silence.

Chapter Twenty-nine

Reagan stood outside Sterling's door, her hand resting on the polished knob, a breakfast tray balanced on her hip. A few hours' sleep had done nothing to clear her head. She was still so confused. She hated Sterling for deceiving her all these months, for putting her through a private hell . . . but deep in her heart she loved him. She loved him and she was proud of what he had done for his country. Quietly, she's slipped into his bedchamber.

Sterling was sitting up in bed, writing on a lap desk. He was bare-chested, the counterpane thrown carelessly over his lap to cover his nakedness. He glanced up and smiled when he saw Reagan.

She was dressed in a freshly pressed sprigged cotton gown, her thick auburn hair tied back in a green ribbon. She was a breath of sunshine.

"Morning," she greeted hesitantly. "I brought you a biscuit and some tea. Some of that English tea Mr. Carleton gave us."

He laid aside his report to Captain Craig and patted the counterpane. "Come sit for a minute."

She set down the tray and came to him, allowing him to take her hand. "Grayson left early to report to Major Burke. I hope he's going to be all right."

Sterling patted her hand. "He's going to be fine. We have to believe that."

She shook her head, looking away. Her hand felt good in his. "I like him, you know. He's so much like you . . . but he's different."

Sterling took a deep breath. He'd gone over and over in his mind how he would broach this subject. "Reagan," he said, deciding directness was his best approach. "It doesn't matter, darling, I'll understand, but I have to know."

"Know what?"

"Did . . . did you make love with him?"

She turned to Sterling, studying his anxious blue eyes. "No," she whispered. "I knew it wasn't you almost immediately."

"How?" He kissed the back of her hand, relief written all over his face.

"I don't know. There was just something different." She broke into a grin. "I was positive when he kissed me. He doesn't kiss as well as you do."

Sterling laughed. "I'll be sure and tell him."

She joined in his laughter. "I already did."

Sterling pulled her into his arms. "Oh, God, Reagan, why does this all have to be so complicated?" He kissed the corner of her mouth and she responded against her will.

"No, you mustn't. Your head," she murmured against his lips. "Sterling, we have to talk."

"I don't want to talk." He brushed his hand over the curve of her breast. "Nothing makes sense when we talk. *This, this* makes sense, though." He pressed his lips against her mouth, his kiss gentle yet demanding.

"Sterling," Reagan said, a husky catch in her

416

voice. "This isn't why I came." Her mind was a jumble. She couldn't think when he was touching her like this, yet she couldn't force herself to stop him. She needed him so desperately.

"Shh," he soothed, easing her gently beside him on the bed. "Love me, Reagie." He sprinkled her face with light, feathery kisses. "Let me take away your pain. Let me tell you I'm sorry."

With a soft cry of abandon, she gave up her resistance. She lifted her head off his pillow, taking his mouth with her own, delving deep to taste him. She ran her hand over his bandaged head, catching a lock of his clean golden hair. She stared up at him, her eyes riveted to his. "Yes, let me love you." Her hand glided over his bare chest, but he caught it.

"No, lie back," he whispered, kissing her fingertips "Relax."

With a sigh, she obeyed. She watched him as his nimble fingers unhooked the front of her gown. She rested her hands on his shoulders as he pulled it over her head and tossed it to the floor. Then came her corset and stockings and finally her shift.

Reagan's cheeks colored. The bright sunlight that poured through the windows made her feel self-conscious. She reached for the counterpane to cover herself, but he pulled it from her hands.

"No, let me look at you," he told her. He stretched out beside her, running a hand over her breasts, down her belly, veering to her creamy thigh. His light, sensuous touch made her shiver, though she was warm. She watched him as he studied her slim form, and a heat began to rise within her.

When Sterling lowered his mouth to a pert nipple, she gave a sigh of relief. Her muscles were tensed, her body a bow strung too tight. She threaded her hands through his shoulder-length hair, encouraging him. Ripples of pleasure radiated outward as he teased her flesh with the tip of his tongue, making her quiver with desire. She savored every shiver of pleasure, every sigh of ecstasy as he stroked her, whispering words of love.

"Sterling, please," she breathed. "No more. Come to me." She lifted her arms. "I need to feel you inside me."

"No," he whispered, nibbling the lobe of her ear, his hot breath taunting her. "Not yet."

She writhed in sweet agony as he traced a pattern across the flat of her belly with his fingertips. Instinctively she lifted her hips as his hand moved closer to the apex of her thighs. When his hand met with the downy red curls, she moaned softly.

All thought of redcoats, lies, betrayal, and pregnancy slipped from her mind. There was nothing but the two of them and this glorious swirl of pleasure.

When Sterling finally lowered his body over hers, she was gasping for breath. He took her with one stroke and she cried out in sheer relief. They quickly began to move as one, faster and faster as they rode each crest of the waves of sensation. But each time Reagan almost reached that final peak of fulfillment, he slowed his pace, drawing out her pleasure until she thought she would die of it.

"No more," she whispered, stroking the wide expanse of his back. "Please, Sterling."

With a soft chuckle, he began to rise and fall again, delving deeper with each stroke. Higher and higher she climbed until finally her senses shattered. Her body tensed in ultimate rapture, once, twice, a third, and still he moved against her.

Sterling gave a cry spilling into her and then collapsed beside her. Reagan rolled over, allowing him to draw her into his arms. She cuddled against him, listening to his breath slow to a normal pace, taking in the tantalizing musky odor of their lovemaking.

Sterling brushed back a tendril of her auburn hair. "I've something to ask," he told her.

She studied him through the veil of her dark lashes. "Yes?"

His eyes fixed on hers. "Reagie, will you marry me?"

"Sterling, I—"

He pressed his fingers to her lips. "Hear me out. I've been assigned to a post in Williamsburg. I want you to go with me. I want you to be my wife."

For a moment she thought she would say yes. But how could she marry him? He'd lied to her. She didn't know this man, Sterling. The man she'd fallen in love with was an imposter—a combination of himself and his brother. The man she loved didn't exist. "I have to have time," she whispered. "So much has happened. You lied to me, Sterling."

His face fell. "I leave tomorrow. I can't give you any time."

419

She slipped out of bed and pulled on her shift. "Then I can't say yes."

"Reagan. You're not being reasonable."

"I can't leave Elsa." She scooped her remaining clothes off the floor. Suddenly her heart was pounding again. She couldn't breathe.

"We'll take Elsa with us, then."

"She said she won't go. She said if I try to make her leave the city she'll run away and she'll keep running way."

"Then let her marry Ethan."

"Don't be ridiculous," Reagan scoffed. Her hand rested on the doorknob. If she didn't escape, she thought she'd faint. She hadn't expected him to ask her to marry him. She'd wanted him to, God knows. But now, she couldn't bring herself to say yes. She'd lived her entire life here on Spruce Street. How could she leave her grandfather's home, her printing press, her life, to follow this man who'd deceived her?

"Reagan, it may be years before I can come back for you. This could be our only chance. Say you'll marry me."

Tears clouded her eyes as she swung open the door. "I can't. I'm sorry," she whispered as she fled the room.

Reagan bolted upright, soaked in perspiration and shivering with cold. Her heart pounded beneath her breast. She clutched at the cotton sheets, shaking with fear. Indian John! He was here! Here in her room! She could smell him!

She fixed her gaze on the window. The light curtains swayed in the breeze, the moonlight illuminating a patch on the floor. Her throat constricted in terror. She had closed that window before she'd retired. She was certain of it!

Reagan waited a long moment, expecting Indian John to come out of the shadows, his razor-sharp knife gleaming in the moonlight. She held her breath, frozen with fear as another minute passed and then a third.

"Don't be ridiculous!" Reagan scolded herself. "He's dead. Sterling said . . ." She let her voice trail into nothingness. Lies, he'd told so many lies. Was that one, too?

She jumped out of bed and grabbed a dressing gown off the chair as she went by. Slipping her arms into the robe, she went down the hall, her bare feet slapping quietly on the wooden floor. She had to know the truth. Her nightmares had become too vivid.

Reagan pushed open Sterling's bedchamber door. "Sterling, I have to . . ." Her voice caught in her throat.

Standing in the moonlight was a man. His silhouette was short and ragged. He was leaning over Sterling's sleeping form, a knife clutched in his hand.

Reagan let out a blood-curdling scream. Sterling rose up out of bed, crying out with alarm.

Reagan flung herself at Indian John, pounding him with her fists. "No." she raged. "Not him, too!

You took my papa, but you'll not take him!" She snatched the washbowl off the table and brought it crashing over his head.

Indian John gave a yelp, losing his balance, and fell backward onto the bed.

Sterling scrambled for his pistol. "Get back, Reagan," he ordered.

Before she could make her escape, Indian John lashed out, catching her arm. Brutally, he pulled her across the bed, putting it between him and Sterling.

"Let her go." Sterling shouted. "This is between you and me, half-breed."

Grayson burst into the bedchamber, a lamp in his hand. He came to a halt just inside the doorway.

Reagan trembled with a mixture of anger and fear. She could feel Indian John's cold knife pressing against her throat. It was just like in her dreams, only somehow the reality was less frightening. This man had terrorized her too long, and tonight it would end . . . one way or another.

"Get back," Indian John answered shakily, confused by Grayson's presence. "Get back the both of ya or I cut her."

The half-breed's stench sickened her. "Shoot him!" Reagan told Sterling. She stood perfectly still.

Sterling kept his eyes fixed on Indian John's scarred face. "No. You're too close."

She looked to Grayson who stood in the lamplight, his pistol drawn. "Come on, Grayson. Kill the bastard!" She could feel Indian John beginning to tremble as his breath quickened. "Kill him," she repeated. "It's an easy shot!"

Indian John took a step back, dragging Reagan with him. "Shut up! You hear me, you little redcoat whore!" He gave her a vicious shake. He was frightened by the twin men . . . bad medicine.

"Let her go and we'll let you go," Grayson bargained. He was moving ever so slowly toward the bed.

Indian John shook his head. "No. I ain't that stupid. Now the two of you get away from the door. I aim to get myself outta here with the girlie, lessin' of course you wanna see her die here." His one good eye darted back and forth between Grayson and Sterling.

Grayson glanced at Sterling who nodded slightly. At his brother's indication, he moved out of the half-breed's path. Indian John dragged Reagan around the bed and toward the door.

"Now you just walk right along here, bitch," he murmured in her ear. "You stay right close. You keep me safe, I keep you alive, least for the time bein'." Indian John backed out of the room and down the hallway toward the stairs.

Grayson and Sterling followed slowly, still hoping for a chance to fire without risking Reagan's life with the shot.

When Indian John and Reagan reached the staircase, he began to back down them, feeling his way along in the semidarkness. "I ain't kiddin' with you two devil's spawn. I don't know which she belongs to, maybe both, but unless you wanna see her bleed all over your floor, you'd best back off."

Reagan waited until Indian John reached the landing where the tall case clock stood. When he turned to descend the final flight of stairs, she rammed her elbow into his stomach, at the same time twisting her leg around his so that he lost his balance.

The two went crashing down the stairs, but Reagan manage to catch hold of the railing and the half-breed fell free of her. His knife flew from his hand as he landed at the bottom of the staircase. He leaped up and fumbled with the lock at the front door.

Grayson raced down the steps past Reagan, firing his pistol. The half-breed gave a groan as the lead ball penetrated his back, but he kept moving. He flung open the door and darted outside.

Sterling came running past Reagan. "Grayson!" He threw his pistol and Grayson dropped his, catching his brother's weapon in midair. "You've got to stop him," Sterling shouted.

Reagan stumbled to her feet with Sterling's aid and they ran down the steps. They reached the front hall in time to see Indian John start across the lamplit street. At the same moment a carriage came careening around the corner. By the time the driver saw the man, it was too late. Reagan turned away just as the half-breed was trampled under the slashing hooves of four galloping horses.

Indian John's agonizing scream echoed in the air as he was caught beneath the carriage and dragged down the cobblestone street. A sickening thud was repeated again and again until his screams ended abruptly.

Sterling wrapped his arms around Reagan, pulling her inside. Grayson came back up the front steps.

"Guess I'd best get dressed," he told Sterling. "I told you I'd take care of the half-breed." He offered Sterling his loaded flintlock. "And see, I didn't even waste a second shot."

Sterling kicked the front door shut. "Anyone see us?"

Grayson gave a snort, already hurrying up the grand staircase. "I hardly think so. Not with that show. But you'd best lay low until the morning when we can get you out of Philadelphia." His face twisted into a scowl. "Grisly sight, wasn't it?"

Reagan pulled away from Sterling, having gathered her wits. He tried to reach for her again, but she slapped at his hand. "I thought you said he was dead," she flung bitterly. "He could have killed you!"

"Let me explain," Sterling pleaded. Nothing was coming out the way he'd expected. He loved Reagan so much that it hurt, yet, he was losing her and he seemed powerless to stop it.

"I'm sick to death of your explanations!" She looked up at him, trying to hold back her tears. Her hand rested on her flat belly. "I could never live with you. How would I ever know what was a lie and what was the truth."

"It wouldn't be like that."

She wrapped her arms around her waist, shivering in the warm night air. "Get out of my way. I'm

425

going to bed. Grayson will have to deal with the soldiers tonight."

"Reagan, don't do this to me, to yourself. I have to leave at first light."

"Godspeed, then," she responded bitterly, brushing past him.

Sterling grasped her arm. "I wasn't the only master of deception here."

She gave a laugh of disbelief. "I hardly think the situations are comparable."

"You knew I was looking for the penman. You could have told me, you knew I'd not have turned you in."

"I knew no such thing." She yanked her arm from his grasp and started up the steps. Her throat was constricted, her heart was pounding. She loved him and yet she knew she couldn't go with him.

"Reagan, I'll ask one last time," he called after her, his voice trembling. His hands were clenched at his sides in anger. After all they'd been through together, how could she treat him like this? She'd said she loved him, for God sakes. "Will you marry me?" he asked.

Reagan turned onto the landing, refusing to meet his gaze. "Go to hell, Sterling."

Chapter Thirty

An hour before dawn, Elsa rose and dressed noiselessly. She ran a hairbrush through her thick dark hair and tied it back in the scarlet ribbon Reagan had bought her. Taking an ancient carpetbag, she packed a clean change of undergarments, her toiletries, the silver-handled toothbrush her father had given her, and her favorite rag dolly.

Her shoes and best bonnet in one hand, the carpetbag in the other, she left her room and went down the steps and through the hall to the kitchen.

Elsa came to a halt, making a small noise. She hadn't expected Grayson to be awake! She knew it was the brother because the Grayson that was now Sterling was still wearing her bandages around his head. "Oh," she whispered.

Grayson looked up from his palm toddie. "I'm sorry, did I scare you, sweetheart?"

Elsa nodded.

Grayson glanced at her bag, bonnet, and shoes in hand, then at her stocking feet. "Going somewhere?"

Elsa nodded. "Going to get married," she said solemnly. "Only Ethan says nobody's supposed to know. Not until it's too late."

"The blacksmith your sister says you can't see?"

She nodded again, shifting her weight from one

foot to the other. "Um hmm. She thinks I'm too dumb too get married. She doesn't understand that me and Ethan, we love each other."

Grayson stared into his pewter mug thoughtfully. "You know Sterling asked your sister to marry him, only she said she couldn't because she had to stay here with you."

Elsa shrugged. "I tried to tell her I wasn't going to need her to take care of me anymore but she wouldn't listen. I think Reagie's the stupid one sometimes, not me. She loves Sterling—even though she can't always remember his new name."

"You certain you want to marry this Ethan fellow and live with him?"

Her face lit up. "Ethan says he'll love me for the rest of time." She lowered her gaze to the floor, squirming. "I don't really know how long the rest of time is going to be, but I bet it's a long, long, time." She looked up at him, a grin on her face.

Grayson couldn't resist a smile. "Sounds like a good enough reason to me."

She chewed on her lower lip. "You won't go tell, then, will you?"

He shook his head. "Not my place to stop you."

She dropped her calfskin shoes on the floor and slipped her feet into them. "You're nice, just like Sterling. I like both of you."

Grayson lifted a blond eyebrow. "You certain you wouldn't like to marry me instead, then?"

She giggled. "Don't be silly. I don't love *you*."

"Can't blame a man for trying. I'll hate to lose a pretty girl like you, Elsa."

"I got to go now because Ethan'll be waiting for me."

"Good-bye, then."

"Good-bye." She turned and started for the front door then stopped short. "Grayson?"

"Yeah, sweetheart?"

"Could you write a letter for me?"

"A letter?"

"For my sister. So she'll understand. I don't write, I just draw pictures."

Grayson contemplated the proposal for a moment. *Why the hell not?* he thought. "Sure, Elsa. Get me some ink, a quill and a sheet of paper, but we'd better hurry. Sterling and that housekeeper of yours will be awake shortly."

"I'll be right back." A few minutes later, Elsa returned with the writing materials.

"All right, tell me what you want to say and I'll write it."

She took a deep breath before starting. "Sister . . . I hope you won't be mad . . ." Elsa looked up anxiously. "You think that's all right? She's gonna be hopping mad."

Grayson lifted a hand. "It's fine."

Nodding, she went on. " 'I hope you're not going to be mad, but I married Ethan this morning. I'm sorry I had to do what you told me not to, but you wouldn't listen.' " She paused. "Have you got that?"

Grayson dipped the quill into the ink again. "Got it. Anything else?"

"Yes. 'Please come to visit us at our house and see how happy I am. Love, Elsa.' " She leaned over him. "But I can write the Elsa part. Ethan taught me."

Grayson handed her the goose quill and watched her concentrate as she strained to scrawl her name.

Finally she handed him back the quill. "I think the 'S' is snaking the wrong way, but it's all right isn't it?"

He waved the paper to dry the ink. "Perfect, sweetheart."

"Oh, and one more thing. At the bottom write, 'I think you should marry Sterling and be happy, too.' "

Grayson chuckled. "Got it. Now you go before she catches you. I'll make sure she gets the letter."

To Grayson's surprise Elsa gave him a peck on the cheek. Before he could speak, she grabbed her carpetbag and bonnet and ran from the kitchen. He heard the front door open and then close a moment later.

Reagan woke to a deafening silence in the house. She knew Sterling was gone. She'd heard him moving about sometime near dawn. She'd half expected him to come to her bedchamber, but he hadn't. She glanced at the small clock on the mantel above the fireplace. Good heavens. It was nearly noon. She'd never slept this late in her life!

She got out of bed, refusing to think about Sterling or her possible pregnancy. If she thought of it now, she'd surely crumble. Methodically, she dressed in her green lutestring gown. It had been one of

Sterling's favorites and had always made her feel good inside. Pulling back her hair with one of his old green hair ribbons, she added a lace mobcap and was finished.

Downstairs, Reagan went into the kitchen, intending to be truly decadent and finish the last of the good English tea Mr. Carleton had left on the step. "Nettie?"

The old woman was pouring a pot of tea. "Here, girl. Thought we could use some tea. There's a pot of porridge if you're hungry."

"No. Just the tea." She frowned. "Where's Elsa? didn't hear her in her room."

The old woman shrugged her bony shoulders. "Don't rightly know. I was going to ask you the same question."

Reagan's cheeks colored with anger. "She must be with that blacksmith, again. Nettie, I don't know what I'm going to do with her!"

The blind housekeeper offered Reagan a cup of tea. "Don't know that you can do anything with her. She's got a head like you . . . like her mother. Once somethin's chilled, she don't change her mind."

Reagan gave a sigh. She wasn't in the mood for Nettie's prophesying this morning. Going to the worktable, she pulled out the old three legged stool to sit on. As she raised her teacup to her mouth she spotted a piece of paper on the other side of the table. Curious, she picked it up.

Reagan took too big a gulp of the steaming tea and choked. The handleless tea cup fell from her hand, shattering on the floor.

"What is it?" Nettie turned to her, startled.

Reagan read the letter slowly, hearing Elsa's voice echoing in her ears. Tears began to slip down her cheeks. "Oh, no, Nettie," she breathed. "She's gone . . ."

"Elsa?" The old woman turned her full attention to Reagan. "Gone where, girl?"

"She says she married the blacksmith this morning." Reagan looked up. "Oh, Nettie. This must have been written hours ago. I don't know by who. The writing looks something like Sterling's, but it wasn't him."

Nettie nodded. "The other one would be my guess."

Reagan crumpled the letter in her hand. Nettie was headed for her own room in the lean-to. "Nettie, where are you going?"

"To pack."

"Pack?" Reagan asked, bewildered. "Pack to go where?"

"To Elsa. She needs me. This big house is gettin' to be too much on these bones anyway."

"But what about me? *I* need you."

The woman gave a wave of her shriveled hand. "Only one person you ever needed Reagan Anne Llewellyn and you sent him packing this morning!"

Reagan's lower lip trembled. "How can you leave your home? You've lived here half your life."

Nettie shook her cane at Reagan. "You sayin' I'm too old for change? A body's never too old for change. Change is what keep a person young and full of life!"

Reagan lowered her head to the table, cradling it in her arms. She'd never felt so alone in her life. Everyone was gone, Papa, Elsa, Sterling, even Nettie was going. Who was left for her? The sound of footsteps made her raise her head.

For a moment, her breath caught in her throat. Standing before her was a strikingly handsome redcoat. But it wasn't the man she loved. "Grayson," she said quietly.

"I've been to Major Burke's. The half-breed's death has been classified as an unfortunate accident. He'll go to his grave with our secrets."

She nodded, then lifted the ball of paper she still held in her hand. "You wrote this." It wasn't a question but more an accusation.

"I did."

"Why?"

"Because the young lady asked me to." He dared a smile. "She was quite hurried."

"You *knew* I'd forbade her to see that man. Now she's gone off and married him, for heaven sakes!"

"She's a damn sight more sensible than you." Grayson yanked off his grenadier cap and set it on the table. From inside his coat he retrieved a silver flask.

Reagan's eyebrows arched defensively. "How so?"

"You were a fool not to go with him."

"He lied to me."

"Oh, don't start that song and dance again. You didn't go with him because you were afraid to."

"No." She shook her head vigorously.

433

He sipped from the flask, savoring the bite of the whiskey. "Yes. You were afraid to leave the security of this house, of your sister, and go into the unknown. You didn't trust him."

"It's not true." She slid off the stool. "He deceived me."

Grayson's eyes narrowed. "Tell me something honestly, Reagan. Had you been in his place, had it been *your* captain who'd been giving you the orders, would you have done the same?"

She couldn't break from his startling gaze, one so much like Sterling's. "Yes," she whispered finally.

"What? I didn't hear you."

She sobbed. "Yes, I'd have done the same. Yes, I was afraid!" She hung her head. "I just didn't know it."

Grayson threw up his hands. "So there you have it!"

She blinked. "Have what?"

He leaned against the worktable, shaking his head. He crossed his lean legs and took another pull on the silver flask. "The understanding. Now that you know you were afraid, you'll be able to face it. What, you don't think Sterling's scared out of his breeches?"

She didn't know what to say. All she knew was that at this moment she wanted Sterling. She was still angry with him, hurt by his deception, but she wanted him more than life itself. "It's too late," she told Grayson, defeated. "He's gone."

"Hell, it's never too late. You ride out now and you can catch him by nightfall."

She looked up at him anxiously. "You think so?"

He shrugged. "I can't promise he'll take you, but was I you, I'd sure as hell give it a whirl."

"I'd have to leave Elsa."

"She's already left you."

"My grandfather's house."

"I can look into renters for you." He shrugged. " 'Course your sister and her new husband might like it here. Elsa said there are several children."

"Where is he?"

"A tavern in New Castle, Delaware."

"I'll need a pass to get out of the city, and a horse."

Grayson winked. "I've got a horse. And I just happen to have a pass here somewhere." He pulled a folded piece of paper out of his scarlet uniform coat. "But if you're going at all, you've got to go now."

"I can't leave now! I'll have to pack, leave instructions with Nettie for the house, cover the furniture—"

"Look," Grayson interrupted. "Either you love him or you don't."

She dropped her hands to her hips. "How do you know so much about this business? I don't see you married!"

He took another sip of his whiskey and then screwed the cap back on the flask. "Only because I haven't met a girl like you yet."

She stood staring at Grayson for a long moment. That was a nice thing for him to say. "I was cruel to him. I thought it was all right for me to have loyalties, but not him. You think he'll take me back?"

"He'd be a fool not to."

She could feel her heart taking flight, soaring again. She dared a smile. "I'll get my riding clothes on. You get the horse."

In less than half an hour Reagan was on Spruce Street outside her grandfather's house and Grayson was handing her up into Giipa's saddle.

"Now you understand how to get there? Those roads should be safe, but if anybody messes with you, you blow a hole through his head with that pistol you're carrying and ask questions later."

Reagan nodded. "Don't worry, I'll be fine. It's not that far."

Grayson gave a nod, stepping back. "Go on then, and I'll tell all of your neighbors that you left me for a Colonial clod."

Her laughter filled the afternoon air. "Goodbye and take care. You'll be in our thoughts." Grayson tipped his grenadier cap and she rode away.

Down two blocks she dismounted and went up to a stately brick-and-frame house. A few minutes later she emerged carrying a covered picnic basket. It was a wedding gift for Elsa. Walking the remainder of the way to the blacksmith's, Reagan carried the basket, taking care with it.

In the blacksmith's yard she tied up Giipa and went to the door. Hesitantly, she knocked.

It swung open and the red-faced man who was now her brother-in-law answered the door. The sound of stringed instruments and laughter filtered through the air. It was celebration — a wedding celebration.

Ethan smiled. "I told my Elsa you would come. Please come into our home and share some wine."

Reagan shook her head. "I'm leaving. I'm going try and find Sterling." She stared at the toe of her riding boot. "I think I may marry him."

"I'll get Elsa," the blacksmith said gently. "But come in."

"No. I'll wait here. I . . . I have a present."

He disappeared and a moment later Elsa came outside. Her cheeks were rosy and her eyes danced. She threw her arms around her sister. "I'm so glad you came. But Ethan says you're going away."

Reagan nodded. Her eyes were getting misty again. "You're married now?"

She nodded excitedly and held up her hand to show a dull gold wedding band.

"You certain this is what you want?"

"I love Ethan," she answered simply.

"Then here's my wedding gift." She offered the basket. "I don't know how long it will be until we see each other again. If Sterling will still have me, I think we'll marry."

Elsa lifted the lid and gave a squeal of delight. She dropped to her knees. "Oh, sister!" Out of the basket she pulled a mewing black-and-white kitten. She held the little fluff of fur against her cheek. "He's so sweet!"

"Better look again, Elsa."

She reached into the basket and pulled out another kitten. "It's orange!" Elsa's eyes widened. "There's still something scratching in there, can you hear it?"

Reagan nodded and Elsa reached into the basket extracting two more kittens. "Four kittens! I can't believe it!"

Ethan stepped outside. "That was a very nice thing to do," he told Reagan. "She really misses Mittens."

Elsa looked up at the bridegroom. "Can I bring them inside at night, Ethan. I don't mind cleaning up the piddles."

Ethan laughed, grasping Elsa by the hand and lifting her to her feet. The kittens ran and tumbled in the grass. "Anything you want, dear. A house full of kittens if you like."

Elsa beamed. "See, Sister. Ethan's going to let me keep them in the house."

Reagan smiled. "Give me a hug and get back to your party. I have to go."

Elsa embraced her sister, then went back to her husband's arms. "Write to me," Elsa said. "Ethan reads good."

"I will. I promise."

Ethan followed Reagan to her horse and helped her into the saddle. He cleared his throat. "I'm not a man for words, but I wanna thank you. I'm sorry we had to marry this way, but I thank you for being so good about it now that it's done. You or Sterling ever need anything, you can count on me."

Reagan offered her hand and he took it in his meaty one. "You take care of her, Ethan, and we'll try to get back soon. In the meantime you two lay low and try not to cause too much trouble. Let someone else be a hero."

Ethan tugged on his sleeveless waistcoat. "We're just doing our share, Miss Reagan. Nothing more, nothing less. You know how Elsa is. She gets something in her head and there's no stopping her."

Reagan joined in his laughter as she sank her knees into Grayson's fine steed.

"Godspeed," Ethan called as she rode out of the yard and down the street, heading south toward New Castle.

Sterling sat in the back of the public room, his head cradled in his hands. An empty ale jack rested in front of him along with a half-eaten plate of stew. "Barmaid!" he bellowed, his speech slightly slurred. "Another."

A dark-haired girl retrieved his leather jack and returned it filled with frothy ale. "Anything else, luv?"

Sterling's eyes narrowed as he tried to focus. He heard the feminine voice. Was it Reagan's? No, some wench, but not his Reagie. His Reagie was gone. She was in Philadelphia with Grayson. She hated him. She'd called him a liar. Sterling gave a hiccup. He *was* a liar.

"No." Sterling waved the barmaid away. "Don't want anything you've got. Don't want anything but what I can't have," he added softly as the servant flounced off.

He took a long drink of the ale. He was drunk, but he thought he just might get drunker. Anything to make him forget. He was so angry at Reagan, but he still loved her. His heart ached for her. She said she wouldn't marry him because he'd deceived her, because of Elsa, but none of that made any sense! If she'd loved him enough, she'd have come, and he supposed that that was what hurt the most.

Sterling drained his jack and pounded the table with it, indicating he wanted another. While he waited he pushed back on the bench, throwing a boot up on the scarred wooden table. He'd removed his telltale bandages and now wore a wool hat to cover his stitches. He wiped his numb lips against the back of his hand.

The door to the public room swung open and a woman stepped inside. She stopped to speak to a grizzled old sailor who stood guard at the door. The man pointed a gnarled finger in the direction of the public room and the woman stepped into the lamplight.

Sterling blinked. Damn! His eyes were playing tricks on him. He could have sworn the woman looked just like Reagan. He licked his dry lips, leaning forward on his elbows. "Reagie?" He formed her name. He *knew* it wasn't her; she was in Philadelphia.

She came closer and he became more confused. *This* was why he didn't drink hard. He just couldn't handle it like Grayson. He squinted. "Reagan?"

The woman's face lit up and he rose slowly to his feet. She was putting out her arms to him. She was laughing, she was crying. He wondered numbly if he'd died and was headed for heaven.

"Reagan, is that you?" His voice sounded odd in his ears.

"Sterling." She threw herself against him and he lowered his face to bury it in her sweet-smelling hair. "I'm so glad I caught you. I was afraid you'd go before I made it here."

He stroked her smooth cheek. "You came . . . you came. Why?"

She laughed, staring up at him, her cinnamon eyes filled with love. "You're drunk."

He gave a hiccup. "Either not drunk enough or too drunk. Are you sure you're real?"

Her laughter filled his ears. *"This* is real," she murmured. She pressed her mouth to his in a searing kiss. When she pulled away they were both breathless. A cheer rose from the tavern patrons.

"Give me another chance," she told him. "Ask me again."

The reality of the situation was wearing away the effect of the ale. "Ask you?"

"To marry you."

He took her hand and kissed her knuckles. He couldn't believe she was really here. "No," he told her.

Her face fell.

"No," he said quickly. "I told you I'd ask that one last time."

"But—"

"Ask *me,*" he whispered.

A smile filled her face with white light. "Will you marry me?" She took his hand, lowering it until it brushed her stomach. "Will you give our child a father?"

He swept her into his arms. "A baby? We're going to have a baby? I thought you said you couldn't have children."

Reagan shrugged. "So I lied," she murmured against his lips.

Epilogue

Nervously, Reagan glanced into the beveled mirror that hung on the wall of her new bedchamber. It had been Sterling's parents' room here in the Georgian brick farmhouse at Thayer's Folly, but after today Reagan and Sterling would be sharing it. Since her arrival in Williamsburg, she'd been staying with his maiden aunt to assure her acceptance in the community. No one would ever know what had passed between them in the winter months in Philadelphia. Their child would simply be born early.

The sound of another carriage rolling up to the front door two stories below caught her attention. She gave her elegant coiffure one last pat and went to the window to see if she recognized the latest arrivals. The last month had passed in a whirlwind of confusion and activity. She and Sterling had come to Williamsburg and opened his parents' home just outside of town. Sterling had settled into his safe, respectable post with the Patriot Army in Williamsburg, and he had begun plans to clear another three hundred acres to grow food for Washington's army.

443

A knock at the door startled Reagan, and she turned away from the window. She didn't know why she was so jumpy! "Yes?"

"Reagie, the reverend is waiting."

"I . . . I'm not quite ready." She felt like a schoolgirl, giddy and breathless.

Sterling laughed, coming through the door. "You're as ready as you're ever going to be, now come on." He offered her his hand but she refused it.

"Sterling Thayer!"

"What?" He looked at her innocently, his blue eyes twinkling with mischief.

"If you think I'm marrying a man wearing that, you're mistaken!"

"What are you talking about? Sterling patted the brocaded scarlet coat he wore. "The dressmaker says its all the rage in Paris."

Reagan rested her hands indignantly on her hips. "Take it off, Sterling, or I'm not coming down."

"There's no time for me to change. I told you, the good reverend's waiting."

"The good reverend can wait until the Second Coming for all I care. I'll marry no man in a red coat!"

Sterling broke into laughter as he pulled off the offensive garment. "You're serious about this, aren't you?"

Her stern expression dissolved. "I can't believe you're making jokes on our wedding day."

Sterling tossed the coat onto their bed and reached out to take her in his arms.

444

"Sterling, you'll crush the silk ribbon," she protested weakly. His embrace was reassuring.

He stroked her cheek, kissing her gently on her rosy lips. "I don't give a hang about your silk ribbons, sweet, all I care about is you."

"Sterling!" She pulled away, but still held on to his hand. "We'd better go down. I hear the music."

"Come along then," he said, feigning exasperation. I guess I'll have to marry you and *then* give you your gift."

"Gift?" She stopped in midstep. "You have another gift? Sterling, you've already bought me enough gowns and jewels to clothe half of Philadelphia!"

He raised a blond eyebrow. "Yes, but this is a *special* gift." He shrugged. "You're right, though. We'd better get this marriage over with first."

Her curiosity piqued, Reagan couldn't resist. "What is it?"

"No, no. Later." He looped her arm through his and started to lead her down the hall.

"Sterling!"

Laughing, he grasped her hand and made a sharp turn, taking her down the servants' back staircase. "There's really no room in the cellar. I thought an office in town might be better."

"An office in town? For heaven's sake, what are you talking about?"

He stopped at a door. "Close your eyes."

"Sterling!"

"Close your eyes, or no present."

She squeezed her eyes shut, letting him lead her

through the door.

"All right, you can open them."

Reagan's eyes flew open. "Sterling!" she gasped. In front of her stood the major components of a new printing press. "For me?" she breathed, running to touch the polished wood and metal.

"For you, my love." He took her hand in his. "To keep you out of trouble . . . or *in* trouble as the case may be."

Reagan's eyes brimmed with tears. "Thank you," she whispered.

"You're welcome. Now shall we go? I believe we have a wedding to attend."

HISTORICAL ROMANCES BY EMMA MERRITT

RESTLESS FLAMES   (2203, $3.95)
Having lost her husband six months before, determined Brenna
Allen couldn't afford to lose her freight company, too. Outfitted
as wagon captain with revolver, knife and whip, the single-
minded beauty relentlessly drove her caravan, desperate to reach
Santa Fe. Then she crossed paths with insolent Logan Mac-
Dougald. The taciturn Texas Ranger was as primitive as the surrounding Comanche Territory, and he didn't hesitate to let the
tantalizing trail boss know what he wanted from her. Yet despite
her outrage with his brazen ways, jet-haired Brenna couldn't sup-
press the scorching passions surging through her . . . and suddenly she never wanted this trip to end!

COMANCHE BRIDE   (2549, $3.95)
When stunning Dr. Zoe Randolph headed to Mexico to halt a
cholera epidemic, she didn't think twice about traversing Comanche territory . . . until a band of bloodthirsty savages attacked
her caravan. The gorgeous physician was furious that her mission
had been interrupted, but nothing compared to the rage she felt
on meeting the barbaric warrior who made her his slave. Determined to return to civilization, the ivory-skinned blonde decided
to make a woman's ultimate sacrifice to gain her freedom — and
never admit that deep down inside she burned to be loved by the
handsome brute!

SWEET, WILD LOVE   (2834, $4.50)
It was hard enough for Eleanor Hunt to get men to take her seriously in sophisticated Chicago — it was going to be impossible in
Blissful, Kansas! These cowboys couldn't believe she was a real
attorney, here to try a cattle rustling case. They just looked her up
and down and grinned. Especially that Bradley Smith. The man
worked for her father and he still had the audacity to stare at her
with those lust-filled green eyes. Every time she turned around, he
was trying to trap her in his strong embrace.

*Available wherever paperbacks are sold, or order direct from the
Publisher. Send cover price plus 50¢ per copy for mailing and
handling to Zebra Books, Dept. 3038, 475 Park Avenue South,
New York, N.Y. 10016. Residents of New York, New Jersey and
Pennsylvania must include sales tax. DO NOT SEND CASH.*

Contemporary Fiction From Robin St. Thomas

Fortune's Sisters   (2616, $3.95)

It was Pia's destiny to be a Hollywood star. She had complete self-confidence, breathtaking beauty, and the help of her domineering mother. But her younger sister Jeanne began to steal the spotlight meant for Pia, diverting attention away from the ruthlessly ambitious star. When her mother Mathilde started to return the advances of dashing director Wes Guest, Pia's jealousy surfaced. Her passion for Guest and desire to be the brightest star in Hollywood pitted Pia against her own family—sister against sister, mother against daughter. Pia was determined to be the only survivor in the arenas of love and fame. But neither Mathilde nor Jeanne would surrender without a fight. . . .

Lover's Masquerade   (2886, $4.50)

New Orleans. A city of secrets, shrouded in mystery and magic. A city where dreams become obsessions and memories once again become reality. A city where even one trip, like a stop on Claudia Gage's book promotion tour, can lead to a perilous fall. For New Orleans is also the home of Armand Dantine, who knows the secrets that Claudia would conceal and the past she cannot remember. And he will stop at nothing to make her love him, and will not let her go again . . .

Available wherever paperbacks are sold, or order direct from the Publisher. Send cover price plus 50¢ per copy for mailing and handling to Zebra Books, Dept. 3038, 475 Park Avenue South, New York, N.Y. 10016. Residents of New York, New Jersey and Pennsylvania must include sales tax. DO NOT SEND CASH.